C000125544

*Emma*
# DARCY

Each volume has three terrific, powerful
stories written by one of the queens of the
genre. We think you'll love them…

**March 2014**

**April 2014**

**May 2014**

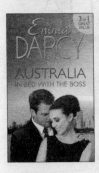

**June 2014**

**July 2014**

**August 2014**

# Emma
# DARCY

## AUSTRALIA
### IN BED WITH A BACHELOR

Published in Great Britain 2014
by Mills & Boon, an imprint of Harlequin (UK) Limited,
Eton House, 18-24 Paradise Road, Richmond, Surrey, TW9 1SR

AUSTRALIA: IN BED WITH A BACHELOR
© 2014 Harlequin Books S.A.

*The Costarella Conquest* © 2011 Emma Darcy
*The Hot-Blooded Groom* © 2001 Emma Darcy
*Inherited: One Nanny* ©1998 Emma Darcy

ISBN: 978 0 263 24584 4

010-0314

**Emma Darcy**'s life journey has taken as many twists and turns as the characters in her stories, whose international popularity has resulted in over sixty million book sales. Born in Australia and currently living in a beachside property on the central coast of New South Wales, she travels extensively to research settings and increase her experience of places and people.

Initially a French/English teacher, she changed careers to computer programming before marriage and motherhood settled her into a community life. A voracious reader, the step to writing her own books seemed a natural progression and the challenge of creating exciting stories was soon highly addictive.

Over the past twenty-five years she has written ninety-five books for Mills & Boon, appearing regularly on the Waldenbooks bestseller lists in the USA and in the Nielsen BookScan Top 100 chart in the UK.

# THE COSTARELLA
# CONQUEST

## Emma
# DARCY

# CHAPTER ONE

FRIDAY afternoon in the office of the man Jake Freedman had every reason to hate, and he could barely contain his impatience to leave. Soon, very soon, he would have all the evidence to indict Alex Costarella for the vulture he was, picking over the carcasses of bankrupted companies to feed his own bankroll. Then he could leave for good. In the meantime, the facade of aspiring to be Costarella's right-hand man in the liquidation business could not afford any cracks.

'It's Mother's Day on Sunday,' the big man re-marked, eyeing Jake with speculative interest. 'You don't have any family, do you?'

*Not since you helped to kill my stepfather.*

Jake managed a rueful smile. 'Lost both my parents in my teens.'

'Yes, I remember you saying so. Difficult for you. Makes it all the more admirable that you pushed on with a career path and have made such a fine job of it.'

*Every step of the way had been burning with the*

*ambition to take this man down. And he would. It had taken ten years to get to this point—accountancy, law, building up experience in Costarella's business, gaining his confidence. Only a few more months now...*

'I'd like you to meet my daughter.'

Shock startled Jake out of his secret brooding and rattled his ruthless determination. He'd never thought about the vulture's family, or what effect his own actions might have on them. He raised his eyebrows enquiringly. Was the daughter about to come into her father's business or...was this some weird attempt at matchmaking?

'Laura is a stunner in any man's language. Smart girl and a great cook,' Costarella declared with an inviting smile. 'Come to lunch at my home on Sunday and find out for yourself.'

A sales pitch! And a set-up for a connection to be made!

Jake inwardly recoiled from an up-close-and-personal involvement with anyone related to this man. His hand moved instinctively in a negative gesture. 'I'd be intruding on your family day.'

'I want you to come, Jake.'

The expression on his face brooked no refusal. It was a strong, handsome face, framed by thick, steel-grey hair and dominated by steel-grey eyes—a face imbued with the confidence of a man who could and did take control of anything and bend it to his will.

Jake knew instantly that if he persisted in

declining the invitation, the approval rating that gave him access to the evidence he needed could be lost. 'That's very kind of you,' he rolled out with an appreciative smile. 'If you're sure I'd be welcome...'

Any doubt on that score was clearly irrelevant. What Costarella wanted, he got. 'Make it eleven-thirty,' he said without hesitation. 'You know where I live?'

'Yes. Thank you. I'll look forward to it.'

'Good! I'll see you then.' The grey eyes glittered with satisfaction. 'You won't be disappointed.'

Jake nodded, taking his dismissal as gracefully as he could, knowing he had to turn up on Sunday, knowing he had to show an interest in *the daughter*, and hating the idea with every fibre of his being.

Why Costarella wanted this, he didn't know. It seemed ridiculously patriarchal in this day and age to be lining up a suitor, as though people were pawns to be moved as he wished. Nevertheless, it was typical of the callous mentality of the man. He moved to his own beat, not giving a damn about anyone else's interests.

Jake had to go along with him, play for time, protect his own agenda. If he had to start dating Laura Costarella he would, but no way would he allow himself to become emotionally attached to her, regardless of how beautiful and smart she was.

*She was the daughter of the enemy.*

He wasn't about to forget that.

Ever.

*Mother's Day...*

Laura Costarella wished it could be what it was supposed to be—a beautiful, memorable day for her mother with her children showing their love and appreciation for all she'd done for them, and their father being happy with the family they'd created together.

It wasn't going to be like that.

Her father had invited a special guest to the family lunch and from the smug little smile accompanying this announcement, Laura strongly suspected that the guest would be used to show up the shortcomings in his son and daughter, as well as the failings of the mother who had raised them.

Jake Freedman—a hard name, and undoubtedly as hard in character as her father was, or he wouldn't have risen so fast to the top of the tree in the Costarella Accountancy Company, which raked in millions from bankrupt firms. Did he know how he was going to be used today? Did he care?

Laura shook her head over the futile speculation. What would happen would happen. She couldn't stop it. All she could do was cook her mother's favourite foods for lunch and try to deflect the barbs of her father's discontent with his family. Keep smiling, she told herself, no matter what.

She hoped her brother would follow that advice today, too, for their mother's sake. No eruption into a resentful rage. No walking out. Just smile and shrug off any critical remarks like water off a duck's back.

Surely it wasn't too much to ask for Eddie to keep his testosterone in check for one short day.

The doorbell rang as she finished preparing the vegetables for baking as she'd seen done on the cooking show that was one of her favourite television programs. They were ready to slip into the oven with the slowly roasting leg of lamb when the time was right. The pumpkin and bacon soup only had to be reheated. The cream was whipped and the lemon-lime tart was in the refrigerator waiting to be served.

She quickly washed her hands, removed her apron and pasted a smile on her face, determined to greet their visitor with all the charm she could muster.

Jake stood at the front door to Alex Costarella's Mosman mansion, steeling himself to be an appreciative and charming guest. The huge two-storey redbrick home was one of Sydney's old establishment houses, set in immaculately kept grounds, oozing solid respectability—a perfect front to hide the true nature of the man who had acquired it by ripping off other people.

He remembered how hard his stepfather had fought the bankruptcy officials to hold back the sale of their family home while his mother was still alive—just a few more months until the cancer finally took her. No caring, no mercy from the money men. And the whole rotten process had been started by Costarella, who had deliberately turned a blind eye to how a company and hundreds of jobs could have been saved, preferring the prospect of lining his own pockets while being in charge of selling off all the assets.

No caring, no mercy.

His stepfather's heart had given out only a few weeks after his mother had died. Two funerals in close succession. Jake couldn't lay both of them at Costarella's door, but he could certainly lay one. It amused him to think of himself as the wolf outside, waiting to be given open entry to another wolf's home.

Taronga Park Zoo was nearby.

But the dangerous animals were right here.

Costarella didn't know Jake was on the prowl, waiting for the right moment to attack. He was holding his daughter out as bait for a bright future with the young gun in the company, unaware that *he* was the targeted prey. As for Laura, herself...

The door opened and Jake was faced with a woman who instantly excited an interest. She *was* beautiful; long black curly hair, incredible blue eyes, a mouth with lush full lips stretched into a greeting smile of perfect white teeth. She wore a clingy top in purple and white, the neckline dipping down low enough to reveal the upper swell of breasts that were more than big enough to fill a man's hands. Tight purple jeans outlined the rest of her hourglass figure and emphasised the seductive length of her shapely legs. The sexual animal inside Jake growled with the desire to take.

It was several moments before he recovered wits enough to identify himself as the expected guest. 'I'm Jake. Jake Freedman,' he said, hoping she hadn't noticed how *taken* he was by her.

Alex Costarella's daughter was a man-trap.

Falling into it did not fit into his plan.

'Hello. I'm Laura, the daughter of the house.'

She heard herself say the words as though from a great distance, her mind totally stunned by how handsome Jake Freedman was. Though *handsome* didn't say it all, not by a long shot. She'd met a lot of good-looking men. Her brother's world was full of them, actors making their mark in television shows. But this man…what was it that had her heart racing and her stomach fluttering?

His hair was dark brown and cut so short the wave in it was barely noticeable. Somehow the lack of careful styling made his dark brown eyes more riveting. Or maybe it was the unusual shape of them, his eyelids drooping in a way that made them look triangular and incredibly sexy. A strong straight nose, a strong squarish jaw and a strongly sculptured mouth added to the male impact of his face. He would have been perfectly cast as James Bond, Laura thought, and had the nervous feeling he was just as dangerous as the legendary 007 character.

He had the physique to go with it, too. As tall as her father but more lethally lean and looking powerfully masculine in his black jeans and black-and-white sports shirt, the long sleeves casually rolled up to the elbows, revealing hard muscular forearms. Jake Freedman was so male, it was stirring everything female in her. Even though she knew he was her father's man, it was impossible not to feel interested in him.

'Pleased to meet you,' he said, offering his hand with a smile that made him even sexier.

'Likewise,' Laura replied, extending her own hand and finding it subjected to an electric sensation that was so shocking she wanted to snatch it away. 'Please come in,' she rattled out, needing movement to excuse the quick extraction from physical contact with him.

'Daughter of the house,' he repeated musingly as he stepped inside. 'Does that mean you still live here at home?'

The curious assessment in his eyes gave her the sense he was summing up possibilities between them. 'Yes. It's a big house,' she answered drily. Big enough to keep out of her father's way most of the time.

Jake Freedman had to be years older than her university friends, given his position in her father's business, and remembering that unpleasant fact she should avoid him like the plague, apart from getting through this visit today. They would have nothing— absolutely nothing—in common.

'The family is enjoying the sunshine on the back patio,' she said, leading him down the wide hallway that bisected the house. 'I'll take you out to Dad, then bring you some refreshments. What would you like to drink?'

'A glass of iced water would be fine, thank you.'

It surprised her. 'Not a Scotch on the rocks man like my father?'

'No.'

'What about a vodka martini?'

'Just water.'

Well, he wasn't James Bond, she thought, swallowing down a silly giggle.

'Do you have a job, Laura?'

'Yes, I'm a Director of First Impressions.' It was okay to let the laughter gurgle out at his puzzled expression. 'I read it in the newspaper this morning,' she explained. 'It's the title now given to a receptionist.'

'Ah!' He smiled at the pretentiousness of it.

'You know what they call a window cleaner?'

'Please enlighten me.'

'A vision clearance executive.'

He laughed, making his megawatt attractiveness zoom even higher.

'A teacher is a knowledge navigator,' Laura rattled on, trying to ignore his effect on her. 'And a librarian is an information retrieval specialist. I can't remember the rest of the list. All the titles were very wordy.'

'So putting it simply, you're a receptionist.'

'Part-time at a local medical practice. I'm still at

uni, doing landscape architecture. It's a four-year degree program and I'm currently making my way through the last year.'

'Working and studying? Your father doesn't support you?' he queried, obviously not quite in tune with a wealthy man who wouldn't finance his children's full education.

She slanted him a derisive look. 'My father doesn't support what he doesn't approve of. You should know that since you work with him.'

'But you're his daughter.'

'Who was expected to fall in with his wishes. I'm allowed to live here. That's as much support as my father will give to my career choice.'

'Perhaps you should have sought complete independence.'

It was an odd remark, coming from a man who had to have made an art form of falling in with her father's wishes. However, she wasn't about to discuss the dynamics of her family with an outsider, particularly not someone who specialised in siding with her father.

'My mother needs me.'

It was a brief reply and all he was going to get from her. She opened the back door and ushered him out to the patio, quickly announcing, 'Your Jake is here, Dad.'

'Ah!' Her father rose from his chair at the patio table, which was strewn with the Sunday newspapers. His whole face beamed a welcome at the man who was undoubtedly performing up to his expectations in every respect. 'Good to see you here, Jake. Beautiful autumn day, isn't it?'

'Couldn't be better,' he agreed, moving forward to shake her father's offered hand.

Confident, smooth, at ease with himself and the situation...and Laura definitely wasn't. She felt dreadfully at odds with the strong tug of attraction that wouldn't go away. It was wrong. It had to be wrong. The last thing she wanted was a man like her father messing with her life.

'Go and fetch your mother, Laura. She's showing Eddie the latest innovations in the garden. You can tell them both to come and meet our guest.'

'Will do,' she said, glad to leave the two men together, though knowing that the stirring of the family pot couldn't be delayed for long. Her father expected instant obedience to his call.

The garden was her mother's refuge. She was never happier than when discussing what could be done next to it with Nick Jeffries, the handyman who shared her enthusiasm for creating wonderful visual effects and did all the heavy work for her. Laura loved this garden, too, loved every aspect of landscape design, making something beautiful instead of tearing something down...as her father did.

And as Jake Freedman did.

It would be stupid to forget that. She could never, never be in tune with a mind that dealt with destruction.

'Mum, Eddie…' she called out. They were by the rockpool, where Nick had installed the new solar lights. 'Dad's guest is here.'

Her mother's smile of pleasure instantly drooped into a grimace. She darted an anxious look at her son, worried about an imminent clash of personalities.

Eddie hugged her shoulders, smiling reassurance. 'I promise I'll be good, Mum. No bad boy today.'

It won a wry little laugh.

Eddie made a great *bad boy* in the soap opera he currently starred in. The wild flop of his thick black hair, the designer stubble along his angular jawline, the dimple in his chiselled chin, the piercing blue eyes…all made him a very popular pin-up, especially on his flash motorbike. He was wearing black leathers today, though he was now carrying his jacket, discarded because of the heat of the morning. His white T-shirt was emblazoned with a Harley-Davidson. He played a bikie and he looked like one, much to her father's disgust.

The three of them started strolling back towards the patio, son and daughter flanking their mother, determined to keep a happy ball rolling for her. Why she stayed with their father was beyond their comprehension. There was no joy in the marriage. Having a very dominant husband who controlled everything seemed to have sapped her of any will for an independent life.

Laura always thought of her mother as a lady,

never anything but beautifully dressed and groomed, imbued with gracious manners, doing everything correctly and tastefully, making a special ritual of keeping fresh floral arrangements in the house, which she did herself. Even her name, Alicia, was somehow very ladylike.

She looked particularly lovely today, her newly dyed blond hair cut into a short, fluffy style, a blue silk tunic giving her eyes more colour. They had seemed so dull and washed out lately, Laura had worried there might be a health problem her mother was not admitting to. She was getting too thin, as well, a fact hidden by the loosely fitting long-sleeved tunic. The white slacks were also loose, affecting a casually elegant look. Certainly no one would notice anything amiss with her, not on the surface. Jake Freedman would probably pigeonhole her as the typical rich man's wife.

'What's he like?' her mother asked.

'James Bond,' popped straight out of Laura's mouth.

'What? Loaded and dangerous?' Eddie queried.

She grinned at him. 'Plus gorgeous and sexy.'

He rolled his eyes. 'Don't you go falling for him, Laura. That's bad territory.'

'Yes, be careful,' her mother quickly warned, her eyes anxious again. 'Your father might want you to like this man. There has to be some motive behind inviting him here today.'

'Could be that marrying the boss's daughter is

on Jake Freedman's agenda,' Eddie put in, grinning wolfishly, then snapping his teeth to make the point.

Marriage?

Never!

She'd walked out of every relationship she'd had once the guy started making demands on her, which always happened sooner or later. From what she'd witnessed at home, marriage was an endless string of demands, plus abuse thrown in if the demands weren't met. No man was ever going to own her as his wife.

She rolled her eyes back at Eddie. 'I'm not so easy to gobble up. I'll be feeding him lunch. He can whistle for anything more from me.'

'Humphrey Bogart,' her mother murmured.

'What?'

'Humphrey Bogart. He whistled for Lauren Bacall. It was in an old movie.'

'Well, I haven't seen it.'

'Did he get her in the end?' Eddie asked.

'Yes.'

'No doubt she wanted to be got,' Laura said, giving her brother a quelling look. 'Different story.'

'I'll be watching the mouth of Dad's man of the moment,' he tossed back at her, wicked teasing in his eyes. 'If he starts whistling...'

'It's more likely the man of the moment is about to be used to show you up as a footloose lightweight, Eddie, so watch your own mouth.'

'I don't know…I don't know…' their mother fretted.

'It's okay, Mum,' Eddie quickly soothed. 'Laura and I have put our walls up and nothing is going to crack them today. Just you relax now. We're both on guard.'

It was a relief to hear Eddie so sure that his protective armour was in place. Laura wished she could say the same for herself. Despite what her mind dictated, as soon as they came into view of the two men on the patio and she caught Jake Freedman's gaze on her, there was no wall at all to hold off the sexual chemistry he triggered in her.

Immediately she felt a wild tingling in her breasts, shooting her nipples into hard bullets. Her hips started swaying provocatively, driven by some primitive instinct to show off her femininity. Heat whooshed to the apex of her thighs and somehow melted the normal strength in her legs. Her toes curled. And turbulent temptation crashed through every bit of common sense that told her to keep away from this man.

She would love to have him.

Regardless of how wrong it would be.

She would love to have him.

Just for the experience!

# CHAPTER TWO

JAKE found it difficult to tear his gaze away from Laura to make a quick assessment of the other two people he was about to meet. The mother was more or less what he expected of Alex Costarella's wife—a lady-of-the-manor type who undoubtedly kept his house as beautifully as she kept herself—but the son was a surprise...unkempt, longish black hair, designer stubble, clothes indicative of a bikie. Obviously Eddie didn't toe his father's line, either.

Two rebellious children and one submissive wife.

Was he supposed to tame Laura, draw her into becoming the kind of woman her father would approve of, sharing his world instead of striking out on her own, pleasing herself?

He looked at her again and felt a tightening in his groin. She was, without a doubt, the most desirable woman he'd ever come into contact with, dangerous to play with, yet the idea of drawing her *away* from her father made her all the more tempting. It was fair justice for Costarella to feel the loss of someone dear to him as well as the loss of the business that gave him the power to wreck people's lives.

He was acutely aware of Laura watching him as her father performed the introductions, weighing up how he responded to her family.

'Alicia, my wife…'

'Delighted to meet you,' Jake rolled out with a smile.

She returned it but there was a wary look in her eyes as she replied, 'Welcome to our home.'

'And my son, Eddie, who obviously didn't bother to shave this morning, not even for his mother.'

The acid criticism was brushed off with a nonchalant grin. 'Couldn't do it, Dad. We're shooting tomorrow. Got to stay in character.' He turned the grin to Jake as he offered his hand. 'I guess you're the son my father should have had, Jake. Happy days, man!'

Jake laughed and took his hand, shaking his head as he replied, 'Don't know about that but thanks for the good wishes, Eddie.'

'You're welcome.'

'Eddie is an actor,' Laura put in proudly. 'He plays the bad boy in *The Wild and the Wonderful*.'

Jake frowned apologetically. 'I'm sorry. I don't know the show.'

Her father snorted. 'It's rubbish. A TV soapie.'

'Rubbish or not, I enjoy doing it,' Eddie declared, totally unabashed. 'How about you, Jake? Do you enjoy doing what you do?'

'It's challenging. I guess acting is, too,' he said, careful to be even-handed in his reply.

'Totally absurd la-la-land,' Costarella jeered. 'Jake and I deal with the real world, Eddie.'

'Well, Dad, lots of people like to have a break from the real world and I help give it to them.' He deftly turned attention back to the guest. 'How do you relax from the pressure-cooker of work, Jake?'

Jake found himself liking Laura's brother. He stood up for himself and was clearly his own man. 'Something physical does the trick for me,' he answered.

'Yeah, got to say sex does it for me, too,' Eddie drawled, eyes twinkling with reckless mischief.

'Eddie!'

The shocked cry from his mother brought a swift apology. 'Sorry, Mum. It's all Laura's fault, saying Jake was sexy.'

'Did she now?' Costarella said with satisfaction.

'Eddie!' Laura cried in exasperation. 'I told you to watch your mouth.'

Jake turned to her, curious to see the reaction to her brother's claim. Her eyes were flashing furious sparks and her cheeks were flushed with embarrassment. As she met his gaze, her chin tilted defiantly and her own tongue let loose.

'Don't look at me as though you haven't heard that about yourself before because I bet you have. It's purely an observation, not an invitation.'

'Laura!' Another shocked protest from the mother.

She threw up her hands. 'Sorry, Mum. I'm off to bring out refreshments. Iced water coming up.'

Jake couldn't help grinning as she turned tail—a very sexy tail—and left the rest of them to patch a conversation together.

'I did try to bring my children up with good manners,' Alicia stated with a heavy sigh.

'No harm done,' her husband declared cheerfully.

'Actually, I like working out at a gym,' Jake said to remove sex from everyone's minds.

''Course you do,' Eddie chimed in. 'Can't get those muscles from sitting at a desk.'

'I do a yoga class,' Alicia offered, anxious to promote non-contentious chat as she gestured for everyone to sit down, tidying the newspapers on the table before sitting down herself.

Jake hadn't expected to find himself interested in Costarella's family. Even less had he expected to *like* any of them. In fact, the only one he'd given any thought to was Laura, whom he'd imagined to be a pampered princess, revelling in the role of Daddy's little girl.

The family dynamics were certainly intriguing and Jake was not averse to exploring them further… watching, listening, gathering information…and maybe, maybe, he might go after what he wanted with Laura Costarella, satisfying himself on several levels.

Laura cursed Eddie for being provocative, cursed herself for reacting so wildly, cursed Jake Freedman

for making her feel stuff that completely rocked any
sensible composure. Her escape to the kitchen should
have settled her nerves but they were still jumping
all over the place even after she'd loaded the traymobile with the preferred drinks and the platter of
hors d'oeuvres.

There was no hiding from the man. He had to
be faced again. She could only hope he wouldn't
try capitalising on her remark or she'd be severely
tempted to pour the jug of iced water over his head.
Which just went to show how out of control she was
and that just wouldn't do. Better to freeze him off
with good manners. She had to keep remembering
that Jake Freedman was her father's man and any
close connection with him could not lead anywhere
good.

Not emotionally.

No matter how good he might be in bed.

And she had to stop thinking of that, too.

Having taken several deep breaths and gritting
her teeth with determination to behave as she should,
Laura wheeled the traymobile out to the patio. It
was a relief to find the four of them chatting ami-
cably about relaxation techniques; meditation, Tai
Chi, massage and flotation tanks. Even her father appeared to be in good humour. She noted glumly that
the only empty chair left for her at the round table
was between Jake Freedman and her mother so she
couldn't avoid being physically close to the man.

She set the platter on the table for everyone to help

themselves, handed the ice-bucket containing a bottle
of her mother's favourite white wine to Eddie and
told him to open it, placed the jug of iced water and
a crystal tumbler in front of Jake, served her father
his Scotch on the rocks, and supplied the wineglasses
before bowing to the inevitable of taking the designated chair and addressing the gaffe she'd made.

'I'm sorry for blowing my stack with you, Jake. I
was annoyed with Eddie. And embarrassed.'

The riveting brown eyes sparkled with amusement, making her stomach flutter again. 'No offence
taken, Laura. I dare say Eddie hears that said about
himself so often, it's lost any currency with him. And
I doubt he thought it had any currency with me, either.'

Letting her know he didn't have tickets on himself, not on that score anyway. Though Laura wasn't
sure she believed him.

Her father snorted in rank disbelief. 'If it didn't
have any currency with Eddie, he'd be out of a job.
It's only because all the teeny-boppers think he's
sexy that he's built up a fan base.'

'Lucky for me!' Eddie said flippantly. 'Though I
do work at it, Dad.'

'Some people just have it,' her mother said, trying
to divert a clash. 'I always thought Sean Connery...'

'Back to James Bond,' Eddie cut in, grinning at
Laura.

She bared her teeth at him in warning.

He stood up to pour the wine, cheerfully saying,

'Mum's a great movie buff, Jake. I bet no one could beat her on that topic in a quiz show. And she's a champion Mum, too. Let's drink a toast to her.' He lifted his glass. 'Mother's Day!'

They all echoed the toast.

Having been handed the movie ball, Jake Freedman proceeded to run with it, giving her mother so much charming attention, Laura couldn't help liking him for it. He was probably working hard at being an amenable guest, showing off his talent for diplomacy to her father. Nevertheless, it was giving her mother pleasure, and her father, for once, was not souring it with any acid comments.

In fact, he looked surprisingly content with the situation.

Laura didn't really care why.

It was good that he wasn't putting her mother down as he usually did.

She slipped away to attend to the lunch preparations, feeling slightly more at ease with Jake Freedman's presence. It was making the day run more smoothly than she had hoped for. The only negative was his sexual impact on her.

She hadn't been able to stop herself from slyly checking him over; the neat curl of his ears, the length of his eyelashes, the sensuality of his lips, the charismatic flashes of his smiles, the light sprinkle of black hairs on his strong forearms, the elegant length of his fingers with their clean clipped nails, the way his muscular thighs stretched the black fabric of his jeans. And long feet! Didn't that mean his private parts would be...very manly?

Which, of course, would be in keeping with the rest of him.

It was all very difficult, knowing he was her father's man. It was also difficult to concentrate on getting everything right for the meal; vegetables to go into the oven, reheating the soup, greens ready for last-minute microwaving, mint sauce on the dining-room table. She would have to sit next to him again; probably a blessing since this table wasn't a round one and he couldn't see what was written on her face unless he turned to her.

So far, he wasn't giving her any special attention and it was probably better if it stayed that way—no dilemma between temptation and caution. He was bound to have a woman in the wings, anyway. Eddie had girls falling all over him and she couldn't imagine it would be any different for Jake Freedman—another reason for not getting involved with him. Being perceived as just one of an available crowd had no appeal.

Although being the boss's daughter, he would have to treat her with respect.

Which she'd hate.

Whatever way she looked at it, having Jake Freedman was no good. Besides, he wasn't exactly holding out the chance to have him, though he might before the day was over. As her mother said, there had to be a purpose behind this visit. If a connection with her was the desired end, she had to be ready for it, ready to say no.

The soup was hot enough to serve. Telling herself she was lucky to have the distraction of being the cook, Laura returned to the patio to invite everyone inside for lunch. Eddie escorted her mother to the dining room. Jake Freedman followed with her father, the two men obviously on congenial terms.

Another warning.

Her father must have once been charming to her mother or she wouldn't have married him. His true character could not have emerged until she was completely under his domination. If Jake Freedman was of like mind, thinking he had the right—the power—to rule others' lives as he saw fit, she wanted nothing to do with him.

Jake continued to get his bearings with the Costarella family over lunch. Eddie had dropped out of school and left home at sixteen, getting himself a job as a backroom boy in one of the television studios.

'One day you'll regret not going on with your education,' his father said balefully.

He shrugged. 'Accountancy was never going to suit me, Dad.'

'No. Head in the clouds. Just like your mother.'

The tone of disgust caused Alicia to flush. She was a more fragile person than her perfectly groomed image presented, very nervy and too anxious to please. He was recalling Laura's comment that her mother needed her when she leapt to Alicia's defence.

'Oh, I think Mum's totally grounded when it comes to her garden.'

'Garden…movies…' Costarella scoffed. 'Alicia has led both of you astray with her interests. I had high hopes for you, Laura. Top of your school in mathematics…'

'Well, I have high hopes for myself, Dad. Sorry I can't please both of us,' she said with a rueful smile.

'Gardening…' he jeered.

'Landscape architecture is a bit more than that, Dad.'

No hesitation in standing up for herself.

Costarella huffed. 'At least you can cook. I'll say that for you. Enjoying the meal, Jake?'

'Very much.' He shot an appreciative smile at Laura. 'Top chef standard. The soup was delicious and I've never tasted better lamb and baked potatoes.'

She laughed. 'Top chef recipes from a TV cooking show. All it takes is dedication to following the instructions. You could do it yourself if you had the will to. It's not a female prerogative. In fact, most of the top chefs are male. Do you cook for yourself?'

'No. Mostly I eat out.'

'Need a woman to cook for you,' Costarella slid in.

It was a totally sexist remark and he saw the recoil from it in Laura's eyes, followed by a derisive flash at him…if he thought the same.

He turned to Costarella and allowed himself one risky remark, grinning to take away any sting. 'Given that most top chefs are male, a man might be better.'

Eddie found this hilarious, cracking up with laughter.

'What's so funny?' his father demanded.

'It's just that lots of guys in the service industry are gay and I don't see Jake as gay,' he spluttered out.

Laura started giggling, too.

'I'm not,' Jake said.

'Certainly not,' Costarella declared emphatically.

'We know you're not,' Laura assured him, still tittering.

'Absolutely.' Eddie backed up. 'Laura wouldn't think you were sexy if you were gay.'

'Eddie, behave yourself,' Alicia cried.

'Impossible,' his father muttered, though his ill humour had dissipated at this affirmation that his daughter was vulnerable to the attraction he favoured.

Laura rose from the table. 'Now that you've embarrassed both of us, Eddie, I'm going to serve sweets, which I hope will be tart enough to glue up your mouth.' She smiled at her mother. 'It's lemon-lime, Mum.'

'Oh, my favourite!' Alicia glowed with pleasure. 'Thank you, dear.'

Jake watched her head off to the kitchen again. It would be risky business, taking on a connection with her, complicating what had been his undeviating purpose for too many years to mess with when he was in sight of the end. She could become a distraction. He'd been single-minded for so long, readjusting his thinking to include a relationship with Costarella's daughter was probably not a good idea, however tempting it was.

Cynically dating her for short-term benefits at work was no longer an option. He was genuinely attracted to her. Strongly attracted to her. She had his skin prickling with the desire for action between them. Costarella expected him to make a move on her. *He* wanted to make a move on her. The tricky part was controlling it.

'How come you're not sharing Mother's Day with your own Mum, Jake?' Eddie suddenly asked.

'I would be if she were still alive, Eddie,' he answered ruefully.

'Oh! Sorry!' He made an apologetic grimace. 'Hope the bereavement isn't recent.'

'No.'

'Guess I'm lucky I've still got mine.' He leaned over to plant a kiss on Alicia's cheek.

'Yes, since you've always been a mother's boy,' Costarella sniped.

There was a flicker of fear in the look Alicia darted at her husband. Jake imagined she had been a victim of abuse for so long, she felt helpless to do anything about it.

'I've been admiring the very artistic centre-piece for the table,' he said, smiling at her to take the anxiety away. 'Are they flowers from your garden, Alicia?'

'Yes.' Her face lit up with pleasure. 'I did that arrangement this morning. I'm very proud of my chrysanthemums.'

'And rightly so, Mum,' Laura chimed in, wheeling the traymobile into the dining room. 'They're blooming beautifully.'

She served the lemon-lime tart with dollops of cream to everyone, continuing her praise of her mother's talent for horticulture.

Jake watched her. She was beautiful. And smart. And so lushly sexy, temptation roared through him, defying the reservations that had been swimming through his mind.

As she resumed the seat beside him, he turned to her, his eyes seeking to engage hers with what he wanted. 'I'd like to see this garden. Will you show it to me when we've finished lunch?'

Startled, frightened, recoiling. 'Much better for Mum to show you, Jake. It's her creation.'

'He asked *you,* Laura,' Costarella immediately bored in. 'Not only should you oblige our guest, but your mother has already shown Eddie around the garden. She doesn't need to repeat herself, do you, Alicia?'

'No, no,' she agreed, her hands fluttering an appeal to her daughter. 'I'm happy for you to do it, Laura.'

Caught.

She had to do it now whether she wanted to or not.

Jake aimed at sweetening the deal for her. 'I'm interested in seeing it through your eyes. You can tell me how it fits your concept of landscape design.'

'Okay! I'll flood you with knowledge,' she said tartly.

He laughed. 'Thank you. I will enjoy that.'

Surrender under fire, Jake thought, but no surrender in her heart. It made for one hell of a challenge… their walk in the garden. The adrenaline charge inside him wanted to fight her reluctance to involve herself with him, yet that same reluctance gave him an out from Costarella's heavy-handed matchmaking…keeping the more important mission on track, without distraction.

He would make the decision later.

In the garden.

## CHAPTER THREE

LAURA told herself it was just a job she had to take on and get through—escort Jake around the garden, bore him to death with her enthusiasm for built environments and deliver him back to her father, who had announced his intention to watch a football game on television in the home theatre.

Eddie helped clear the table, following her to the kitchen to have a private word with her as they stacked the dishwasher. 'You're the main target today, Laura. No doubt about it now,' he warned. 'I'd say Dad wants Jake as his son-in-law.'

'It's not going to happen,' she snapped.

'He's a clever guy. Been playing all sides today. And I've been watching you. You're not immune to him.'

'Which made it very stupid of you to tell him what I thought.'

'Obvious anyway. Believe me, a guy like that knows women think he's sexy. He would have had them vying for his attention from his teens onwards. Just don't say yes to him.'

Easy for him, sitting on the sidelines, Laura thought savagely. 'What if I want to?'

Eddie looked appalled.

'He *is* sexy,' she repeated defiantly, fed up with being put on the spot.

He grimaced. 'Then make damned sure you keep it at sex and don't end up hooked on him. The way Mum is should be warning enough for you.'

'I will never be like Mum.'

He shook his head. 'I wish she would leave him.'

'She can't see anything else. Better play a game of Scrabble with her while I'm doing my duty with Jake. She likes that.'

'Will do. That's a lot more fun than duty.'

Laura heaved a deep sigh, trying to relax the tension tearing at her nerves. 'I don't want to want him, Eddie.'

He gave her a look of serious consideration. 'Go for it if you must. You'll always wonder otherwise. Sooner or later he'll turn you off and I think you're strong enough to walk away.'

'Yes, I am,' she said with certainty.

'But you'd be better off not going there.'

'I know.' She made a rueful grimace. 'Maybe he'll turn me off out in the garden.'

'Unlikely.'

'Well I won't be falling at his feet, that's for sure. And you let Mum win at Scrabble, but don't be obvious about it.'

'No problem.' He grinned his devil-may-care grin. 'Let's go and fight the good fight.'

She grinned back at him. 'The *gay* bit was good.'

He laughed and hugged her shoulders as they returned to the dining room, where he immediately put their plan into action. 'Better get out the Scrabble, Mum. Since you beat me last time, I want a return match, and heaven help me if I'm swamped with all vowels again.'

'I'll leave you to your game,' her father said good-humouredly, rising from his chair, smiling at Jake Freedman. 'I'm sure you'll enjoy my daughter's company.'

'I will,' he agreed, rising to his feet, as well, ready to take on the garden seduction scenario.

Resentment suddenly raged through Laura. Jake Freedman was playing her father's game, but she didn't have to. He wasn't *her* guest. It was after three o'clock. Lunch had gone off reasonably well. The trickiest part of being together for Mother's Day was over. Her father was sparing them his presence. His wrath wouldn't fall on all of them if she didn't remain polite to the man. She could put Jake Freedman on the spot, instead of being the target herself.

She smiled at him. 'Let's go.'

He accompanied her outside, making easy conversation to start with.

'*Was* it your mother's pleasure in her garden that led you to your choice of career, Laura?'

He seemed genuinely curious and she didn't mind

answering him. 'Partly. Nick probably had more influence, the creativity he uses to generate Mum's pleasure.'

'Who's Nick?'

'The gardener and handyman Dad employs to maintain everything, but he actually does more than maintain.'

'Like what?'

'He thinks about what will delight Mum and does it. Like the solar lights he's just put around the rockpool. I'll show you. It's over this way.'

He strolled beside her, apparently content to bide his time, ensure she was relaxed with him. Which was totally impossible, but at least he didn't know it and wouldn't know it until he made a move on her.

'A waterfall, too,' he remarked as they came to the pool.

'Yes. It makes a soothing sound. Most people enjoy sitting near falling water...fountains in a park. Also reflections in water. The lights placed around the pool shimmer in it when it's dark.'

'Does your mother come out here at night?'

'Sometimes. Though she can also see this part of the garden from her bedroom window. What's really special is how Nick lit up the figurines of the Chinese water-carriers coming down the rocks at the side of the waterfall. There's another light at the back of the pot-plant below them. It bathes them in a ghostly glow. Quite a wonderful effect.'

'Landscape architecture,' he said, slanting her a

rueful smile. 'I've never thought about it but I can see why it should be appreciated.'

'I guess in the career you've chosen, you don't take the time to smell the roses,' she shot at him.

'True. I haven't,' he conceded readily enough, as though it didn't matter to him.

It niggled Laura into asking, 'Is it worth it?'

There was a subtle shift of expression on his face, a hardening of his jaw, a determined glint in his eyes. 'Yes, it is. To me,' he answered in a tone that didn't allow for a different point of view.

Laura couldn't leave it alone. 'You like working for my father?'

'Your father is part of a system that interests me.'

It was a clever sidestep, depersonalising her question.

'The system,' she repeated, wanting to nail down his motivation. 'I can't imagine any pleasure in dealing with bankruptcy.'

'No, it can be very traumatic,' he said quietly. 'I would like to make it less so.' The dark brown eyes drilled into hers. 'Not even the most beautiful parks in the world resonate with people in that situation, Laura. All they see is their lives crumbling, their jobs gone, their plans for the future shattered. It can lead to divorce, suicide, violence, depression so dark there is no light.'

She shivered at the intensity of feeling coming from him, a depth of caring she hadn't expected in this man. It didn't sit with coldly calculated ambition.

Not only that, but he'd also somehow turned the tables on her, making his job much more seriously special than hers.

'I know that people going through trauma do find some solace in a pleasant environment,' she argued with conviction. Her mother, for one.

'I didn't mean to undervalue it.' He gestured an appeal. 'I'm not your father, Laura. Perhaps we can both work on having open minds about each other.'

'Why did you come here today?' she asked point-blank.

'Your father wanted me to meet you and I was curious enough to accept the invitation,' he answered, his eyes gently mocking the hard challenge in hers.

She planted her hands on her hips, sick of how he was churning her around and wanting open confrontation. 'So what do you think of me?'

His mouth moved into a very sensual smile. 'I think you're *very* sexy.'

A tidal wave of heat rushed through Laura. She snatched at his own words to her and threw them back at him. 'That doesn't have much currency with me.'

He laughed and stepped forward, sliding an arm around her waist and scooping her into body contact with him, his eyes glittering with reckless intent. 'I've been wanting to do this from the moment we met, so I'll do it, and you can slap me down afterwards.'

There was time—a few seconds—for her to slam

her hands against his shoulders and push away. His mouth didn't crash down on hers. It seemed to her he lowered his head in slow motion, moving his free hand to tilt her face upwards. She did nothing, waiting for the collision of the kiss, wanting it, wanting to know if it would be better than any other kiss a man had given her.

A weird exhilaration was buzzing through her at being held in his embrace, as though he was the right man for her, the perfect man—a sensation she'd never felt until now. Whether it was his intense maleness, his strength, his aggressive confidence, his sexy physique...Laura couldn't pin it down, but curiosity held her totally captive.

His lips brushed over hers with surprising gentleness, tantalising her, exciting her with a sensuality she had not expected. She *did* move her hands to his shoulders, but not to push away, to touch, to feel, to slide around his neck and hold his head to hers. She liked the shape of it, liked the clean, bristly thickness of his short hair—no gel.

He started tasting her, little flicks of his tongue slipping seductively between her lips, and she responded with her own provocative probing, wanting to taste him, a pulsing primitive streak urging her to goad him into less control. It was as though he was testing how good she was for him, whether she would be worth pursuing beyond today, and everything female in her wanted to blow him out of his mind.

A wild exultation zinged through her when he plunged into a far more passionate kiss. No more holding her face. Both arms were around her, pressing her into intimate contact with him and she revelled in the hard evidence of her desirability. He was very definitely aroused, and so was she, as fiercely passionate as he was in the meshing of their mouths, seeking and driving for more and more excitement.

He clutched her bottom, grinding her even closer, and she was so hot for him she didn't care how intimate they were. Her heart was pounding, her thighs were quivering, and the only thought she had was *yes, yes, yes*. It was powering through her. More than desire. Need that craved instant satisfaction. Urgently.

It was he who pulled back, breaking the kiss, lifting his head, sucking in air like a runner at the end of a marathon. She gulped in oxygen, too, the dizziness in her head demanding it. Her breasts were still crushed against his chest and she could feel his heart thumping in unison with hers. Then his cheek was rubbing against her hair and his voice vibrated in her ear.

'I want you, Laura, but it can't be here.'

Here…in the garden…in open view of anyone who wandered outside. Madness. She couldn't take him inside, either. Everyone would know. She recoiled from giving her father the satisfaction of thinking his plan was working. It would worry her mother. Eddie, too. It couldn't be done. The time and place wasn't right. But the man was. Which was very confusing because he shouldn't be.

'I need to sit down,' she said, acutely aware of how shaken she was. 'There's a garden bench...'

'I see it.'

He shifted, tucking her tightly against him, walking her to the bench. Laura had to concentrate on putting one foot in front of the other. He saw her seated then sat beside her, leaning forward, elbows on knees, still recovering himself from the rage of desire that had swept through both of them.

Laura breathed in the scent of the nearby lavender bush. It was supposed to be calming. It did help to clear her head to some extent. Jake Freedman might be his own man but he *was* closely connected to her father. However *right* he might feel to her, she couldn't overlook that situation.

'If you think this means I'm a pushover for the taking, it doesn't,' she blurted out. 'The chemistry between us is just chemistry and I won't be losing sight of that, so don't imagine it gives you any power over me.'

He nodded a few times, then shot her a wry smile. 'Well, you've certainly slapped me down.'

Not for the kiss. For the possible motive hidden behind it because the kiss had got to her, more powerfully than she cared to admit. She tore her gaze away from his tantalising little smile and stared at the waterfall, wishing it could soothe the deep disturbance this man had caused.

'Not so much a slap, Jake,' she said more calmly. 'Just letting you know how I feel about it. My father is obviously pushing me at you. Maybe he wants you as his son-in-law. No way will I be used as a step up your career ladder.'

No comment from him.

His silence went on for so long it began to shred her nerves. 'Sorry if I've dashed your hopes,' she said bitingly.

'Not at all.' He sat up, hooking his arms on the backrest of the bench in a totally relaxed manner, smiling at her as though he was perfectly at peace with her decision. 'I'm not looking for a wife at this point in my life and you're not looking to fill that position. With that understood, do you want any part of me, Laura?'

Which put her right back on the spot.

His eyes glittered with the knowledge that she did, but wanting and taking were two different things. As Eddie said, she'd be better off not going there. Jake could be lying, secretly thinking he could seduce her into becoming his wife. Not that he'd be able to, but if she entered into any kind of relationship with him, he could report to her father that everything was sweet between them, and she'd hate that.

Yet looking at him, remembering how it had felt with him, the thought of not experiencing more of him actually hurt. Which was probably another danger signal. He *did* have power over her.

'I want you,' he said quietly, seeing her struggle

with his question. 'Not because you're your father's daughter. I think the chemistry between us makes that totally irrelevant. I want you because I can't remember wanting any other woman quite as much.'

It echoed her response to him. Jake Freedman was definitely the ultimate ten out of ten. But he could be saying those words because they were what any woman would like to hear. He was such a sexy man, he might affect every woman this way and she was no exception at all to him. *Clever, playing all sides,* Eddie had said.

She eyed him sceptically. 'Is that the honest truth, Jake?'

'Much to my own dismay, yes,' he said with a rueful grimace.

It was an odd thing to say and she looked at him in puzzlement. 'Why to your dismay?'

The riveting brown eyes bored into hers with heart-stopping intensity. 'Because I don't want to want you, Laura. Any more than you want to want me. And with that said, why don't we both take time to think about it?'

He rose from the garden bench, apparently preparing to leave her. Laura was so startled by the action, she simply stared up at him.

'Do you have a mobile phone?' he asked.

'Yes.'

'Give me your number. I'll call you at the end of the week if I'm still thinking of you and you can then say yes or no.'

It was so abrupt, hard, cut and dried, and the turbulent feelings it set off inside her made it difficult to think. Time…yes…time to decide if she couldn't bear not to know more of him…or time to have his impact recede to something less significant.

He took a slim mobile phone out of his shirt pocket and she rattled out her number for him to enter it in his private file.

'Thank you,' he said, pocketing the phone again and flashing an ironic smile at her. 'I've seen enough of the garden. You might like to join Eddie and your mother playing Scrabble. I'll say goodbye to them and then to your father on my way out.'

Relief poured through her. No more stress today. Decision-making could wait. She returned his smile as she rose from the bench. 'I didn't have you pegged as a garden man.'

'I shall take up smelling roses.'

'You need a garden for that. The hothouse ones don't have much scent.'

He raised one eyebrow in a lightly mocking challenge. 'Perhaps we can give each other new experiences.'

She shrugged, deliberately noncommittal. 'Perhaps we can.'

No more was said.

He accompanied her back to the dining room and with every step she sensed him withdrawing from her, wrapping himself in self-containment. It was a weird, cold feeling—in sharp contrast to the wild heat of their physical connection. He was leaving her alone and that troubled her far more than it should.

Eddie and her mother said all the polite responses to his polite appreciation of the day spent with them. Her mother took him in tow to the lounge room so he could say goodbye to her father and she was left behind in the dining room with Eddie, whose eyes were full of questions.

'So?' he asked, as soon as their visitor was out of earshot.

'So, nothing,' she answered. 'I showed him the garden.'

She couldn't bring herself to open up a discussion on what had happened between her and Jake Freedman. Somehow it was too personal, too private.

Besides, it would probably come to nothing.

And it was probably better that way.

Probably.

# CHAPTER FOUR

*THE end of the week,* he'd said.

It was the first thought Laura had when she woke up on Friday morning.

*If he was still thinking of her,* she mentally added, half-hoping that he wasn't so she wouldn't be faced with the decision of whether or not to see him again.

It had been impossible to get him out of her head. She couldn't look at a guy without comparing him to Jake Freedman. None of them measured up to him. Not even close. Her uni studies had suffered with him slipping into her mind when she should have been concentrating. As for being a Director of First Impressions at her receptionist job, no impressions at all had got through to her. Directing the doctors' patients had all been a matter of rote this week. It was like her whole life was revolving around waiting for his call.

Which was really, really bad.

What had happened to her strong sense of independence? It should be rising above this obsessive thinking about a man, putting him in a place of relative unimportance. She didn't like not being in full control of her life. It was as though a virus had invaded her system and she couldn't get rid of it. But as all viruses did, it would run its course and leave her, she told herself.

Especially if Jake didn't call.

However, if he did…

Laura heaved a fretful sigh and rolled out of bed, unable to make up her mind on what she should do. Would she always wonder about him if she didn't try him out?

It was an unanswerable question. Nevertheless, it plagued her all day, distracting her from the lectures at uni. By late afternoon she had decided it was best if Jake didn't call so a choice wasn't even available. She felt so woolly-headed, it was a relief to board the ferry from Circular Quay to Mosman and stand on the outside deck, needing a blast of sea breeze to whip away the fog in her mind.

The ferry was halfway across the harbour when her mobile phone rang. Her heart instantly started hammering. It might not be him, she told herself, plucking the phone out of the side pocket of her bag. He would not have finished work yet. It wasn't quite five o'clock. Her father rarely arrived home before seven.

Gingerly she raised the phone to her ear and said, 'Hello.'

'It's Jake, Laura.'

His voice conjured up his image so sharply, her breath stuck in her throat.

'Would you like to go out to dinner with me tomorrow night?'

Dinner! Her head whirled. To go or not to go…

'I thought we could try Neil Perry's Spice Temple. A new experience for both of us if you haven't been there.'

Neil Perry…one of Sydney's master chefs! His restaurants were famous for their wonderful food. The Rockpool. The Rockpool Bar and Grill. The Spice Temple. She would love, love, love to eat there, but…

'I can't afford it.'

'My treat. You gave me a great meal last Sunday.'

True. He owed her. 'Okay. I'd like that very much,' she said recklessly. A Neil Perry dinner was worth one evening with the man, regardless of what inner turmoil he caused. And maybe that would stop on further acquaintance. 'I'll meet you there,' she quickly added, not wanting her father to know she was seeing Jake Freedman again. 'What time?'

'Will seven o'clock suit?'

'Yes.'

'You know the address?'

'I'll look it up.'

'It's a basement restaurant. Go straight downstairs. I'll wait for you inside.'

'I won't be late. Thanks for the invitation.'

She ended the call, quite pleased with herself for handling it with a fair amount of control. This meeting could be contained at the restaurant…if she wanted it to be. Eddie would let her stay over at his apartment in Paddington on Saturday night so being taken home by Jake could be avoided, too.

Excitement buzzed through her…wicked, wanton excitement.

A sexy man, a sexy meal…impossible not to look forward to experiencing both.

Jake steeled himself for the Friday afternoon wrap-up meeting in Alex Costarella's office, suspecting there was only one issue of real interest on the agenda. He was right. After a half-hour chat about the week's work, Costarella leaned back in his executive chair, a smug little man-to-man smile on his face as he asked, 'Will you be seeing Laura this weekend?'

'Yes. We're having dinner together tomorrow night,' he answered, hating this matchmaking farce, but knowing that going along with it was to his advantage, keeping his position in the company ripple-free until he was ready to strike.

'Good! Good!'

Jake smiled back, playing the game to the hilt. 'Thank you for introducing me to her.'

'Pleasure. Laura needs a man to take her in hand and I hope you're the man to do it, Jake.'

The only way he was going to take her in hand was in bed, if she agreed to it. 'She's certainly very attractive.'

It was a noncommittal statement but Costarella found it encouraging enough to let the matter pass. 'Enjoy your weekend,' he said, and Jake was free to leave.

He'd thought a lot about Laura Costarella since last Sunday. She was hostile to her father, hostile to his wishes, and he'd anticipated her saying no to the dinner invitation. Since he very much wanted her to say yes, he'd deliberately used the Neil Perry drawcard, knowing that her interest in cooking had to make her something of a foodie.

Temptation…

The stronger it was, the harder it was to resist.

She wanted him, too. No doubt about that. If she was up for a wild fling with him, Jake would be only too happy to oblige. He'd been itching to oblige all week. Satisfying the lust she'd triggered in him was fast becoming a must-do, though he did feel ambivalent about taking on Costarella's daughter. He hadn't counted on liking her and he certainly didn't want to begin caring about her.

Spicy company, spicy food, spicy sex.

That had to be the limit of his involvement with the daughter of his enemy because a line would be driven between them when he brought charges against her father, ensuring that the corrupt insolvency practitioner could never again bury another struggling business to secure his obscene liquidator's fee.

Lust always burned out after a while, he assured himself.

In the meantime, the fire had been lit for tomorrow night and he looked forward to some very spicy heat.

Laura stood in front of the billowing turquoise hologram that gave an exotic curtain illusion to the doorway leading to the Spice Temple. It should have added pleasure to her dressing up for this dinner date. She was wearing her sexiest dress—a short turquoise silk bubble skirt attached to a tightly fitting black silk bodice—and the gorgeous black-and-turquoise high heels her mother had bought her for Christmas. Nothing, however, could dispel the anger festering in her mind and churning through her stomach.

Jake Freedman deserved to be stood up. Only the lure of Neil Perry's food had brought her here and she *was* owed a dinner. As for her outfit, she hoped it made Jake Freedman want her all the more because he could eat his heart out for sex tonight. No way was he going to get as much as a piece of her.

'Have a nice night with Jake!'

Her teeth gnashed over those words—accompanied by her father's beaming smile of approval. He'd been told about this date. Maybe the two men had plotted it together. Whatever… Tonight was no longer a private and personal meeting. It reeked of other agendas in the wind and she hated the thought of playing a part in either man's scheming.

Determined on focusing on the food and giving

Jake Freedman a very cold shoulder, she stepped past the doorway and made her way downstairs. Red dominated the decor of the basement restaurant. The scent of joss-sticks wafted through it. Definitely the hot, *in* place to be, Laura thought, noting that most of the tables were already occupied, even at this relatively early hour.

Jake had a table for two. He rose from his chair as he saw her being led to it, his gaze swiftly raking over the high points of her femininity, before shooting her a look of sizzling appreciation. Laura sizzled, too, not only with the acute, physical awareness he sparked off, but also with resentment at the sheer animal magnetism that clutched at her heart and turned her insides to jelly.

His clothes were completely nondescript—white shirt, grey slacks. They were irrelevant to the stunning impact of the man, as though it was his natural right to hold centre stage anywhere, in any company without any effort whatsoever. He waited for her with easy confidence and Laura wished she could knock him down and sweep him out of her life as though his existence was of no account.

Somehow she had to make it of no account.

'You look spectacular,' he said in greeting, grinning wickedly as he added, 'Great shoes!'

'They're good man-stomping shoes,' she replied, doing her best to appear cool and collected.

One black eyebrow quirked upwards. 'About to do some stomping?'

She returned a glowering look. 'I'll eat first.'

'Good idea! Work up some energy.'

He was amused.

Laura seethed over his amusement as she sat down. They were handed menus by a waitress who offered to help them make choices if they wanted anything explained.

'Not yet,' Laura said firmly. 'I want to salivate over every dish before I start choosing.'

'We'll call you when we're ready,' Jake put in, smiling his charming smile, which, of course, would bring the dazzled waitress running the moment he caught her attention.

Laura fixed her attention on the menu. She read the Spice Temple philosophy first. It described what the restaurant aimed for—unique and special dishes, seasoned by an unmistakable Chinese flavour and driven by a long-fostered passion for Asian cuisine, all designed to delight the senses with their contrasting tastes and textures. She hoped they would dominate her senses and block Jake Freedman out.

'Why do you want to stomp on me?'

She set the menu down and glared at the curiosity in his eyes. 'How many brownie points did you get for telling my father we were meeting for dinner tonight?'

'Ah!' He made a rueful grimace. 'I didn't offer the information, Laura. He asked me directly if I was seeing you again. Did you want me to lie about it?'

She was unappeased. 'I bet you knew he would

ask. That's why you called me when you did. Before you left work yesterday.'

He cocked his head on one side, the dark brown eyes challenging her stance on this issue. 'I thought you were determined on not having your father rule your life.'

'He doesn't.'

'He's influencing your attitude towards me right now.'

'Because you told him.'

He shook his head. 'You should make decisions for yourself, Laura, regardless of what anyone else knows or says. You made yours yesterday. Why let him change what you want? You've brought him here with you instead of moving to your own beat.'

She frowned, realising she had let her father ruin all her pleasure in anticipating this date. Although how could she be excited over being used?

'What about you? Are you here for me or for him?' she asked, watching for any shiftiness in his eyes.

He grinned a wickedly sexy grin. 'When I was watching you walk to this table, I can assure you I was not thinking of your father.'

Heat bloomed in her cheeks at the provocative statement. She lifted her chin, defying the desire he wanted her to share. 'I decided to flaunt what you weren't going to get.'

'Decisions, decisions,' he mocked, gesturing an appeal. 'Can we leave your father out of them for the rest of this evening? Just enjoy all there is to enjoy just between ourselves?'

He was very appealing.

The man had everything—looks, intelligence, the sexiest eyes in the world, and he was undermining her prejudice at a rate of knots. Nevertheless, she couldn't quite set aside an ulterior motive for this date with her. On the other hand, why shouldn't she take pleasure in being with him, move her father to the sidelines, denying him any power to influence the play between her and Jake? After all, she was the one with the power to decide how far she would get involved with this man.

She gave him a hard look of warning. 'As long as it's kept between ourselves, I'm happy to take a more positive attitude towards you.'

'And I'm happy to be your secret lover,' he replied, his eyes dancing with unholy teasing.

Her heart performed a somersault. 'I didn't say anything about becoming lovers.'

'Just assuring you that private moments will be kept private.' He opened up his menu. 'Let's salivate over what's on offer together. Did you see that the hottest dishes are printed in red?'

*He* was the hottest dish.

Laura dragged her mind off visualising him as her lover and reopened her menu. 'I prefer spicy to hot, hot,' she said, looking at the list of entrées.

'Okay. We cross out the red print ones.'

'You don't have to. Choose whatever you like.'

'There's so much to like, it will be better if we can share, don't you think? Have a taste of each other's choices? Broaden the experience?'

Sharing the taste... Laura's stomach curled. It sounded intimate. It was intimate. And suddenly she didn't care about other agendas. She wanted this experience with him.

'Great idea!' she said, and allowed herself to smile.

His eyes twinkled with pleasure, completely dissipating the anger she had carried to this meeting.

'You're incredibly beautiful when you smile,' he remarked. 'I hope I can make you smile all evening for the sheer pleasure of looking at you.'

She laughed. 'No chance! I'm going to be busy eating.'

'I'll try for in between bites.'

'I'll be drooling over the food.'

He laughed. 'Speaking of which, what entrées would you like to try?'

A smile was still on her face as she read the yummy list. The happy excitement about tonight with Jake had come bouncing back. He was right about making decisions for herself. She should trust her own instincts and go with what instinctively felt right.

# CHAPTER FIVE

THE waitress advised them to choose only one main course with a side dish of vegetables to share since they were ordering two separate entrées. The helpings were large and they would surely want to leave room for dessert.

'Definitely,' Laura agreed. 'I have to try the sesame ice cream with candied popcorn and chocolate.'

'And I want the Dessert Cocktail,' Jake said with relish. 'Sounds wonderful—caramelized pear, London gin, lillet blanc and crème de cacao shaken and served with the chocolate, sesame and cashew bark.'

It sounded very James Bond to Laura who couldn't help grinning over the thought. Jake might not be 007 but he was certainly tall, dark, handsome and dangerous, especially to any peace of mind. Somehow peace of mind wasn't rating highly at the moment. A thrilling buzz was running through her veins and she was now determined on milking maximum enjoyment out of the night, throwing caution and the Machiavellian shadow of her father to the winds.

'That's a big smile,' Jake commented, his eyes simmering sexily.

'Loving the idea of having a piece of your dessert,' she tossed back, knowing she wanted a piece of him, too.

'Food, glorious food!' he quoted from the musical *Oliver*, half singing the words and making her laugh.

'We have to decide on which one of our main courses to go for now,' she reminded him.

'We'll go with your choice—the stir-fried pork, bacon, smoked tofu, garlic shoots, garlic chives and chilli oil—and I'll pick the vegetable dish.'

'Which will be?'

'Stir-fried wild bamboo pith, snow peas and quail eggs with ginger and garlic.'

'We'll probably end up with garlic breath.'

'We can try washing it away with wine.'

He ordered an expensive bottle of sauvignon blanc.

The waitress departed, having assured them of prompt service.

Laura heaved a satisfied sigh as she sat back and relaxed, happy to enjoy the ambience of the restaurant and the company of the man she was with.

'How was your week?' she asked.

He gave her a very sensual smile. 'All the better for ending here with you. How was yours?'

'Annoying.'

He raised a quizzical eyebrow.

She made a rueful grimace. 'I couldn't get you out of my head.'

He laughed. 'I'm glad the problem wasn't entirely mine. The question is whether to feed the fever or starve it?'

'I'm all for feeding tonight.'

'So am I.'

His eyes said he wanted to eat her all up and Laura couldn't deny she wanted to taste him again, too, but she wasn't ready to commit herself to becoming lovers on such short acquaintance.

'I meant here at the restaurant, Jake. I don't really know you, do I?' She eyed him seriously. 'My father obviously likes you very much, which isn't a great recommendation. I think from your visit last Sunday, you can draw a fairly clear picture of my life, but I don't have one of yours, apart from your mentioning that your mother has passed away. What about the rest of your family?

He shrugged. 'Both my parents died when I was eighteen. I was their only child. I've been on my own ever since. My life is not complicated by having to manage relationships, Laura. As I saw you doing last Sunday.'

'You move to your own beat,' she said wryly.

'Yes.'

'No live-in girlfriends along the way to here and now?'

He shook his head. 'I haven't met anyone I wanted to be with every day.'

She nodded, extremely wary of the live-in situation herself. 'It's a big ask, day in, day out. I can't see myself even wanting to try it.'

He smiled, eyes twinkling with understanding. 'You wish to be a free spirit.'

'I've seen my mother compromise too much,' she shot at him.

'Not all men are like your father, Laura,' he said seriously. 'My parents' marriage was very happy. I grew up in a loving home. I wish I still had it.'

She felt a stab of envy, though his loss triggered sympathy, as well. 'You were lucky to have what you did, Jake, but I guess missing that home life leaves you feeling very lonely.'

His eyelids dropped to half-mast, narrowing the flash of dangerous glitter. Some powerful emotion was coursing through him, belied by the offhand tone he used in his reply. 'It's been ten years, Laura. I've learnt to live with being alone.'

She didn't think so. She sensed anger in him at the loss, a deep abiding anger, so intense there was an edge of savagery to it. The image of a lone wolf endlessly prowling for some measure of satisfaction leapt into her mind.

Had he been looking for it in the career he had chosen? The bankruptcy business was centred on loss and he'd spoken almost passionately about the trauma of it and wanting to help when she'd taken him out to the garden last week. It had surprised her at the time. The conviction started to grow in her that he was not like her father. Not at all like him.

Which made the pleasure she could share with him much more acceptable.

'The self-sufficient man,' she said, smiling. 'Who doesn't want to be alone tonight.'

His smile was definitely wolfish, exciting her with the wild thought of howling at the moon together, mating on top of a mountain under the stars. Ridiculous since they were in the middle of a city, but the female animal inside her was strongly aroused, wanting to explore intimate possibilities with Jake Freedman.

The waitress returned with the bottle of wine and filled their glasses for them. Jake lifted his in a toast. 'To learning a lot more about each other.'

Laura nodded agreement. 'I'll drink to that.'

She clicked her glass to his and they both sipped the wine.

'I heard you tell Eddie that you worked out at a gym. Do you go often?'

'Usually after work. It's a good way of winding down.'

And every woman in the place would be eyeing him off, Laura thought, wondering if he also used the gym for casual pick-ups. She couldn't imagine him not having a very active sex life. Which, she strongly suspected, he kept completely separate from his work life.

'You said last Sunday you didn't want to want me,

Jake,' she reminded him. 'Is that because it's difficult to avoid it touching on your career with me being my father's daughter?'

He made an ironic grimace. 'I think it's a complication we'd both prefer not to have.' He leaned forward, his dark riveting eyes shooting a blaze of purpose at her. 'Let's shut the door on it. Just do what we want to do together, regardless of other issues. Are you brave enough to go down that road with me, Laura? Strong enough to make the choice for yourself?'

The challenge propelled her pulse into overdrive. Brave? Strong? She wanted to belief that of herself, but was it really true? She'd always shied clear of intimate entanglements, afraid of how they might affect her. The couple of sexual experiments she'd allowed herself had been more out of curiosity—a desire for knowledge—than a wish for a closer, more possessive attachment.

Jake Freedman tapped something far more primal in her and that was scary because it was uncontrollable. She wanted to explore it, to feel whatever he could make her feel, but she couldn't quite override the sense of danger with him. Already he had taken up far too much possession of her mind. Would that go away with passion spent or would she end up losing the mental independence she needed for self-survival?

She could not—would not—end up like her mother.

'I like to come and go as I please, Jake,' she said firmly. 'I don't think I'd mind joining you along the road now and then, but...'

Her mouth dried up as a dazzling grin spread across his wickedly handsome face.

'Fine...perfect...we can draw a map and meet when the time is right for both of us.'

She laughed with nervous excitement. He was so obliging, so tempting, so incredibly sexy, and surely there was nothing too scary about having an intermittent adventure with him.

The waitress arrived with their entrées. Laura had chosen the fried salt-and-pepper silken tofu with spicy coriander salad and Jake had decided on the Northern-style lamb and fennel dumplings. Both dishes looked and smelled deliciously enticing.

'We divide them in half. Right?' she said eagerly.

'Sharing is the deal,' he agreed, obviously enjoying her keen anticipation. 'Go ahead. Divvy up.'

Jake watched her halve the portions on each plate, liking her meticulous care, liking everything about her, especially the determination to run her own life as she saw fit. It freed him of any guilt over pursuing what he wanted with her. She was not looking for a happy-ever-love with him. She didn't believe in it.

Given what he'd seen of her parents' marriage, he understood where she was coming from and why she would shy clear of serious attachments. Alex Costarella had wrought damage on his own family, as well as on many others'. He'd robbed Jake of his parents, but unlike them, Laura was alive and kicking. She would survive. An intermittent relationship with him should not create a problem for either of them.

'We should start with the dumplings and finish with the salad,' she said authoritatively.

'Yes, ma'am.'

It startled her into a laugh. 'I didn't mean to be bossy.'

He grinned. 'I don't mind taking advice from a serious foodie. In fact, I would like you to extend my education on gourmet delights.'

She blushed. 'You're teasing me. I think I'll just shut up and eat.'

'Enjoy.'

She ate with obvious relish. It was a pleasure watching her appreciating each different taste. 'Please feel free to comment,' he urged. 'I wasn't really teasing you, Laura. I want you to share your thoughts on these dishes with me.'

'Tell me what *you* think,' she countered.

He did and she happily responded.

The whole meal was a pleasure, not only for the wonderful variety of tastes, but also Laura's delight in them. She made it a great sensory experience and not only on the palate. The licking of her lips, the heavenly rolling of her eyes, the rise and fall of her lush breasts when she sighed with satisfaction, the warm smiles that fuelled a burning lust to have all of her…Jake itched to sweep her off to bed and take his fill of Laura Costarella.

He couldn't recall ever having enjoyed an evening with a woman so much. It was impossible to tolerate the thought of it ending here. He had to persuade her to want what he wanted. And not just tonight. He knew one night wouldn't satisfy him. Not now.

They finished up with nougatine and rum truffle candy bars to nibble as they sipped the last of the German Riesling he'd ordered to accompany their dessert.

'This has been fantastic, Jake. Thank you so much for giving me the experience.' Her beautiful blue eyes twinkled. 'Definitely a more than fair exchange for my Sunday lunch.'

'Apart from Neil Perry, what other top Sydney chefs would you like to try out?' he asked, determined on tempting her into his company again.

She reeled off a number of names, then shook her head. 'I can't afford to go to their restaurants but one day I hope to. In the meantime, I drool over their cook books.'

'I can afford them, Laura, but I don't want to go alone. Nor do I know as much about food as you do. I'm happy to pay for you to be my educator, my companion, to share your knowledge and pleasure with me. Will you do that?'

She hesitated, frowning over his proposition.

'An adventure into fine dining,' he pressed.

'With you footing the bill,' she said, wincing over the inevitable cost.

'Why not? It's my idea.' Not to mention the desire running hot behind it.

'It's like…you're buying me, Jake.'

He shook his head. 'Buying your interest, your knowledge. Expanding my own. Say yes, Laura. It will be fun together. As tonight has been.'

Which was undeniable.

'You're right,' she said on a sigh of surrender. 'It's no fun alone. I'm sorry I can't pay my way but I simply don't earn enough with only a part-time job.'

He waved a dismissive hand. 'Don't worry about it. I'll consider it an investment in broadening my life.' He flashed her a mischievous grin. 'You could bring a garden rose for me to smell at our next restaurant. You're right about the hothouse ones sold by street vendors. They have no scent.'

She laughed, a lovely ripple of sound that was headier than the wine. 'You actually went out and tried them?'

'I did.'

'Well, there's hope for you yet.'

'Hope for what?'

'For being more aware of nature's beautiful gifts.'

'I'm very aware of one sitting directly opposite me.' He reached across the table and took one of her hands in his, lightly rubbing his thumb over its palm as his eyes bored into hers, every forceful atom of his mind willing her to concede to the strong sexual attraction between them. 'Spend the night with me, Laura. I've booked a room in the Intercontinental Hotel. It's only a short walk from here. Let's satisfy what was left unsatisfied last Sunday.'

It was blunt.

It was honest.

It promised nothing more than it said.

It had to be this way or no way.

Despite all he liked about her, she was still Alex Costarella's daughter and that fact would separate them when the time for retribution came. Jake had been moving towards that destination for ten years. Whatever he had with Laura could only be a brief sidetrack.

# CHAPTER SIX

A WILD MÊLÉE of emotions pumped through Laura's heart. The response of her body to Jake's proposition was instantaneous; her stomach contracting in sheer yearning for the satisfaction he promised, her thighs pressing together to contain the rush of excitement at their apex, her breasts tingling with the need to be touched, held, given the same sensual caressing he was using on her hand.

The simple answer was yes.

She wanted to go with him, wanted to feel how it would be, wanted to know, but the surge of desire was so compelling it frightened her. This wasn't just curiosity. Nor was it an experiment over which she had control.

And there were other considerations.

She was supposed to be spending the night at Eddie's apartment. Her brother would worry if she didn't turn up there so he would have to be told, though she need not actually speak to him. A text message would suffice. Eddie would undoubtedly repeat what he'd said before—*make damned sure you keep it at sex and don't get hooked on him.*

Good advice. Except Laura had the fluttery feeling that she was hooked. Deeply and irrevocably hooked. Although if Jake ever demanded too much of her, surely she had enough backbone to walk away. He was offering her great dinners and very probably great sex. It shouldn't be a problem for her to take both and enjoy both.

His thumb pressed into her palm. 'What reservations do you have, Laura?' he asked quietly, the dark brilliant eyes scouring hers for answers, challenging whatever barriers were in her mind.

Pride wouldn't allow her to admit she was scared of his power over her. It suddenly seemed terribly important to appear brave and strong, not only to him but also to herself. She forced a smile. 'None. I was just thinking I don't want to be left wondering, so let's do it.'

He relaxed into a laugh—a deep rumble of pleasure that thrummed along her shaky nerves, promising all would be well between them. His eyes sparkled delight in her as he said, 'You are one amazing woman.'

She raised her eyebrows in arch surprise. 'Why?'

He grinned. 'Before I met you I was expecting a pampered princess or a calculating miss, used to getting to her own way. It was a surprise to find you were neither. But you are quite strikingly beautiful,

Laura, and beautiful women tend to use that power to see how far a man will go for them.'

'I don't like power games,' she said sharply, hating any form of manipulation.

'No. You're wonderfully direct with what you think.' He lifted his glass in a toast to her. 'May you always be so.'

She cocked her head on one side consideringly. 'Were you buttering me up with the foodie thing?'

He shook his head. 'I want more than a one-night stand with you. I'm quite certain I'll enjoy our adventure into fine dining.'

'So will I.'

'Then we're agreed on our points of contact.'

She laughed, happily giddy with the sense that this wasn't so much a dangerous trap she might fall into but a course of action that could give her tremendous pleasure. Her whole body zinged with excitement at the points of contact soon to be made.

'Will you excuse me for a few minutes?' she said, rising from her chair. 'I need to go to the ladies' and call my brother.'

'Why your brother?' he asked, frowning over the possibility of third-party interference.

'I arranged to stay overnight at his apartment. I don't want Eddie worrying about me.'

'Ah! Of course! You didn't want your father to know. He won't know any more from me, Laura,' he quickly assured her.

She paused a moment, eyeing him with deadly

seriousness. 'If you don't keep to that, Jake, I won't see you again.'

'Understood.'

A secret affair, Laura thought, liking the idea of it as she made her way to the ladies' room. Somehow it was less threatening than a relationship she would be expected to talk about. Eddie would have to know but she could trust him to keep it private if she asked him to. They had a solid sister/brother pact about running their own lives—away from their father.

However, she had no sooner sent the necessary text than her mobile phone rang in response. With a rueful sigh, she reopened it, knowing Eddie was going to express concern.

'You said you weren't going to fall at his feet,' he snapped in disapproval.

'I'm standing upright and walking to where I want to go. Just like you do, Eddie,' she reminded him.

'You're younger than I am, Laura. Not as street-hard. I tell you, that guy knows how to play all the angles. You should be standing back a bit, more on guard.'

She knew it was Jake's connection to her father making her brother overprotective but she had dealt with that issue. Until it raised its head again—if it did—she was determined on ignoring it and pleasing herself. 'I want this, Eddie. Let it be. Okay?'

In the short silence that followed she had a mental image of him grinding his teeth over her decision, not liking it one bit but forced to respect it. 'Okay,' he said grudgingly. 'Will I see you tomorrow?'

'If you're at the apartment when I come to pick up the things I've left there.'

'I'll be in. Hope this isn't one hell of a mistake, Laura.'

'I hope so, too. 'Bye for now.'

She stared at her reflection in the mirror as she refreshed her lipstick. Her eyes were very bright. Feverishly bright? Earlier this week she had likened Jake to a virus that had invaded her system, knocking her out of kilter. The invasion was much stronger tonight, both physically and mentally, and she didn't want to fight it. Surrendering to all the clamouring feelings inside her had to be right. By tomorrow she would know for certain if it was a mistake. That was better than wondering.

Jake rose from his chair as she approached their table again. 'Ready to go?' he asked as she reached it.

'Yes. Have you paid...?'

He nodded. 'And tipped. The service was excellent.'

'Absolutely. We didn't have to wait too long for anything.'

He smiled, the sexy simmer back in his eyes as he hooked her arm around his, drawing her into close physical contact with him and intimately murmuring, 'I'm glad you don't like waiting.'

Her ear tingled from the warm waft of his breath.

Her heart leapt into a wild hammering as the thought jagged through her mind that she was being too easy for him—not waiting, plunging headlong into bed with him. Probably all women were *easy* for him and she would be no different to any of the others. But did that really matter? Wasn't she going after what *she* wanted? She didn't have to be different. She just had to be true to herself.

She sucked in a deep breath to calm herself as they moved towards the exit. 'I daresay you don't have to wait for much, Jake,' she said drily.

'You're wrong.' He slid her an ironic look. 'Some things I've been waiting years for.'

'Like what?'

She caught a savage glitter in his eyes before he turned his head away and shrugged. 'Just personal goals, Laura. I guess you're impatient to make a start on your career, but you have to wait until you get your degree under your belt.'

'It will be good to finally strike out on my own,' she agreed, wondering what his personal goals were and why they sparked such a flow of strong feeling in him. A dangerous man, she thought again, dangerous and driven, but driven by what?

'I'm sure you'll find your work-life very rewarding, caring about the environment as you do,' he remarked, sliding straight back into an admiring expression, shutting the door on what he obviously wanted to keep private.

Laura decided not to try probing. Later in the

night when his guard was down and he was more re-laxed, he might reveal more about himself. It could wait. Or maybe his goals were connected to her fa-ther. In which case, she didn't want to know. Not to-night. Tonight was about exploring something else entirely and she didn't want anything to spoil it.

As they emerged onto the street she hugged his arm, secretly revelling in its strongly muscled mas-culinity. Her imagination conjured up images of him naked—the perfect male in every respect. Every woman should be allowed to have one, she told her-self, and this was simply seizing the opportunity. This connection to Jake Freedman didn't have to get complicated. In fact, she shouldn't let it become complicated. It was much safer to keep it simple.

'The hotel is about three blocks away,' he said, his mouth moving very sensually into a teasing lit-tle smile. 'Can you manage to walk that far in those gloriously erotic shoes or shall I flag down a taxi?'

She laughed, giddy with the thought of his mouth moving erotically all over her. 'I can walk, as long as it's a stroll and not a forced march.'

'I wouldn't force anything with you, Laura. This is all about choice,' he said seriously.

It was nice to have that assurance, to know she wasn't at physical risk with him. Strangely enough, it hadn't even occurred to her that she might be. It was the emotional risk she'd been concerned about. No man had ever affected her as Jake did.

'Why choose a hotel?' she asked as they walked towards it. 'We could have gone to your place.'

'My place is barely habitable. It's an old run-down terrace house that I'm in the process of renovating. There's stuff everywhere. I hope I can make it look great when it's finished, but that's not tonight or any night soon. I only have time to work on it at week-ends.'

'You're doing the renovating yourself?'

'Not all of it. Only the carpentry. My father taught me all the skills of the trade and I'm enjoying doing the work myself.'

'Your father was a carpenter?'

'No, he was an engineer but he loved working with wood. It was a hobby he shared with me in my growing-up years.'

The tone of deep affection told her he'd shared a very special bond with his father while Eddie had only ever known criticism and disapproval from their father and she had learnt to avoid the kind of contact that inevitably led to acrimony. Such different lives...

Possibly working with wood kept the family bond alive for Jake, though he'd also said last Sunday he liked to relax by doing something physical. Going to the gym was not his only outlet, and she liked the idea of him being involved with something creative. Renovating a house was similar to building an environment to a pre-designed plan.

Jake worked for her father but he definitely wasn't like him.

She would tell Eddie so tomorrow.

In the meantime, she couldn't resist lifting her free hand to slide her fingers across Jake's. 'Your skin isn't rough,' she remarked.

He was amused by her checking. 'I wear gloves for heavy work. You must do, too.' He caught her hand and held it, caressing it as he had before, smiling into her eyes. 'Definitely no calluses.'

Laura had difficulty catching her breath he was so utterly gorgeous and her mind was spinning with the wonder of how excited he made her feel. Only belatedly did it click into the line of conversation and produce a reply, the words coming out huskily. 'My mother's training. A lady should always protect her skin from damage.'

He stopped walking, halting both of them as he released her hand to lift his to her cheek, stroking it with exquisite softness. 'No damage,' he murmured.

His thumb slid under her chin, tilting it up. He unhooked his arm from hers and wrapped it around her waist. His head bent and Laura watched his mouth coming closer and closer, her heart hammering in wild anticipation for the kiss she had been remembering all week.

It didn't matter that they were standing on a public sidewalk in the centre of the city with people passing by. Everything beyond this moment with Jake faded into insignificance. The desire, the need to feel what he'd made her feel before, was pulsing through her.

His lips grazed over hers, igniting a host of electric tingles. His tongue flicked over them, soothing, seductively seeking entry, which she eagerly gave, wanting the deeper sensations, the erotic tasting, the rise of feverish passion that would blow away any lingering doubt about choosing to have this night with him.

Eagerly she surrendered her mouth to the intimate connection with his and almost instantly her inner excitement escalated, wiping all thought from her mind, making her super-aware of physical contact with him, the delicious pressure of touching points; breasts, stomach, thighs, a wild vibrancy pouring through her, making her ache with the intensity of feelings that had never been so overwhelmingly aroused.

This kiss was not just a kiss. It was total invasion, possession, wildfire sweeping beyond any control, burning her up with the need to have all of this man. Laura lost all sense of self. She was completely consumed by her response to him, and the response was too immediate, too powerful, too real for her to reason it away.

She wanted him.

More fiercely than she'd ever wanted anything.

It was a dizzying shock when he tore his mouth from hers and pressed her head onto his shoulder, making the separation decisive. Her heart was pumping so hard, the drumming of it filled her ears. Only vaguely did she hear him suck in breath. His chest expanded with it. He rubbed her back, probably an instinctive calming action. Her quivering nerve ends were grateful for it.

'Shouldn't have done that but I've been wanting to all evening,' he muttered. 'Are you okay to walk on, Laura?'

Hotel…alone together in private…bed…uninterrupted intimacy… 'Yes,' she breathed on a sigh that relieved some of the tense ache in her chest. 'As long as you hold on to me.'

A deep sexy laugh rumbled from his throat. 'Letting you go will be the problem, not holding on to you.'

His words struck a vulnerable chord in her that Laura instantly shied away from examining. 'Let's not think about problems,' she said quickly, lifting her head to shoot him a look of needful appeal. 'I only want to think about what we can have together.'

'So do I,' he answered, tenderly cupping her cheek as though she was something very precious, his dark eyes shining with pleasure in her. 'It's not far to the hotel now.'

'Okay. Give me your arm.'

He tucked her close to him. The shakiness in Laura's legs gradually lessened as they walked the rest of the way to the Intercontinental. Neither of them spoke. They moved in a haze of mutual desire, impatient for the fulfilment of it, everything else irrelevant.

The hotel had been built around the old treasury building, making spectacular use of its special features. Laura had shared an afternoon tea with her mother there after a shopping day in the city. The main gathering place was The Cortile, a marvellous two-storeyed area covered by a huge glass dome, with colonnaded walkways surrounding it. Tonight, as Laura and Jake headed around it to the reception area, elegantly dressed people were indulging in a late supper, enjoying the ambience and the music being played on a grand piano.

It was a classy hotel and Laura couldn't help feeling pleased that Jake had chosen it. Somehow it made tonight with him more special. He collected their door-key from the receptionist and as they moved to the bank of elevators, he murmured, 'I took a Bayview room. It overlooks the Botanical Gardens. I thought you'd enjoy the view over breakfast.'

Laura's heart swelled with happiness. He'd been thinking of her, planning to give her pleasure. This wasn't just about sex with him. They were going to share more. Much more. She had made the right decision. A journey with Jake Freedman was well worth having. She no longer cared about how far it might go or where it might end. He was the man she wanted to be with.

# CHAPTER SEVEN

JAKE quickly slid the door-key into the slot just inside the room and the lights came on. Everything looked fine—classy, welcoming, and most important of all, providing a private oasis, not touching on Laura's home environment nor his, completely separate to the lives they normally lived.

It had to be this way.

Bad enough that he was in the grip of uncontrollable desire for Alex Costarella's daughter. Boundaries to this affair had to be set and kept. He couldn't allow it to take over too much of his life. But right here and now he could satisfy his hunger for her, and to his immense relief she was up for it, no further delay to what they both wanted.

She walked ahead of him, moving towards the window seat with the view on the far side of the room. He watched the provocative sway of her hips, felt the tightening in his groin, started unbuttoning his shirt, impatient for action. She set her handbag on the desk as she passed it. Jake tossed his shirt on the chair in front of it, took off his shoes, his gaze fastening on her turquoise high heels with their seductive ankle straps. She had great legs and the thought of having them wound around him brought his erection to full tilt.

'Lots of city lights but it's too dark to see the botanical gardens,' she remarked.

'Won't be dark in the morning,' he muttered, unzipping his trousers.

She glanced back over her shoulder. 'I think I like this view better,' she said with sparkling interest, her eyes feasting on his bare chest and shoulders. 'I've been wondering how you'd look naked.'

He laughed, exhilarated by the honesty of her lust for him. He whipped off the rest of his clothes, dumping them on the chair with his shirt. 'Hope you're not disappointed,' he said, grinning with confidence, knowing his physique invariably drew attention from women at the gym.

'Not one bit,' she answered emphatically, examining all his *bits*, which raised the already high level of Jake's excitement.

She lifted an arm and hooked the long tumbling fall of her black curls away from her neck, her other hand reaching for the top of the zipper at the back of her dress, obviously intent on removing her own clothes.

'Let me,' Jake said hastily, finding the bared nape of her neck incredibly erotic and wanting the pleasure of slowly uncovering the rest of her, visually feasting on her lush femininity.

A few quick strides and he was taking over the task, opening up the snugly fitting bodice, exposing the satin-smooth, elegant slope of her back, which, delightfully, was uninterrupted by a bra. The line of her spine created an intriguing little valley that compelled his finger to stroke the lovely length of it. His touch raised a convulsive shiver of pleasure and he smiled, knowing her body was as taut with excitement as his own, every nerve alive with sensitivity.

Eager to see more of her, he unzipped the top of the skirt and peeled it from her hips, letting it fall to the floor. The sight of a sexy black G-string encircling her small waist and bisecting a totally luscious bottom sucked the air from his lungs and blistered his mind with urgent desire. He barely stopped himself from moving forward and fitting himself to the tantalising cleft.

Better to remove the last scrap of clothing first. He hooked his thumbs under the waistband and glided it over the soft mounds, down the long, lissom thighs and the taut curves of her calves, every millimetre raising the raging heat in his blood. The flimsy fabric caught on the straps of the erotic shoes. Couldn't leave them on. The stiletto heels could do him a damage in the throes of passion and Jake was already envisaging a huge amount of fantastic activity in bed.

'Sit down, Laura. Makes it easier to take your shoes off.'

He was still crouched, ready to free her feet when she swivelled around and sat on the window seat.

The eye-level view of her beautiful full breasts was a mind-blowing distraction. She leaned back so they tilted up at him, large rosy aureoles with peaked nipples shooting temptation. He stared, captivated for several moments before gaining his wits to lift his gaze to see if she was deliberately teasing him.

Her thickly lashed blue eyes looked darker than before, simmering with an inviting sultriness. She wanted him enthralled by her fabulous femininity, wanted to drive him wild for her. Whether it was a deliberate exertion of her woman-power or not, it reminded Jake of who she was and how careful he had to be not to become ensnared by this woman.

He fixed his attention on the shoes, forced his fingers to undo the ankle straps. In a few moments he could take all he wanted of her, revel in having it, and he would, all night long, but come the morning he had to be sane enough to walk away from her and keep her at a mental distance until the next time they were together.

Shoes off.

They were both completely naked now.

He stood up, and the act of towering over her triggered his sense of man-power. He was in charge of this encounter. He'd brought her to this cave and he would control everything that happened between them. With a surge of adrenalin-pumped confidence he leaned over, gripped her waist and lifted her off the window-seat, whirling her straight over to the bed, laying her down, positioning himself beside her with one leg flung over hers, holding her captive so he could touch the rest of her at will.

'Kiss me again,' she commanded, her voice huskily inviting, her eyes glittering with the need for passion to blow them both away.

'I will,' he promised, but not her mouth, not yet.

The rose-red nipples were pointed up at him, hard evidence of her arousal and he wanted her more aroused than he was. He closed his mouth around them, drawing on the distended flesh, sucking, his tongue swirling, lashing. She wrapped her hands around his head, fingers thrusting through his hair, dragging on his scalp, her body arching, aching for a more consuming possession.

Not yet... Not yet...

He swept a trail of hot kisses down over her stomach to the arrow of dark springy curls leading to the most intimate cleft between her thighs. He could smell the wonderfully heady scent of her desire for him as he dipped his mouth into the soft folds of her sex, intent on driving this centre of excitement to fever pitch. He exulted in tasting her hot wetness, exulted even more as she writhed to the rhythm of his stroking, crying out at the frantic tension building up inside her, jack knifing up to grab his shoulders and tug his body over hers.

He was ready to oblige now, knowing her entire being was screaming for him and he was still in control, though bursting to unleash his own knife-edge desire. As he lifted himself up, her legs locked around him, her hips already rocking, and there was no more waiting. He surged into the slick passage to the edge of her womb and dropped his head to ravish her mouth, wanting total invasion, absolute domination of this intimate togetherness.

Yet she met the attack of his kiss with an assault of her own, a fusion of heat that turned aggression into a melting pot of exploding sensations and he lost every vestige of control. Her legs goaded him into a series of fast thrusts, clamping around him at the point of deepest penetration as she moaned at the intense satisfaction of it, then rolling her hips around the hard heated fullness of him as he withdrew to plunge again, driven to hear and feel her pleasure in him over and over, wildly intoxicated by the sense of being drawn from peak to peak, each one raising the stakes to a higher level of fierce feeling.

It was like riding a storm, hurtling towards the eye of it at breakneck velocity, their lives hanging on holding on to each other until they reached beyond the violent shattering that threatened every escalating moment and landed in a place where they could peacefully return to themselves again. Jake didn't care how long that took...minutes, hours.

It was a fantastic journey—her response to him, what he felt himself, a host of primal elements whipping them towards a final crescendo. The breakthrough was a totally cataclysmic moment, both of them crying out as the storm released them into a free fall of exquisite delight and they floated down on a sweet cloud of ecstasy, still clamped together as they shifted into a more relaxed embrace, prolonging what they had shared as long as they could.

Even just cuddling her close to him was sweet, smelling the scent of her hair, winding strands of it around his fingers, rubbing his cheek over its silkiness, feeling the rhythm of her breathing in the rise and fall of her breasts against his chest, the sensual stroking of one of her legs between his, knowing she was still revelling in feeling him.

Eventually thoughts drifted through Jake's mind, carrying a need to make sense of why this sexual experience with Laura had been so incredibly intense. Never before had he been completely locked into having a woman like this, driven to take, driven beyond what he'd previously known. His liaisons with other women had been more casual pleasures, enjoyable, relaxing—what he'd considered normal. Why did the animal chemistry go deeper with Laura Costarella?

She was definitely the most beautiful woman he'd ever taken to bed. Had that heightened his excitement? Somehow he couldn't quite believe that would affect him so much. His mind kept niggling at her family connection to Alex Costarella. Was it because of *who* she was, linking her to the passion for retribution, which had consumed most of his life for the past ten years? Or did the fact that she should have remained forbidden to him cause the difference?

Impossible to pin it down. All he absolutely knew

was he couldn't allow this affair to escalate into a serious relationship. If he kept to that, surely he could simply enjoy what she gave him—her companionship over the dinners he would arrange, and the intense physical pleasure they would share in bed together afterwards.

Settling on this determination, Jake shut down on the questions, intent on making the most of this night together. 'Feeling good?' he asked, wondering what she was thinking, if she was happily satisfied with her decision to set aside her reservations about him.

'Mmmh...very good.'

There was a smile in her voice.

He didn't need to know any more. He smiled his own contentment with the situation.

She began an idle stroking of his body—slow, erotic caresses, which instantly stimulated him into touching more of her, lingering over every voluptuous curve, loving the wonderfully sensual feel of her womanliness. Touching moved into kissing as they explored each other in intimate detail, arousing the need to merge again, to feel all that could be felt between them.

It was marvellous, less frenzied this time but still incredibly exciting with the mutual abandonment of all inhibitions. It left Jake feeling flooded with pleasure, and the gradually ebbing waves of it lulled him into a deep untroubled sleep.

\* \* \*

Laura woke to morning light. They'd forgotten to draw the curtains last night, too consumed with each other to think of anything beyond the sensational intimacy they'd shared. She rolled over to look at the man who had taken her to heights of pleasure she had never even imagined, let alone known.

He was still asleep. Despite the brilliant dark eyes being shut, his face was still strongly handsome and his body... She sighed over how perfectly manly it was, just the right amount of muscularity and everything ideally proportioned. Absolutely gorgeous. Sex appeal in spades. What a fantastic night she'd had with him! No regrets, that was for sure! Whatever happened next between them, this was one experience she would never forget.

Careful not to wake him, she slid off the bed and padded quietly to the bathroom, wanting to freshen up and look good when he did open his eyes. She grabbed her handbag off the desk in passing, glad that it contained a small hairbrush and lipstick. With no change of clothes to wear, it was a relief to find bathrobes provided for guests. She could lounge around in one of them until it was near time to leave the hotel.

Having showered and groomed herself as best she could, Laura returned to the bedroom to find Jake still asleep. Quite happy for a little time on her own, she settled on the window-seat, her back against the side wall, feet up on the cushion, arms hugging her knees, instinctively wanting to hug in all the lovely feelings generated by last night with Jake.

It wasn't just the sex, although that had been unbelievably awesome. Even now her heart swelled with the sheer joy of learning how marvellous it could be with the right man. Nothing could have felt more *right* to her, which made her wonder if it was wrong to stand back from a serious relationship with Jake. So far she liked everything he had shown of himself, and definitely wanted to know a lot more. Maybe they could have something great together.

The view of the botanical gardens caught her eye. A stroll through them would be a pleasant way of continuing the day—time to chat about their interests and look for more common ground between them. She would like to see the house he was renovating, too, the kind of home he was making for himself. The environment people chose to live in could speak volumes about them. Sharing the private life of Jake Freedman was an exciting prospect and Laura was hugging that to herself, too, when his voice broke into her hopeful reverie.

'Happy with the view this morning?'

She laughed, bubbling over with high spirits and looking at him with sparkling pleasure. 'It's lovely! The sun is shining and it's going to be a beautiful day.'

He grinned at her as he rolled out of bed, saying cheerfully, 'So let's make a start on it. Call room service and order breakfast for both of us while I freshen up in the bathroom.'

'What would you like?'

'You choose. I have great faith in your food judgement.'

He left her grinning, enjoying the back view of him as he headed off to the bathroom. Only when this vision was cut off did she swing her legs off the window-seat and set about ordering their breakfast, choosing what she wanted herself and hoping Jake would be pleased with everything.

He came out of the bathroom, wearing the other bathrobe and checking his watch. 'It's eight o'clock now. How long before room service arrives?'

'About another twenty minutes.'

The dark eyes twinkled sexily. 'Only time for a good-morning kiss then. And no disrobing.'

'We have the rest of the day,' she suggested happily as he drew her into his embrace.

He frowned. 'No. No we don't. There's work I have to get done on the house before the plumber comes tomorrow.'

'Can I help you?' she asked impulsively, wanting to be with him.

He shook his head. 'You would be a major distraction, Laura. I'll work more efficiently on my own.'

He grazed his lips over hers—a distraction that didn't quite soothe the stab of disappointment over the rejection of her offer. She told herself his reasoning was fair enough and opened her mouth for a whole-hearted kiss. He'd given her a wonderful night and there would be more in the future. No need to be greedy, asking for today, as well.

It was a soft, very sensual kiss, and he withdrew from it before it escalated into wild passion, brushing her hair tenderly from her face, smiling into her eyes. 'Thank you for last night. We'll do it again soon,' he promised her.

'Thank *you*. I'll look forward to it,' she said, inwardly craving much more from him but doing her best to accept the situation gracefully.

'I'll book a taxi to take you from the hotel to Eddie's apartment after we've had breakfast.' He stepped back from her and moved towards the telephone on the desk, asking, 'Where does he live, Laura?'

'Paddington.'

'That's handy.' He grinned at her as he picked up the receiver. 'We can share the taxi. I'll see you to his place first before going on home.'

'Where do you live?'

'Next suburb. Woollahra.'

Virtually in walking distance from Eddie's apartment, she thought, watching him make the call. She wanted to ask what street, but held her tongue, knowing she would be tempted to go there and suddenly frightened of how deeply she was being drawn by this man.

Jake didn't want a full-on relationship. He'd told her so at dinner last night. And she had been super-cautious about going down that road, too. Obviously nothing had changed for him. It shouldn't have changed for her, either. She had to keep her head straight about this, not get twisted up by emotions that could mess with the decisions she'd made about her life.

A journey with meeting places.

Best to keep to that.

But somehow she couldn't really take pleasure in the breakfast they shared. It didn't sit right in her stomach. And she hated the taxi trip to Paddington, knowing Jake was travelling on without her. It took an act of will to smile her goodbye at him. And then, of course, she had to face Eddie and say everything had been fine.

Which was the truth.

Though not quite.

It had been fantastic, brilliant, totally engaging.

Too engaging.

And that was dangerous.

# CHAPTER EIGHT

To Eddie's inevitable query about her night with Jake Freedman, she breezily answered, 'Great food, great sex, and marriage is not on the menu for either of us so don't worry about my becoming a victim of secret agendas. That's definitely out!'

Later in the day, she settled her mother's concern with, 'It won't become a serious relationship, Mum. It was just a dinner date, which I might or might not repeat.' With a mischievous smile, she added, 'Depends on how good the restaurant is if he asks me out again.'

It made her mother laugh. 'Oh, you and food!'

And she cut off her father's probe into the personal connection by regaling him with details of every spicy dish she'd tasted, virtually dismissing Jake's company as pleasant enough but relatively unimportant.

However, it was easier to establish in other people's minds that an involvement with Jake was not a big issue than it was to convince herself. Life simply wasn't the same as before she met him. He dominated her thoughts, especially at night when she was alone in bed, her body restless with memories of their intense intimacy. It was impossible to block him out for long and she grew angry and frustrated with herself for not being able to set him at a sensible distance, especially as day followed day without any contact from him.

He hadn't given her *his* mobile telephone number.

He obviously had a silent land number at his Woollahra home because his name wasn't listed in the telephone directory.

No way could she call him at work because her father might get to hear about it.

Control of any connection between them was all on *his* side and she had no control whatsoever over yearning to be reconnected. Which was turning her into a stupid, love-sick cow and she hated being like that, hated it so much when he did finally call her on Friday afternoon, the zoom of pleasure at hearing his voice was speared through by resentment at his power to affect her so deeply. She only grudgingly managed a polite 'Hi!' to his greeting.

He didn't seem to notice any coldness in her response, rolling straight into the business of the call without any personal enquiries about her or her well-being. 'I've been trying all week to book us a table at one of your top restaurants for tomorrow night. Can't be done. They're all booked up and there hasn't been any cancellations. However, I have managed to get us a table at Peter Gilmore's Quay restaurant for next Saturday night. Is that okay with you?'

Peter Gilmore's Quay—listed as one of the top fifty restaurants in the world! It was a totally irresistible invitation. A rush of excited enthusiasm flooded over all other feelings.

'Fantastic!' tripped off her tongue. 'I saw his amazing Snow Egg dessert on a television show. It started with a layer of guava purée mixed with whipped cream. On top of that was guava-flavoured crushed ice. Then a meringue shaped like an egg and an inside that was creamy custard apple. It was topped off with a thin layer of toffee melted over it. Absolutely to die for!'

His laughter flowed through her like a fountain of joy. She couldn't help smiling, couldn't help feeling happy.

'Shall we meet there at seven o'clock? Same as last time?' he asked.

'Yes.'

'Great! See you then, Laura.'

Click!

That was it from him.

The happiness deflated into a rueful sigh. It was what they had agreed upon—meetings for an adventure into fine dining. Jake probably thought of any sexual follow-up as icing on the cake. And she should, too. She couldn't fault him for not suggesting they do something else together this weekend.

The problem of wanting more was entirely hers and she had to deal with it, get over it.

On the whole, Laura thought she managed that fairly well over the following week. Probably knowing they had a definite date to meet made it easier to concentrate on other things. She promised herself that at this meeting she would not expect an extension of their time together beyond the night, nor hope for it. After all, it was better for her to maintain her independence and not become slavishly besotted with the man.

Despite all her sensible reasoning, she could not control the fizz of excitement as she prepared for the big evening out. In an attempt to lessen its importance to her and show Jake she was taking this journey as casually as he was, she chose a far less dressy outfit—her best jeans, which were acceptable almost anywhere, and a peasant-style top with some wild costume jewellery she'd bought at the markets. Beaded sandals completed the look she wanted—fun, not seriously formal or serious anything else.

Eddie had been warned she would be staying overnight at his apartment again. Before leaving home she deliberately picked a yellow rose, not a red one, from her mother's garden. It was a Pal Joey rose and it had a fabulous scent. Jake might not remember asking her to bring one to their next dinner together but it definitely showed she was keeping to her side of their deal.

The ferry ride across the harbour from Mosman

to Circular Quay brought her close to the site of the restaurant. There was an excited lilt in her step as she walked around to the overseas passenger terminal where all the big cruise ships docked. Jake would be waiting for her inside Quay on the upper level and tonight would undoubtedly be brilliant all over again.

For Jake it had taken rigid discipline to wait through the fortnight before indulging himself with Laura again. It would only be a week next time, and the next, and the next, provided, of course, she wanted to go on with it. Why shouldn't he have as much of her as he could within reasonable limits? As long as he kept the end in mind, his involvement with her would not get in the way of what he had to do. It was no good wishing she wasn't Alex Costarella's daughter. Nothing could change that.

She walked into the restaurant looking like a wonderfully vivid gypsy with her black curly hair all fluffed out around her shoulders, lots of colourful beads around her neck and a peasant blouse that clung to the lush fullness of her breasts. Tight jeans accentuated the rest of her sexy curves and the instant kicks to his heart and groin told Jake she was having too big an impact on him.

He shouldn't have started this.

Shouldn't be going on with it.

But she smiled at him as he stood up from their table to greet her and a rush of pleasure had him smiling back. Just before she reached him, her hand dived into the bag she carried and brought out a full-blown yellow rose.

'For you to smell,' she said, her blue eyes sparkling a flirtatious challenge.

It surprised him, delighted him, and the pleasure she brought him intensified as he took the rose and lifted it to his nose. 'Mmmh...I shall always connect this glorious scent with you.'

She laughed. 'And I shall always connect glorious food with you. I can't wait to salivate through Peter Gilmore's menu.'

He laughed and quickly held out her chair with an invitational wave. 'At your service.'

Once they were both seated, a waiter arrived, handing them menus, and Jake asked him to bring a glass of water for the rose to keep it fresh.

As soon as they were left alone together, Laura leaned forward with another heart-kicking smile. 'I'm glad you like it.'

He grinned. 'I have plans for this rose.'

'What plans?'

'For later tonight.' Like rubbing it all over her skin and breathing in the scent as he kissed her wherever he wanted. 'I've booked us a room at the Park Hyatt at Campbell Cove....'

'Another hotel,' she broke in with a frown.

'My place is still a mess,' he explained with an apologetic grimace. 'Can't take you there, Laura.'

He never would. He *had* to keep her separate from his real life.

'But I know that hotel is terribly expensive, Jake. And on top of this dinner tonight, which will undoubtedly cost the earth…'

'The cost is not a problem to me,' he assured her.

Still she frowned. 'Does my father pay you so well?'

He shrugged. 'Well enough, but I don't count on him for my income.' *Because that was always going to end and quite soon now.* He would probably become unemployable in the bankruptcy business after he'd blown the whistle on how corrupt some of it was and he'd prepared for that outcome. 'I have a side interest that has proved very profitable.'

It piqued her curiosity. 'What is it?'

There was no harm in telling her. He doubted she would tell her father and it didn't really matter if Costarella knew, not this close to his resignation from the company. 'I buy run-down houses, renovate them in my spare time, then sell them on.'

'Ah!' She looked pleased. 'The property ladder. That's another show I sometimes watch on TV. It's always fascinating to see how each property is improved before reselling. How many houses have you done?'

'I'm currently on my fifth.'

'I'd love to see it sometime. See what you're doing to it,' she said with eager interest.

He had to clamp down hard on the strong impulse

to share it with her, to hear her views on the renovations he was doing, enjoy her interest. She was so attractive in so many ways. But anything beyond sexual intimacy had to be discouraged or he risked becoming far too hooked on Laura Costarella. Bad enough that he couldn't go to bed without wanting her in it.

'Maybe when it's further along,' he said ruefully. 'It's virtually a shell right now. Nothing to see but mess.'

She grimaced in disappointment. 'Okay. I guess you'd prefer to feel some pride in showing off your work. I take it you've made a good profit from each house you've done.'

'Good enough not to worry about paying for a great night out with you, Laura, so don't you worry about it, either. I can well afford special treats like this and having you share them doubles the pleasure.'

She visibly relaxed, smiling her heart-kicking smile at him again as she picked up her menu. 'In that case, I'm very happy to share your pleasure. I shall have no inhibitions about ordering whatever I want to try.'

No inhibitions in bed, either, Jake thought happily, relieved that she wasn't pressing the house issue. Their time together had to be time out from his real life. He couldn't consider anything else with her however much he would like to.

Laura let herself wallow in the pleasure of being with Jake. He was so attractive in every respect—looks,

wit, charm. There was nothing about him she
didn't like. However, he was big on control, and
she shouldn't forget that. Although there was a plus
side to that, too. It had obviously taken a great deal
of inner strength to set the trauma of losing his parents aside and drive himself towards establishing a
professional career, and his enterprise in climbing
the property ladder, as well, was truly admirable.

Something Eddie had said popped into her
mind—*sooner or later he'll turn you off*—but she
honestly couldn't see that happening, definitely not
tonight. In fact, she was so turned on, it was impossible to find any wrongness in him.

He was the best company over dinner, relishing
and enjoying the amazingly wonderful food as much
as she did. The conversation between them was fun.
The sexy twinkle in his eyes kept her excitement
bubbling. She loved every bit of him, which should
have set warning signals off in her head, but it was
so giddy with delight, no sense of caution was even
registered.

Again it was an easy walk to the hotel. Her body
was humming with delicious anticipation. Her feet
wanted to dance all the way. Jake had brought the
rose she'd given him at the restaurant, twiddling it in
his fingers as they walked, smiling down at it, and
she smiled at it, too, imagining he intended taking
it home with him as a romantic reminder of her.

She knew this wasn't supposed to be a romantic
relationship. It was probably crazy wanting it to turn

into one, yet all her female instincts were insisting this man was the right man for her. He wasn't *demanding* anything of her. It was simply great being together.

The hotel was brilliantly sited right below the harbour bridge. A set of glass doors on the far side of their room showcased a fabulous view of the opera house. Laura couldn't help loving the luxury of it, couldn't help loving the man who was giving it to her. As soon as the door was closed behind them, she turned to hug him tightly and kiss him with every fibre of her being, unable to wait another second to feel all he could make her feel.

Almost instantly they were on fire for each other, quick hungry kisses turning into fierce, needful passion. The barrier of clothes was unbearable. She broke away to get rid of hers and laughed as she saw Jake clamping the stem of the rose between his teeth to free his hands for the same purpose.

'Just as well I picked off the thorns,' she tossed at him.

'Mmmh...' was all he could answer.

Naked and still laughing with wild exhilaration, she raced him to the bed, landing and rolling until her caught her, trapping her into stillness with one strong leg flung over hers. She looked up into wickedly glittering eyes, her chest heaving for breath, her heart hammering with excitement.

'You can't kiss me with that rose between

your teeth,' she teased, her lower body wriggling provocatively against his.

He plucked the rose free and started caressing her face with it. 'I've been fantasising about doing this all evening. Lie still, Laura. Close your eyes. Feel the petals gliding over your skin. Breathe in the scent of them.'

It took enormous control to follow his instructions but it was worth the effort, focussing on the amazing sensuality of what he was doing, the soft graze of the rose, tantalisingly gentle, followed by a trail of kisses that had all her nerve ends buzzing. It made her feel like a pagan goddess being worshipped, anointed with perfume and brought to tingling life by a ceremony of slowly escalating physical ministrations.

She had never been so acutely aware of her body, hadn't realised she had erotic zones below her hipbones, behind her knees, on the soles of her feet. To be touched like this everywhere, to be kissed as though every inch of her was adored…it was an incredible experience, mesmerising, heavenly.

Finally he came to her most intimate parts, caressing her to an exquisite tension, making it impossible for her to lie still any longer. Her body arched in need for release and she cried out his name, desperately wanting him to take her to the end now.

He moved swiftly to oblige and it was wondrous all over again, the ebb and flow of extreme sensations gathering momentum to a fantastic climax, then the delicious aftermath of sweet contentment, the scent of the yellow rose still lingering on her skin, adding its heady pleasure to their intimate togetherness.

Laura had never felt so blissfully happy. To have a lover like Jake…she was incredibly lucky to have met him. She could even find it in her heart to be grateful to her father for bringing him into her life. This journey was definitely worth taking and she hoped it would go on for a long, long time.

As they were leaving the hotel the next morning Jake asked, 'Will you be free to join me next Saturday night? I've booked a table at Universal, Christine Manfield's restaurant.'

*Free for you anytime,* she thought, her heart skipping with pleasure at not having to wait more than a week to be with him again. Glorious food was no longer the seductive temptation it had been, though she would absolutely enjoy it, having Jake as her dining partner.

'That would be lovely,' she said, trying not to sound too eager for his company, which was now the main drawcard. This relationship did have to be controlled. Jake was not falling all over himself to be with her every free moment he had and it was better for her if she could hold him at a distance, too, in between their meeting points,

'Same time?' he asked.

'Suits me.'

'Good!'

He gave her his brilliant, sexy smile and Laura

managed a smile back though her insides clenched, wanting, needing much more of him. She had to bite down on her tongue to stop herself pleading, *Why can't we be together today? I won't get in the way of your working on the house renovations. I'll help. We can chat, laugh, enjoy being with each other.*

The words kept pounding through her mind as they settled in the taxi that would take her to Eddie's apartment before driving on to Jake's place, but she couldn't let herself voice them. It would put Jake in a position of power over her, knowing she wanted him more than he wanted her.

Had her mother fallen into that trap with her father, showing how needy she was? If so, he'd certainly taken advantage of her vulnerability. She wasn't sure if Jake would be like that or not, but her gut feeling told her not to show any weakness that could be exploited.

It was best to keep to what they had agreed upon. If anything changed further along the line, the change had to come from him, not from her and certainly not today.

# CHAPTER NINE

TETSUYA'S, a Japanese-French fusion eatery many times listed amongst the top fifty restaurants in the world, was Jake's choice for his last night with Laura. It had the longest waiting time to secure a table—two months—and he'd actually held back his own agenda, just to have this very special dinner together before he took her father down.

He checked his watch as he waited for her to arrive, conscious of not wanting her to be late, not wanting to have a minute of this final encounter wasted. It wasn't quite seven o'clock. The hell of it was he would miss the pleasure of her company, miss the fantastic sex they had shared even more, but knew it was stupid to try spinning out their time with each other any further.

It had been good. Great. But she was her father's daughter and once the axe fell on Costarella he would come out fighting for blood in return and the first casualty would be any personal association with his accuser. Laura would be turned out of the Mosman mansion if she didn't toe that line. Even if she chose not to and fled to her brother's apartment… No, she wouldn't do that. She would stay by her mother to deflect as much of her father's venom as she could.

Tonight was it—the end.

No point in looking for any way around it.

Besides, once he'd achieved the objective he'd set for himself he wanted to move on, find the kind of relationship he'd seen between his mother and step-father, have a family of his own, hopefully sharing good times with his wife and children. Regardless of how powerfully drawn he was to Laura Costarella, he couldn't fit her into that picture.

As hot she was in bed, she kept a cool head out of it, content to go about her own life without trying to get him involved in it. This was confirmation to Jake that marriage had no appeal to her—understandable given *her* family background. Part-time lovers was as far as any man would get with Laura. It made the end of their affair easier in so far as he knew it carried no deep importance to her. He'd given her pleasure. He hoped the memory of it would not get too tainted by the angst his actions would inevitably cause in the Costarella household.

All this past week he'd been tossing up whether to tell her, warn her what was about to happen, explain why. Somehow that smacked too much of justifying himself and he didn't need to do that, not when he was meting out justice, which would eventually be evident to everyone. Besides, he'd told Laura right from the beginning he didn't want to want to her.

Understanding would come soon enough. Better for them both to enjoy this one last night.

Laura was smiling, aglow with excited anticipation as she entered Tetsuya's. She was ten minutes late, due to the public transport connections needed to get to Kent Street in the inner city—where the restaurant was located—but she was finally here for another night with Jake. And there he was, rising from the table where he'd been seated.

Her heart skipped a beat. Every time he had this impact. And his smile of pleasure on seeing her... it was like a fountain of joy bursting through her. She loved this man, loved being with him, fiercely wished they could be sharing much more than one night a week.

Though she told herself it was sensible not to get too involved, not when she still had to earn her university degree. It was halfway through the year now. In a few more months... Was Jake waiting for her to be fully qualified before inviting her into more of his life? There was quite an age gap between them. Maybe he was conscious of that, too. Whatever his reasons for keeping their relationship so strictly limited, Laura felt sure they would wear out eventually. They were too good together—great together—for this journey to ever end.

She couldn't resist planting a greeting kiss on his cheek before sitting down. 'Sorry I'm a bit late. The bus trip was slow. Lots of people getting on and off.'

'No problem,' he assured her, his deep rich voice curling around her heart, warming it with pleasure. 'You're here. And I've been perusing the menu. This promises to be a fantastic dining experience.'

'Oh, wow! I've been *so* looking forward to it.'

He laughed at her excitement as they both took their seats. Laura loved his laugh, the sexy male rumble of it, the way it lit up his handsome face, the dancing twinkles in his eyes.

'I want us to do the gustatory menu—all eight courses of it. Are you up for it?' he asked.

Laura goggled at him. 'Eight courses!'

'They won't be big. Just a marvelous range of tastes.'

'Let me see.' She held out her hand for the menu and he passed it over. The list of dishes Jake wanted proved irresistible. 'I'm up for it,' she said decisively.

It would obviously cost Jake another small fortune, but also obviously he didn't care so Laura refused to feel guilty about the expense. It was his choice. He grinned at her, knowing she was happy to succumb to temptation.

She sighed. 'You're spoiling me rotten with all this, Jake.'

An oddly rueful expression twisted his grin. 'You've given me more than money can buy, Laura. I should probably thank you for being you.'

Why did that sound…almost as if he was saying goodbye to her? Laura frowned over the uncomfortable niggle. Surely he was just trying to balance out what they had together, make it feel okay to her. 'It's no big deal being me,' she said critically.

He shook his head, his eyes gently mocking her. 'I can't imagine enjoying our dinners so much with anyone else.'

She relaxed into a relieved smile. 'Then I should thank you for being you because I can't imagine it, either.'

'Good to be in accord on that point.'

She laughed. 'I think we're in accord on many points.'

'True. Shall we order now?'

He signalled their readiness to a waiter while Laura happily assured herself that everything was fine between them.

Again it was another brilliant evening with Jake. The dinner was sensational. It was great fun enjoying and discussing the various tastes, comparing it to what they'd eaten in other restaurants. Laura visited the ladies' room just before they were about to leave and on her way back to their table, she was struck by another little stab of uncertainty.

Jake was not looking for her return. He sat in pensive mode, a dark, bleak expression wiping out all the sparkles he'd shot her way during dinner. It didn't take much intuition to realise something was wrong—something in the private life he didn't share with her. Wasn't it time that he did? They'd been seeing each other on a very intimate basis for almost three months now. Surely he knew her well enough to trust her with what was in his mind.

He brightened as she reached the table, pulling himself back from the place he'd travelled to without her, but Laura's fighting spirit had been pricked into taking a stand. 'What were you thinking of just now, Jake?'

He shook his head, a wry little smile curling his mouth as he rose from his chair. 'A piece of the past. Nothing to do with you, Laura. I've called a taxi for us. It's waiting outside.'

He tucked her arm around his as she frowned over his evasive reply. 'I want to know,' she said, shooting him a searching look.

He grimaced at her obstinacy, but did answer her. 'I was thinking of my parents. How much they enjoyed sharing meals together.'

'Oh!' Laura's heart instantly lifted. The memory had obviously saddened Jake but she felt it did have something to do with her—a connection to what *they* were doing, which he enjoyed with her! It made her feel their relationship was more meaningful to him than he was willing to admit at this point.

'I've booked us into the Park Hotel tonight,' he told her as they made their exit from the restaurant.

Another hotel. She knew it overlooked Hyde Park in the city centre, which gave them only a short trip to Paddington and Woollahra in the morning. It always disappointed her that he didn't ask her home with him but she'd decided never to push it. Besides, she was still cherishing that link to his parents, whom he'd loved very much.

They didn't chat in the taxi. Laura was keenly anticipating the sexual connection with Jake and she imagined his mind was occupied with it, too. It seemed to her he held her hand more tightly than usual, his long fingers strongly interlaced with hers, their pads rubbing her palm. She silently craved more skin-to-skin contact, barely controlling her impatience to dive into bed with him.

Certainly their desire for each other hadn't waned at all. As soon as the door of the hotel room was closed behind them they were locked in a fierce embrace, kissing like there was no tomorrow, shedding clothes as fast as they could on their way to the bed, totally consumed with a wild passion that demanded to be slaked before easing into a more sensual lovemaking.

Even that seemed to carry more intensity than usual, more need for continually intimate contact, and Laura revelled in it, believing it meant Jake felt more for her now, on a personal rather than just a sexual level. It was a long time before they fell asleep and in the morning she woke to the sense of having her body being softly caressed by a loving hand. She rolled over to fling her arm around Jake, who proceeded to arouse her more acutely. They'd never had sex *the morning after* but they did this time, and Laura took it as another heart-hugging sign that their relationship was beginning to change to a closer one.

They ate a very hearty breakfast.

Showered, dressed and ready to leave, they were at the door of their hotel room when Jake turned and kissed her again, a long, passionate kiss that left Laura tingling with excitement on their elevator ride down to the foyer. Her mind swam with the hope he was going to ask her home with him instead of their going separate ways today.

A taxi was waiting outside the hotel entrance. Jake opened the passenger door for her and she got in, sliding along the back seat to make room for him. Instead of following her he leaned in to tell the driver Eddie's address and hand him a twenty dollar note.

Startled, Laura blurted, 'Aren't you coming with me?'

His dark eyes met hers, flat dark, almost black, devoid of any brilliance. 'No. I have somewhere else to go, Laura,' he stated decisively. He reached out and touched her cheek. 'It's been good. Thank you.'

Then the brief caress was withdrawn, as swiftly as Jake withdrew himself, shutting the passenger door and signalling the driver to take her away. Which he did, given no reason not to.

Laura was too stunned to protest the move. She sat in total shock, her hopes, her dreams, her expectations crashing around her. That was a goodbye! Not a *see you next time*. Jake hadn't mentioned a next time. Her hand lifted and clapped her cheek, holding on to what a creeping tide of panic was telling her had been his farewell touch.

Her mind railed over why it should be so. Surely there was no reason to give up what had been good. He would call her during the week. This couldn't be the end. Yet the more she thought about it, the more she felt he had been saying goodbye to her all last night. And this morning. Last dinner, last sex, last kiss, last touch!

But maybe she had it wrong. Maybe, maybe…

The taxi pulled up outside Eddie's apartment. Laura pulled herself out of her mental torment enough to thank the driver and step out onto the pavement. A glance at her watch showed almost eleven o'clock. She hoped Eddie was having a Sunday brunch with his friends somewhere because she wasn't up to chatting normally with him, not when her mind kept running on this awful emotional treadmill.

No such luck!

He was seated at his dining table in the living room, a cup of coffee to hand as he perused the newspapers. The moment she let herself into the apartment he looked up to shoot an opening line at her. 'Hi! Had another great night with Dad's golden boy?'

'Yes. A great night.' Even to her own ears it was a hollow echo of Eddie's words. It was impossible to work any happy enthusiasm into her voice.

He looked at her quizzically. 'Tetsuya's up to your expectations?'

'Yes. Absolutely.' That was better, more emphatic.

'Are you sick or something?'

'No.'

He sat back in his chair and gave her his wise look. 'Then why do you look like death warmed up, Laura?'

She sighed, accepting the fact there was very little she could hide from Eddie. He had a very shrewd talent for boring straight through any camouflage she put up. 'I think Jake said goodbye to me this morning and I'm not ready to say goodbye to him,' she said, shrugging in an attempt to minimise her dilemma.

Eddie grimaced and rose from his chair, waving her to the table. 'Come and sit down. I'll get you a cup of coffee. It might perk you up a bit.'

She slumped into a chair, feeling weirdly drained of energy.

'Why do you *think* he said goodbye?' Eddie asked as he poured coffee from the percolator.

Laura relived the scene in her mind. 'He put me into the taxi at the hotel, touched my cheek and said, "It's been good. Thank you." Usually he shares the taxi with me and tells me where we'll meet next week, but this morning he shut the door on me and waved me off.'

'It's *been* good,' Eddie repeated, musing over the past tense. He shook his head as he brought her the shot of caffeine and resumed his seat across the table from her. 'If he'd said *was* good...'

'No, it was *been* good. I'm not mistaken about that, Eddie.'

He grimaced. 'Got to say it sounds like a cut-off line to me. Do you have any idea why?'

'No. None. Which is why I'm so...in a mess about it.'

'No little niggles about how he was responding to you? Like maybe getting bored with the routine you'd established?'

'I'm not stupid, Eddie. I'd know if he was bored,' she cried, though right now she didn't feel certain about anything.

'Okay. He wasn't bored but he was saying good-bye regardless of the pleasures you both shared. That only leaves one motive, Laura,' Eddie said ruefully.

'What?'

'You've served your purpose.'

She shook her head in helpless confusion. 'I don't understand. What purpose?'

'You can bet it's something to do with dear old Dad.'

'But we've kept our whole relationship away from him,' she protested.

'You have, but how can you possibly know that Jake has?'

'He promised me...'

'Laura, Laura...' Eddie looked pained. 'I warned you from the start that this is a guy who plays all the angles. He's not our father's right-hand man for nothing. He's obviously worked at winning Dad's trust. He's worked at winning yours. But let me re-mind you, James Bond plays his own game and I think you've just been treated to one of them—*love 'em and leave 'em.'*

*James Bond*... She'd stopped connecting Jake to the legendary 007 character. He was the man she wanted, the man she loved, the man she'd dreamed of having for the rest of her life. Had she been an absolute fool, getting so caught up with him? Hadn't Jake felt anything for her beyond the desire to take her to bed? How could the strong feelings he'd stirred in her be completely one-sided?

The intensity of his love-making last night and this morning had made her believe he felt a lot for her. Eddie had to be wrong. She couldn't think of any purpose Jake could have in loving her and leaving her. He might very well have somewhere else he had to be this morning—somewhere he wished he didn't have to go because of wanting to be with her—and that past tense he'd used could have been simply a slip of the tongue. Maybe she'd worked herself into a stew for nothing and he would call her during the week.

Eddie shook his head at her. 'You don't want to believe it, do you?'

'I guess time will tell, Eddie,' she said flatly. 'Let's leave it at that. Okay?'

'Okay.' He gave her a sympathetic look. 'In the meantime, chalk up the positives. You've had the experience of dining in some of the finest restaurants, staying in very classy hotels, plus a fair chunk of great sex. Not a bad three months, Laura.'

She managed a wry smile. 'No, not bad at all.'
*But I want more.*
*Much more of Jake Freedman.*
*And I desperately hope I get more.*

## CHAPTER TEN

THE rest of Sunday went by without a call from Jake.

No contact from him on Monday, either.

It would probably come on Friday, Laura told herself, doing her best to concentrate on her uni lectures and not get too disturbed by the lack of the communication she needed. Regardless of the situation with Jake, she still had to move on with her life, get the qualifications necessary for her chosen career. Yet all her sensible reasoning couldn't stop the sick yearning that gripped her stomach when her thoughts drifted to him. And telling herself he would call soon didn't help.

It surprised her to see her father's car parked in the driveway when she arrived home on Tuesday afternoon. He never left work early and it wasn't even five o'clock. A scary thought hit her. Had something bad happened to her mother? An accident? Illness? She couldn't imagine anything but an emergency bringing her father home at this hour.

She ran to the front door, her heart pumping with

fear as she unlocked it and rushed into the hallway. 'Mum? Dad?' she called anxiously.

'Get in here, Laura!' her father's voice thundered from the lounge room. 'I've been waiting for you!'

She stood stock-still, her heart thumping even harder. He was in a rage. No distress in that tone. It was total fury. The only concern she need have for her mother was being subjected to his venom again.

The double doors from the hallway into the lounge room were open. Laura stiffened her spine, squared her shoulders and forced her feet forward, knowing that her mother would be spared the full-on brunt of savage remarks when he turned them onto her. It didn't matter how much she hated these vicious scenes. Better for her to be here than not here.

On entering the war zone, she found her mother cowering in the corner of one of the sofas, white-faced and hugging herself tightly as though desperately trying to hold herself together. Her father was standing behind the bar, splashing Scotch into a glass of ice. *His* face was red and the bottle of Scotch was half-empty.

'Are you still seeing Jake Freedman?' he shot at her.

No point in trying any evasion when her father was in this mood. He'd dig and dig and dig.

'I don't know,' she answered honestly.

'What do you mean "you don't know"?' he jeered, his eyes raking her with contempt. 'Don't pretend to be stupid, Laura.'

She shrugged. 'I was with him on Saturday night but he made no plans for us to meet again.'

Her father snorted. 'Had a last hurrah, screwing my daughter.'

'Alex, it's not Laura's fault,' her mother spoke up, showing more courage than she usually did. 'You introduced him to her.'

It enraged him into yelling, 'The bloody mole played his cards perfectly! Anyone would have been sucked in by him!'

'Then don't blame Laura,' her mother pleaded weakly, wilting under the blast.

What had Jake done? Laura's mind was in a whirl as she crossed the room to where her mother was scrunched into as small a space as possible and sat on the sofa's wide armrest next to her. 'What's going on, Dad?' she asked, needing to get to the crux of the problem.

He bared his teeth in a vicious snarl. 'That bastard has taken all my business to the Companies' Auditors and Liquidators Disciplinary Board and had me suspended from any further practice in the industry, pending further investigation.'

'Suspended?' This was why he was home, but… 'Investigation of what?'

His hand sliced the air in savage dismissal. 'You've never been interested in my work, Laura, so it's none of your concern.'

'I want to know what Jake is accusing you of.'

He shook a furious finger at her. 'All you have to

know is he was hell-bent on taking me down every minute he was supposedly working *for* me. Rolling you was icing on the cake for him.'

'But why? You're making it sound like a personal vendetta.'

'It *is* a personal vendetta.' His eyes bitterly raked her up and down. 'How personal can you get with his hands all over you, exulting in taking every damned liberty he could.'

'Alex!' her mother cried in pained protest.

She was ignored.

'And you let him, didn't you? My daughter!' her father thundered.

Laura refused to answer.

He sneered at her silence. 'He would have revelled in every intimacy you gave up to him.'

'This isn't about me, Dad,' she said as calmly as she could. 'I'm obviously a side issue. Why does Jake have a personal vendetta against you?'

'Because of JQE!' The words were spat out.

'That doesn't mean anything to me,' Laura persisted.

He glared at her contemptuously as though her ignorance was another poisonous barb to his pride.

Her chin lifted defiantly. 'I think I have the right to know what I've been a victim of.'

'JQE was his stepfather's company,' he finally informed her in a bitterly mocking tone. 'He believes I could have saved it and chose not to. The man died of a heart attack soon after I secured the liquidator's fee.'

*Step*father! 'Was his surname different to Jake's?'

'Of course it was! If I'd had any idea they were related, he would never have been employed by me.'

'How long has he been working in your company?'

'Six years! Six damnable years of worming his way through my files, wanting to nail me to the wall!'

A man with a mission…James Bond… Dark and dangerous…

Her instincts had been right at their first meeting, but she hadn't heeded them, hadn't wanted to.

'Could you have saved his stepfather's company, Dad?' she asked, wanting to know if the mission was for justice or some twisted form of vengeance. Jake had loved his stepfather, possibly the only father he had known.

'The man was an idiot, getting in over his head,' her father snarled. 'Even with help he was in no state to rescue anything. His wife was dying of cancer. Trying to hang on was stupid.'

A judgement call. Had it been right or a deliberate choice for her father to make a profit out of it, charging huge fees to carry out the liquidation process?

What was the truth?

Laura knew she wouldn't get it from her father. He would serve his own ends. Always had.

As for Jake, he must have been totally torn up

with grief when the seeds of his mission had been sown—his mother dying of cancer, his stepfather driven into bankruptcy and dying of a heart attack. It must have been a terribly traumatic time, having to bury both parents in the midst of everything being sold up around him. She had sensed the darkness in him, seen signs of it, heard it in his voice that first day in the garden when he'd described the terrible downside of bankruptcy, but hadn't known how deep it went, hadn't known that she was connected to it by being her father's daughter.

The bottle of Scotch took another hit. A furious finger stabbed at her again. 'Don't you dare take his side in this bloody whistle-blowing or you are out of this house, Laura! He used you. Used you to show me up as even more of a fool for trusting him with my daughter.'

Had that been Jake's intention behind tempting her into an affair? An iron fist squeezed her heart. He'd controlled every aspect of their meetings, kept their involvement limited to Saturday nights. Had he been secretly revelling in having her whenever he called? Because of who she was?

'What there was between us is over,' she said flatly.

'It had better be, my girl!' Threat seethed through every word. 'If he contacts you…'

'He won't.' Laura was certain of it. He *had* been saying goodbye on Sunday morning.

'Don't bet on it! It would be an extra feather in his cap if he sucked you in again.'

'He won't,' she repeated, sick to her soul. She'd loved him, truly deeply loved him, and the thought of having been used to drive a dagger further into her father was devastating.

'You be damned sure of it, Laura, because if I ever find out otherwise, you'll pay for it!'

'I'm sure.'

'You're looking sick around the gills. He got to you all right.'

The savage mutter was followed by another hefty swig of Scotch.

'I'm not feeling well,' her mother said shakily. 'Will you help me up to my bedroom, Laura?'

''Course I will.' She quickly moved off the arm-rest to give support.

'Running away as usual,' her father said scath-ingly. 'We'll be living with this hanging over our heads for months, Alicia. No escaping it.'

'It's just the shock, Dad,' Laura threw back at him. 'Mum needs some recovery time.'

'Recovery! I'll never recover from this! Never! That bastard has me hamstrung!'

Not for nothing, Laura thought as she helped her mother from the room. Jake must have presented a considerable body of hard evidence against her fa-ther for him to be suspended from practice. And had still been gathering it while he was seeing her on the side.

She needed recovery time, too.

Her mother felt terribly frail. Laura put her to bed and tucked the doona around her. 'It's not your fault, either, Mum,' she said gently.

The pale blue eyes were teary and fearful. She grasped Laura's hand. 'I don't think I can bear it if your father is home every day.'

'You don't have to. Eddie would take you in. You have only to ask.'

She shook her head fretfully. 'It wouldn't be fair on him. You don't understand, Laura. Your father wouldn't tolerate my leaving him. He'd...do something.'

Laura hated the fear but she knew there was no reasoning against it. She and Eddie had tried many times. 'Well, I don't think Dad will be at home all the time. He'll be out networking with people, fighting this situation with everything in his power.'

'Yes. Yes, he will. Thank you, Laura. I'm sorry... sorry that Jake...'

'Let's not talk about him. You just rest, Mum.'

She kissed the slightly damp forehead and left the room before her own tears welled up and spilled over—tears of hurt and shock and grief that pride had insisted she hold back in front of her father. And her mother.

In the safe haven of her bedroom she wept until she was totally drained of tears. Her mind was wiped blank for a long time as she lay in limp misery, but gradually it began to turn over everything that had happened between her and Jake in the light of what she now knew and it kept coming back to the one line that felt critically important—the line he'd spoken after their first kiss in the garden.

*I don't want to want you.*

But he had.

He most definitely had wanted her, and quite possibly not because of who she was but *in spite of* who she was.

Which made a huge difference to her father's interpretation of Jake's conduct where she was concerned.

It meant she was not part of his vengeance plot.

She was an innocent connection to the man whom he saw as the prime cause of the darkest time of his life. The words he'd used describing bankruptcy came back to her—lives crumbling, futures shattered, depression so dark there is no light. The emotional intensity that had surprised her in that forceful little speech had obviously erupted from personal experience.

Looking back, she began to make much more sense of how Jake had run their affair, always keeping the end in sight, ensuring their involvement was limited, not escalating into something too serious. He'd known it was ill-fated from the start, but he'd found her as irresistible as she'd found him and he'd taken the small window of opportunity for them to enjoy each other before circumstances made it impossible.

*It's been good. Thank you.*

He hadn't been *using* her.

They'd both chosen to give themselves the pleasure of mutual desire and it had been good. The more Laura reasoned it out, the more she believed the journey they'd taken together was completely separate from the road Jake had been travelling to put her father out of business.

She remembered the intensity of his love-making on Saturday night, the long passionate kiss before they left the hotel room, the flat darkness—no... light—of his eyes as he touched her cheek in the taxi.

Maybe he hadn't wanted to say goodbye.

Maybe he loved her as deeply as she loved him.

Maybe he just couldn't see a future for them, given what he was about to do.

That might be true...or it might not.

It depended on how much he felt for her.

She had to see him, talk to him, find out the truth.

# CHAPTER ELEVEN

LAURA wished she could have borrowed Eddie's car to tour the streets of Woollahra, looking for the houses that were being renovated, noting them down for further investigation. It would have been the most time efficient way of searching for Jake's current home, but she knew her brother would not have been sympathetic to her quest. Better not to ask. Better to go on foot, however long it took.

When she'd broken the news to Eddie, he'd leapt to the same interpretation of Jake's interest in her as her father, being quite smug about having been right that Laura should never have *gone there*, right about Jake having a mission, too. The latter was impossible to deny, but Laura could not set aside the need to *go there* again.

At least Eddie had taken their mother out today, giving her a break from the wretched tensions at home. It left Laura enough free time to cover a fair bit of ground in her search, though it was now Sunday—no tradesmen's trucks around to mark possibilities. After three hours of walking one street after another, and feeling somewhat dispirited at her lack of success, she decided to take a break for lunch and give her feet a rest.

Heading up another street that led to a public park where she could sit and eat her home-made sandwiches, Laura could hardly believe her eyes when she actually spotted Jake. He was on the upstairs balcony of a terrace house, painting the iron-lace railings—the same shade of green as the front door and the window frames. It was a rich forest green that looked really good against the old red bricks of the house.

He looked good, too, a fact her heart was registering by thumping painfully. She stood still, staring up at him, wracked by a terrible uncertainty now that the moment of truth was at hand. Was she being an utter fool, coming to him like this? So what if she was, she fiercely argued to herself. A sharp dose of humiliation wouldn't kill her. And she wasn't about to die wondering, either.

His head lifted, his gaze suddenly swinging to her as though some invisible force had drawn it. 'Laura!' He spoke her name in a tone of angst, jerking up from his crouched position on the balcony, frowning down at her. 'What are you doing here?'

'I need to talk to you,' she blurted out.

He shook his head. 'It won't do you any good.' His gaze shot to a van parked on the other side of the street. 'That's been here since Wednesday. I'd say your father has me under surveillance and he won't like getting a report of your coming to me. Just keep walking and maybe nothing will come of it.'

Her father's threat jangled through her mind—*you'll pay for it.*

Right now Laura didn't care. Jake had just proved his caring for her. That was more important than anything else. Or was he just trying to get her out of his life again as fast as possible?

'I have to know,' she said with immovable determination. 'I won't go until you lay out the truth to me.'

A pained grimace twisted his mouth as his hand waved in a sharp, dismissive gesture. 'You already know it had to come to an end. Remember it for what it was and move on.'

'What was it, Jake?'

'You know that, too,' he shot back at her.

'No, I don't. You kept me in the dark about what meant most to you. I don't know if it gave you a thrill to have me while plotting to bring my father down, if I was some kind of sweet icing on the cake for you. I want to know that before I move on.'

Jake stared at the woman he should never have touched, his mind torn by the deep hurt emanating from her. She was still the most beautiful, most desirable woman he'd ever known, quite possibly would ever know, and he hated having to part from her. It had to be done, but did it have to be done with her mind poisoned against what they'd shared?

He wanted her to have a good memory of him, not a bitter one. Yet how was he to soothe the hurt and protect her from her father's wrath at the same time? The surveillance man was surely watching, taking note of this encounter. The longer it went on, the worse it would be for Laura at home.

'There's a public park at the end of this street,' he said, pointing the direction as though she had asked for it.

'I know!' she cried in exasperation. 'Can't you just answer me?'

He shot a warning look at the van. 'I'll meet you there when I've finished this painting. Go, Laura. Go now.'

He turned his attention to the work in hand, bending down to the tin of paint again, hoping the intense urgency in his voice would spur her into moving away from him. After a few moments' hesitation that tied his gut into knots, she did walk on, hopefully proving there was nothing in this meeting worth reporting.

He maintained a steady pace with the brushwork, exhibiting no haste to finish the job. It gave him time to think, time to reason out he should keep his answers to Laura short, avoid the tempting impulse to take her in his arms and prove his passion for her had been real, was still real. The ache in his groin had to be ignored. This meeting had to be limited to setting her straight, then letting her go. Anything else could not be sustained in the climate of her father's venomous animosity.

The narrow alley that ran along the back of this row of terraces allowed him to leave his house unobserved. He would return the same way. A last meeting. No more.

*He does care for me. He does.*

It was like a chant of joy in Laura's mind, making every step towards the park a light one for her tired feet. Jake would have no reason at all to give himself the trouble of meeting with her if she meant nothing to him. If she'd been part of his vendetta against her father, he would have shamed her in the street. He had certainly not been amused by her coming to him nor titillated by his power to draw her. He'd been pained by her presence, reminding him of what they'd shared, what he'd been trying to shut out as finished.

Except it wasn't.

Not for her and not for him.

The connection was too strong to obliterate.

Laura was sure of it.

She found a park bench under a tree and sat down to wait, not bothering to unpack the sandwiches in her handbag. Her heart was too full of other needs for eating to be a priority anymore. Jake would come to her soon—Jake, whom she loved…whom she would always love. Did he feel the same way about her?

Was it only the situation with her father that had driven him to break it off with her?

She had no idea how long she waited. Her mind was obsessed with finding some way to continue their relationship—safe places to meet, secret places, whatever it took for their journey not to end. When she spotted him approaching her at a fast stride she leapt to her feet, barely quelling the urge to run to him and fling her arms around his neck. Talking had to come first, she told herself, though if he wrapped her in his embrace...

He didn't. There was no smile on his face, no joy at seeing her, no sexy twinkle in his eyes. When he reached her he took hold of her hands, squeezing them as though to prevent any other touching. 'I never meant you to be hurt, Laura,' he said gruffly. 'I thought we could simply satisfy ourselves with the pleasures we could give each other. None of that had anything to do with your father. It was all about you, the woman I wanted to be with, not whose daughter you are.'

His thumbs were dragging across the skin on the back of her hands, wanting his words to sink in, go deep, expel the nastiness of the motivation that her father had given him. The earnest sincerity in his voice, the blaze of need to convince her in his eyes... Laura believed he spoke the truth. She *wanted* to believe.

'You should have told me what you were about to

do, Jake,' she blurted out. 'It wouldn't have been so bad if you'd told me.'

His mouth twisted into a rueful grimace. 'I didn't want to spoil our last night together, bringing your father into it, bringing my family background into it. And telling you wasn't going to change anything.'

'It would have prepared me.'

'Yes. I see that now. I'm sorry. I thought you'd understand. What we had was time out of time, Laura.' He squeezed her hands hard. 'You must let it go and move on.'

'I don't want to, Jake. It was too good to let go. You must feel that, too,' she pleaded.

He jerked his head in a sharp negative. 'There's no way. Your father will see to that and bucking him would make things much worse for both you and your mother. You told me she needs you. And you still have to get your uni degree for the career you want. Any association with me will cost you too much.'

If he was under surveillance… Yes, it would be too risky. The tensions at home were volatile enough already. Yet letting this connection she felt with Jake go… Everything inside her railed against giving it up.

'What about when this is all over, Jake. Could we pick up again then?'

He shook his head but there was a pained expression on his face as he answered, 'The process of indicting your father for corruption may go on for years, Laura.'

'Is he guilty?'

'Without a doubt.'

'Will he go to jail?'

'He'll be ousted from the industry. It's unlikely that any further action will be taken.'

No relief for her mother. No escape unless…

'Once I get my degree and hopefully a well-paid position, I'll be independent. And perhaps I can persuade my mother to come and live with me. We'll be free and clear of my father.'

'Perhaps…' he repeated, but there was no belief in his eyes.

Her hope for at least some distant future with him was being crushed. It begged for a chance to survive. 'Do you really want this to be goodbye, Jake?'

'No. But I can't honestly see any good way forward,' he said flatly.

'You have my mobile phone number. You could call me from time to time, check on how things are going,' she suggested, trying to keep a note of desperation out of her voice.

He wrenched his gaze from the plea in hers and stared down at their linked hands. Again his thumbs worked over her skin. After a long nerve-tearing silence, he muttered, 'You should close the door on me, Laura. You'll meet someone else with no history to make your life difficult.'

'I won't meet anyone else like you,' she said

fiercely, every instinct fighting for a love she might never feel with any other man.

He expelled a long breath with the whisper, 'Nor I, you.' Then he visibly gathered himself, head lifting, meeting her gaze squarely again. 'I won't call you from time to time. I won't keep any hold on you. When I'm done with your father—however long that takes—I'll catch up with you to see where you are in your life and how we feel about each other then.'

She knew there was no fighting the hard decision in his eyes, in his voice. 'Promise me you'll do that, Jake. Whatever happens between now and then, promise me we'll meet again.'

'I promise.' He leaned forward to press a soft warm kiss on her forehead. 'Stay strong, Laura,' he murmured.

Before she could say or do anything, he'd backed off, released her hands and was walking away. She stared at his retreating figure, feeling the distance growing between them with each step he took, hating it yet resigned to the inevitability of this parting.

He'd promised her they'd meet again.

It might be years away but she didn't believe any length of time would make a difference to how she felt with him.

And she did have things to achieve—her qualifications, building a career and hopefully persuading her mother that there was another life to be led, free of abuse and oppression.

It would not be time wasted.

She would be better equipped to continue a journey with Jake Freedman when they met again—
older, stronger, more his equal in everything. She
could wait for that.

# CHAPTER TWELVE

*STAY STRONG...*

Laura repeated those words to herself many times as she tried to minimise her father's savagery over the next few weeks, protecting her mother from it as best she could. She had half expected a vicious blow-up about her visit to Jake's house, but that didn't eventuate. Either there hadn't been a surveillance man at all, or he hadn't reported the incident, not seeing anything significant in it.

Strangely enough her mind was more at peace with Jake's promise. She didn't fret over his absence from her life. It was easier to concentrate on her landscape projects than when she was seeing him each week. Knowing what he was doing, knowing why, helped a lot, as did good memories when she went to bed at night. Besides, there was hope for a future with him, which she kept to herself, not confiding it to her mother or Eddie, both of whom would probably see it as an unhealthy obsession with the man.

She spent as much time with her mother as her uni studies and part-time receptionist work would allow. Nick Jeffries seemed to be finding a lot of maintenance jobs that had to be done, coming to the house two or three times a week. Laura wondered if he knowingly provided a buffer between her parents, giving her mother an excuse to be outside with him, supervising the work. He was a cheerful man, good to have around, in sharp contrast to her father, who was never anything but nasty now.

One evening she was in the kitchen with her mother, helping to prepare dinner, when he arrived home bellowing, 'Laura!' from the hallway, the tone alone warning he was bent on taking a piece out of her.

Her heart jumped. What had she done wrong? Nothing she could think of. 'I'm in the kitchen, Dad!' she called out, refusing to go running to him or show any fear of his mean temper.

*Stay strong...*

She kept cutting up the carrots, only looking up when he announced his entry by snidely commenting, 'Good sharp knife! You might want to stick it into someone, Laura.'

Like him? He had a smug smile on his face, in no doubt whatsoever that she wouldn't attack him physically. He was the one who had the power to hurt and that knowledge glittered in his eyes. He stood there, gloating over whatever he had in mind to do. Laura waited, saying nothing, aware that her mother had also stopped working and was tensely waiting for whatever was coming next.

'I've had Jake Freedman under surveillance,' he announced.

The visit to Jake's house! But that was so long ago. It didn't make sense that her father would keep such a tasty titbit until now.

He waved a large envelope at her. 'Hard evidence of what a slime he is.' He strolled forward, opening the envelope and removing what looked like large photographs, and laid them down on the island bench in front of her.

'Thought you'd like to see Jake Freedman's steady screw, Laura,' he said mockingly, pointing to a curvy blonde in a skimpy, skin-tight aerobic outfit, her arms locked around Jake's neck, her body pressed up against his, as was her face for a kiss.

It was like a kick in the gut, seeing him with another woman.

'Meets her at the gym three times a week.'

Every word was like a drop of acid eating into her heart.

The pointing finger moved to the next photograph. 'Goes back to her place for extra exercise.'

There was the blonde again, the pony-tail for the gym released so that her shiny hair fell around her face and shoulders in soft waves. It was a very pretty face. She was opening the door of a house, smiling back invitingly at Jake, who was paused at the foot of the steps leading up to the front porch.

'Woman works at a club on Saturday nights,' her father went on. 'Very handy. Left him free to have his delectable little encounters with you. Shows what a two-faced bastard he is in every respect.'

She didn't speak, couldn't speak. Sickening waves of shock were rolling through her. It was a huge relief that her father didn't wait for some comment from her.

'Need a drink to drown the scumbag out,' he muttered and headed off to make his usual inroads into a bottle of whisky, leaving the damning photographs behind to blast any faith she might have in Jake's love for her.

Laura stared at them. It was only a month since her meeting in the park with him—a meeting he hadn't wanted, a meeting to ensure she wouldn't pester him again, coming to his house where she had never been invited. She had accepted his reasoning, believed in his promise, and here he was with another woman, enjoying her company, having sex with her.

Two-faced…

Of course he had to be good at that—brilliant—to fool her father.

Fooling her, too, had probably been a fun exercise in comparison.

A dark, dangerous man… She should have trusted that instinct, should have said no to him, should never have allowed him to play his game with her because it had been *his* game all along, *his* arrangements, *his* rules. She had read into them what she wanted to believe and he had let her with his rotten promise.

Tears welled up and blurred her vision. She shut her eyes, didn't see her mother move to wrap her in a comforting hug, only felt the arms turning her around, a hand curling around her head and pressing it onto a shoulder. She wasn't strong in that moment, couldn't find any strength at all. She gave in to a storm of weeping until it was spent, then weakly stayed in her mother's embrace, soaking up the real love coming to her from the rubbing of her back and the stroking of her hair.

'I'm sorry you've been so hurt by this,' her mother murmured. 'Sorry you were caught up in your father's business, in past deeds you had nothing to do with. So wrong…'

'I loved him, Mum. I thought he loved me. He promised me we'd meet again when this was all over,' she spilled out, needing to unburden the pain of the soul-sickening deception.

'Perhaps that was a kinder way of letting you down than telling you the truth. You're a wonderful person, Laura. Even he had to see that, care for you a little.'

'Oh, Mum! It's such a mess!' She lifted her head and managed a wobbly smile. 'I'm a mess. Thanks for being here for me.'

Her mother returned an ironic little smile as she lifted her hand to smear the wetness from Laura's cheeks. 'As you are for me. But please don't think you always have to be, my dear. I want you to have a life of your own, away from here. Like Eddie.'

'Well, we'll talk about that when I'm through uni. Now let's do this dinner. I don't want Dad to know I've been upset.'

Pride lent her strength again. She snatched up the photographs. 'I'll just take these up to my room as reminders of my stupidity, clean myself up and be right back down to help. And don't worry about me, Mum. I'll be okay now.'

She dumped the photographs on her bed, bitterly thinking how *easy* she had been for Jake, how vulnerable she had been to his strong sex appeal, how willing to go along with *his* journey, letting him call all the shots. He'd probably had this other woman all along. Even if the pretty blonde was only a more recent acquisition for his sex life, the very fact of her spelled out that he felt no deep attachment to Alex Costarella's daughter.

Washing her face, she wished she could wash Jake Freedman right out of her head.

*Stay strong...*

Oh, yes, she would. She had to. Nobody was going to wreck her life; not her father, not Jake, not any man. This steadfast determination carried her through dinner, sharpening her wits enough to dilute her father's barbs with good-humoured replies. It also formed her resolution when she returned to her bedroom and was faced with the photographs again.

She scooped them up and shoved them straight back into the envelope her father had left with them.

It was a blank envelope and she wrote Jake's address on it, grimly pleased that the search for his house had not been completely wasted time. She wanted him to know that she knew about his other woman and he would not be sucking up any more of her time.

To underline that fact, she wrote an accompanying note—

> *As for any future meeting between us, you can whistle for me, Jake. I'm moving on. Laura.*

No angst in those words. She liked the *whistle* bit. It carried a flippant tone, as well as implying he was just another jerk to be ignored.

Having slipped the note into the envelope, she sealed it and put it in her briefcase to be posted tomorrow. Over and done with. Her life was her own again.

Jake sorted his mail, frowning over the business-size envelope with the handwritten address. It wasn't standard practice to handwrite anything that wasn't personal these days. Curious about its content, he slit it open and drew out the photographs and the damning little note from Laura.

A lead weight settled on his heart.

He'd been sucked in by the dancer at the gym. She'd been Costarella's tool. That was bleeding obvious now. He hadn't suspected a set-up when she'd

grabbed at him as he was leaving the gym, expressing what seemed like genuine fear of being stalked
and pleading with him to walk her home—just a few
blocks to where she knew she'd be safe. It wasn't
much to ask, wasn't much to do—a random act of
kindness that was coming back to spike him with a
vengeance.

Then the embrace of gushing gratitude a week
later, an over-the-top carry-on that he'd backed away
from, not wanting it, not liking it, certainly not encouraging any further involvement with the woman.
But that didn't show in the photograph. It didn't serve
Costarella's purpose to give Laura shots of his reaction.

He carried the mail into his house, despondently
dumping it on the kitchen bench on his way to the
small backyard, which provided a sunny haven from
the rest of the world. He slumped into one of the deck
chairs he'd set out there, still holding Laura's note
that brought their journey to a dead end.

He stared at the words—*I'm moving on.*

It was what he had meant her to do, advised her
to do, and most probably it was the best course to
chop him completely out of her life. Costarella was
not about to tolerate any future connection between
them. Even if he explained this photographic set-
up to Laura and she believed him, Costarella would
look for other ways and means to drive wedges into
their relationship. It gave him a focus for getting

back at Jake for bringing him down and he'd relish that malicious power.

Definitely best that what he'd had with Laura ended here and now.

No future.

He folded the note and tucked it into his shirt pocket.

He'd known all along that this was how it would have to be, but it was still damned difficult to accept. Achieving what he'd set out to do to Alex Costarella felt strangely empty. Like his life after his mother and stepfather had died. But he'd picked himself up then and moved forward. He could do it again.

There should have been warmth in the sunshine.

He couldn't feel it.

The emptiness inside him was very cold.

## CHAPTER THIRTEEN

For the rest of the year Laura applied herself so thoroughly to her uni course, she not only attained her degree, but also graduated with honours in every subject. This gave her an extra edge over other students entering the workforce for the first time. She was snapped up by a firm of architects, wanting a landscape specialist to enhance their designs. It was a wonderful buoyant feeling to know all her hard work had paid off and she was actually going to begin her chosen career.

The phone call notifying her of her successful interview came in the first week of December and her new employers wanted her in their office the following Monday. After revelling in the news for a few moments, she rushed out to the back garden to tell her mother, who was trailing after Nick Jeffries as he checked the sprinkler system.

'Mum! I got it! The job I interviewed for!' she called out, causing both of them to turn and give her their attention. She grinned exultantly at them as she added, 'And they want me to start next week!'

Her mother's face lit with pleasure. 'That's fantastic, Laura!'

'Fantastic!' Nick repeated, grinning delight at her. 'Congratulations!'

'And before Christmas, too,' her mother said with an air of relief, turning her face up to Nick's and touching his arm in an oddly familiar manner. 'Can we do it?'

He nodded. 'The sooner, the better.'

'Do what?' Laura asked, bemused by what seemed like an intimate flow of understanding between them.

Nick tucked her mother's arm around his and they faced Laura together as he told her their news. 'Your mother is leaving your father and moving in with me. We've just been waiting for you to have some freedom of choice, Laura, and now you're set.'

She was totally thunderstruck. Her mother and Nick? She had never imagined, never suspected there was anything beyond a casual affection between them, born out of sharing the pleasure of a lovely garden. She knew Nick was a widower, had been for years, but he'd always been very respectful to her mother, caring about what she wanted but never taking liberties that might not be welcome. When had their relationship moved to a different level?

'I can see you're shocked,' her mother said on a deflated sigh.

Her air of disappointment jolted Laura into a quick

protest. 'No! No! Just surprised! And pleased,' she quickly added, beaming a smile at both of them.

'It's not good for Alicia here,' Nick said, appealing for her understanding.

That was the understatement of the year!

'I'm sure Mum will be a lot happier with you than with Dad,' Laura said with feeling. 'Both Eddie and I have always liked you, Nick. And appreciated how much you've lightened Mum's life. I think it's brilliant that you're stepping in and taking her away, but I've got to warn you, Dad's bound to be horribly mean about it. He's not a good loser.'

Which was another huge understatement.

Nick patted her mother's hand reassuringly. 'Alicia doesn't need to take anything from him. I can provide for her.'

'There's very little I want to take from this life, Laura. Nick can fit it into his van,' her mother said, looking brighter now that her decision had been so readily accepted by her daughter. 'But you'll have to move on the same day. Either come with us or go to Eddie's until you can afford a place of your own. I can't leave you here, not with your father finding out I've walked out on him.'

'No, that would not be a good scene,' Laura heartily agreed.

The biggest understatement of all!

'I'll go to Eddie's, let you two start your lives together on your own,' she decided. 'It won't be for long. As soon as I get my first pay cheque, I'll look around for an apartment close to my work.'

'We must tell Eddie now,' her mother said anxiously, looking to Nick for his support again.

'Yes, he has to be brought into the plan,' Nick agreed.

'No problem. I'll call him, let him know,' Laura suggested. 'And don't worry, Mum. Eddie will be all for it.'

She shook her head. 'I must tell him, dear. It's only right.'

'Okay. Just trying to save you trouble, Mum.'

'I know. It's what you've been doing for years,' she said sadly. 'But no more, Laura.'

'That's my job from now on,' Nick said with a cheerful grin. 'All you have to do, Laura, is choose what you want to take with you, pack it up and be ready when Alicia nominates the day.'

'A day when I'm sure your father will be out. I'm not going to face him with this. I'll leave him a letter. Let him rage to an empty house.'

'Best course,' Nick said decisively. 'I wouldn't put it past him to stoop to physical violence and I won't have Alicia subjected to any risk of that.'

'Definitely the best course,' Laura agreed. 'What about Friday, Mum? I'm sure Dad said that was when he was meeting with his barrister to plan the counter-attack to the accusations against him.'

*Give him some dirt on your lover-boy, Laura,* he'd

jeered. *Jake Freedman won't come out of this clean, I can promise you that.*

*None of my business,* Laura had firmly recited to herself, determined not to encourage her father into elaborating on *the dirt,* refusing to go anywhere that involved Jake. Despite all the intervening months, she hadn't been able to bury the hurt of her disillusionment with him and it was quite impossible to become interested in any other man.

'Yes, Friday!' her mother cried excitedly.

*The day of freedom.*

She turned to the man who had opened another door for her. 'No way will Alex miss that meeting, Nick. As soon as he's left the house I'll call you.'

'And I'll be here,' he assured her.

It was really heart-touching seeing the caring for her mother written on Nick's face, seeing her open trust in him. Laura had to clear a lump in her throat before she could speak.

'Now we've got that settled, I'm off to my room to start selecting what I want to take with me. You two can start planning a happy future together.'

She kissed them both on their cheeks and skipped away feeling even more light-hearted at the prospect of her mother's escape to a new life. No more oppressive abuse, no more fear, no more misery. Nick Jeffries was not an impressively handsome, wealthy man, but the kindness running through his veins was obviously more attractive to her mother than anything else.

And maybe that was what she should look for in a man.

Forget Jake Freedman's strong sex appeal.

Forget everything she had loved about him.

There had been no real kindness in him.

A kind man would never have used her as Jake had.

Next week she would be starting a new phase of her life, leaving everything and everyone connected to her father behind, and that would surely make forgetting Jake easier. She would be busy working her way into her career, forging a path of her own without having to worry about her mother's well-being, and looking forward to a really happy, tension-free Christmas for once!

*Joy to the world!*

Smiling over the words that had sung through her mind, Laura raced upstairs to her room to start organising the big move. Having perused the contents of her wardrobe, she decided large plastic garbage bags were needed for easy transportation. A lot of old stuff need not be taken. She stared down at the turquoise shoes Jake had called erotic on her first date with him at Neil Perry's Spice Temple. Gorgeous shoes. A gift from her mother. But could she ever wear them again without remembering him, remembering how it had been in the hotel after he'd taken them off?

A knock on her door interrupted the miserable train of thought.

'It's just me,' her mother called.

'Come in,' Laura quickly invited, wanting some private time with her mother, mostly to feel totally assured that going with Nick Jeffries was the right move for her, not an act of desperation or some kind of sacrifice to her children's peace of mind.

'Nick has stacked some boxes in the laundry for us to use,' she said, her blue eyes sparkling with happy anticipation.

'Mum, you are sure about this?' Laura asked earnestly. 'You're not just taking some...some easy way out?'

'No, dear. I'm very sure.' She walked over to the bed and sat on the end of it, looking at Laura with a soft, dreamy expression on her face. 'I lost myself with your father. I want to find the person I could have been and Nick will let me do that. I know I'm different with him and I like the difference. He touches my heart and makes me feel good, Laura, good in a way I've never felt before.'

She'd felt good with Jake until... But this wasn't the time to be thinking of him. She had to *stop* thinking of him. 'That's great, Mum,' she said warmly, giving her an ironic smile. 'I guess I'm still a bit surprised. When did you two open up to each other?'

'It was just after my birthday...'

*Tenth of October*

'Your father had been particularly nasty to me and I was sitting out on the garden bench near the pool, weeping over my miserable existence, wishing I were dead. Nick had come to work and he found me there.

There was no hiding my wretched state and he was so kind, so comforting. We talked and talked....'

She sighed, shook her head as though it was too difficult—or too private—to explain, but the reminiscent smile on her face spoke of unexpected pleasure found and treasured. 'Anyhow, the more we talked, the more I realised *I* wanted to be with him, and *he* wanted me to be with him, too. We both believe we can make a beautiful little world together. You can't imagine, Laura. Everything feels so different with Nick. So very different...'

Yes, she could imagine. No problem at all in imagining how it was or how it could be. She pulled her mother up from the bed for a hug. 'I'm so glad for you, Mum. Make sure you tell Eddie all that so he won't worry about you.'

'I will, dear. And you must both come to Nick's house for Christmas. We'll have a lovely celebration of it this year.'

'Mmmh...' Laura grinned. 'We'll be able to have fun together.'

'Yes, fun!' Her mother seized the concept with delight and sailed out of the room, no doubt eager to share it with Nick.

Over the next few days Laura and her mother secretly packed what they wanted to take, storing the boxes in Laura's room, where her father never ventured. Eddie was cock-a-hoop about the plan and in total agreement that it be carried out without their father's knowledge, not risking any explosive confrontation.

Friday morning came. Alex Costarella duly left for his meeting. Nick arrived in his van within minutes of the all-clear call. He and Laura packed the boxes and bags into it while her mother removed her personal papers—birth and marriage certificates from her father's safe—and made a last-minute check that nothing important had been missed.

There were absolutely no regrets on driving away from the Mosman mansion. It was like having a huge weight lifted off their hearts. The sense of freedom was so heady they couldn't help laughing at everything said between them. Laura called Eddie on her mobile phone to inform him of their successful escape and he was out on the street waiting for them when they arrived at his apartment block.

They all moved her belongings into his second bedroom and once that task was complete, she and Eddie accompanied their mother and Nick back to the van to say goodbye and wish them well. Oddly enough her mother looked strained as she nervously fingered a large envelope she'd left on the passenger seat, finally thrusting it at Laura.

'I don't know if it's right or wrong to give you this,' she said anxiously. 'It was in your father's safe and I looked into it while I was searching for my papers. It holds more photos of Jake Freedman—ones he didn't show you, Laura. I think he lied about those he did. Lied to drive a wedge between you and Jake, wanting to hurt. He always wanted to hurt when he didn't get his own way. Maybe seeing these will lessen the hurt a bit. I hope so, dear.'

It felt like a knife was twisting in her heart as she took the envelope, but she managed a smile, quickly saying, 'Don't worry, Mum. What's done is done and it's all in the past anyway. Go with Nick now. Be happy.'

They drove off and she stood so long staring blankly after the van, Eddie picked up the vibes of her distress and hugged her shoulders. 'It might be in the past but it's not done with, is it, Laura?' he said sympathetically. 'I know you haven't got over the guy. So let's go inside and look at what Dad's Machiavellian streak came up with to destroy what you had together.'

They were before-and-after photographs—before and after the damning shots that had driven her to reject any future with the man she had loved. Jake hadn't followed the pretty blonde into the house. She'd gone inside alone. Even the shots of them walking down the street together had no hint of any intimacy between them—just a man accompanying a woman.

As for the kiss at the gym, it was clear that the woman had thrown herself at Jake. There were snaps of his face showing surprise, annoyance, impatience, rejection, none of which had been visible in the photo her father had shown her.

'It was a set-up,' Eddie muttered, tapping a clear

shot of the blonde. 'I've seen this woman around the traps. She's a fairly high-class working girl. This would have been an easy gig for her and no doubt Dad paid her well for it.'

A set-up…and she'd fallen for it; hook, line and sinker.

'I didn't give Jake a chance to explain,' she said miserably. 'I posted him the incriminating photos with a message that wrote him out of my life.'

'Don't fret it, Laura. I'm sure Jake was smart enough to realise Dad wasn't going to tolerate a connection between the two of you. He probably thought he was saving you grief by letting it go.'

Yes, he would think that. But he wouldn't contact her when the business with her father was all over. Not now.

'I didn't believe in him enough. I didn't *stay strong*,' she cried, gutted by her failure of faith in his caring for her.

Eddie frowned. 'You think there was genuine feeling for you on his side?'

'Yes! It was just the situation making everything too hard. He promised me we'd meet again but I've messed it up, Eddie, taking Dad's word instead of his. I've completely messed it up!'

'Not necessarily. You must have his home address if you posted the photos to him,' he said thoughtfully. 'You're free of Dad now, Laura, and so is Mum. Why not pay Jake a visit, find out where you stand with him? Better to know than not know.'

'Yes!' She jumped up from her seat at Eddie's table where they had laid out the photographs, gripped by a determination to set everything right, if she could. 'I'll go. It's a chance to nothing, isn't it?'

He nodded. 'If you have to go there, go there.'

She did.

A wild hope zinged through her heart every step of the way, right until the front door of Jake's house was opened and she was faced with a young woman holding a baby on her hip.

'Hello. Are you one of our new neighbours?' the woman asked with bright-eyed interest.

'No, I…I was looking for Jake Freedman,' Laura blurted out.

'Oh, I'm sorry. He's gone, I'm afraid, and I don't have a forwarding address. We bought the house from him two months ago and moved in last week. I have no idea where you can find him.'

'It's okay. Thank you. Have a nice life here.'

A nice life in the house Jake had worked on and sold…and he had now moved on.

And Laura had no idea where to, either.

But it wasn't the absolute end, she told herself on the long trudge back to Paddington. The case against her father was set down to be heard in March next year—three more months away. Jake was the prime witness against him. He had to attend the court hearing, give evidence—fulfil the mission that had driven them apart.

A court of law was a public place.
She could go there.
She would go there.

## CHAPTER FOURTEEN

LAURA dressed carefully for the first day of the hearing, choosing to wear the professional black suit she donned for business meetings. She wanted Jake to see her as a fully adult woman, established in her career and capable of standing on her own. However, the suit was figure-hugging, accentuating her feminine curves, and she left her hair loose, wanting him to see her as sexy, too, reminding him of the pleasures they had shared.

She had all week to make contact with him, having arranged for the time off work, but her heart was set on sooner rather than later. Arriving early at the court house, she tensely searched the waiting rooms and corridors, hoping to cross paths with Jake. Having no luck at even catching a glimpse of him, she entered the inquiry room, settling on one of the back seats, sure that she would see him here sometime today.

Her father was seated beside his barrister. He saw her, giving her a bulletlike stare before turning away.

She didn't care what he thought of her presence. Only what Jake thought mattered.

The hearing started. Jake had not entered the room. Laura set aside her frustration and listened to the accusations her father had to answer. This was what Jake had been secretly working on—more important to him than their relationship.

Sixteen companies were named—JQE amongst them. Struggling companies that could have been saved by arranging bridging loans but which her father had chosen to bury, gouging millions out of selling off their assets by charging outrageous fees for his services as liquidator.

The judge described it as 'Churning and burning.'

The day dragged on with no sight of Jake, not in the morning session, not in the lunch-break, not in the afternoon session.

Her father was the only witness called. He admitted to earning between four and six million dollars a year from failing companies but belligerently insisted it was by carrying out due process and he was innocent of any wrongdoing. His air of contempt for the court did not endear him to the judge. Laura hated listening to him. She kept darting glances around the room, hoping to see Jake, willing him to appear.

Why wasn't he here?

Surely this was the culmination of his mission for justice.

Shouldn't he be listening to what her father said so he could rebut it?

Jake was sitting in the consultation room, waiting for the prosecuting barrister to report on the afternoon session, feeling buoyantly confident that Alex Costarella would finally be nailed for the fraudulent bastard he was. The glass panels of the door gave him a view of the area directly outside the enquiry room. A rush of people into it signalled that the session was over.

Jake recognised the reporters who had tried to interview him. The case was drawing quite a bit of interest from the business sector of the media. Which was good. Too much skulduggery was hidden from the public. The more people were aware of what went on, the more they could guard against it, or at least question what was happening.

Laura!

Jake bolted to his feet, shocked at seeing her amongst the departing spectators, his mind instantly torn by uncertainty over what she was doing here and the wild urge to stride out and sweep her into a fiercely possessive embrace. It had been so long—almost a year—but just the sight of her had his body buzzing with the need to have her again.

She looked stunning, the black suit barely confining her voluptuous curves, her glorious hair bouncing around her shoulders. His fingers itched to rake through its silky mass. His groin was tingling hotly from a swift rush of blood. He'd never wanted a woman so much. If he reached out to her now, would she happily respond, or…?

More likely she would spurn him, he realised, the surge of excitement draining slowly away. Given that she had believed whatever story her father had spun around the photographs she'd sent him, no doubt believing she'd been used as a malicious thrill on the side, as well, the probability was she was here to support her father against him.

Love…hate—they could colour anyone's judgement.

He watched her join the group of people waiting for the elevator, watched her until steel doors closed behind her, and ached inside for what had been lost. He'd let the past rule his decisions, the long-burning need for justice. It was a crusade for good over evil, yet he knew he would feel no joy in the victory. Satisfaction, perhaps, but no joy.

He had to take the witness stand tomorrow. If Laura attended the hearing again… A violent determination rampaged through him. He would make her believe every word he said, every revelation of the kind of man her father was. It might not win him anything from her on a personal level, but at least she wouldn't be able to sustain any support for her rotten father, who had ruined any chance they might have had for a future together.

*The second day...*

Laura had no sooner settled on a back-row seat in the inquiry room than her father was on his feet, pushing back the chair he had occupied at his barrister's table so violently it tumbled over. He ignored it, glaring furiously at her as he strode down the aisle, obviously intent on confrontation.

She sat tight, steeling herself to ride out his wrath. Since she and her mother had left the Mosman mansion before Christmas, none of the family had had any personal contact with him. No doubt he contemptuously considered them rats that had deserted the sinking ship, but he had no power over them anymore. He couldn't actually *do* anything to her, not here in public, but if looks could kill, she'd certainly be dead.

'What the hell are you doing here?' he demanded, the thunderous tone of voice promising punishment for her sins against him.

'Listening,' she answered curtly, refusing to be cowed.

Burning hatred in his eyes. 'Are you on with Jake Freedman again?'

'No.'

His lips curled in a sneer. 'Chasing after him.'

She met his vicious mockery with absolute self-determination. 'You lied to me about him, Dad. I've come to hear the truth.'

'Truth!' he scoffed. 'You benefited from his

stepfather's fall. That's the truth. And Freedman isn't about to forget it, not when he's been brooding over it for years.'

The judge's entrance demanded her father's return to his barrister's side. Laura was shaken by the encounter. She'd been all keyed up, hoping that a meeting with Jake might lead to a resumption of their relationship. Fixated on the photographs, she hadn't given any thought to other factors. When all was said and done, she was still her father's daughter, and Jake may well have killed any feeling he'd had for her and moved on, especially after she'd used false evidence to blow him away.

A chance to nothing, she'd said to Eddie, and the truth was she was probably fooling herself about having any chance at all. She sat in a slump of silent despair, not hearing anything until Jake's name was called.

Tension instantly stiffened her spine and pressed her legs tightly together. Her eyes automatically drank in everything about him as he entered the room and was led to the witness box. He wore a sober grey suit and the air of a man all primed to carry out deadly business. James Bond—sleek, sophisticated, sexy, making her heart kick at how handsome he was, making her stomach flutter at how devastating this day could be to her. Even the sound of his voice as he was sworn in evoked memories of intimate moments, making her ache for more.

He shot his gaze around the room before sitting

down. For one electric moment it stopped on her. There was no smile, not the slightest change of expression on his face at seeing her. She didn't smile at him, either. The feelings inside her were too intense. She fiercely willed him to know she was here for him. The moment passed all too quickly, his gaze flicking to the prosecuting barrister as he settled on his chair.

He didn't look at her again.

Not once.

Laura listened to his testimony, hearing a biting edge in every word. It became perfectly clear that her father's intent as a liquidator was exploitation, without any regard to the interests of any company or its creditors. Billable hours extended to clerical staff, even to the tea and coffee lady—each at three hundred dollars an hour. At one meeting with creditors, the coffee served to them came to eighty dollars a cup.

'Nice cup,' the judge remarked acidly.

'Not exactly sweet when the creditors never get their entitlements,' Jake said just as acidly.

The flow of evidence went on and on, backed up by facts and figures that could not be denied. They painted a picture of shocking corruption. Laura felt ashamed of her connection to the man who hadn't cared how many people he hurt in amassing more and more money for himself. She'd known he had a cruel nature. She hadn't known his contempt for others extended so far.

It was sickening.

She understood now how much this mission had meant to Jake, especially given what had happened with his parents. Apart from the personal element, it was right to take her father down, saving others from suffering similar situations. He was doing good, more good than she had ever done in her life, showing up the faults of a system that was a feeding ground for liquidators without any conscience.

It took a big person to stand up and blow the whistle on it, regardless of any cost to himself. She admired Jake's drive to get it done. But her father was right about one thing. She was his daughter and her life had been cushioned in the luxury of his greedy profiteering. It wasn't her fault but she was definitely tainted by it in Jake's mind.

*I don't want to want you.*

And there was no sign of him wanting her now. He wouldn't even look at her, though she had been willing him to all day. He probably hated the sight of her—a memory of weakness on his part, not to be revisited.

*Stay strong.*

His whole demeanour, his voice, his laying out of undeniable facts, had been relentlessly strong today. He was not going to reconnect with her. Laura slipped out of the inquiry room as soon as the afternoon session ended, carrying the misery of lost hope with her. There was no point in coming back tomorrow. Jake had obviously shut the door on her and she must now do it on him.

She forced her legs to walk straight to the elevator, forced her finger to jab the *down* button. Other people clustered around her, waiting for the elevator to arrive. Minutes crawled by. There was a buzz of voices commenting on the hearing. Laura heard her father called *one hell of a shark*. No sympathy for him. Nor should there be.

Her own heart suddenly rebelled against leaving Jake believing that she had been here to support her father. The elevator doors opened. The surge forward carried her into the compartment but she wriggled out again, telling herself there was one last stand she had to make—a matter of self-respect if nothing else.

Jake emerged from the inquiry room with his barrister, the two men conferring with each other as they walked out. Laura didn't care if she would be interrupting something important. What she had to say would only take a couple of moments and it was important to her. Her hands clenched in determination. Her chin instinctively lifted. Every nerve in her body was wire-tight as she closed the short distance between them.

As though sensing her approach, Jake's head jerked towards her. His gaze locked on hers, hard and uninviting, twin dark bolts boring into her head. The barrister murmured something to him. Jake's hand sliced a sharp dismissive gesture, his attention not wavering from Laura. She stopped a metre short of him, close enough to be heard, her mind totally focussed on delivering a few last words.

'I found out that my father lied about the photographs. I'm sorry that I let him influence my belief in you, Jake. I wish you well.'

That was it.

She turned and walked back to the elevator where another group of people had gathered, waiting for its return. She could go now, having righted the wrong she had done Jake. And she did wish him well. He was a good man.

*She didn't hate him!*

The steel guard Jake had put around his feelings for Laura Costarella cracked wide open at this stunning realisation. He was in instant tumult over her apology, wanting to know more, but she had already turned away and was heading for the elevator, not waiting for any response from him. What did that mean? She didn't want one? Didn't expect one?

How long had she known about her father's lie? If it was before this hearing, she wouldn't have attended it to support him. Was it simply curiosity that had drawn her here, a need to know everything that had limited their relationship and made it so impossible to sustain? But surely she wouldn't have bothered unless…she still had feelings for him.

*I wish you well….*

It was a goodbye line.

He didn't want it to be. He wanted…

The elevator doors opened. Laura was following the group of people into it. She was going and everything within him violently rebelled against letting her go.

Without any conscious thought at all he lifted two fingers to his lips and whistled the most piercing whistle he'd ever produced in his life.

## CHAPTER FIFTEEN

THE whistle startled everyone who heard it. Conversations were momentarily cut off. Feet stopped moving. Heads turned. Laura's heart felt as though it had been kicked. Her mind instantly recalled the kiss-off line she'd written to Jake.

*As for any future meeting between us, you can whistle for me.*

Had he done it?

Please…let it be him wanting a meeting with her.

A meeting with a future in mind.

The other people resumed their movement into the elevator. Laura didn't. She had to turn around, had to see. If it was Jake who had whistled, he'd be looking at her, perhaps holding out a hand in an appeal for her to stay where she was, wait a minute.

A chance to nothing, she told herself, her heart hammering as she acted on her need to know, throwing a quick glance over her shoulder. Jake had left his barrister's side and was striding towards her, determined purpose burning in the eyes that locked onto hers, holding her still until he could reach her.

The elevator doors closed. Laura was the only person left behind. But Jake was coming to her. They hadn't talked to each other for almost a year. She had no idea what was on his mind, yet the leap of hope in hers was so strong, it was impossible to put a guard of caution around it. He could probably see it in her eyes, the wanting, the needing. Pride couldn't hide it. She had none where he was concerned.

He stopped about a metre away from her, tension emanating from him, making her nerves even tighter.

'It's been a long time,' he said.

'Yes,' she agreed, the word coming out huskily. Her throat was choked up with a mountain of tumultuous emotions.

'There's a good coffee shop on the corner of the next block. Can I buy you a cappuccino?'

She swallowed hard to get rid of the lump. He was offering time together, wanting time together. A meeting. 'I'd like that very much,' she answered, her voice still furred with feelings that were totally uncontrollable.

'Good!' he said and stepped around her to press the elevator button, summoning it to this floor again.

Third time lucky, Laura thought giddily.

Jake flashed her a smile. 'I wish you well, too, Laura. I always have.'

She nodded, yearning for far more than well-wishing from him.

'Are you still living with your father?' he asked.

'No. I have a full-time job now. Landscape

designer for a firm of architects. I can afford my own apartment.'

'What about your mother?'

'She moved out the same time I did. She's okay. Much happier.'

'Sharing your apartment?'

'No. Nick Jeffries, our former handyman/gardener, carried her off to his home. He's a widower and they're very much in love.'

'Wow!' Jake grinned, surprised and seemingly delighted by this turn of events. 'I guess you don't have to worry about her anymore.'

'No, I don't. Having nothing to fear from Nick, she's already blooming into a far more positive person.'

'That's good. Great!'

He really did look pleased—pleased because he didn't want anyone to be her father's victim, or pleased because she was completely free and clear of any continuing connection with her father? Was he checking to see if he could reasonably resume a relationship with her with no negative fallout from it? Did he want to? She was still her father's daughter. Nothing could change that.

The elevator arrived and Jake waved an invitation to precede him into it. They were the only people occupying the small compartment on this ride. Jake stood silently beside her on the way down. Laura was too conscious of his close presence to think of anything to say. She had been intensely intimate with this man and the memories of it were flooding through her mind—the passionate kisses, the exquisite sensitivity of his touch. She had to press her thighs tightly together to contain the hot, searing need to have him again.

As they walked out to the street she was fiercely wishing he would take hold of her hand but he didn't attempt even that simple physical link with her. The evening rush hour hadn't quite started. The sidewalk wasn't crowded. There was no reason for Jake to take her arm to keep them together and he didn't. They reached the coffee shop without touching at all and Jake led her to a booth, waiting for her to slide in on one bench seat before seating himself across the table from her.

'Like old times,' she remarked, managing an ironic smile to cover the sick feeling that this might be the last time she shared a table with Jake.

He returned the smile. 'A lot of water has passed under the bridge since then. Are you happy with the career you've chosen?'

She nodded. 'It's very challenging but I'm loving it. What about you, Jake? Have you moved on to renovating another house?'

'Yes. I sold the last one.'

'I know.'

He looked quizzically at her and she flushed, realising she had given away the fact that she had tried to visit him. Too late to take back those revealing words. She heaved a sigh to relieve the tightness in her chest and plunged into telling the truth. What point was there in holding back?

'On the day we left Mosman—it was just before last Christmas—Mum found a bunch of other photographs of you in Dad's safe. They made me realise he'd set you up, then spun a false story to make me believe...' She hesitated, inwardly recoiling from repeating the horribly demeaning picture her father had drawn.

'That I was a liar and a cheat,' Jake finished for her with a wry grimace. 'I didn't blame you for believing him, Laura. It was my fault. I should never have touched you. It put you in a rotten position when I made my move against him.'

His use of the past tense hurt. If he regretted their relationship, what hope was there for a future one? But she was halfway through her explanation and she wanted to finish it.

'Anyhow, it made me feel really bad about how I'd completely written you off, so I went to your house at Woollahra, wanting to apologise, except you were gone and other people had moved in. I had no means of contact with you unless I came to the hearing, and I'm glad I did. Listening to everything being laid out made me understand why you had to take my father down. You were right to do it. And I do wish you well, Jake.'

There!

Definitely water under the bridge now!

And she'd managed it with reasonable dignity.

A waiter arrived to take their order and Jake asked for two cappuccinos, quickly inquiring if she wanted something to eat as well—a toasted sandwich? Laura shook her head. Her stomach was in knots. After the waiter had left them, Jake regarded her seriously for several moments, making the knots even tighter.

'It's not over, Laura,' he said quietly. 'There will be ugly things said about me in the days to come.'

*The dirt her father had up his sleeve.*

'Will they be true?' she asked.

'Not on any professional level. He can't deny the evidence against him. It's too iron-tight. So I'm confident that nothing will change the eventual outcome. He's gone from the industry, regardless of what he uses in an attempt to discredit me.'

'Do you know what he'll try to use?'

He made a wry grimace. 'You were my only weakness, Laura. I'm anticipating an attack on my character revolving around my involvement with you.'

She frowned. 'But that had nothing to do with how he ran his business.'

'I think he'll try to link it up.'

A fierce rebellion swept through Laura. Her father had been too successful in hurting others, deliberately doing it and taking malicious pleasure in it. She wanted him to fail for once, and be shown up as the liar he was—some justice for the months of misery he'd given her.

She leaned forward, earnestly pressing for Jake

to agree with her. 'I've taken this week off work. I could testify on your behalf. I know you didn't do me any wrong, Jake.'

His face tightened in instant rejection. 'This isn't your war, Laura. It was wrong of me to put you in the line of fire and I won't do it again. I'll ride it through.'

'It *is* my war,' she cried vehemently. 'I've taken the bullets and I want to return them. I'm not ashamed of my involvement with you. It makes a much stronger stand if we ride this through together. Publicly together. Surely you can see that any capital my father might think he could make out of our connection becomes utter nonsense if we're still connected.'

He didn't offer any quick rebuttal this time. The riveting dark eyes scoured hers with blazing intensity. Laura had the sinking feeling he was unsure of her staying power. She hadn't remained strong against her father's manipulation in the past.

'There's no other man in your life, Laura?' he asked quietly.

The question startled her—not what she had been expecting. It offered hope that Jake was considering her suggestion. 'No. I'm free and clear,' she stated firmly.

It suddenly occurred to her that he might not be. He hadn't touched her. Just because the memory of him had made her disinterested in other men didn't mean he'd felt a similar detachment. She'd certainly opened the door for him to move on when she'd shut it on her life.

'I'm sorry. I didn't think,' she blurted out, flushing self-consciously over her single-mindedness, her hands fluttering an apologetic dismissal of her impulsive ideas. 'If you're in another relationship, of course this won't work.'

'I'm not,' he said swiftly, reaching across the table to take one of her hands in his, long strong fingers stroking, soothing her agitation. 'There's nothing I'd like more than to be connected to you again, Laura. I just want to be sure it's right for you.'

A wild joy burst through her heart. She stared at him, scarcely able to believe she did have another chance with him. Warmth from his touch ran up her arm and spread through her entire body, a blissful warmth, promising her the loving she craved. She wanted this man so much, yet it hadn't really been right for her before, not with him limiting their relationship to great dinners and great sex. The temptation to take whatever she could of him played through her mind, but she knew that would never be enough.

'Will you show me the house you're now working on?'

It was a critical question, challenging how much he wanted to be connected to her.

His face relaxed into a smile, his eyes twinkling sexy delight. 'Would after we drink our coffee be too soon?'

She laughed in sheer ecstatic relief. 'No, not too soon. Where is it?'

'Petersham. It's about ten minutes in the train from Town Hall, then a short walk from the station. An easy commute to the city centre.'

'Is it another terrace house?'

'No. A two-bedroom cottage with a yard, both of which have been neglected for years.' He grinned. 'Maybe you can give me some ideas on what to do with the yard.'

It was so wonderful that he was willing to share this project with her, she grinned straight back. 'I'd love to design a cottage garden. Something delightfully old-fashioned. All I've done so far at work is very modern landscape.'

'Then you'll have to go shopping for plants with me,' he said decisively. 'Guide me into buying the best.'

More sharing. Laura's cup of happiness was suddenly bubbling to the brim. 'No problem,' she assured him, revelling in allowing herself to love this man all over again.

The waiter returned with their cappuccinos. Jake released her hand and they sat apart again, but another journey had begun—one that shimmered with the promise of far more than the first they'd taken together. Laura couldn't remember a coffee ever tasting so good.

Jake could scarcely believe this incredibly fortunate turn of events. Laura hadn't moved on. Not from him. And the time apart had not been wasted. She had achieved complete independence from her father and quite clearly would never allow herself to be subjected to his influence again. It was now totally irrelevant that she was Alex Costarella's daughter. She was simply herself—the beautiful, strong, giving woman he had come to love. And since her mother no longer needed her in any protective sense, the way ahead for them was free of any insurmountable complications.

He could throw caution to the winds, share whatever he wanted with Laura without any sense of guilt over how hurt she might be from associating with him. The whole truth was out in the open now. There was no reason to hold back on anything. Where the future might take them as a couple was entirely in their own hands. The most important thing was he could have her again. Nothing else really mattered.

Froth from the cappuccino coated her upper lip. He wanted to lick it off. Her tongue slid out and swept it away. Her beautiful blue eyes twinkled at him teasingly as though she knew what he'd been thinking.

'I haven't wanted any woman since you, Laura,' he said softly. That was the truth, too, and he needed her to know it. The damning photographs could have left doubts in her mind about how deeply he'd felt connected to her. This was a new start and he couldn't bear anything marring it.

She smiled, happiness lighting up her lovely face.

'It's been the same for me, too, Jake, though I did have a lot of bad thoughts about you.'

'The woman in the photographs…she said she was being stalked and pleaded with me to walk her home from the gym. It was an act of kindness, Laura, nothing more.'

The smile broadened. 'I like kindness in a man. Nick is very kind to Mum. She never had that from Dad.'

*Neither did you. Only demands and abuse if they weren't met.*

Jake understood where Laura was coming from, why marriage was not an attractive proposition to her, but maybe he could change her view of it, given enough time together. She was certainly seeing the difference for her mother.

He wanted a family in his future. The loss of it had driven him all these years and now that the goal he had set himself had been reached, he could plan a different scenario for his life, hopefully with Laura. It was like a miracle that it was possible at all.

She put down her cup and gave him a look of eager anticipation. 'Are we done here? Ready to go?'

Desire roared through him like an express train. He couldn't get her out of the coffee shop fast enough. They started the walk towards Town Hall hand in hand, a joyous bounce in their step. It was rush hour, people crowding past them either way. They came to a building with a recessed entrance and Jake instantly pulled Laura out of the mêlée on the sidewalk and into his embrace against a sheltered side wall.

'I've been wanting to do this ever since I saw you yesterday,' he murmured, his eyes blazing with naked need.

'Yesterday?' she echoed quizzically.

'I thought you'd come for your father. If I'd known you'd come for me…'

He couldn't wait. Like in the garden the first day they'd met, like on their first date on the way to the hotel…he had to kiss her and she wrapped her arms around his neck and kissed him right back, their passion for each other as wildly exhilarating as ever, more so with the freedom from all restrictions.

But they couldn't give it full expression in this public place.

They had to move on.

And they did.

Together.

\* \* \* \* \*

# THE HOT-BLOODED
# GROOM

## Emma
# DARCY

# CHAPTER ONE

'I WANT you married.'

Bryce Templar gritted his teeth. It wasn't the first time his father had made this demand. Undoubtedly it wouldn't be the last, either. But he hadn't come out of his way to visit the old man, still convalescing from his recent heart operation, to have another argument about his bachelor state.

He kept his gaze trained on the view, ignoring the contentious issue. The sun was setting, adding even more brilliant shades of colour to the stunning red rocks of Sedona. His father's winter residence was certainly sited to capture one of the most striking panoramas nature had to offer, here in the Arizona desert. And of course, communing with nature was another thing Will Templar preached—spiritual peace, clean air, clean living...

'Are you hearing me, boy?'

Bryce unclenched his jaw and slid his father a derisive look. 'I'm not a boy, Dad.'

'Still acting like one,' came the aggressive grumble. 'Here you are with your hair going grey and you're not settled with a woman yet.'

'I'm only thirty-four. Hardly over the hill. And you went grey in your thirties. It's genetic.'

It wasn't the only physical aspect of his father he'd inherited. They were both well over six feet tall, big men, though his father had lost quite a bit of weight over the past year and was looking somewhat gaunt in the face. They had the same strong nose, the same determined mouth, closely set ears, and while his father's hair was now white, it was still as thick as his own.

The only feature he'd inherited from his mother was her eyes—heavier lidded than his father's and green instead of grey. Will Templar's eyes had been described in print as steely and incisive, but right now they were smoking at Bryce with irritable impatience.

'I was married to your mother in my twenties.'

'People married earlier in those days, Dad.'

'You're not even looking for a wife.' He shook an admonishing finger. 'You think I don't hear about your bed-hopping with starlets in L.A.? Getting laid indiscriminately doesn't sit well with me, son.'

Bryce barely stifled a sigh as he thought, *Here comes the clean living lecture.* 'I don't bed-hop and I'm not indiscriminate in my choice of playmate,' he bit out. Hoping to avoid a diatribe on morals, he added, 'You know how busy I am. I just don't have the time to put into a relationship what women want out of it.'

It brought his father up from his lounger in a burst of angry energy. 'Don't tell me women don't want marriage. They all want marriage. It's not difficult to get a woman to say *yes* to that. And I'm living proof of it with five wives behind me.'

All of them walking away with a bundle, Bryce thought cynically. Except his mother who died before she'd got around to divorce. The billion dollar empire of Templar Resources could absorb the cost of hundreds of wives. It just so happened Bryce didn't like the idea of being taken for the pot of gold at the end of the rainbow ride.

If a woman wanted him…fine. Especially if he wanted her. But the occasional pleasure in bed did not warrant a gold ring and a gold passport to a hefty divorce settlement. Apart from which, he certainly didn't need the aggravation of a demanding wife. He much preferred a walkaway situation.

'You get married, Bryce, or I'll put Damian in control of business, right over your head. Make him CEO until you do get a wife. That will free up your time,' his father threatened.

'And give you another heart attack when he messes up,' Bryce mocked, knowing his half-brother's limited vision only too well.

'I mean it, boy! Time's slipping by and I'm feeling my mortality these days. I want to see you married, and married soon. With a grandchild on the way, too. Within a year. Just get out there and choose a wife. You hear me?'

He was going red in the face. Concerned about his father's blood pressure, Bryce instantly set aside the argument. 'I hear you, Dad.'

'Good! Then do it! And find a woman like your mother. She had a brain, as well as being beautiful.' He sank back onto the cushions of the lounger, taking quick shallow breaths. The high colour gradually receded. 'Worst day of my life when your mother died.'

Bryce couldn't remember it. He'd only been three years old. What he remembered was the succession of stepmothers who had waltzed into and out of his childhood and adolescence.

'Got to think of the children,' his father muttered. 'Damian's mother was a featherhead. Charming, sexy, but without a thought worth listening to.' His eyes closed and his voice dropped to a mumble. 'Damian's a good boy. Not his fault he hasn't got your brain. At least he's guidable.'

Watching fatigue lines deepen on his face, making him look older than his sixty years, Bryce was troubled by the thought there was more to his father's remark on *feeling his mortality* than he was letting on. Just how bad was his heart condition?

While they'd had this argument over marriage before, there'd never been a time-frame stipulated.

*Within a year.*

And the threat about Damian—empty though it was—added more weight to the demand, carrying a measure of desperation.

The sun had slipped below the horizon as they'd talked. The massive red rocks were darkening with shadows. Nothing stayed the same for long, Bryce reflected, and if time was running out for his father...well, why not please him by getting married?

It shouldn't be too much of a problem.

He wouldn't let it be.

# CHAPTER TWO

SUNNY YORK's heart did not leap with joy when she spotted her fiancé shoving through the crowd of delegates waiting to enter the conference room. His appearance sent a shudder of distaste down her spine and she found herself gritting her teeth as a host of blistering criticisms clamoured to be expressed.

It was the last day of the conference, the last day to try and smooth over the bad impressions he'd made on others, and the most important day for her, which Derek knew perfectly well. And he turned up like this?

She shook her head in disgust, thinking of how early she had risen this morning, determined on presenting a perfect, go-getting image. It had taken an hour to get her unruly mane of rippling curls under reasonable control, carefully blow-drying out any tendency to frizz and ensuring the whole tawny mass of it looked decently groomed. Her make-up was positive without being overdone, and her sharp yellow suit was a statement of vibrant confidence.

There was absolutely nothing sharp about Derek. His suit looked rumpled, as though he'd dropped it on the floor and dragged it on again. His eyes were bloodshot, he'd nicked his chin shaving, and he was obviously in no state to get anything out of the morn-

ing session. She actually bristled with rejection as he
hooked his arm around hers.

'Made it,' he said, as though it were an achievement she should be grateful for.

Never mind that he'd broken every arrangement for
them to spend private time together. Turning up for
her sales presentation did not make up for treating her
like nothing all week. And turning up like this was
the last straw to Sunny.

Her sherry-brown eyes held no welcoming warmth
as she tersely replied, 'I expected to see you at breakfast.'

He leaned over confidentially. 'Had it at the roulette table. Free drinks, free food all night. They sure
look after you at these casinos and I was running hot.'

Sunny's heart felt very cold. 'I'm amazed you tore
yourself away.'

He grimaced as though *she* was acting like a pain
to him. 'Don't nag. I'm here, aren't I?'

Four days they'd been in Las Vegas and he'd been
gambling every spare minute, even skipping conference sessions when he thought he could get away
with it. 'I take it the hot run ended,' she bit out, barely
controlling a fiery flash of temper at *his* criticism of
*her* attitude.

'Nope. I won a packet,' he slurred smugly. 'But I
happened to see the big man come in last night and
if he's showing this morning…'

'What big man?' she snapped, losing all patience
with him.

'The head of the whole shebang. Bryce Templar

himself. He dropped into the L.A. conference last year to give us a pep talk, remember?'

Sunny remembered. The CEO of Templar Resources was the most gorgeous hunk she'd ever seen, almost a head taller than she was and with a big muscular frame that telegraphed *all man* to her, eminently lust-worthy, but so far beyond her reach, he was strictly dream material.

She hadn't heard a word he'd said at L.A. She'd sat in the audience, imagining how it might be in bed with all that strong maleness being driven by the charismatic energy he was putting out in his address to them.

His father had founded Templar Resources, back in 1984, and it was now the largest networking company in the world, producing and servicing software in most languages. Obviously the son was building on that, not just inheriting his position, which added even more power to his sex appeal. On any male evolution scale he was definitely the top rung.

'Guess he'll do the same today,' Derek babbled on. 'Thought I'd better turn up for it.'

Sunny cast a severely jaundiced look at the man she'd cast in the future role of her husband and father to the family she wanted. Having seen her two younger sisters married and producing adorable babies, she'd become hopelessly clucky, and when Derek had walked into her life, he'd seemed the answer to her dreams.

Those dreams had received an awful lot of tarnishing this week, and right at this moment, the reminder of a man as powerfully impressive as Bryce Templar did nothing to shine them up again.

Derek was the same height as herself—if she wore flat heels—and quite handsome on better days when his blue eyes were clear and his face more alive. His dark blond hair was still damp from a very recent shower so the sun-bleached streaks weren't showing so much this morning. He usually kept his rather lean physique toned up with sessions in the gym but he hadn't been anywhere near the hotel's health club this week.

All in all, he was much less a man in Sunny's eyes than he'd been four days ago. Whether this gambling fever was a temporary madness or not, he'd completely lost her respect, and she'd hand him back his diamond ring right now, except it might cause a scene that she could do without in front of the other delegates whose respect *she* wanted when she gave her presentation in just another hour's time.

Deeply disillusioned and angry with the assumption she would overlook everything, she unhooked her arm from Derek's as they moved into the conference room and gave him a stony warning. 'Don't think you can lean on me if you fall asleep.'

'Oooh, we are uptight, aren't we?' he mocked, looking uglier by the second. 'Nervous about performing in front of the CEO?'

'No. I just don't want to prop you up,' she grated.

'Fine! Then I'll sit at the back and you won't have to worry about it,' he sniped, sheering away from her side in a blatant huff.

Sunny walked on, rigidly ignoring him. No doubt

a back-row seat suited Derek very well. If Bryce
Templar didn't show, he could easily slip outside and
get on with his gambling. Though if he thought other
people besides herself hadn't noticed what was going
on, he was a fool.

The managing director of the Sydney branch had
already commented on his absence from conference
sessions, as well as his failure to attend any of the
social functions at night. Derek might be considered
a top consultant but playing the corporate game was
important, too. He was earning a big black mark here
in Las Vegas, not only on a personal level, but a
professional one, as well.

Still inwardly fuming over his behaviour, Sunny
made her way to the very front row of tables in the
auditorium, where she was entitled to sit as one of
the presenters this morning. Having settled herself
and greeted the other delegates in the team she'd been
attached to all week, she did her best to push Derek's
disturbing behaviour out of her mind, concentrating
on listening to the buzz about Bryce Templar's arrival
on the scene.

Had he come to announce some new technologies
being developed by the company? Was he here to
reward someone for outstanding performance? Speculation was running rife.

It ended abruptly as the man himself made his entrance, accompanied by the conference organisers. A
hush fell over the room, attention galvanised on the
CEO of Templar Resources. He took the podium
without any introduction but whatever he said floated
right over Sunny's head.

From a purely physical viewpoint, she couldn't help thinking that Bryce Templar had to have the best gene pool in the whole world, and if she could choose any one man to be the father of the baby she'd love to have, he would top the stud-list.

The woman in yellow kept attracting Bryce's eye. She was the only spot of colour amongst a sea of grey and black business clothing. Since she was seated right at the front, he couldn't miss seeing her, and as women went, she was definitely worth a second look.

Great hair. Lush wide mouth. Big dreamy eyes. A strong impression of warmth, which stayed with him as he left the podium, niggling at the bitterness his lawyer had stirred with the call about yet another change Kristen was demanding in the prenuptial agreement. His fiancée was fast dissipating any warmth he'd felt for her.

As he sat down at the official table with the conference organisers, he reflected on the black irony of having thought he'd picked the ideal wife. Kristen Parrish had enough beauty and brains to meet his father's criteria, plus a very stylish career as an interior decorator, which meant she wouldn't be hanging on having a husband dance attendance all the time. She had a business of her own to run. Which suited Bryce just fine.

The problem was, her sharp brain was proving to be one hell of a calculating machine, and Bryce fiercely resented the way she was manipulating the situation. Just one mention that he wanted a child, preferably within the first year of marriage, and she'd started using it as a bargaining chip to ensure she would always have funds to raise their child should the marriage fail. She was literally bleeding him for all she could get, and if it wasn't for his father, he'd tell her to get lost.

Then she'd probably sue him for breach of promise.

And would he find anyone better?

His gaze flicked to the woman in yellow and caught her looking at him. Her head instantly jerked away, thick dark lashes swept down, and her cheeks bloomed with heat. Quite an amazing blush. She had to be in her late twenties or early thirties, and very committed to a career to be here at this conference. Hardly the shy type. She wouldn't be wearing yellow if she was shy.

Her cheeks were still burning, lending even more vivid colour and warmth to her face. It was a very appealing, feminine face, finely boned, though not quite perfect with the slightly tip-tilted nose. Her hair drew his attention again, copper and corn colours tangled through a tousled riot of waves and curls, the thick mass of it falling from a centre parting and tumbling down over her shoulders. It looked…very touchable, unlike Kristen's ice-blond sculptured bob.

He wondered what the woman in yellow would be like in bed, then put a firm clamp on those thoughts.

He'd made his bed.

Besides, would the woman in yellow prove any different to Kristen when it came to the money angle?

With a cynical shake of his head, Bryce reached

for a glass of iced water. No point in getting heated about anyone he didn't know…or Kristen's greed.

His forthcoming marriage was a done deal. Almost a done deal. He didn't have the time to settle with someone else. The doctors had told him it was a miracle his father was still alive and they were using experimental drugs to treat his condition. Such risky medication held out no guarantees, and Bryce didn't want to delay giving what peace of mind this marriage might bring, at least in the short term.

No point in brooding over the outcome for himself, either. He'd flown to Vegas to hand out awards and get a feel of how the rank and file were dealing with the company products. His mission this morning was to listen and observe. Which he proceeded to do.

First up was a panel who role-played selling the concepts of particular products to customers who have no idea how they would work in business, or that they even existed to be used. Bryce was favourably impressed by their understanding and the concise way they focused on customer needs to adopt and apply more profitable business practices.

Next came a sample presentation to a company board level, delivered by a Business Development Manager from Sydney, Australia. The program noted that Sunny York had the enviable record of always achieving her quota of sales. *Her*…a woman? His interest piqued, Bryce waited curiously to assess why she was so successful.

The conference organiser finished his patter on her, raised his arm in a welcoming gesture, and in a typically hyped-up voice, announced, 'Miss Sunny York.'

Up stood the woman in yellow!

She had a smile on her face that would captivate and dazzle even the hardest-headed financial directors. And she was tall—six feet tall, Bryce estimated—and more than half of that height was taken up by the longest legs he'd ever seen on a woman. He couldn't help watching them as she stepped up to the podium. Her skirt ended above her knees but it wasn't a mini. It simply looked like a mini on those legs, and she wasn't even wearing high-heels, just comfortable court shoes with enough of a heel to look elegant.

His gaze travelled slowly upwards from her feet...what would it be like to have those long, shapely legs wrapped around him...the curvy cradle of her hips underneath him...plenty of cushion in those nicely rounded breasts, too...that mouth, so full-lipped and wide, made for sensual pleasure...and her hair tumbling everywhere.

'Hi!' She spread her smile and twinkling eyes around the audience, drawing everyone to her with a flow of warmth that sparked responding smiles. 'I'm here to help you make money...and save money.'

She had them in her hand from that very first delivery and didn't let them go for one second in the whole forty minutes of her presentation. It didn't feel like a hard-sell. She came over as concerned to serve the customer's very best interests, her voice carrying a very natural charm, allied to a mobility of expression which was almost mesmerising. The line of logic she injected into selling sounded so simple and convincing, she left no doubt this was a winning move, and her own positive energy literally generated positive energy through the whole auditorium.

Bryce found himself totally entranced.

Even her Australian accent was endearing.

Sunny…

He could certainly do with a bit of that sun in his life. A lot of it. All of it. His stomach clenched as his mind skidded to Kristen. He didn't want a coolheaded calculator. Taking her as his wife went against every grain in his entire body…and that very same body was craving what Sunny York might give him.

His eyes feasted on her as she stepped down from the podium. He'd invite her to join him for lunch…test possibilities. Seize the day. Seize the night. A night with Sunny York would at least satisfy the compelling fantasies she'd been stirring, and if she was all she promised to be…

The flash of a diamond on her left hand pulled the hot run of thoughts up with a jolt. Bryce stared at the ring that declared Sunny York was engaged to be married, committed to another man, whom she probably loved. Her whole performance demonstrated she put her heart into everything she did. Heart and soul.

Bryce wasn't used to feeling like a loser. It hit him hard, the sick hollowness following on the wild surge of excitement she had evoked in him. He sat back in his chair and grimly reviewed his options.

He might be able to seduce her away from her fiancé. Inducements marched through his mind…

powerful attractions for most women. But if he did win her like that…would he still want her?

Give it up, man, he told himself savagely.

Kristen was ready and willing…so long as he paid the price she demanded. Which he could well afford. Settle with her and be done with it.

# CHAPTER THREE

SUNNY headed for the ground-floor casino, determined on having a showdown with Derek. He hadn't come to the lunch—not even waiting outside the conference room to give her a courtesy comment on her presentation before skipping off—and he hadn't shown for the last session, regardless of the fact that Bryce Templar had been giving out awards. His respect for *the big man* obviously hadn't extended that far.

She didn't like the casino floor. The assault on her ears from countless bell-ringing slot machines was horrific. It was bad enough walking through it. Actually spending hours here was beyond her understanding. Having finally located the roulette tables, she scanned them for Derek and was frustrated at not finding him. Could he have gone to bed—the need for sleep catching up with him?

Frowning, Sunny moved from foot to foot, too worked up to walk away with so much angst playing through her mind. She shot her gaze in every direction, not really expecting to resolve anything, simply at a loss to know what to do next. It came as a shock when she actually spotted Derek, seated at a *blackjack* table, watching the cards being played by the dealer with an intensity that cramped her heart.

He was caught in a thrall that nothing was going to break.

It seemed that nothing else mattered.

Sickened by the realisation of how destructively addictive gambling could be, Sunny hesitated over confronting Derek, yet the relationship they had shared up until this week demanded that he at least recognise how he was treating it. The need to get through to him drove her over to the blackjack table. She waited until he threw down his cards in disgust, apparently having lost his bet, then tapped him on the shoulder.

'Derek...'

He sliced an impatient frown at her.

'...could I speak to you, please?'

'Can't you see I'm playing?'

'It's important.'

Grimacing at the interruption, he heaved himself off his chair and tipped the back of it onto the edge of the table to hold his place. 'What's so damned important?' he demanded, his bleary eyes snapping with frustration.

'It's the last night...'

'I've just lost the roll I won at roulette. My luck's got to turn...'

'Derek, we've got seats for the *Jubilee* show. And dinner beforehand.'

'The action is here. I'm not leaving it.'

'Don't I mean anything to you anymore?' she cried, trying to get through the obsessive glaze to some grain of perspective on what he was doing.

The personal tack clearly irritated him. 'I sat

through your presentation. You slayed 'em as you always do. Is that what you want to hear?' he said ungraciously, then waved a sharp dismissal as he added, 'If you're hot to go and watch some showgirl extravaganza, fine. But as you just pointed out, this is our last night here and I want to win my money back.'

'And what if you don't? What if you lose more?'

He looked shifty.

'Derek, just how much have you lost already?'

Feverish need flashed at her. 'I'll win it back. It's only a matter of time.'

An icy fear struck her. 'Have you been gambling on credit?'

'That's my business. We're not married yet.'

No sharing. No desire to share. Complete shut-out. Hurt and disappointment held her silent for a moment as she realised beyond any doubt that there could be no happy future for them. A bitter urge to show him what he'd done, how low he had fallen, had her wrenching the diamond ring off her finger.

'Here!' She held it out to him. 'You can pawn it. Get some more money to throw down the drain.'

It rocked him. 'Now look here, Sunny…'

'No. Try looking at yourself, Derek. It's over for me.'

'Well, if you feel that way…' His eyes glittered as he took the ring. 'You'll change your mind when I win a bundle.'

He was unreachable on any level. 'I won't change my mind. We're through, Derek,' she said with absolute finality.

His gaze had dropped to the diamond in his hand,

and Sunny had the gut-wrenching impression he was assessing what he could get for it. Her eyes blurred—all the inner torment of hopes and dreams being just swept away suddenly catching her by the throat. For their eight-month-long relationship to come to this…

She swung away, swallowing hard to stop herself from bursting into tears and making a spectacle of herself. Her legs moved automatically, driven by the need to get out of the casino, out of this dreadful playground which trapped people and drained them of any soul she could relate to.

The slot machines jangled around her, a cacophony of sound that seemed to mock her misery. She completely lost her bearings, not knowing what direction led to an exit. A moment's enforced reasoning told her to head for the hotel's reception desk from where the lobby was definitely in view.

It was such a relief to break free of the vast gambling area, tears swam into her eyes again. This time she simply put her head down and followed the walkway to the lobby, hoping not to run into anyone who knew her.

The limousine was waiting. His plane was waiting to fly him back to L.A. Kristen was waiting for him to return to her, no doubt ready to sweeten her prenuptial demands with how well she would accommodate his needs. Bryce Templar told himself that what he'd just witnessed didn't change anything, but still he lingered in the lobby, watching Sunny York.

She'd taken off the diamond ring.

The man she'd handed it to wasn't following her.

Her haphazard flight from what was clearly a distressing scene had finally been checked and she was heading towards him. Not consciously. She hadn't seen him. She wasn't seeing anything except the floor stretching ahead of her.

'Your bag is in the car, sir,' the bellhop informed him.

He nodded, unable to tear his eyes away from the long beautiful legs of Sunny York, walking her towards him. The memory of her warm vibrancy played havoc with his usual cool decision-making processes. Here was opportunity. The guy at the blackjack table was one hell of a big loser and that loss was right in front of Bryce to be capitilised upon. The urge to do so was more compelling than any urge he'd had for a long time.

She was free.

*He* wasn't, Bryce sternly reminded himself. Kristen was wearing *his* ring. But not a wedding ring yet. And before he could have any further second thoughts, a fierce surge of highly male instincts moved him to intercept Sunny York's path to the exit doors.

'Miss York...'

Legs were planted in front of her—the legs of a big man—and that voice...her heart quivered as a weird certainty crashed through the daze of misery in her mind. Bryce Templar was addressing her. Bryce Templar!

Her feet faltered, hesitating over making a wild sidestep to escape him. Even blinking furiously, she couldn't hide the moisture in her eyes. Impossible to face him…yet impossible not to. A man like Bryce Templar would not be snubbed. Not by an employee of his company.

'I was looking for you after the awards presentation,' he said purposefully.

It surprised her into raising her gaze to his. 'Looking for me?' His eyes were green, pouring out interest in her, and despite her embarrassment, Sunny found she couldn't look away.

He smiled. 'You impressed me very much this morning.'

At the vivid memory of how he had impressed her, heat whooshed up her neck and scorched her cheeks. It reduced her to total speechlessness.

'You have a remarkable gift for selling,' he went on.

Somehow she managed to get her mouth around, 'Thank you.'

'I wondered if I could interest you in a proposition.'

*Like having a baby with me?*

Sunny blushed even more furiously at that terribly wayward thought. Her mind was hopelessly out of control. Bryce Templar had to be talking about a business proposition, which was stunning in itself…the big man thinking she had a special talent for sales.

'Were you on your way somewhere?' he asked.

Realising her gauche manner was probably putting him off—*putting Bryce Templar off!*—Sunny tried desperately to adjust to this totally unexpected situation.

'I...I was just going for a walk. Out of the hotel. We've been closeted inside all day...'

'Yes, of course,' he said understandingly. 'I'll walk with you. If you'll just excuse me a few moments while I rearrange my schedule...' He smiled again, showering her with warm approval. '...I would like to talk to you.'

She nodded, completely dumbstruck at the prospect of strolling down the street, accompanied by Bryce Templar. Her whole body started tingling as she watched him stride over to the concierge's desk. He was rearranging his schedule to be with *her!* It was incredible, world-shaking.

Green eyes...she hadn't been close enough to see their colour before. They gave his face an even more striking character. Or so it seemed to her.

She watched him command the concierge's attention. He would naturally command attention anywhere, Sunny thought, even without the weight of his name and position. His height, the breadth of his shoulders, the sheer physical authority of the man, drew the gaze of everyone around him.

For once in her life, Sunny had the uplifting feeling of her own tallness ceasing to be a burden that had to be bypassed in her reaching out to others. She was short enough to hold her head high next to Bryce Templar without diminishing his sense of stature in any shape or form. Not that her height would be of any concern to him—a man of his power—but it was a relief to her not to feel conscious of it.

He made some quick calls on a cell phone, then spoke again to the concierge. Sunny was grateful for

the time to pull herself together. A business proposition, he'd said, which was what she should be focusing on instead of letting foolish personal responses
to him turn her into a blithering idiot. She had a future
to consider…a future without Derek.

Yet when Bryce Templar turned back to her, his
green eyes targeted her with an intensity that didn't
feel business-like at all. Sunny was instantly swamped
with an acute awareness of being a woman, every
feminine instinct she had positively zinging with the
electric possibility that *he* found her worthy of mating
with.

It blew her mind off any consideration of business.
Her pulse was a wild drumbeat in her temples. Her
stomach clenched at his approach. He stretched one
arm out in a gathering-in gesture and some madness
in her brain saw him naked and intent on claiming
her. Then his other arm pointed to the exit doors and
the crazy anticipation rocketing through her was
countered by a blast of sanity.

A walk…

That was the sum of his invitation.

Somehow she pushed her shaky legs into walking.

Bryce Templar did not, in fact, touch her. A bellhop rushed to open the door. When they emerged
from the hotel, the big man fell into step beside her
and Sunny instinctively chose to turn right because
he was on her left and bumping into him was unthinkable in her dreadfully hyped-up state with fantasies
running riot.

'Have you enjoyed being in Las Vegas?'

It was a perfectly natural question but his voice

seemed to purr in her ear, heightening her awareness of him. Sunny kept her gaze trained straight ahead, not trusting herself to look at him and keep sensible. *Business, business, business,* she recited frantically.

'I haven't really had much time to explore the city,' she answered carefully. 'The conference has been pretty much full-on. Which is what we're here for,' she quickly added in case it sounded like a criticism. 'And I have learnt a lot.'

'You apply what you know extremely well,' he remarked admiringly.

She shrugged. 'I like giving our customers the best deal I can.'

'Well, you've certainly done an excellent job of serving Templar Resources.'

'I'm glad you think so.'

'Oh, I think you'd be an asset to anyone, Miss York. Or may I call you Sunny?'

'If you like,' she gabbled, trying not to read too much into his charming manner.

'It suits you. You project a warmth that makes everyone want to bask in it.'

*He* was projecting a warmth that was sending her dizzy. She was tempted to glance at him, to check the expression on his face, but didn't quite dare. It was difficult enough to remain reasonably sensible when she was so affected by his close presence. If he caught her looking at him and held her gaze, she might melt into a mindless heap.

'What do you wish to see on our walk?' he asked pleasantly.

She had no plan. Her only thought had been to get

out of the casino. 'I…I just wanted…more of a feel for the city…before I leave.'

'I suppose, in a way, you could call it a very romantic city…full of dreams.'

*Shattered dreams if you're a loser.*

The flash of Derek was unwelcome, bringing with it the empty feeling of no marriage and no babies to look forward to. But she could never accept Derek as a husband or the father of her children now. It was definitely for the best that she'd found out what she would have been getting in him.

'The re-creation of romantic cities in the newer hotels—Venice, Paris, New York. They're quite fantastic facsimiles of the real thing,' Bryce Templar remarked, continuing his *romance* comment. 'Have you had a look at them?'

Sunny struggled to get her mind back on track with his. 'The Venetian and Paris, yes. They're amazing.'

'Well, we're walking in the right direction to see New York, New York. The Excalibur and the Luxor are further on beyond it. Very striking with their Medieval and Egyptian architectural themes.'

Suddenly struck by his indulgence towards what he perceived as her wishes, Sunny began seriously wondering what he wanted with her. Here he was, strolling along the Boulevard, playing guide to her tourist…what was it leading to? They reached an intersection and had to stop for the traffic lights to change. Taking a deep breath, and steeling herself to cope with the nerve-shaking magnetism of the man, Sunny turned to face him.

'Your time must be valuable,' she stated, her eyes quickly searching his for a true response.

'Isn't everyone's?' he replied.

'Yes. But...' She floundered as he smiled, showing obvious pleasure in her company.

'You need to relax. So do I. Is there any reason we shouldn't relax together?'

'No,' she answered breathlessly, her pulse going haywire at the realisation he *was* attracted to her, man to woman attraction. No mistake. No flight of fancy. The spark of sexual connection was in his eyes—the keen interest, the desire to know more, the hunter's gleam that said she was worth pursuing and he meant to pursue.

'Good!' There was a wealth of satisfaction in that one simple word. He reached out and gently cupped her elbow. 'The lights have changed. Let's go with the flow.'

The flow Sunny felt had nothing to do with the stream of people crossing the street with them. She was barely aware of them. The hand lightly holding her arm had the mental force of a physical brand...like Bryce Templar was claiming possession of her, burning his ownership through the sleeve of her suit-coat and making her sizzle with possibilities she would not have believed in a few moments ago.

Bryce Templar...wanting *her*. She hadn't been completely crazy back in the hotel lobby. But what did it mean to him? Was it his habit to pluck a woman out of a crowd—someone he fancied—and just go after her? It probably was that easy for a man like him. What woman would refuse the chance to...?

Shock stopped that thought from reaching its natural conclusion. Fanciful lusting was one thing. Real
flesh-and-blood lusting was something else. Did she
want to be a one-night stand for Bryce Templar, finishing off his trip to Las Vegas—a bit of relaxation,
satisfying a sexual urge? Surely that was all it could
be. She was an Australian, on her way back to Sydney
tomorrow. An easy goodbye.

'How would you feel about transferring to the U.S.,
Sunny?'

It startled her into a fast re-think. 'You
mean…leave Sydney…for here?'

'Not here. Your base would be Los Angeles. Or
New York. They hold our biggest operations.'

*Business!*

Was she hopelessly out of kilter, imagining the sexual stuff?

Totally confused, Sunny tried to come to grips with
this new question. A career move…an upward career
move…out of her own country.

'Would you find that too much of a wrench?' he
asked quietly. 'I realise it's a big ask, particularly if
you're close to your family.'

Her family…Sunny almost groaned as she envisaged telling her mother and sisters she'd broken her
engagement to Derek. No wedding. No marriage. No
babies. She'd been a failure as a woman in their eyes
for years and there she'd be, proving it again. Almost
thirty and couldn't find Mr. Right. Sympathy would
be directed to her face, pity behind her back, and
she'd hate every minute of it.

'I have my own life to lead,' she said on a surge of proud independence.

'No family?' he queried.

'I have two married sisters and my mother is very involved with her grandchildren. My father died some years ago. I'd be missed...and I'd miss them...' She flashed him a look of self-determination. '...but I would certainly consider an offer.'

Triumph glinted in his eyes. 'Then I'll make it as attractive as I can.'

Her heart jumped into another gallop. It wasn't her imagination. This was highly personal. And he wanted her on hand *for more than one night!*

'The package would include a generous travel allowance,' he assured her. 'Which will enable you to visit your family on a reasonably frequent basis.'

Behind her, music suddenly boomed out over loudspeakers. So dazed was Sunny by the revelation that Bryce Templar was very intent on getting her where he wanted her, she almost leapt out of her skin at the fanfare of trumpets, her head jerking around, half expecting to see a triumphal parade for the victory being planned in the green eyes.

'It's heralding the dance of the fountains at the Bellagio,' Bryce informed her. 'Come...it's worth seeing.'

His arm went around her waist, sweeping her with him and holding her protectively as he steered her through the crowd gathering along the sidewalk to enjoy the promised spectacle. He didn't push or shove. People simply gave way to him, standing back to let him and his companion through to a prime watching position against the Italian-style balustrade that edged the man-made lake in front of the Bellagio Hotel.

He stood half behind her, dropping his hand onto the balustrade on her far side to keep her encircled in the shelter of his arm, though no longer touching her. It was an extraordinary feeling—being protected and cared for by this big man. Sunny couldn't help revelling in it. She was so used to fending for herself, it was wonderful to wallow in the sense of being a woman whose man was looking after everything for her, ensuring her pleasure.

Except he wasn't actually *her man*. But could he be? In a very real sense? The very male solidity of the body so close to hers was real enough. So was her response to it. If she leaned back...made deliberate contact...what would happen?

Recognising the wanton recklessness in that temptation, Sunny held still, telling herself to wait for his moves. It ill behove her to instigate anything, especially when she wasn't in his social league. She'd made a fool of herself, believing she could share her life with Derek. How big a fool might she be, reading far too much between the lines of Bryce Templar's proposition?

A row of high water spouts started running right across the lake. Circles of fountains shot into the air. The music moved into the tune of 'Big Spender' and the high lines of water looped and swayed and bopped to the rhythm like a human chorus line, dancing to a choreography that required perfect timing.

It was an entrancing sight, yet the song being used

struck a raw place in Sunny, reminding her this city revolved around gambling and all the lavish glamour, luxury and service were designed to draw people into big spending. Derek could very well be ruining himself here. Though the responsibility for that lay squarely with him, no one else.

Would she be ruining her life, impulsively linking it to whatever Bryce Templar wanted?

A gamble, she thought. A big gamble on a big man. An absolutely magnificent man who made her feel…exceedingly primitive.

The fountains whooshed high in a fabulous finale, then seemed to bow before gracefully dropping back under the surface of the lake, their dance over.

'That was lovely,' Sunny breathed, and with her eyes still sparkling appreciatively, turned to look directly at the man who was fast infiltrating every aspect of her life. She realised instantly that his gaze had been fixed on her hair. It slid from the soft mass of waves to meet hers, transmitting a sensual simmering that caught what breath she had left in her throat. The rest of her words emerged as a husky whisper. 'Thank you for showing it to me.'

For one electrifying moment he looked at her mouth. The blast of raw desire she felt emanating from him scrambled her mind. Her lips remained slightly parted, quivering in wanton anticipation.

Then he dragged his gaze back to hers, locking onto it with searing force as he murmured, 'Your pleasure is my pleasure.'

Her breasts prickled. Her stomach clenched. A tremor of excitement ran down her thighs. Her only conscious thought, rising out of the raging desire he stirred was…

It *was* real…his wanting her…as real as her wanting him right back…and if she didn't take this gamble she might be missing the experience of a lifetime.

# CHAPTER FOUR

BRYCE only just managed to stop himself from kissing Sunny York right then and there. The desire to ravish the mouth she seemed to be offering him was totally rampant. Only a belated sense of where they were—on a public street with a crowd of tourists around them—gave him pause, and his brain seized the pause to flash a neon-bright danger signal.

He was out of control.

Even so the physical rebellion against the warning was sharp and intense. But being in control had ruled his life so long, his mind automatically equated that factor with success, and losing this woman with rash action at this point was unacceptable. She had been skittish up until now. Moving too fast might frighten her off. It wasn't smart to assume too much too soon, not when so much was hanging on the outcome of one night with her.

Dumping Kristen.

Marrying Sunny York.

Persuading her into a pregnancy she might not want.

It was a huge leap for him to take. How much bigger for her, without his cogent reasons firing the impulse to take this alternative road?

He stepped back, gesturing a continuation of their

stroll. 'A little slice of New York awaits you up ahead.'

Her beautiful amber eyes reflected inner confusion. Her vulnerability to what he was doing smote his conscience for a moment. She was afloat from her broken engagement, undoubtedly wanting an escape from the hurt to both heart and pride, and he was ruthlessly intent on drawing her into his net.

But he would look after her and give her a life full of riches if she came his way.

With that soothing justification riding on the advantage he knew he was taking, Bryce slid into charm mode, offering a whimsical little smile as he sought to ease her personal turmoil with outside interests.

'The Statue of Liberty, the Brooklyn Bridge, and the Empire State Building are somewhat scaled down since they're merely dressing up a hotel, but very recognisable,' he said encouragingly.

She gave her head a little shake, alerting Bryce even more forcefully to the danger of moving too fast. She'd have to be totally insensitive to miss the sexual signals he'd been giving out and he suspected she was all too aware of them, given the way she'd been evading looking at him and the tension emanating from her. Although part of that could have been the need to hide her distress over the guy she'd just broken with.

'Have you had any first-hand experience of New York?' he quickly asked, talking to re-establish a more comfortable connection for her.

'Yes, but only a few days' sightseeing.' She hesitated, her eyes scanning his uncertainly. 'Not…not business.'

'What was your impression of it?' he pressed, relieved when she stepped forward, indicating her willingness to go on with him.

'It had an exciting energy…the sense of a lot happening.' Her mouth curved into a musing smile. 'Extra-wide sidewalks. Hot dogs, with an amazing range of choices for spicing them up. Delicatessens with exotic food. Caramel apples…'

He laughed. 'You must really enjoy food.'

'Yes, I do.' Her smile turned lopsided. 'My sisters accuse me of having hollow legs.'

'That has to be envy.' Her incredibly sexy legs were an instant source of erotic fantasies.

'Oh, I doubt they envy me much…except not having to diet.'

'Then I hope you'll have dinner with me. I shall enjoy eating with a woman who likes food and doesn't see it as the enemy to be kept at bay.' He slanted her a teasing glance. 'You will eat more than lettuce leaves?'

She laughed. It was a delightful gurgle, spontaneous, warmly responsive. 'We can skip salad altogether if you like.'

'I take it that's a yes to dinner?'

She scooped in a big breath. 'Yes.'

Elation zoomed through him. He didn't care if this was some kind of emotional payback to the guy back in the casino, who clearly hadn't valued her enough. She was coming *his* way…plunging ahead with reckless disregard for caution.

After all, he triumphantly reasoned, what did she have to lose? His cynical side told him if it was pride driving her, he represented a top replacement in the lover stakes. What he was offering had to be all gain from her point of view—better prospects for her career, a transfer away from her erstwhile fiancé, and an enviable reason to remove herself from any criticism by her family with the CEO of Templar Resources taking a personal interest in her.

But falling into bed with him might not be on her agenda.

She might not see that as wise—in her position as his employee—or, indeed, desirable in a personal sense, given her very recent disillusionment with her fiancé. On the other hand, there was always *impulse*.

Bryce started planning a seduction scene as he continued chatting to her, building a rapport to bridge what *he* had in mind.

Sunny couldn't believe her luck. Dinner with Bryce Templar. Dinner for two. Beautiful man, beautiful food, beautiful wine—probably the finest champagne to celebrate her taking up his proposition. Except she didn't quite know what his proposition was, apart from its involving her transfer to the U.S. *And the personal element.*

A convulsive little shiver ran down her spine. Was sex on the side the pay-off for a big career promotion? She quickly shut her mind to that creepy-crawly thought. Bryce Templar *liked* her. She could tell from the way he was talking to her. He wasn't just making conversation. He was enjoying the to-and-fro, smiling, laughing, connecting on *all* levels.

He was clearly interested in her as a person—what level of education she'd had, the various positions she'd held, leading to her current one, everything she'd done with her life so far, her likes, dislikes. In fact, Sunny was so intoxicated by his charm, it took her a while to realise he was actually conducting an in-depth interview while they wandered along the boulevard.

This was a somewhat sobering thought. Though reassuring, as well. It had to mean he was seriously considering where she could best be used in the company business, and more importantly, he didn't seem at all put off by anything she'd said.

He wasn't touching her, either. From the moment he'd stepped back from that highly charged moment in front of the Bellagio Hotel, he'd made no physical contact with her. Plenty of exhilarating eye contact, but nothing physical. Perhaps he had stepped right back from sexual temptation, deciding an intimate liaison with her was inappropriate.

Which, of course it was, Sunny told herself. If she held his high esteem, well…that was something very positive. Yet she couldn't stop her gaze from surreptitiously wandering over him whenever he paused in his role of tourist guide, pointing things out to her.

The muscular breadth of his chest caught her eye as they lingered under the Statue of Liberty at New York, New York, watching the roller-coaster that looped around the hotel, its riders screaming their excitement. A woman would surely feel safe, held to all that strength, and as a father, he would easily be able to carry two or three children, clutched in his arms or perched on those shoulders.

Then his hand captivated her attention, directing her to look at the figure of the magician, Merlin, in the windows of one of the turrets forming the Medieval castle which was the Excalibur Hotel...a large strong hand, deeply tanned, long fingers, neatly buffed nails. To have such a hand holding her breast, stroking her...did it know how to be gentle? Was he a caring lover?

When they stood between the giant Sphinxes that flanked the great pyramid of the Luxor Hotel...he didn't look at all dwarfed by them...more like a powerful pharaoh of his time...a man astride the world he was born to...and what would spring from the loins of this king of kings?

Sunny had to take a stern grip on herself. Secretly lusting over Bryce Templar was bad enough. She had to stop thinking about babies, especially connected with him. Whatever the deal he had in mind for her, babies would most certainly not be part of it.

They took the pedestrian overpasses to cross the street to the other side of the boulevard. The second one led them into the vast MGM complex, and an Elvis Presley impersonator strutting ahead of them and revelling in the notice he drew, evoked a bubble of shared amusement.

'I've never understood that,' Sunny murmured.

'What?'

'Why people want to be someone else.'

'You never entertain a dream world?'

She blushed, guiltily conscious of her x-rated dreams about him. 'Not to the extent of actually copying another person.'

'You're content to be you.'

'I guess I think…this is *my* life, however imperfect it is.'

The twinkling green eyes intensified to a sharp probe. 'What would make it perfect?'

Sunny couldn't reveal that, not when her idea of perfection revolved around the man he was. She could feel her blush deepening and frantically sought some kind of all-purpose answer.

'I don't think we can expect perfection. Making the most of who we are is probably the best aim.'

'So a good career in your chosen field would satisfy you?'

Was he testing how long she might stay in his employ? She couldn't bring herself to lie. A career that interested her was great but it wasn't *everything*. 'Well…not completely,' she admitted, hoping he didn't need total dedication to her work. 'I think most of us would like to have a…a partner…to share things with.'

Surely he would, too. Being alone was…lonely. Though he probably never had to be alone if he didn't want to be. Here she was…providing him with company, simply because he chose to have it, and he hadn't even met her before today. Maybe he was self-sufficient enough not to need any more than a bit of congenial company whenever he cared to fit it in.

'What about children?' he asked, jolting her out of

her contemplation of what she wanted for herself, and hitting directly on a highly sensitive need.

'Children?' she echoed, unsure where this was leading.

'Do you see yourself as a mother some time in the future, or are babies a complication you don't want in your life?'

She sighed. It probably wasn't the smart answer but she simply couldn't pretend that missing out on having a family—at least one baby—wasn't any big deal to her.

'I would like to have a child one day...with the right father,' she added with a wry wistfulness.

'What would encompass *right* to you, Sunny?'

This was getting too close to the bone. Having envisaged *him* as the genetically ideal father, Sunny's comfort zone was being severely tested by his persistence on these points.

They had descended the staircase from the street overpass into the MGM casino area, and were now moving past a café with a jungle theme. Unfortunately Tarzan did not leap out and provide a distraction, and Bryce Templar's question was still hanging.

'What relevance does that have to my job?' she asked, deciding some challenge should be made on the grounds of purpose.

'It goes to character,' he answered smoothly. The green eyes locked onto hers, returning her challenge with an intimate undercurrent that flowed straight around her heart and squeezed it. 'I'm very particular about the character of anyone I bring into close association with me.'

*Close.*

The word pounded around her bloodstream, stirring up a buzz of sexual possibilities again.

'Some women's prime requirement of *right* would be a certain level of income. The child-price, one might say,' he said sardonically.

Sunny frowned. 'I could support a child myself. That's not the point.'

'What is?'

She rounded on him, not liking the cynical flavour of his comment, and hating the idea of him applying any shade of it to her. '*You* have a father. What was right for you as a child?'

His mouth curled with irony. 'For him to be there when I needed him.'

Which she could no longer trust Derek to do. The clanging casino noise around her drove that home again.

'You've just said it all, Mr. Templar,' she stated decisively.

Her eyes clashed with his, daring him to refute that this quality overrode everything else. It carried the acceptance of responsibility and commitment, displayed reliability and caring, and generated trust...all the things Derek had just demonstrated *wrong* about himself.

Bryce Templar didn't refute it. He stared back at her and the air between them sizzled with tense unspoken things. Sunny had the wild sense that he was scouring her soul for how *right* a mother she would be, judging on some scale which remained hidden to her but was vibrantly real in the context of mating.

'Let's make that Bryce,' he said quietly.

And she knew she had passed some critical test. They stood apart, yet she could feel him drawing her closer to the man he was, unleashing a magnetism that tugged on all that was female in her...deep primitive chords thrumming with anticipation.

He smiled...slowly, sensually, promisingly. 'You must be hungry by now. I am.'

'Yes,' she replied, almost mesmerised by the sensations he was evoking. She was hungry for so many, many things, and every day of this week in Las Vegas she had felt them slipping away from her, leaving an empty hole that even the most exciting career couldn't bridge. Maybe she was crazy, wanting this man to fill the emptiness so much, she was projecting her own desire onto him.

'This way,' he said, and proceeded to guide her around the casino area to the MGM reception desk.

Sunny was barely conscious of walking. She was moving with him, going with him, and he was taking her towards a *closer* togetherness. Dinner for two. On first-name terms. Sunny and Bryce.

She expected him to ask about restaurants at the desk, but he didn't.

'Bryce Templar,' he announced to the clerk. 'A suite has been booked for me.'

'Yes, Mr. Templar. The penthouse Patio Suite. Your luggage has been taken up. Your key?'

'Please.'

It was instantly produced. 'If there's anything else, sir...'

'Thank you. I'll call.'

He was steering Sunny towards the elevators before she recollected her stunned wits enough to say, 'I thought you were staying at the conference hotel.'

'I'd already checked out when I saw you in the lobby.'

She frowned, bewildered by this move. 'Couldn't you check in again?'

'I preferred to keep my business with you private.'

*Private…in a private penthouse suite.*

A penthouse for playboys?

The elevator doors opened and Bryce Templar swept her into the empty compartment…just the two of them…doors shutting off the crowded casino, closing them away from all the people who had surrounded them on their walk, and suddenly there was silence…except for the hum of the elevator and the thundering beat of Sunny's heart.

# CHAPTER FIVE

SHE stood rigidly beside him. Bryce willed the elevator to go faster. He knew she had expected a public restaurant, not this, but he had to get her alone with him. Close the net. His mind worked double-time, producing a string of soothing words, ready to answer any protest she might make about the situation he'd set up.

He saw her hand clench. She took a deep breath. Her face turned to him, her stunning amber eyes swimming with questions. Her mouth moved, tremulous words slipping out. 'I don't think…'

'Don't think!'

The growled command came from nowhere. Before any sophisticated reasoning could stem the urge that exploded through him, Bryce scooped Sunny York into his embrace and kissed her with such devouring intensity, there was no possibility of any more words being uttered by either of them.

He was so hungry for her—for all that she was—the raging desire coursing through him directed all movement. The elevator stopped. The doors slid open. He swung his woman off her feet, hooking her legs over his arm, and it felt absolutely right as he carried her to his suite because her hands were linked around his neck and her breasts were pressed to his chest, and she was kissing him back as wildly as he was kissing her.

The slot-card in his hand opened the door. He kicked it shut. No bed in sight. The suite was a two-storey apartment. Catching sight of the staircase he charged up to the intimate rooms on the next level and straight into the bedroom. Seduction did not enter his head. There was no finesse at all in the need that had him put Sunny on her feet so he could get her clothes off. And his own.

He couldn't wait to have her naked with him, to feel every luscious curve of her, skin to skin, her lovely long legs in intimate entanglement around him. It excited him even more that she was as eager as he was to be rid of all barriers, her hands just as frantically busy with undressing, wanting to feel him and know everything there was to know.

Her eyes were a blaze of gold, burning him up. Her mouth was sensationally passionate in its hunger for his. Her hands were wildly erotic in their touch. Her glorious hair was pure sensual pleasure, its scent, its silky mass, its flashing colours. And fully naked, she was stunningly perfect, her whole body so lushly female, soft and supple, calling on him to perform as a man, and he was so ready to, the drive to take and possess was overwhelmingly immediate.

He laid her on the bed, kneeling over her for a moment, savouring the sight of her—all her sizzling warmth lying open to him, every inhibition abandoned in the sheer craving for this mating with him. Her arms lifted, winding around his neck, pulling him down, wanting him as much as he wanted her.

No foreplay. It wasn't needed by either of them. They were both poised for a completion that had to come. He drove forward, sheathing himself in her moist heat, revelling in her ecstatic welcome, loving the sense of being deep inside her. And her legs wrapped around him, holding him in, exulting in the sensation of feeling him there, then urging him to repeat the action, to move into the rhythm that would take them both on the upward climb to where they had to be…together.

It was an incredible feeling—this compulsive copulation with her—his intense arousal, the sense of being so aggressively male, primitively needful of having *this* woman. Somehow she embodied everything he had to have, and it drove him into a frenzy of possession.

The amazing, the wonderful, the totally exhilarating thing was, she was just as frenzied as he was in wanting what he was giving her, and when he could no longer stop himself from climaxing, she was right there with him, joining him in a fantastic meltdown that seemed to fuse them as one.

For a few moments he spread his body over hers, wanting to feel the whole imprint of her femininity as he kissed her again, sealing their oneness—all of him, all of her, together, as deeply and totally as they could be. The satisfaction of it was euphoric. He wished he could stay where he was, but it wasn't fair to subject her to his weight for long.

He rolled onto his side, scooping her with him to lie in the cradle of his arm, holding her snuggled close to him. He was swamped by a sense of tenderness for her, this woman who made him feel as a man should feel, wanted for what he was, not *who* he was…an instinctive, compulsive wanting.

His hands moved over her, gently caressing, loving the soft texture of her skin, soothing the endearing little tremors his stroking aroused. His fingers threaded through her hair, enjoying the winding spring of curls around them. The urge to bind her to him was so strong, he didn't even pause to wonder what she was thinking—or feeling—about what had happened between them. The words simply spilled straight out.

'Marry me!'

He didn't even realise he spoke in a command. Her head was resting just under his chin. He felt it jerk slightly, a startled little movement.

'What…' The question was choked with disbelief. He heard her sharply indrawn breath, then, '…what did you say?'

Bryce was not about to back off from having the advantage of their intimacy to press his suit. He rolled Sunny onto her back and propped himself up on his elbow beside her, meeting her stunned gaze with an intensity of purpose that was not to be shaken. He lightly traced the line of her full-lipped mouth with his finger as he delivered a clear and firm statement.

'I want you to marry me, Sunny York.'

Sunny could scarcely believe her ears. But he'd said it twice and his eyes were serious. Her sensitised lips were tingling and she couldn't get her mind thinking in any order at all. It didn't help when he lowered his head and grazed his mouth over hers, his tongue sliding seductively across the soft inner tissue, and the hand that had caressed her lips, moved down to cup her breast, gently kneading it as his thumb fanned her nipple with tantalising tenderness.

He knew how to do it right. Sunny's mind completely glazed over again, mesmerised by the rightness that had swamped it from the moment she had been seized by lustful madness in the elevator. He kissed her more deeply, re-igniting all the exciting sensations of previous kisses.

'I want you to be my wife,' he murmured against her lips, his breath still mingling with hers.

*His wife.*

Then he was trailing kisses down her throat, to the breast he hadn't touched yet, covering it with the hot excitement of his mouth, sucking it erotically, pumping pleasure through her in delicious spasms, building a craving for more and more.

'I want you to have my child,' he said, moving to her other breast, sliding his hand down to caress her stomach in circular sweeps, as his mouth played sweet havoc and her mind flashed images of...

*His child.*

His child in her womb, his child at her breast...the baby she'd love to have...with this man as the father...the man she'd secretly thought would be the *best* father.

And now he was kissing her stomach, as though he was imagining his baby in there, and his hand was between her thighs, stroking them apart, making room for him to come to her again, exciting the need to have him there. Such intense sensations of pleasure, demanding the fulfilment only he could bring, but when he moved again, it was to drive the need higher, his mouth closing over her sex, setting her on fire with the exquisite brushing of his tongue, the desire for him quickly reaching exploding point.

She heard herself cry out for him, begging, pleading, desperate for him to answer the ache inside her, and he responded immediately, filling her with a glorious rush of satisfaction as he plunged himself deeply into the quivering place that yearned for him.

It felt so good, so right, and she revelled in every stroke of him inside her, loving the hard fullness that kept pushing the pleasure of his possession higher and higher until she felt herself shattering around him, moving into a sea of bliss, and he rocked her there, bringing wave after wave of beautiful feelings that spread through her entire body. The spasms of euphoria kept coming even after he had climaxed and they were simply lying together, luxuriating in the intimate peace of needs fulfilled.

Feather-light fingers stroked the curve of her spine. His cheek rubbed over her hair. She felt his warm breath fan her temples as he spoke, gruffly demanding a reply from her. 'Say you'll marry me, Sunny.'

*Marry him.*

It was a huge step to take. Her still-floating mind struggled with the enormity of it, hardly believing it was real. It was still difficult to believe all she'd done with him was real. But here she was, lying naked on a bed with him, having been brought alive sexually to a fantastic extreme she had never imagined possible. Nevertheless, this…this hasty plunge into intimacy, did not warrant a hasty plunge into marriage!

'Bryce…'

She hadn't even called him by his first name before! The unfamiliarity of that alone had her hauling herself up to look at him, face to face…this man who seemed intent on marrying her…Bryce Templar, the CEO of Templar Resources, whom she had thought so far removed from her normal life, the idea of a marriage between them had been inconceivable.

His green eyes were simmering with pleasure in her. A sensual little smile curved his lips. 'You're even more beautiful with your hair all tousled,' he murmured.

He thought her *beautiful?* Her hair was probably a tangled mop with all the threshing around she'd done in the heat of passion. And that memory brought a flush to her face.

'We've barely met,' she rushed out, embarrassed by her terribly wanton behaviour.

'So?' He stroked her hot cheek, his eyes smiling reassurance. 'What has time got to do with anything? When something is right, it's right.'

The conviction in his voice eased her troubled sense of having acted out of character. This *was* different—what anybody could excuse as extraordinary circumstances.

'You might not feel it's so right tomorrow,' she said cautiously, still finding his proposal too stunning to really accept it could be genuine.

'Sunny, you said you wanted a partner. So do I, and *everything* about you feels right to me.' His eyes flashed absolute conviction as he added, 'And I don't believe you're the kind of woman who'd go to bed with a man *you* didn't feel right with.'

That was true. She'd never been promiscuous, and one-night stands were definitely not her scene. It was a relief to hear him reading her correctly. Although she'd never been hit by such overwhelming lust before. But lust wasn't love, more an instinctive thing running right out of control. She couldn't believe getting married should be based on *instinct*. There were many more factors involved in making a partnership work well.

'We're even in the same business,' he went on. 'All the more to share with each other, understanding what's involved in our lives.'

She'd thought she had that with Derek. It should be a plus in a relationship. But then she'd believed a lot of things about Derek—for months!—and only found out differently this past week. What seemed right could turn out very wrong indeed.

'And I want a child,' Bryce Templar pressed. 'A child who is wanted just as much by its mother. That's you, Sunny, isn't it? You want to be a mother.'

She couldn't deny it.

'We're not getting any younger,' he pointed out. 'How old are you?'

No harm in answering that question. 'Twenty-nine.'

'I'm thirty-four and I don't want to be an old father. The sooner we make a baby, the better.' He cocked a quizzical eyebrow. 'Any chance we might have already made one?'

It shocked her that protection had not entered either of their heads. Unsafe sex... 'I hope you're not a health risk,' she shot at him.

He laughed. 'No, I'm clean. And I have no doubt you are, too, Sunny York.'

She sighed her relief. 'Well, at least I'm on the pill.'

'Why not throw the pills away?' His eyes twinkled wickedly. 'We can try again. All night...'

Just like that? Plunge into pregnancy with him as the father? Her fantasy answered? Yet fantasies were one thing, realities quite another. People didn't make life commitments, virtually on the spur of the moment. She frowned at him, thinking that stopping contraception would be a very reckless decision, especially when she was feeling all at sea about what had already happened with him, let alone what he had in mind now.

'Do you really want that, Bryce?' she queried, uneasy with the way he seemed to be rushing decisions that shouldn't be hurried. It still sounded strange, using his first name, yet she could hardly call him Mr. Templar in this situation.

'Oh, yes,' he said decisively, a gleam of determination in his eyes. 'I wouldn't play you false about such serious things, Sunny. You're the woman I want as my wife, in every sense. Give me my way and we'll be married tomorrow.'

'Tomorrow!' She shook her head dazedly.

'Easily done in Las Vegas and I see no point in wasting time.'

'I'm on a flight home to Sydney in the morning.'

'You don't have to be on it. And I certainly don't want you on it. In fact...' He reached for the telephone on the bedside table. '...I'll make arrangements for your luggage to be packed and brought here.'

'Bryce!' she cried, grabbing his arm, totally rattled by how fast he was moving.

He shot her a piercing look. 'Do you *want* to go back to that hotel, Sunny?'

And break up what was happening here?

Run into Derek?

'No.' She withdrew her hand, fluttering a helpless gesture. 'It's just...'

'Leave it to me. I'll fix everything.' He grinned at her. 'How about running us a bath while I make the calls? I'll notify the Sydney manager that you're staying on and I'll get the hotel staff to pack everything for you and get it delivered here. Okay?'

Sunny took a deep breath.

It felt as though Bryce Templar was taking her on a wild roller-coaster ride and it was scary to think of where it would lead next, yet to get off...without knowing more...and the grin on his face made him *so* attractive, inviting her into his private and personal world, delighted to have her with him.

Besides, getting on the plane with Derek in the morning was not a happy prospect, seated next to him on the flight to L.A., then the long haul to Sydney. Arguments, stress, wondering what might have been if she'd stayed...

'Okay,' she echoed, the word torn out of her need to escape a miserable return to Sydney, as well as the strong temptation to stay right where she was with

Bryce Templar, at least long enough to see what the end of the ride might be like. 'But what about my ticket home if...'

'Do you imagine I wouldn't make good on that for you, should you want to go?' he cut in quietly.

Her heart cringed at her unwitting impugning of his integrity. 'I'm sorry. This is all so fast...'

'I promise I'll look after you. Whatever you need. Whatever you want. All you have to do is tell me, Sunny.'

She took another deep breath to steady her whirling mind. 'Okay. I'll stay on...for a while.'

His grin sparkled with triumph this time, putting a host of butterflies in her stomach. She had the wild sense that Bryce Templar had carried her into his cave and was now busily shutting off all exits until he had his way with her. Which clearly meant she needed some space to calm herself down and start thinking rationally about her immediate future with him.

'I'll go find the bathroom,' she said, remembering his suggestion of running a bath...*for both of them!*

'You do that,' he approved heartily, reaching for the telephone again. 'This won't take long.'

She slid off the bed, and very conscious of her naked state with his eyes watching her, headed straight for the most likely door to an adjoining bathroom. It proved to be precisely that and she shut it behind her to ensure at least a few moments' privacy.

As caves went, this was certainly a sumptuous one, Sunny couldn't help thinking as she noted the Italian marble accents, the positively decadent Roman tub, even a television set to watch while bathing. Life with

Bryce Templar could be very seductive with such luxuries. All the same, she was not going to be rushed into any rash decisions. The old saying—*marry in haste, repent at leisure*—was a good warning.

On the other hand, she might as well enjoy what was here. Having turned on the taps to fill the bath, she sprinkled in some scented grainy salts from a very elegant jar, then added a blue syrupy mixture that instantly frothed into bubbles. Satisfied that she wouldn't feel quite so naked with a mass of foam to hide behind, Sunny moved around the other facilities.

Beside the toilet was a European bidet—very civilised sophistication—and in a drawer of the vanity table she found a packet of hairpins which she proceeded to use, hoping not to get her hair wet in the bath. *Tousled* might look beautiful to Bryce but *wet* was definitely not her best look.

For a few moments she stared at her own face in the mirror. What did Bryce Templar see in her that he hadn't seen in the many many women who must have traipsed through his life? Why should he suddenly decide she was the one to marry?

She was passably attractive. Her eyes were probably her best feature. Her nose had that irritating tilt that always got sunburnt if she wasn't careful and her mouth was too wide. The hair he admired was the bane of her life. And she'd hated her legs in her teens, so long and gangly, though they did have more shape to them now she was older and her figure more mature.

Shaking her head, the puzzle of Bryce Templar's choice still unresolved in her mind, Sunny stepped over to the bath, which was now well filled. She turned off the taps and lowered herself gingerly into its warm foamy depths. A sigh of sheer pleasure relaxed the tension raised by too many uncertainties. Sinful pleasures, she thought, wondering if she would end up rueing her decision to stay.

A knock on the door preceded its being pushed slightly open. 'May I come in?' was courteously asked.

'Yes,' she answered, her heart jiggling nervously at the thought of sharing this bath with him. But since she'd already shared far more, it was way too late to start feeling shy.

The door swung wide open and Sunny's breath caught in her throat at the sight of him coming towards her. He had been naked on the bed, but she hadn't really seen him like this. They'd been too wrapped up in other things. His physique was stunningly male, magnificently proportioned and power-packed with just the right amount of masculine muscle.

He looked...fantastic.

And she could have *him* as her husband!

But there was more to marriage than the physical, Sunny hastily berated herself. This terribly strong desire he inspired was probably the most sinful pleasure of all.

'Brought the menus with me for us to choose dinner from,' he said with a smile, waving the large folders he held in his hand. 'I'm hoping your appetite will match mine. I think we should order a feast to celebrate our coming together.'

Dinner! She'd forgotten all about it.

'Yes. That would be good,' she agreed, trying to get her mind focused on an appetite for food instead of the very distracting appetite for him.

He laid one folder on the floor beside her, fetched a towel for her to dry her hands, then lowered himself into the bath, facing her from the other end. 'Your luggage should be here within the hour and I've let the Sydney people know you won't be on tomorrow's flight with them,' he tossed at her as he opened his menu to peruse its contents.

She wondered what reaction that announcement from Bryce Templar had caused amongst her colleagues. Had Derek been told? Her stomach suddenly clenched. What would Derek think? What would he do?

*I don't care,* she told herself on a surge of violent anger for the uncaring way he had treated her. She grabbed the towel, dried her hands, picked up the menu and opened it, determined on ordering a veritable feast.

The die was well and truly cast now.

One way or another, she'd thrown in her lot with Bryce Templar.

Dinner for two!

# CHAPTER SIX

BRYCE saw the belligerent tilt of her chin and her mouth compressing into a line of determination as she reached for the menu. He had no difficulty in reading what those telltale expressions meant. The boats were burnt. There was no way back. Not tonight nor tomorrow. No point in not making the most of her time with him.

He smiled to himself. The net was closed. Not exactly how he'd meant to do it. In fact, he'd lost the plot completely in his somewhat intemperate need to have her, but he was now satisfied he hadn't hurt his end purpose by it. He may well have improved his chances of convincing her to marry him. Mutual desire was a strong persuader. And he had the rest of the night to capitalise on it.

He moved his legs to lie in tandem with hers, enjoying the long silky slide of her calves and thighs. She was certainly built perfectly for him. The way they fitted together was especially satisfying. He looked forward to much more of it.

'What are your favourite foods?' he asked, wanting eye contact with her.

Her lashes slowly lifted. From this distance the colour of her eyes looked darker, more a warm brown. They still lit up her face. She had a wonderful face. Not classically beautiful, like Kristen's, but Kristen's

61

was like a smooth mask in comparison. Sunny's was alive, projecting a wealth of fascinating expression.

'I *love* lobster,' she stated with open fervour. 'I see they've got Maine lobster on the menu, so I'm definitely having that.'

He laughed at the rich satisfaction in her voice. She truly was a delight in every sense. He would enjoy having her as his wife. 'What else?' he prompted.

She listed everything she found tempting, displaying a relish for food that whetted his own appetite. He couldn't remember ever having such fun, discussing a menu. They were discussing the merits of a selection of sweets when the telephone rang, interrupting the pleasurable anticipation of a superb meal.

'Probably announcing the arrival of your luggage,' Bryce commented, hauling himself out of the bath to deal with the call since the telephone, although in the bathroom, was out of his reach and he didn't want Sunny answering it.

She laughed at the foam flaking off him as he moved. 'You make a great snowstorm.'

'Maybe we should have the Bombe Alaska for sweets,' he tossed at her, grinning as he snatched up a towel.

'No. I really fancy the raspberry soufflé.'

'It'll probably sink before it gets here. Think about it.'

Her eyes chided him. 'Spoilsport.'

He laughed, loving the natural interplay between them. Sunny was much more relaxed with him now, not on guard at all. Which had to bring her closer to what he wanted.

Having wiped his hands, he picked up the receiver, expecting a quick communication. 'Templar here.'

'Ah, Mr. Templar. Miss York's luggage has arrived. And so has a Mr. Derek Marsden, demanding to see Miss York. He claims she is his fiancée.'

'No way,' Bryce returned tersely.

'He is being very insistent, sir. One could say threatening, if you take my meaning.'

Bryce tensed, a savage aggression instantly gripping him. The last thing he needed was Sunny's ex-fiancé hanging around, creating scenes, and possibly swaying Sunny off the course she had chosen. He had to protect the ground he'd won.

'I'll come down and deal with it. Give me a few minutes.'

'Thank you, sir. I'll hold the gentleman here. Should I send the luggage up?'

'No. Not yet. I'll deal with that, too.'

'As you wish, sir.'

He slammed the receiver down, startling Sunny. 'Something wrong?' she asked, wide-eyed at his change of mood.

He grimaced an apology. 'A business problem.'

'Not my luggage?'

'Still coming,' he answered, quickly towelling himself dry. 'I have to go and meet an associate in the lobby, Sunny. It should only take ten minutes or so. While I'm gone, call room service and order what we've decided upon.' He forced a smile to put her at ease with the situation. 'You get to choose the selection of sweets. Okay?'

She caught the undercurrent of urgency. 'Is it a bad problem?'

'No.' He relaxed his face into a wry expression. 'Just vexing that it's come up when I'd rather be with you.'

She smiled. 'Then I'll try not to miss you.'

'Think of great food,' he teased, and was off, striding for the bedroom and the clothes he had to put on before facing the rival he had to dismiss.

He couldn't allow this Derek Marsden any room for worming his way back into Sunny's affections. Bryce frowned, wondering how Marsden had picked up on where she was. He hadn't given out that information.

He dressed at lightning speed, his mind ticking over possibilities. Marsden had arrived at the same time as Sunny's luggage. Possibly he had gone to her hotel room, found her clothes and toiletries being packed by staff, then followed the trail, greasing palms with big tips to learn what was going on.

Dog in the manger stuff, Bryce decided. If Marsden had really valued Sunny, she wouldn't be here in this suite. No doubt it was *his name* being involved that was sticking in Marsden's craw. In any case, he had no claim on her. She had given him back his ring. The break was clear-cut and Bryce aimed to keep it that way. No second chance for Marsden.

Sunny was still in the bathroom, happily ignorant of her ex-fiancé's intrusion on the scene. Hoping to make his absence as brief as possible, Bryce made a fast exit from the suite, summoned the elevator, and waited impatiently for its arrival. His mind skated through his impression of the man he'd seen at the blackjack table this afternoon—about the same height as Sunny, fairish hair, clean-cut type of college-man looks, lean build.

Physically, Bryce knew he was the far more intimidating man. He didn't expect a fist-fight, but Marsden could turn ugly, faced with the frustration of losing out. The trick was to get him to accept defeat, and if possible, allow him some dignified retreat.

The elevator arrived. The descent to the lobby was uninterrupted. Bryce spotted Marsden near the reception desk but proceeded there without giving any sign of recognition. They had never personally met and Bryce had no intention of displaying any knowledge of him. He directed an inquiring gaze to the clerk who had handled his check-in.

Marsden stepped forward before an introduction was made. 'Mr. Templar,' he called aggressively.

Bryce paused, raising a challenging eyebrow at the man accosting him. His suit was crumpled, his eyes bloodshot, and he was clearly the worse for having imbibed too much alcohol. Possibly a belligerent drunk.

'I'm Derek Marsden,' he announced. 'Of the Sydney branch of Templar Resources.'

'Indeed?' Bryce returned frostily. 'I understand you're causing a problem here. What concern do you have?'

He rocked back on his heels, glaring at Bryce. 'I want to see Sunny.' His hand lifted, pointing an accusing finger. 'I know she's here. I know she's with you. And you have no right to stop me from seeing her. She's my fiancée.'

'Miss York is certainly with me,' Bryce acknowledged. 'We are negotiating her transfer to a new position in Los Angeles. As to her being your fiancée, Miss York has declared herself free of commitments and she is certainly not wearing an engagement ring.'

He flushed. 'We had an argument. She took it off. That's what I want to see her about. Fix it all up again.'

'Then I'd be obliged if you'd try doing so in your own time, Marsden. Not mine. This is a business meeting and you are interrupting without invitation.'

'So what is her luggage doing here if it's business?' he jeered, turning nasty.

'It was brought here at Miss York's request,' Bryce replied, keeping a cool calm. 'I understand she does not wish to return to the conference hotel. Perhaps you are the reason why, Marsden.'

The edge of contempt stung him into defence. 'I just want to talk to her. Get things straight. She's gone off half-cocked if she's discussing a transfer and that won't do *you* any good when she comes to her senses.'

'Miss York has presented herself to me as a free agent and I see no reason to give you the opportunity to harrass her. She is at liberty to contact you if she so wishes. Now if you'll excuse me...'

Bryce started to turn away.

'She's mine!' came the seething claim as Marsden grabbed him by the arm.

Bryce squared his shoulders and cast a quailing

look at the slighter man. 'You work for Templar Resources, Marsden?' he said quietly, threat embodied in every word.

The angry glaze in the bleary blue eyes wavered.

'You are not doing yourself any favours here,' Bryce continued quietly. 'I suggest you return to your hotel, sleep off this…unwise burst of aggression…and catch your flight back to Sydney in the morning…where you may still have a job.'

The hand dropped away.

Marsden stood slack-jawed, not having foreseen these consequences.

Bryce had no compunction whatsoever in using the power of his position to get this man out of Sunny's life. He signalled the concierge who instantly hurried over. 'Please get Mr. Marsden a taxi and see him into it,' he instructed and nodded towards a couple of security guards who could assist if necessary. 'Put the fare on my tab.'

'I'll pay for it myself,' Marsden blurted out in fierce resentment.

Bryce subjected him to one more icy look. 'As you wish. Goodnight, Marsden. I hope you have a safe trip home.'

He shouldered past the concierge and marched off towards the exit doors. Bryce watched him out, not quite sure he'd read the man correctly. Australians had a reputation for bucking authority, going their own way. Still, he'd given Marsden something to think about and he hoped it was enough to make him realise there was no chance of a reconciliation with Sunny.

He moved over to the clerk he'd dealt with at the reception desk. 'The bellhop can bring up Miss York's luggage now. If there's any more trouble from Mr. Marsden, let me know.'

'Certainly, Mr. Templar.'

He shared the elevator with the bellhop. Sunny's luggage comprised a medium-sized suitcase and a standard carry-on, obviously an economic travelling wardrobe, enough to suit what was required for a conference with its various functions, but not enough for a prolonged stay. Some shopping would need to be done.

He dismissed the bellhop at the door to the suite, carrying in the luggage himself. Seeing no sign of Sunny in the living room, he took the bags upstairs, expecting to find her there. She was not in the bedroom. Nor the bathroom. The yellow suit was gone from where it had been dropped on the floor. So were her other garments.

Bryce stared at the empty space that was no longer littered with her clothes. Unfamiliar feelings—fear, panic, an intolerable sense of loss—started screwing him up inside. His mind literally jammed over the thought she had gone…left him…was even now on her way back to Derek Marsden. He should not have given her any time alone to reconsider what she was doing.

Or maybe he was jumping the gun.

He hadn't searched the entire penthouse.

With his heart pounding harder than if he'd run a marathon, Bryce made a fast sweep through the other upstairs rooms. Nothing! No sign of her presence anywhere!

'Sunny!' he roared as he reached the staircase and started down it.

'Yes?'

He stopped dead, his head swivelling to her voice. She was there, standing in the opened doorway to the outside patio. Her hair spilled in glorious disarray around the huge collar of an oversized white bathrobe. She hadn't dressed. Her feet were bare.

For several moments they stared at each other. It hit Bryce that she looked very vulnerable, caught in a time-warp between the past and the future, not knowing quite where she was or what she was doing here. He was her only focus right now.

Was he being fair to her?

Would she take Marsden back if the guy cleaned up his act and grovelled enough?

'Is everything all right?' she asked, seeking guidance.

'Yes,' he asserted, determination sweeping back. He'd be a better husband for her than Marsden. 'Everything settled,' he assured her, walking down the rest of the stairs. 'I took your bags up. They came when I was in the lobby.'

'Thank you.' She looked discomforted by that information, half turning back to the patio as she added, 'I was out looking at the view. All the neon lights along *The Strip*...'

'You're the best sight of all, Sunny,' he said warmly, crossing the living room to reach her. 'I was just thinking how much I'd like to come home to you every night. Exactly like this.'

Her gaze veered back to his and he caught the sense she wanted to believe him, but was uncertain of filling that role. He smiled, wanting to convince her of his pleasure in her. It was no lie.

'Did you get onto room service and order our dinner?'

She smiled back. 'I did. And I hope you're really hungry, Bryce.'

'I am.'

*For you.*

*And that was no lie, either.*

He drew her into his embrace. Her eyes were liquid amber, silently, eloquently asking if this was right, or was she hopelessly astray in being here with him.

He kissed her to burn away the doubt.

There was no doubt in his mind.

He wanted her as his wife and she was going to be his wife. Whatever he had to do to win her, he'd do.

# CHAPTER SEVEN

SUNNY woke slowly, savouring the sense of a warm delicious languor…before she remembered why her body felt so replete and relaxed. A little electric jolt went through her brain. She sucked in a deep breath and carefully, quietly turned her head.

Her breath whooshed out on a relieved sigh. She didn't have to face him yet. The rest of the bed was empty. He'd obviously wakened before her and left her to sleep on. She resettled herself and started thinking.

Bryce Templar…

Her hand drifted over her naked body…remembering. He was certainly a fantastic lover. She closed her eyes, recapturing the incredible sensations in her mind, the power of them, the intensity of the pleasure that had rolled on and on through so much of the night.

*What time was it?*

Her head jerked up, eyes flying open again. The clock-radio on the bedside table read 9:14. The flight she should have been on from Las Vegas to Los Angeles had already left. Panic galloped through her heart, stirring up the enormity of what she had done…cutting herself off from all she had known…Derek…

She struggled to get a grip on herself. It wasn't all

irreversible. She could still go home if she wanted to. Bryce had promised that decision was hers anytime she chose. As for Derek...

She dropped her head back onto the pillow. Unaccountably tears pricked her eyes. Derek hadn't even tried to change her mind when she'd handed him back her ring. All those months of planning to marry...and they'd had many good times together. Her family had liked him. She had really believed they would make a good marriage together.

But he hadn't even tried to get her back.

He could have tracked her to the MGM hotel if he'd wanted to. Gambling had obviously meant more to him than she did. And always would, now that he'd caught the bug for it, Sunny savagely reasoned. Her chin set with determination. She would not mourn his passing out of her life.

Which left her with...Bryce Templar.

And his proposal of marriage.

She heaved a huge sigh. He was definitely a marvellous lover but she couldn't marry him on that basis alone, however tempting it might be. As it was, plunging into this intimacy with him was probably going to complicate any career decisions she made. Nothing was clear-cut anymore.

But...he certainly made her feel good about herself. For him to desire her so much...to want her as his wife... It was quite mind-boggling.

How could *he* make up his mind so fast? Wasn't he taking a big risk in committing himself to a marriage with a woman he'd only known for a day? Not even a full day! Surely a man in his position should take more care in choosing a life partner.

Not that there was anything wrong with her, Sunny quickly reasoned, but how could he know that? On such short acquaintance? Was he so confident of reading her character correctly? Maybe that was a skill CEOs had to have—choosing the right people for the right positions.

Deciding that lying here by herself wouldn't give her any answers, Sunny rolled out of bed and headed for the bathroom. She took a quick shower, all the time wondering what Bryce was doing downstairs—reading the newspaper, making business calls, having breakfast, *waiting for her?*

Grateful to have her own toiletries, she brushed her teeth, applied a light make-up, and did what she could to get her hair in reasonable order without taking too much time with it. She hesitated over dressing, not knowing what plans Bryce might have. Easier just to wrap herself in the bathrobe until some decisions were made.

She heard Bryce speaking to someone as she started down the stairs and paused, not wanting to interrupt anything important.

'Just do your best to keep the cost to a minimum.'

It was a terse command, showing impatience with the caller.

'No, I won't change my mind.'

Even more terse. Whoever was on the phone to him was stirring Bryce's ire and whatever was put to him now evoked an icy reply.

'Understand me very clearly, Sherman. It's finished. We simply write this off. No more negotiation. Nothing—absolutely nothing—will get me to reconsider this decision. Now you take it from there, knowing my position on this is irreversible.'

The cut-off click created a pool of silence that seemed to echo with the ruthlessness with which Bryce had ended the deal that had been in negotiation. Someone had pushed too far, Sunny thought. All the same, it was an insight into the character of the man. He wielded command with an iron fist when the occasion demanded it.

She couldn't imagine him ever being seduced by gambling. He would make a limit and stick to it. Yet he was gambling on her with his proposal of marriage, wasn't he? Perhaps that, too, had a limit. He'd give so much time to her, then...

Shaking off the thought which only time could prove right or wrong, Sunny proceeded down the stairs. Bryce was pacing back and forth across the living room, a frown of deep concentration on his face. Then, either hearing her soft footsteps or sensing her presence, he stopped, his face clearing as his gaze zeroed in on her.

'Ah! Some morning sunshine!' he said warmly. 'You slept well?'

'Very well.' He was wearing his bathrobe, too, so Sunny didn't feel uncomfortable about not being dressed. 'Have you been up long?'

He shrugged. 'There were a few things I wanted to get out of the way so I could concentrate entirely on you.'

His eyes were eating her up and Sunny's heart was

doing cartwheels. It was so incredibly flattering to be desired by him, and she couldn't help remembering how magnificent he was, under that bathrobe.

'All done?' she asked, trying to sound matter-of-fact.

'All done.' He grinned as he swept her into his embrace, his eyes teasing her caution. 'So here it is—the next morning—and I still want to marry you, Sunny York.'

'Mmm…have you had breakfast?'

He laughed. 'I was waiting for you.' His mouth grazed over hers with tantalising sensuality. 'And you taste so good,' he murmured.

'Food is good, too,' she choked out, struggling to keep her mind clear of the seductive web he was weaving again.

'Then we shall order breakfast right now.'

Everything she wanted, when she wanted it… It was terribly difficult to keep her head on straight around Bryce. He swamped her with such tempting attractions, most of all himself.

Over a sumptuous breakfast, she finally managed to focus on addressing the question of business. 'We haven't settled on the kind of position you're offering me, Bryce.'

'First and foremost, the position of my wife,' he answered, his eyes unmistakably reflecting very determined purpose.

Sunny's heart skipped a beat. 'What if I say no to that?'

'You haven't said no yet. Until you do, Sunny, I'll

be doing everything within my power to persuade you to say yes.'

She could feel his power winding around her and wondered if it would prove irresistible in the end. 'I really don't know much about you, Bryce,' she stated defensively.

'What do you need to know?'

His heart, she thought, then doubted her own ability to judge that, given her terrible misreading of Derek's heart. Needing to start somewhere, she said, 'Well, I know you have a father. What about the rest of your family?'

'My mother died when I was three. I was her only child.'

No wonder he'd counted so much on his father being there for him! 'I'm sorry. That must have been hard…to be left without a mother,' she said with sincere sympathy.

His mouth twisted with irony. 'Oh, my father kept trying to provide me with mothers. He married four more times, resulting in four divorces. I have a half-brother and two half-sisters, but their respective mothers took their children with them. I was…am…the only constant in my father's life as far as family is concerned. We are…very attached to each other.'

'I see,' she murmured, thinking his father hadn't exactly set an example on how to make a marriage work.

'Do you see that I don't want an easy-come, easy-go marriage?' he countered as though he could read her thoughts. 'That I want a wife who is as committed to me and our children, as I would be to her?' he pressed on. 'Parents together, Sunny. A stable home.'

All that he felt he hadn't had himself? It was strong motivation, but was motivation enough when faced with a clash of needs? Sunny suspected Bryce was very used to getting his own way on most things.

His eyes glittered knowingly as he added, 'You've come from a stable home, haven't you? It means something to you.'

'Yes. It's why I don't want to rush into such a serious step as marriage.'

'What reservations do you have about me?'

Sunny frowned, not having any criticisms to make except... 'I don't understand why you're so keen, so quickly.'

Her eyes flicked to his in sharp challenge, determined on getting a reply that satisfied her sense of reality—a reality that was not wrapped in hothouse passion or persuasive patter.

He leaned back in his chair but it was not a move that held relaxation, more putting a weighing distance between them as he considered what answer to give her. She could almost feel the wheels clicking around in his mind, and there was no mistaking the tension emanating from him as he came to a decision.

'I'll tell you why, Sunny,' he said quietly, and she tensed, every intuitive instinct telling her that something important was about to be revealed, and he was counting on her understanding, counting on a positive response from her, as well.

'My father has a heart condition. Every day he lives is a medical miracle. For some time he has been agitating for me to marry, have a child. I know this is a symptom of his own rather immediate sense of his mortality, but it is his dearest wish and I would like to give him that sense of our bloodline going on before he dies.'

*A bloodline!* It sounded almost Medieval. Like feudal lords securing a succession. 'You want to marry me for your father's sake?' she asked incredulously.

'No. I could have married any number of women for my father's sake. I am considered...' His mouth took on a cynical curl. '...very eligible in the marriage stakes.'

Sunny did not doubt that truth.

'But I didn't want just any woman as my wife, Sunny. I wanted a woman who felt right to me. A true partner on many levels.' His eyes blazed with conviction. 'Every instinct I have is shouting that I've found her in you.'

Her heart jiggled with an intemperate burst of joy. It took a tremendous effort to override the wild response and keep boring in on her misgivings. 'You trust your instincts so much?'

'In every aspect, you shine with rightness. No other woman ever has. Not to me.'

'Then I'll still be right to you in a month's time,' she argued.

'And my father might be dead in a month's time.'

It was softly said, yet it hit Sunny hard, making her remember her own father's death. He'd been a volunteer fire-fighter, supervising a burn-off. The wind changed unexpectedly, trapping him and two others. No goodbyes. No chance to tell him how much he'd given her and what it had meant. Not even a few moments to show him she loved him.

Bryce leaned across the table and took her hand in his, pressing his sense of urgency, his *caring*. 'I want to marry you now, Sunny. Today. And present you to my father as my wife for him to see what I see...so he won't fret about the future anymore.'

What she saw was how much it meant to him to answer his father's need, and she remembered him saying his father had always *been there for him.*

She understood the urgency he felt, and was moved by his reasoning, honoured that he had chosen her to be the wife he took home to his father, yet she could not get over the uneasy sense of being an instrument to resolve a situation, rather than a woman who was loved for herself.

It was difficult, knowing where Bryce was coming from, to set his proposal aside. The impulse to give him what he wanted was strong. She'd always wanted a marriage based on the kind of values she believed in, and in a way, Bryce *was* offering that—solid family values—yet...

'I'm sorry. I...I need to think about this.' Her eyes eloquently pleaded his patience. 'I can't do it today, Bryce. I can't just...walk straight into it.'

He brushed his thumb over the back of her hand, as though wishing—willing—to get under her skin. 'What's troubling you most, Sunny?' he asked quietly, his eyes meeting her plea with a caring concern that stirred more emotional confusion.

She shook her head, thinking she was probably being a fool, putting what had proved to be an illusion with Derek over the substance Bryce probably represented.

'Tell me,' he softly pressed.

'I always thought I'd get married for love,' she blurted out. 'Not...not for convenience.'

'Convenience,' he repeated with a harsh edge, frowning over the accusation implied in it. 'If I'd wanted convenience...' He bit off the thought, shaking his head. His gaze flashed to hers, searing in its intensity. 'I swear to you this marriage is not a convenience to me, Sunny. I want you. I want you in my life. How can I make that more clear to you?'

'It's too fast!' she cried. 'It's just too fast!' She pulled away from him, pushing up from the table in her agitation, gesturing a helpless apology. 'You've made it clear and I...I know this must be frustrating to you, but...I need time to feel sure I'm doing the right thing for me, too. I'm sorry...'

'It's okay,' he quickly assured her, rising from the table and holding out his hands in an open gesture of giving. 'I didn't mean to make you feel pressured. I guess my own decision is so clear-cut to me...' He grimaced an apology. 'I'm not about to force you into marriage, Sunny. It has to be your choice, too, and if you're not ready to make it...'

'I'm not. Not yet,' she quickly added, acutely aware she didn't want to shut the door on his proposal, however many doubts were clouding it for her.

'Then we'll make other plans for today,' he offered, smiling to soothe her agitation. 'Simply spend time together. Are you happy to go along with that?'

She nodded, her chest feeling too constricted to

find breath for more words. He was the most stunningly attractive man she'd ever met and one side of her was clamouring it was madness not to accept him on face value alone. Only the painful thud in her heart argued that *want* wasn't love, and she craved real love from the man she married—the kind of love that lasted a lifetime.

'Have you seen the Grand Canyon?'

'No,' she whispered shakily.

'Would you enjoy a ground/air combination tour—a helicopter flight, as well as travelling around the rim by road, hiking where you want to?'

Sunny scooped in a quick breath. 'Yes. I'd like that very much.' Outside distraction...more time...

'Shall I book it for an hour's time? Can you be ready to go that soon?'

She nodded, grateful to seize on quick action. 'It won't take me long to get dressed. I'll start now.'

Eager to be on the move, she was already heading for the staircase when he paused her with the words...

'One last thing, Sunny...'

'Yes?'

He had stepped over to the telephone table and had picked up the receiver to make the booking. His head was cocked quizzically and she was anticipating a further question about the trip they had agreed upon.

'You said...*married for love.* What, in your mind, is love?'

Her mind went completely blank, then tripped into a welter of needs that Derek's defection had wounded, very badly. Out of the miserable emptiness of bitter disillusionment came the one thing love had most represented to her, and precisely what Derek had torn away.

'Emotional security,' she said, with all the passion of having been stripped of it.

'I see,' he murmured, as though weighing her answer against what he could balance it with.

'What is love to you, Bryce?' she shot at him, wanting him to feel some of the vulnerability he had stirred with his question, though she couldn't really imagine him feeling insecure about anything.

He seemed to consider his answer carefully before giving it, perhaps gearing it to her own. She didn't want that. She intinctively shied from thinking he would pursue his purpose relentlessly, calculating every word, every move.

'I think it's something that grows,' he said slowly, his eyes holding hers with hypnotic intensity. 'It begins with strong mutual attraction, and is fed by the caring each person demonstrates towards the other. It's a commitment to caring, and without that commitment it dies a quick death.'

Derek, she thought, not caring enough for her.

While Bryce...how much did he care? His answer sounded genuine, a deeply held personal belief, not a reply designed to win her over.

His mouth quirked into an appealing little smile. 'A fair assessment?'

'Fair enough,' she agreed. 'I'll think about it.'

He nodded and turned away to make telephone contact for the tour booking.

He cared a lot about his father, Sunny thought, and

as she continued on upstairs, she decided he would care a lot about any child he fathered, too.

But how much for her?

Would love grow between them?

Could she take that gamble?

# CHAPTER EIGHT

BRYCE clamped down on his impatience. Rushing Sunny was not going to work. Marsden had obviously caused too much emotional damage for her to trust easily. Yet he was quite certain her instincts sided with him. She would never have responded as she had without feeling the same deep attraction he felt.

Or was it rebound stuff—an overwhelming need to be desired?

That was one need he could certainly answer. Desire was simmering through him right now as they waited for the arrival of the elevator to take them down to the limousine which would transport them to the helicopter base. The stretch jeans and T-shirt Sunny had pulled on showed every delectable line and curve of her. She'd crammed one of the conference caps over her rioting curls, and it, too, seemed provocative on her, like a perky invitation to whip it off and free her hair.

Free everything!

The elevator doors slid open. Sunny glanced nervously at him as she stepped into the empty compartment. Bryce's chest tightened as he followed and hit the control panel for the ground floor. What good was restraint? Pouncing on her the last time they had been in this elevator together had propelled them into an intimacy that was working for him. Why should he hold back now?

The doors closed.

Driven once more by the urge to claim her as his, Bryce reached out and wrapped her in his embrace. Her lovely amber eyes lit with alarm. 'No pressure,' he gruffly promised, lifting a hand to gently stroke the tension from her face. 'I just have a need to feel you with me.'

The amber softened into a golden glow as he bent his head to kiss her and there was no hint of resistance when his mouth touched hers. The hands that had rested warily on his shoulders, slid quickly to link around his neck, an eager signal of her desire to feel him with her, too.

It was more than enough to push Bryce into seeking all she would give him and her active response as he deepened the kiss instantly ignited a passionate drive to break the emotional barriers in her mind, to draw all her feelings towards him with such dominant force, nothing else existed for her but the two of them together.

He pressed her closer, exulting in the long, feminine legs clinging to his, the soft fullness of her breasts spreading across the hard muscle of his chest, the whole delicious pliancy of her body as it seemed to crave every contact with his. He was so strongly aroused, so exhilarated by the fervour of her response, he wasn't aware of the elevator having come to a halt at ground level.

The whirr of the doors opening did belatedly register in his consciousness, but by the time he'd lifted his mouth from Sunny's, the doors were closing again, which was fine by him. He didn't want to stop what he was doing. They could ride straight back up to his suite and...

'Bryce...' An urgent gasp.

'Mmm?'

'We're down!'

He sighed, swiftly deciding he had regained some ground with her and playing for more might be a bad idea. He swung aside, reached out and pressed the Open Doors button just as the elevator was being sealed shut again.

Her hands dropped from his neck as she turned to face the exit, but she made no move to distance herself from the arm he'd left around her waist. They stepped out to the lobby together, which was a far more satisfying situation to Bryce than the apartness she'd been subtly maintaining since their breakfast conversation. It was clear he had to keep stoking this very mutual desire and sweeping her along with him until she accepted he was the man for her.

*'You slut!'*

The ugly words sliced through Bryce's pleasurable mission-plan, and the sight of Derek Marsden advancing on them switched his mind to red alert! Beside him he felt Sunny's whole body jerk with shock and her feet came to an abrupt halt, which halted him, as well, since no way was he about to let go of her.

*'Derek?'*

The name spilled from Sunny's lips, even as her mind recoiled from the horrible name he had called her. The shock of seeing him was stunning enough, having expected him to fly out on the plane to Los Angeles, but to be so insultingly labelled in public...

'Yeah,' he jeered. 'Thought you'd neatly got rid of me, didn't you? Sneaky bitch!'

'That's more than enough!' Bryce rapped out in a steely voice.

Sunny felt the surge of aggressive tension whipping through him, his hand on her waist gripping harder, pulling her protectively closer.

'She's taking you for a ride, Templar,' Derek threw at him, his eyes shooting daggers. 'Want to see the ring she gave back to me yesterday so she could go after you?'

'That's not true, Derek!' Sunny cried, appalled by this attack on her integrity.

He ignored her, plucking the engagement ring out of his shirt pocket, holding it in his clenched fist with the diamond pointing at Bryce, shaking it at him as he poured out more venom. 'No doubt you can buy one bigger than this.'

'That has nothing to do with why I broke with you, Derek, and you know it!' Sunny fiercely protested.

He turned on her in vicious accusation. 'You left me and went straight off with him.'

Sunny shook her head, bewildered by the totally unfair interpretation of the situation.

'At my instigation,' Bryce sliced in. 'You are mistaken. It was I who approached Miss York, not the other way around.'

'Miss York...huh!' Derek snorted derisively.

'Think I didn't see you in a clinch in the elevator just now?'

'I have asked her to marry me,' Bryce stated with icy dignity.

'*Marry* you?' Sheer fury twisted Derek's face. 'Well, let me tell you she was marrying *me* this time yesterday.' His eyes blazed at Sunny. 'What did you do? Give him the eye all the time you were sitting in the front row of the conference room?'

'No! I didn't do anything!' she cried, flushing with the guilt of having nursed lustful thoughts. But only in a fantasy way, not aimed to draw Bryce's attention to her.

'Like hell you didn't!' came the bitter rebuttal. 'You got your eye on the main chance and goodbye Derek.'

The sheer injustice of his slurs on her character whipped up Sunny's fury. 'It was goodbye Derek because all you could think about was gambling!'

'Well, it's you who's gambling now, you scheming little gold-digger! And I hope Templar sees you for what you are before he's fool enough to marry you.'

'I am not a gold-digger! It's you who wanted easy money.'

'At least I earn what I spend. I don't trade in sex for it.'

'Oh! Oh!' Sunny gasped, reduced to speechlessness.

'That is too offensive!' Bryce growled, his whole body clenching, ready to spring.

But it wasn't his fight, Sunny thought frantically. It was hers. And she had to fight back.

'Offensive!' Derek hurled at Bryce, too aroused to be intimidated. 'I track her here and discover there's no room in the name of Sunny York. She spent the night with you, sleeping her way to the top. That's *offensive*.'

'You're right!' Sunny snapped, leaping in to defend herself. 'I did sleep with him. *He* found me more attractive than a roulette wheel.'

'Well, you just keep spinning for him. I don't want a whore as my wife.'

'You insult Sunny once more and I'll ram the words down your throat,' Bryce bit out, violence shimmering in the air.

'No!' Sunny instantly swung towards him, slamming a hand on his chest, desperate to prevent any movement towards Derek who was shaping up to slug it out.

Fists wouldn't resolve anything. It would only make the whole scene uglier and more public than it already was.

She glared at her ex-fiancé over her shoulder. 'We have nothing more to say to each other. Please go, Derek.'

He glowered at Bryce to prove he wasn't intimidated, then sliced a look of contempt at Sunny. 'Screw you! I'll have plenty to say to everyone else about why you ditched me.'

'You keep your filthy mouth shut or I'll shut it for you,' Bryce threatened, his chest swelling against Sunny's hand.

'You don't have that much power, sucker!' Derek challenged, and on that jeering note, turned his back on both of them and strutted off as though he was cock-of-the-walk.

'Don't do anything, Bryce,' Sunny pleaded, frightened by the aggressive jut of his chin and the fighting strength that was teetering on the edge of exploding.

His gaze lowered reluctantly to hers, eyes glittering. 'You want me to let him get away with that slimy slander?' he demanded, rage clipping every word.

'It's true I broke my engagement to him yesterday,' she said, trying to excuse some of the offence.

'And none too soon,' Bryce ground out. 'There was no *love* for you in that outburst, Sunny.'

No...no love...just wounded ego and vile nastiness. Her stomach felt sick with it. 'Did you believe...' She anxiously scanned the glittering green eyes. 'Did you believe anything of what he said about me?'

The question brought a beetling frown. 'You know I don't. How could I? I've been with you every step we've taken together.'

But her staying with him as she had *was* open to misinterpretation. 'You don't think I'm a...a gold-digger? Out for what I can get?'

'Not you, Sunny,' he declared with ringing certainty.

She felt intensely grateful for his belief in her. Into her distressed mind flashed the image of Bryce always standing by her, ready to defend, to protect, caring with the kind of strength Derek had never had.

'Do you still want to marry me?' she asked.

'You think *he* could change what I feel?' came the incredulous challenge.

'No. Not you,' she answered, somehow knowing that very deeply. Bryce Templar trod his own path, and suddenly she wanted very much to share that path with him. It looked safe. It looked secure.

He cupped her face in his hands, commanding her full attention as his eyes blazed into hers. 'I want you, Sunny York. I'd marry you right this minute if I could.'

The warmth of his skin took away the dead coldness left by Derek's emotional kicks in the face. Bryce's desire for her sizzled into her bloodstream, bringing a vibrancy that re-energised her whole body.

'Then I will...I will marry you, Bryce,' she heard herself say, as though the words were drawn from a place she was barely conscious of, yet she knew even as she said them, she wouldn't take them back.

Bryce knew instantly it was a rebound decision. Her eyes were focused on him but they had a calm, almost distant expression in them, not one sparkle of happiness or even warm pleasure in the thought of being his wife. He should have felt an exhilarating zing of triumph, having achieved his goal so quickly, but the achievement wasn't his. It was Marsden's. Nevertheless, the prize was there to take, and Bryce was not about to let it slip away.

'Today?' he pressed.

'Yes.' Her mouth quivered into a challenging little smile. 'Right this minute if you like.'

He grinned, determined on being cheerful. 'We do have to get a wedding licence first.'

'Is that a problem?'

'A quick trip to the courthouse. No problem at all.'

'Then let's do it.'

As simple as that! Except Bryce was acutely aware of the complex undercurrents to this apparent simplicity. As he linked Sunny's arm around his and steered her out of the hotel to the waiting limousine, he asked himself if it was wise to take advantage of a decision she may well think better of, given a few hours' distance from Marsden's backlash.

Which reminded him that Marsden had to be dealt with before he caused more damage. He'd call Sherman as soon as he had a free minute. His crafty lawyer could speak to Marsden in L.A., pound home enough unpleasant legalities to demonstrate that silence held the greater good.

'Mr. Templar and Miss York,' the chauffeur greeted them affably, holding the passenger door open. 'Lovely day for a trip to the Grand Canyon.'

Bryce paused, hit by an unaccustomed sense of wrongness. It was a rare moment of indecision for him, yet this choice did involve Sunny very intimately and he did not want her to be unhappy as his wife. He lightly squeezed the hand resting passively on his arm, drawing her gaze to his and watching intently for any hesitation on her part.

'Are you sure about marrying me, Sunny?'

'Yes, I'm sure,' she stated decisively.

'You don't want to go to the Grand Canyon and take some time to think it over?'

'No.' Her chin was set in determination. 'I want to marry you today.' Her eyes sparked into vehement life. 'If it's right for you, it's right for me!'

It snapped Bryce straight into positive action. He turned to the chauffeur. 'Use your car phone to cancel the tour and take us straight to the courthouse.'

'Yes, sir.'

Bryce handed Sunny into the limousine and followed to settle beside her.

'The courthouse,' the chauffeur repeated, grinning happily at the change of plan as he closed the door.

It has to be right, Bryce fiercely told himself, taking Sunny's hand and lacing their fingers in a grip of togetherness.

*I'll make it right.*

# CHAPTER NINE

SUNNY was amazed how easy it was to get a wedding licence. All she had to do was produce her passport, fill out a form and sign her name. No wonder Las Vegas was called the marriage capital of the world, she wryly reflected. Here it was a totally hassle-free procedure—no other certificates required, absolute minimal red tape, no enforced waiting time.

Her mind quickly flitted over that last consideration. Waiting was not good in this case. Bryce's father wanted to see him married. Not that Will Templar would actually be at the ceremony, but the *fait accompli* would ease his mind and hopefully be beneficial to his heart condition. And then...no waiting any longer to have a baby. No more waiting at all.

As they emerged from the courthouse, the licence safely tucked in Sunny's handbag, Bryce took out his cell phone and made a call, asking to speak to a wedding consultant. Sunny frowned at him, not wanting any delay, not wanting some hypocritical fuss, either. This was a straight-out marriage of convenience, not a love affair to be celebrated in the traditional way.

'Don't we just go to one of the wedding chapels?' she said bruskly, much preferring to get it over and done with.

He shook his head, determination flashing from his

eyes as he answered, 'We do it right. Down to every detail.'

Sunny listened incredulously as he spoke to the consultant, listing off the kind of detail she would have thought important…if she'd gone ahead and married Derek. But that would have taken months of planning and scheduling and decision-making—chapel, flowers, kind of ceremony, photographer. Bryce was taking it upon himself to organise the whole wedding deal in a matter of minutes, *without even consulting her!*

Sunny burned with resentment. Wasn't her consent enough for him? Why did he have to make a production out of a wedding based on mutual purpose?

Having completed the call to his satisfaction, he put the phone away, tucked her arm around his and grinned, clearly delighted with his planning. 'Next stop,' he said, hurrying her towards the waiting limousine.

'What stop?' she demanded to know, beginning to feel truculent.

He addressed the chauffeur who was once again holding the door open for them. 'The Top of the Town Bridal Boutique.'

'A bridal boutique!' Sunny gasped.

Bryce bundled her into the limousine, still grinning from ear to ear. 'Going to get you the wedding dress of your dreams.'

'It's not necessary,' she gritted out, rebellion stirring.

'Yes, it is.'

'There's just the two of us getting married,' she

argued, turning to face him, to hammer home the truth as she saw it. 'It's not as if we're doing it in front of a whole pile of guests.'

It wiped the grin off his face. With a far more serious expression, he quietly asked, 'Aren't we the most important two, Sunny?'

Somehow that point steadied the angry whirl of protest in her mind. 'Yes, we are,' she conceded, though this was not the wedding of her dreams and she didn't want to pretend it was.

'Do you want to look back on our wedding and think of it as some hole-and-corner ceremony?'

She frowned, not having thought of what they were doing in *those terms*. 'It...it means the same,' she argued, still feeling out of step with his grand plan.

His green eyes seemed to glow like emerald fire as he softly said, 'I want my bride feeling beautiful, and knowing she is beautiful to me.'

Sunny's heart turned over.

'And I want you to be proud of the photos of our wedding when you show them to our children—their mother and father on the day they were married.'

Their children? They swirled in the mists of Sunny's imagination—a little boy and girl, examining their parents' wedding photos.

'We owe it to ourselves and them to do it right, Sunny,' Bryce pressed.

She hadn't been looking ahead. The blind need for positive action had seized her, and nothing else had really entered the equation. Selfishly blind, Sunny suddenly realised. This was Bryce's wedding, too.

And the intent of their marriage was to have a child...children.

As he said, love could grow out of caring for each other. He wanted her to feel like a beautiful bride, and why shouldn't she? She would have wanted that with Derek, and Bryce was better husband material than Derek had ever been.

She could send a wedding photo to her family. That would make her marriage to Bryce more right for them, as well. And shift any nasty cracks from Derek into the sour grapes category. A *fait accompli* would certainly help to put a stop to criticism.

'Okay. We'll go for all the trimmings,' she agreed, glad now that he had thought of them for her. 'But I pay for my own wedding gown, Bryce.'

He laughed. 'One last stroke of independence?'

It was more a matter of pride. 'I'm not coming to you on a free ride.'

He instantly sobered, his eyes flashing darkly. 'Wipe that guy and everything he said out of your mind, Sunny. This is our day. I know what you're worth to me and in that context, counting money is meaningless. I'm not buying you.'

Shame wormed around inside her, raising a flood of heat to her cheeks. 'I'm sorry, Bryce. I...I guess that really stung me.'

'Let it go,' he advised quietly. 'Don't let it spoil what we can have together.'

'I won't,' she promised fervently, her eyes begging his forgiveness. It was Derek who had humiliated her, not this man. Bryce made her feel good about herself.

He smiled, chasing the painful shadows of Derek away.

She smiled back, determined that she *would* feel beautiful as his bride. And she wouldn't count the cost of anything because that was how Bryce wanted it. Pleasing her husband-to-be was important.

When they arrived at the bridal boutique, he instantly commandeered a saleslady, instructing her to show Miss York the very best stock she had, and he expected to see the selection of gowns paraded in front of him so he could judge for himself which one most suited her very unique style of beauty. He then settled himself on a white satin sofa and waved them on to the business of looking at what was available.

'Now there is a guy I could really take to,' the saleslady remarked to Sunny, rolling her eyes in maxi-appreciation. 'You sure have won yourself a prize in him.'

'Yes. Yes, I have,' Sunny agreed, determined to believe it.

'Hmm...' The woman eyed her up and down. 'With your height and legs, we certainly don't want a crinoline-style skirt. Too much. Slim and elegant with a fabulous train, I'd say. Shall we start with that?'

Sunny nodded. 'Sounds good.'

'Perhaps something off the shoulder to frame that gorgeous mass of hair.'

Sunny barely stopped herself from rolling her own eyes at this description of her unruly mop. Reminding herself that Bryce liked her hair, just as it was, she simply said, 'Let's see.'

Maybe because it all seemed rather unreal, it was actually fun, parading the gowns for Bryce, striking poses for his studied opinion. His running commentary on the detail of everything made her laugh and he scored each showing out of ten. Oddly enough, his scores matched her own judgment, demonstrating like minds, which also helped to push any misgivings about her decision aside.

The fifth gown, however, brought the sense of fun to an abrupt halt. It wasn't exactly a *traditional* bridal dress, not silk nor satin nor even white, and it didn't have a train, either. But Sunny loved it and to her eye it looked perfect on her, nothing to be fixed or altered. It also made her feel more…*female*…than anything she'd ever worn before.

This time she didn't prance out of the dressing-room to show it off to Bryce. She walked self-consciously, knowing the slinky ankle-length gown in cream garter lace was moulded to her every curve. The long sheer sleeves added an elegant grace and the scooped neckline was just low enough to reveal the uppermost swell of her breasts. The image of a sexy swan floated into her mind and she couldn't help thinking this was how she would have wanted to look—to feel—if she was marrying for love.

Bryce was not alone on the sofa. Another man had joined him, apparently showing off the contents of an attaché case. They both turned to look at her. Bryce's face instantly lit up with pleasure.

'That one!' he said, almost on a note of awe, his eyes drinking in the whole lovely flow of it on her.

It mightn't be love but the blaze of desire in his

eyes was warming. Sunny slowly twirled around to give him the benefit of every angle, basking in the heat of his approval and the sexual response he stirred in her…needing to take the chill off her heart.

'Ten out of ten?' she asked.

'About ten thousand out of ten!'

'Good! Then I'll buy it.'

'You do that,' he fervently approved. 'But first come and have your finger sized for the wedding ring so our jeweler here can get moving on it.'

A wedding ring! A convulsive little shiver ran down Sunny's spine. This wasn't a game of fantasy dress-ups. They really were doing this…getting married!

It only took a few moments to get her finger sized. Then she was swept into choosing a bouquet from a book of photographs. There were so many pictures, they became a blur to her. When a bridal nosegay was suggested as the ideal accompaniment to her dress—complimenting it rather than distracting from it, Sunny simply let herself be guided.

It was also suggested that a pretty coronet of flowers matching those in the bouquet, would look better than a veil. Sunny instantly agreed. No veil. Somehow a veil was going too far, a mockery of what a wedding should stand for. Not even for her future children would she wear a veil. She simply couldn't bear it…Bryce lifting it off her face as though she were a true bride.

No!

She would pledge herself to him bare-faced.

Let there be at least that honesty between them.

With everything decided upon, delivery to the hotel was promised within the hour.

Back at the hotel, Bryce had lined up a hairdresser, a beautician and a manicurist to give Sunny every bit of pampering a bride could possibly want. Although the whole process felt more and more like a charade, since it all took place in their suite, it was easy enough to submit to it.

Trays of tempting finger food were brought to her, meant to satisfy any hunger pangs. Champagne was served. Sunny forced herself to nibble a few delicacies since fainting at the altar was hardly a good start to any marriage. The champagne was a good nerve-soother, but she was careful only to sip it occasionally. Being a drunk bride wasn't a good start, either.

The whirl of activity centred on her kept Sunny from thinking too much. She had to make more choices about her fingernails, her hair, her make-up, how the coronet of flowers was to sit. Only when all the preparations had been completed, and a fully dressed and meticulously groomed bride looked back at her from the mirror, did her nerves stage a revolt against any possible soothing. They plunged straight into an agitated tangle.

All the helpers had retired from setting the scene. The show was about to go on, except it wasn't a show. It was real, and the lines she would speak—the vows she would take—would affect the rest of her life.

'You take my breath away.'

Bryce...standing in the doorway...shaking his head as though she were a miracle he couldn't quite believe in. He took her breath away, too, looking utterly superb in a formal grey morning suit, a touch of cream in his silk cravat and a cream boutonniere to match the exquisite little flowers in her bouquet.

'Time for our photo call in the chapel studio,' he said huskily, pushing forward to collect her and take her with him.

Sunny took a deep breath and turned towards him, managing a somewhat shaky smile as she said, 'I'm ready.'

'Not quite.' His smile was a warm caress, driving off the rush of goose bumps on her skin. He took her left hand and slowly slid a magnificent emerald ring onto her third finger. 'I chose this for you. I hope you like it.'

'Bryce…' She could barely choke out his name.

Not a bigger diamond than Derek's. An emerald…and she felt his green eyes burning into her heart, willing her to take it without question, and wear it because it was *his* gift to her, *his* promise which would not be shabbily broken as Derek's had.

She swallowed hard to remove the constricting lump in her throat. 'It's…it's wonderful. Thank you.'

He wrapped his hand around hers and heaved a satisfied sigh. 'Let's go and get married.'

*The final act.*

Somehow his ring and his hand sealed it for Sunny.

The decision was made…the outcome inevitable.

The half-hour photographic session in the chapel studio seemed to pass in a matter of minutes. Bryce was there with her every second, showing his pleasure in her, making her feel beautiful, making her feel…*loved*.

And the brilliance of the ring he'd placed on her finger kept dazzling her whenever she rested her hand on his chest or shoulder or next to her bouquet…a pear-shaped emerald—almost a heart—its vivid green hue emphasised by a border of white diamonds set in yellow gold. She had never seen anything like it…so very special, unique…and he'd chosen it for *her*.

For Bryce to value her so much…*she did want to marry him!*

*It felt right.*

They moved on to the chapel.

It was decorated with sumptuous floral arrangements.

A pianist sat at a grand piano, playing Celine Dion's song—'I've Finally Found Someone.'

A marriage celebrant smilingly beckoned them forward.

Somehow it didn't matter that the chairs on either side of the aisle were empty. Sunny thought fleetingly of her mother and sisters, but they had had their weddings. This was hers and Bryce's, and it belonged to them, no one else.

The civil ceremony performed was a simple one. There was no sermon, no gushy sentiments. To Sunny, the words seemed all the more meaningful for their straightforward simplicity.

When Bryce spoke his vows, his gaze remained steadfast on hers, and his voice carried a quiet solemnity that seemed to seep into her soul, spreading a sense of peace and dispelling any worries about a future with him.

She spoke hers just as solemnly, meaning every word of her commitment to him and their marriage. It was very real now. There was no going back from this moment. They would go forward together and make the best of whatever life served out to them.

Bryce had bought two gold wedding rings, one for her, one for him. It touched her that he wanted to display the fact that he was married—a bachelor no more—a husband who cared about his commitment to her.

'With this ring, I thee wed...'

He had to take off the emerald ring to slide the gold band into place, but the removal was only momentary. Sunny stared down at the dual rings on her finger, fitting perfectly, brightly shining proof that she now belonged to him.

*'I now pronounce you husband and wife.'*

Such fateful words...

Sunny poured all her hope for a good future with Bryce into the kiss that followed, and from him flowed a fervent eagerness to get on with it.

The wedding certificate was filled out, placed in a special holder, and given to Sunny—a lasting memento of a momentous day. The pianist was playing 'All The Way' as they thanked the marriage celebrant and the official witnesses.

They turned as a wedded couple to walk back down the aisle, and the words of the song were running through Sunny's mind, echoing what she hoped would prove true. At least she wasn't carrying any false illusions about this marriage. It was a matter of making it right, not expecting it to just turn out that way without having to work at it.

'Where is the Bryce Templar wedding?' a woman's voice shrieked, blowing the music right out of Sunny's ears.

Her step faltered as Bryce squeezed her hand hard, having come to a halt himself. Not only was tension ripping through him but any trace of a benign expression was gone, replaced by grim anger.

'Too late? Just finishing?' the woman's voice shrilled, then broke into furious determination. 'We'll see about that!'

Sunny jerked her gaze from the startling reaction from Bryce, just in time to see the woman burst through the entrance to the chapel, charging at battle pace before coming to a heaving halt at the start of the aisle, her gaze ripping Sunny up and down, then stabbing at Bryce.

'How could you?' she screamed at him.

The wild intrusion and the ear-piercing outrage was a total show-stopper. Sunny could only stare at the woman in a tumult of confusion. Who was she and why was she on the attack?

'How could you do this to me?' the woman demanded fiercely of Bryce, apparently deciding to ignore the bride beside him as though Sunny were nothing.

'Very easily, Kristen,' Bryce answered coldly.

Kristen? He knew her, then? It wasn't some complete madwoman on the loose?

'You ruthless, callous pig!' came the blistering indictment. Her face screwed into vicious fury. 'You'll pay for this!'

'Oh, I expect to,' Bryce drawled, a fine edge of contempt in every word. 'But not as much as I would have paid...*had I married you.*'

# CHAPTER TEN

MARRIED!

Bryce had been going to marry *this woman?*

Even as Sunny's mind jammed with shock, her eyes swiftly took in everything there was to take in about his first choice—very, very classy with her polished blond hair falling in smooth perfection to her shoulders and cut to feather inwards from her ears to her throat, a stylishly artful frame for a face that was classic model material.

So was her body, though she wasn't quite as tall, nor as long-legged as Sunny. In fact, she was much better proportioned, her figure looking very sexy in a straw linen wrap-around dress and lots of gold accessories—chain belt, sandals, bag, bangles, necklace— all shouting the kind of money Sunny had never had at her disposal.

Bryce's contemptuous comment had acted like a smack on the face, but the jolt of it only lasted a few seconds. The pent-up fury was unleashed again, propelling the woman forward, her arm upraised to deliver a very physical slap to Bryce's face.

He caught her wrist before violent contact was made, holding it in a vice-like grip. 'Back off, Kristen!' he commanded in his steely voice, lowering her arm and slowly releasing it as he emphatically asserted, 'It's over. I told you it was finished this morning.'

*This morning?* Sunny glanced sharply at Bryce. Before or after she had agreed to marry him? There was a very disturbing question of integrity here.

He sensed her glance, caught the worry in it, and instantly answered, 'Before you woke up, Sunny.'

Even so, he had gone to bed with her first. Had he been testing her out before giving up Kristen?

'Damn you, Bryce!' his ex-fiancée stormed. 'I would have backed down if you'd given me the chance.'

'No chance.' He released Sunny's hand to put his arm around her shoulders in a very possessive and reassuring hug. 'I now have the wife I want.'

'A bargain basement bride, no doubt,' Kristen jeered, switching her gaze to Sunny, her grey eyes blazing scorn. 'You didn't even have the sense to marry him in the State of California.'

Which totally bewildered Sunny. What did California have to do with getting married?

'I'm sure it's beyond your comprehension, Kristen,' Bryce bit out coldly, 'but Sunny didn't marry me with an eye to a divorce settlement. Nor did she put a price on having a child.'

*Money?* Was that the currency of marriage in California?

'Then more fool her, with your record of using women as you please. Sucked her right in, did you, Bryce?' Kristen mocked savagely.

Sunny's mind whirled around this hasty marriage in Nevada—all Bryce's doing...except for her consent…which he'd started working for as soon as he'd had sex with her!

'I think women tend to draw from men what they put out themselves,' Bryce commented coldly. 'Users do get used, Kristen. It so happens Sunny is a different breed to you.'

'And such a convenient windfall *for you,*' she flashed back at him. 'Except this cheap move of yours is going to cost you, Bryce. Cost you big!'

A *windfall*…Derek's blow-up…her hasty consent…

'Go ahead and sue me, Kristen. Buying you out of my life will be worth every cent I have to pay.'

She bared her teeth, hissing, 'I'll take you down for as much as I can.'

'Your demonstration of greed in the prenuptial agreement leaves me in no doubt you'll money-grub as far as you can.'

Sunny's mind boggled over a prenuptial agreement. She'd always thought such things horribly cynical with their implication that the marriage commitment was inevitably a transitory thing and a division of property had to be worked out beforehand. If Bryce had even mentioned one, she would have backed off so fast…yes, she was a different breed. A *convenient windfall?*

'It's a straight breach of promise,' Kristen argued in fierce resentment, again sneering at Sunny as she added, 'throwing me over for her.'

'Oh, I think any judge would find good reason for that,' Bryce drawled, hugging Sunny even closer. 'My wife is such a warm contrast to you, Kristen…'

'I'm a Parrish!' she declared with belligerent arrogance. 'That name *means* something. I'll be listened to, Bryce Templar!'

'Yes, you undoubtedly will be,' he agreed uncaringly. 'The media will gobble up every bit of it as you prove you've been badly done by, revealing your avaricious little soul to the whole world in a public courtroom. You think you'll win their sympathy?'

Angry heat speared across her cheekbones. 'So...you figure you've got all the angles covered so you can cheat me.'

The words were flying so fast and furiously, Sunny was only catching the fact that Kristen was a gold-digger. Big time! Despite the name she set such store by.

'No agreement was reached, Kristen,' Bryce stated bitingly. 'You weren't content with what was offered.'

'What about *this agreement?*' She thrust her left hand up in a clenched fist, showing off the huge diamond ring on her engagement finger. '*It* shows something.'

'Yes. It shows my good will, which you proceeded to flout.'

She tossed her head defiantly. 'Well, don't think you're getting it back!'

'I don't want it back. I don't want anything remotely associated with you. We have nothing left to say to each other.'

'Except through our lawyers!'

'Agreed. Now if you don't mind...'

Sunny was subjected to a scathing look. 'Congratulations! You've got yourself a cold, calculating pig and you're welcome to him!'

Having delivered her best exit line, Kristen Parrish flounced a quick about-turn and strode out of the chapel, her stiff back eloquently denying any wounds whatsoever.

Just like Derek, Sunny couldn't help thinking. Rejection was never a palatable situation, but rejection in favour of someone else…that could definitely bring out the worst in some people.

Both she and Bryce had been badly misled in choosing their first partners for marriage. The question was…had they made the right choice now?

Sunny hoped so. With all her heart she hoped so. Yet she couldn't shake the feeling they had both been driven into this choice by a rebound effect…Bryce seemed to be everything Derek wasn't…and she was a *warm contrast* to Kristen Parrish.

A windfall marriage…

She shivered.

Bryce's arm instantly tightened around her. 'I'm sorry you were subjected to that, Sunny,' he said ruefully. 'My big mistake…'

She sighed, lifting her gaze to his in anxious query. 'Am I a windfall, Bryce?'

'Yes.' His eyes simmered with hot possessiveness. 'The best windfall that's ever come my way and I consider myself the luckiest man alive to have you as my wife, Sunny.'

Instead of Kristen, she thought.

'And I need, very much, to be alone with you,' he added softly.

He drew her with him, out of the chapel, into the elevator, back to their suite, and while Sunny took comfort from his desire for her, she couldn't stop the questions whirling around in her mind.

When had he calculated the difference between her and Kristen?

When had he decided to marry her instead?

And the bottom line—marrying to please his father—was she simply a better candidate? A cheaper candidate? *The bargain basement bride?*

# CHAPTER ELEVEN

THE moment they were in their suite with the rest of the world shut out, Bryce turned her into his embrace. Sunny didn't mean to stiffen up, but she couldn't quite feel right, pretending nothing had happened to colour things differently. Her hands pressed nervously against Bryce's chest, holding her bouquet between them, her heart thumping painfully instead of happily.

'It's worrying you, isn't it…all that Kristen said?' Bryce quietly probed.

'Not…not all of it.' She fiddled with his boutonniere, wishing Kristen hadn't turned up. But there was no joy in hiding her head in the sand, now that she was more aware of circumstances.

'Tell me what's preying on your mind, Sunny. Let me fix it.'

'You didn't tell me about her.'

'She was irrelevant to us.'

No, she wasn't irrelevant, Sunny thought, and such a ruthless wipe-out of a woman he'd planned to marry—without any second chance offered—did not sit well with her. It was too…too uncaring.

'You were still engaged to her until this morning,' she reminded him, shying away from Kristen's accusation of him being a cold, calculating pig, yet calculation had to have come into his actions, given his need for a wife and the time pressure involved. To give up Kristen before he had secured Sunny's consent…had he? Had he really?

'Technically I was still engaged to her, yes,' he answered. 'In my heart, no.'

'In your heart, Bryce?' She lifted her eyes to scan his, to see how much he meant by that.

'When I asked you to marry me last night, *you* had completely obliterated any possibility of my ever marrying Kristen. I could never have gone back to her after you, Sunny.'

He looked and sounded genuinely sincere.

His grimace held a wealth of distaste as he added, 'I called Kristen at seven o'clock this morning, making it absolutely clear that everything was ended.'

She frowned, remembering similar words he'd spoken much later. 'I heard you talking on the phone to someone just as I was coming downstairs.'

'My lawyer. He had to be notified.'

'Because of the…the prenuptial agreement?'

'Yes.'

'Why did you do that with her? Was it the only way for you to get a wife and child…to buy them?'

His mouth twisted in a fleeting expression of bitter self-mockery. Then his whole face seemed to harden, his eyes reflecting a deep inner cynicism as he replied, 'Prenuptial agreements are quite common in the States, Sunny, especially since divorce has become a national pastime and a boon to lawyers who are out to get their cut. In a financial sense, such agreements offer both protection and security.'

They weren't common in Australia. Or perhaps

they were amongst the very wealthy. Not having ever moved in those circles, she simply didn't know.

'If that is your practice here, Bryce, why didn't you offer one to me?' she queried, *the bargain basement bride* tag nagging at her sense of self-worth.

He didn't have a ready reply. Sunny had the disturbing impression that the wheels had just fallen off his train. The silence reeked of a massive recalculation being made. It totally unnerved her. She broke away from him, frightened now of this marriage she had entered into, feeling hopelessly alienated by an attitude of mind she could never be sympathetic to.

She dropped the pretty bridal nosegay onto an armchair. The rings he'd placed on her finger glinted up at her, mocking the 'forever' sentiments she'd given them. Her heart bled for the dream he wasn't giving her and she cursed herself for having been so hasty in choosing this man to be her husband.

'Do you want a financial agreement, Sunny?' he asked in a flat, weary tone. 'I'll see to it right now if it will make you feel more secure.'

*Secure!* That was such a black joke she might have laughed if it had involved anyone but herself. 'No!' she exploded, wheeling on him as a turbulent rush of emotion demanded he at least understand where *she* was coming from. 'I would be the whore Derek said I was if I let myself be bought like that, and don't you dare treat me like one, Bryce Templar.'

He frowned. His hands lifted in appeal. 'I thought…you seemed upset that I hadn't brought it up with you.'

'If you had, I would never have married you,' she shot back at him in towering contempt. 'It's looking for the out before you're even in. It makes a mockery of the commitment that marriage is supposed to stand for. Especially when children are planned. Especially!' she repeated with passionate conviction.

'That's precisely why I didn't bring it up, Sunny,' he declared, his concern clearing.

'Is it?' she hotly challenged. 'Or am I the windfall that won't cost you as much as Kristen Parrish would have? *The bargain basement bride!*'

He flinched.

For one heart-cramping moment, Sunny thought she had hit the nail right on the head.

Then he exploded into violent rebuttal, his arms slicing the air in scissor-like dismissal. 'I will not have you thinking that of yourself! Nor of me!'

Sunny quivered in shock as he came at her, not having expected to stir such a storm of emotion in him. A calculating man surely stayed in control, but there was nothing at all controlled about his wild gesticulations or the passion pouring from his voice.

'Money didn't once enter into my wanting you. *You,* for yourself, Sunny. I sat there in that conference room yesterday morning, watching you give your presentation, and the whole vibrant warmth of you called to me so strongly...'

'Then?' she squeaked. 'You wanted me then?'

'Yes! So much I was planning to ask you to join me for lunch! Anything to have more of you!'

'But you didn't.'

'No. Because when you stepped off that podium I

saw the engagement ring on your finger. Which meant you belonged to someone else. And I didn't think you were the kind of woman I could *buy* away from a man you were committed to.'

She shook her head, stunned by these revelations.

'You made me hate the thought of marrying Kristen.' His mouth curled around the name in savage disgust. 'Kristen, who kept putting a higher and higher price on having a child in the prenuptial agreement she insisted upon.'

He tore off the silk cravat and unbuttoned his collar as though it were choking him. 'Then…then I was on my way out of the hotel and I saw you confronting some guy at a blackjack table. I saw you take off your ring and hand it back to him.'

'You saw?'

'It stopped me in my tracks. I watched you come towards the lobby and all I could think of was…I *can* have her. I *will* have her.'

She hadn't been mad for thinking what she had in the lobby—Bryce Templar determined on claiming her as his woman.

'If that feels wrong to you, I'm sorry, but it felt very right to me. And I acted on it. What's more…' He hurled off his coat and his fingers attacked the buttons of his vest with speedy efficiency. '…I'll keep acting on it.'

The vest went flying. In an instant he was right in front of her, grasping her upper arms, his eyes blazing with the need to burn away anything standing between them. 'You came with me, Sunny. You wanted me last night. You wanted me this morning. You agreed to marry me. You're my wife.'

It was all true. She stared back at him, overwhelmed by the passion he was emitting. Somehow it didn't matter that there had been ruthless calculation behind everything he'd done, because it was for her...because he wanted her.

'My wife,' he repeated, his voice throbbing with fierce possessiveness. 'And that's how it's going to be.'

He kissed her, and his need poured from his mouth to hers, igniting her own need to have all the worries of this day obliterated, to simply lose herself in the primitive heat of being one with him, as she had been last night, as she could be now...

With a low, animal growl, he scooped her off her feet, carrying her with him, clutching her to his chest, raining kisses on her face and muttering, 'I'll make it right. I'll make it right.'

The frenzied refrain pounded through Sunny's heart, making it swell with a wild kind of joy. She clung to him, kissing him back as feverishly as he kissed her. Nothing had to make sense. This frantic desire had a momentum all its own.

Beside the bed they had shared before, Bryce stood her on her feet to peel off her clothes, and he slowed himself down, taking care, his eyes glittering over her as he removed each garment. 'You are so beautiful to me. Do you know that? Have I told you?'

His hands caressed, sending delicious quivers of anticipation through her. He knew how to touch. He knew how to do everything.

'Yes,' she said. 'Yes. You're beautiful to me, too, Bryce.'

And she did the same to him, stripping off the rest of his clothes, taking the time to glide her hands over his marvellous male body, revelling in his perfect musculature, the gleaming tautness of his skin. She exulted when she felt little tremors running under it, knowing he was as excited by her touch as she was by his. It was especially wonderful to run her finger-tips up the impressive strength of his thighs, to hold and stroke and feel the power of his sexuality.

'Sunny...' It was a furred breathing of her name, threaded with barely contained longing. His hands spanned her waist, lifting her up, sliding her body against his. 'Wrap your legs around my hips. I want to feel you hugging me, wanting me...'

She did, with both her arms and her legs, holding his head to the soft cushion of her breasts as he dropped an arm to support her where she was, instinc-tively balancing both their bodies so he could join them, the insertion so slickly smooth, so incredibly satisfying, so intensely *right,* Sunny closed her eyes and breathed a sigh of utter bliss.

His arms slid up on either side of her spine. 'Lean back. I won't let you fall.'

There was no question of not trusting his strength to hold her wherever he wanted to hold her. She leaned back and his penetration went deeper, increas-ing the sense of intimate union so exquisitely, Sunny was unaware that angling away from him left her bare breasts tilted perfectly to be reached by his mouth. The heightening of pleasure was enormous when he started kissing them, swinging her body from side to side as he moved from one to the other, creating arcs of intense sensation and building such a rapid escalation of excitement, she was swamped in huge rolling waves of it.

'Oh…oh…oh…' she heard herself gasping, totally beyond doing anything active herself. It felt as though she were absolutely possessed by him, enthralled by the sweet havoc he wrought inside her, and wanting more and more and more of every fantastic sensation he imparted.

He lowered her wildly palpitating body onto the side of the bed, still holding her pinioned to him, and the voluptuous roll of him inside her changed to a fast plummeting rhythm that brought surges of sheer ecstacy, a fierce tumbling of pleasure that engulfed her, and the deep inner beat of him went on and on until suddenly it ebbed into a delicious sea of peace.

She was hopelessly limp when Bryce gathered her to him and moved them both fully onto the bed, turning to lie on his back with Sunny half sprawled on top of him. She could feel his heart thumping under her cheek and it seemed to pulse through her own bloodstream. Into the haze of her mind slid the thought…*This is my husband*…and a sweet contentment accompanied it and lingered.

Sexually, what more could she ask for in a partner? He excited her beyond anything she had ever felt before. And she loved his physique. It was such a pleasure to look at him, feel him, and he was now hers to have and to hold—a fantasy come true—so she had every reason to feel content.

'I think, if you want to save this bridal coronet of flowers, I'd better unpin it,' Bryce gruffly remarked.

'Mmm...'

'It's got a bit bruised, but it did look fantastic on you with the rest of you naked, Sunny. Still like a bride.'

Sexy pleasure in his voice—visual satisfaction as well as physical. Sunny smiled as she felt his fingers move gently through her hair, removing pins. She must have looked like some kind of pagan bride. Which led her to the thought that probably in primitive times, mating for life was all physical. The choice of instinct. Survival.

She certainly would have picked *him* out of any bunch of men. Why should it be any different now? The saleslady at the bridal boutique had it right. She'd won the prize.

Though, in a way, she'd won it because the sleekly glamorous status-holder, Kristen Parrish, had defaulted in the marriage stakes, demanding too big a bride-price. A child-price, as well. Which was particularly offensive to Sunny's way of thinking. In fact, it was a cold, callous calculating thing to say—I won't have your baby unless you pay me big bucks.

If anyone was 'the pig' in this agreement, Sunny decided it was Kristen.

Which raised a niggly little question.

'Bryce?'

'Mmm?' Having removed the coronet of flowers, he was busy gently massaging her scalp where the pins had been.

'Would you have married Kristen if you hadn't met me?'

His chest rose and fell as he deeply inhaled and breathed out a heavy sigh. 'She's gone, Sunny. This is us,' he said emphatically.

She hitched herself up to assure him she wasn't being jealous or going down some negative path. 'I know. And I'm glad it's us. Truly I am.'

'Good!' He looked and sounded relieved.

'I just want to know if you would have gone through with it, lacking me to replace her?'

His face tightened. She saw a flash of grim ruthlessness in his eyes. 'Yes, I would have married her. But given the fortune she was demanding, I would have insisted on getting uncontested custody of any child we had.'

*His* child. Sunny believed him. In his world, his father's marriages had come and gone, so Bryce probably didn't set much store by them, but a child—*his child*—meant a great deal. And she understood he much preferred a wife who *wanted* to be a mother to his child, simply because being a mother was important to her, having a value beyond money.

His expression softened as he lifted a hand to her face, gently stroking the contours of it. 'I know you'd never hold a child to ransom, Sunny. You want to share. You care what happens. You want what's best. You'd ensure our child has…' He smiled. '…emotional security.'

'Money doesn't give that, Bryce.'

'I know. I want to give our child emotional security, too. Are you willing to throw your pills away now, Sunny?'

Decision time.

It had been a whole day of decisions.

There seemed no point in hesitating over this last one now.

'Yes,' she answered firmly. 'It's what we both got married for, isn't it? To be parents.'

He laughed, his eyes twinkling wickedly. 'Well, there are some fringe benefits, wife of mine.' And he rolled her onto her back, exuding happiness as he began kissing her again. 'I'm going to love every minute of every effort needed for us to make a baby.'

Sunny had no doubt she would revel in the process, too.

'Though the sooner I get you pregnant, the better,' Bryce murmured. 'I want to take that load off my father's mind. And give him a grandchild.'

*His father...* Bryce's whole motivation for marrying.

A dark concern sliced into Sunny's mind.

What if she didn't get pregnant?

What if she couldn't have children at all?

Everything hung on it.

Everything!

# CHAPTER TWELVE

BRYCE was smiling as he picked up the telephone to call his father. *His wife* was still upstairs, getting ready for their flight to Sedona, and he'd left her smiling, too.

No problems left unresolved.

Everything was on track, just as he wanted it.

He dialled the number and Rosita Perez, the resident housekeeper, picked up at the other end.

'Bryce Templar, here. How is my father this morning?'

'A bit poorly, Señor Bryce, but I'd say it's more grumpy humour than anything else. Do you want to speak to him?'

'Yes, I do.'

Bryce waited, happily anticipating improving his father's humour. Good news, it was said, was the best medicine of all.

'About time you called,' came the curt and typical greeting.

Bryce grinned to himself. 'I'm flying to Sedona to have lunch with you. Does that suit?'

'Of course, it suits. Darned carers won't let me get up to anything myself. Doctors meddling all the time. Pack of quacks, if you ask me.'

'I'm bringing my wife with me.'

'Wife? Did you say *wife?*'

'I did. We got married yesterday.'

'Well, now...'

Bryce could hear his father smiling through the mellowed tone. Without a doubt, being presented with what he wanted was a fine lift to his heart.

'...a done deed, eh!' He actually chuckled. 'Smart move, talking Kristen out of the big showcase wedding she was planning. Lot of nonsense.'

'I didn't marry Kristen.'

'What?'

'I said...*I didn't marry Kristen.* I broke off my engagement to her and married a much better choice for me—Sunny York.'

'What? Who?' His voice rose several decibels.

'Calm down, Dad. You wanted me married. I'm married. To a woman who not only has beauty and brains, but also a warm heart. Even her name is warm—Sunny. Please remember it when we visit.'

'Sunny who?'

'Sunny York. Now Sunny Templar.'

'I don't know any Yorks.' His tone had dropped to querulous.

'You'll get to know her if you treat her nicely.'

'Where'd you meet her?'

'Here in Las Vegas.'

'She's not a showgirl, is she?' Dark suspicion winging in.

'No. Sunny actually works for our company. From the Sydney branch. An Australian.'

'That's going a bit far afield, isn't it? What's wrong with a good American woman?'

'There's nothing wrong with a good American

woman. It just so happens that this Australian woman has more appeal to me than any other female inhabitant of this planet.'

'This sounds too impetuous.' A muttered grumble. 'Good stock, the Parrishes. What do you know about this York family? Do they breed well?'

'Sunny has two sisters with children. Satisfied?'

'Better to have tests done.'

'Did you get *my* mother to have a fertility test?'

'Different times then. You said so yourself. Besides, I was younger than you. How old is this wife of yours?'

'Plenty young enough to have children. And so am I.'

'Huh! Grey in your hair already. Better get started.'

'We intend to.'

'Good!'

'I'm glad you approve,' Bryce said very dryly.

'Don't come that tone with me, boy. You needed pushing into doing the right thing. You just bring this wife along to me and I'll see if you've done it.'

'Her name is Sunny, Dad. You'd better get it right, too, or we won't be staying long.'

'Are you threatening me?'

'No. Just telling you how it is.'

'I hope you're not being led around by the brain below your belt, Bryce.'

'Oh, I think both brains are in fine operation.'

His father snorted. 'When can I expect you?'

'Around noon.'

'I'll be looking forward to it.'

'That was the idea.'

He heard his father chuckling as he put the receiver down.

It gave Bryce's heart a lift.

It *was* good that he'd got married. All the better that he was married to Sunny—a wife worth having in every sense. Producing a grandchild for his father would be no hardship. The trick was to get Sunny pregnant immediately. He'd wasted three months on Kristen. His father was counting his life in terms of one year, which meant there were only nine months left.

Bryce decided he could afford to take a week off work for a honeymoon. Making a baby with Sunny was more important than anything else.

Sunny was all packed and ready to leave for Sedona. Meeting and having lunch with Bryce's father—Will Templar himself—was scary enough without getting her nerves into more of a twist. She didn't have to check her laptop computer for e-mail. It was probably better not to.

Back home in Sydney it was still the middle of the night, so if there was some response from her family about her marriage to Bryce, they wouldn't be looking for any reply from her for many hours yet. Although she'd sent the announcement and the scanned wedding photograph over twelve hours ago, there was no guarantee that her sister, Alyssa, or her husband, John, had even turned on their home computer since then.

Better not to look.

She checked the bathroom once more in case she'd

left something behind. She re-checked her appearance, hoping Will Templar would not find any fault in his new daughter-in-law. Her hair hadn't moved too much out of yesterday's styling for the wedding. Her make-up looked good, if anything understated, but that would probably meet more approval than overstated.

She was wearing one of her conference suits—not the yellow one which she considered too business-like for such a personal meeting. This was a pantsuit in a terracotta gaberdine mixture that didn't crush. Smart casual. The cream silk blouse with its geometric print in green and gold and terracotta gave it a classy touch. She hoped she looked right as Bryce's wife.

Bryce Templar's wife...

Her mind flitted to the e-mail she had sent to her family—short and to the point.

'Today I married Bryce Templar, CEO of Templar Resources. See attached wedding photograph. Will explain everything when I see you. Bryce simply swept me off my feet. As soon as we can he'll be flying home with me to meet the family and help me settle everything there. We'll see you then.'

She walked back into the bedroom and stared at the laptop computer again. What could they say, anyway? A whole pile of recriminations wasn't going to change anything. It was a done deed. Maybe they'd congratulate her.

The laptop stared back—Pandora's box.

Sunny took a deep breath. Not looking was really cowardly. Besides, her nerves couldn't get into much more of a twist. She acted fast, slinging the laptop onto the dressing-table, plugging it in, opening up, switching on, her fingers moving like lightning over the keyboard. The dialling tone seemed to mock her impatience, playing its infuriating little ditty.

Checking incoming messages.

One clicking across the screen.

From Alyssa!

Sunny's heart skipped all over the place as her eyes skated over the words.

Wow! Some bombshell! I called Mum and she cried over missing the wedding but she says to tell you if you're happy she's happy for you and she'll look forward to meeting your new husband.

I called Nadine and she thinks you're crazy for rushing into it. You should have brought him home first. But she wishes you all the best and hopes you haven't made a *big* mistake.

I took one look at the wedding photograph and thought, If I didn't have John—that guy you've married could sweep me off my feet any day. Or night. And that sure is some ring on your finger! Good for you, Sunny.

Lots of love and I can't wait to see him in the flesh!

Sunny breathed a sigh of huge relief. It was okay. They accepted it. And after a while her mother may well be relieved not to have had the expense of another wedding. Paying for her sisters' weddings had been a struggle financially. Sunny had helped out as much as her mother would let her.

She smiled down at the fabulous emerald ring on her finger. It was certainly a statement that none of her family would miss, with its obvious message that Sunny had done very well for herself with the CEO of Templar Resources. Not that money was any yardstick for a successful marriage. It bought things but it couldn't buy happiness.

As for Nadine's hope that she hadn't made a big mistake, well, Sunny hoped that, too, but she wasn't going to let her mind drift down that negative path. She and Bryce had a lot of positive things going for them and they both wanted the marriage to work, especially with becoming parents. Rather than hoping she hadn't made a big mistake, Sunny hoped she'd made the best decision she'd ever made in her life.

She quickly typed a reply—'Thanks, Alyssa. I'll be in touch with details before Bryce and I fly home. 'Bye for now. Love, Sunny.'

Having sent it off, she packed up the laptop again and was just setting it down with the rest of her luggage when she heard Bryce coming up the stairs. She swung to face him as he came through the doorway and was instantly hit anew by his strong sexual impact. Dressed in fawn slacks and a clingy green sports shirt, his magnificent physique seemed to leap out at her, and the grin on his handsome face gave it a magnetic attraction.

Alyssa's words zipped through her mind—*he could sweep me off my feet any day. Or night.*

He'd done just that, Sunny thought, and she didn't

regret a second of it. In fact, if he wanted to do it right now...

'I've called for a bellboy. Are you all packed, ready to leave?'

Her hands fluttered, appealing for his opinion. 'Do I look right to meet your father?'

His eyes simmered over her, causing her breasts to peak into hard nubs and sending tremulous little ripples down her thighs.

'Perfect!' he declared huskily, his gaze finally lifting to sear away any doubts or fears in hers. 'Don't worry about what my father thinks, Sunny. You're *the wife* I want. He'll see that fast enough.'

He walked towards her, emanating a ruthless determination that she was coming to recognise. Nothing was going to shake Bryce from what *he* wanted. Her heart quivered with the knowledge that he'd wanted her from the moment she'd come to his notice, and now she was his.

*But would she stay his if she couldn't give him the child he wanted?*

No negative thoughts, she savagely berated herself as he drew her into his embrace, the green eyes warmly smiling at her, promising there was no possible conflict of interests in this meeting with his father.

'He's looking forward to our visit.'

'Yes...well...it will be interesting.' She managed a teasing little smile in response. 'Father and son.'

Bryce laughed. 'Always a testing ground.' He raised quizzing brows. 'Any reply from your family?'

'Shock/surprise, but best wishes and looking forward to meeting you.'

'So...no problems there.' His eyes glittered satisfaction. 'I've booked us into the L'Auberge Inn at Sedona for tonight.'

This was startling news. 'We're not staying with your father?'

'What? On our honeymoon?'

'We're having a honeymoon?'

'After the wedding comes a honeymoon,' Bryce asserted. 'We are going to do everything right, Sunny.'

And as he bent to kiss her, Sunny was thinking, surely nothing could go wrong when Bryce was so intent on making everything right.

# CHAPTER THIRTEEN

THE fantastic red rock formations around Sedona just seemed to suddenly rise out of the Arizona desert, as startling and as stunning as The Olgas rising out of the desert in the red centre of Australia. Sunny was amazed by what was wrought by time and nature, and the likeness to parts of the Outback.

She had a marvellous view of it all from the plane before it set down at the airport, which was surprisingly situated on top of a hill overlooking the township. They were met by Will Templar's chauffeur who loaded both them and their luggage into a very plush Cadillac. It was a very scenic drive, down the hill, through the town which seemed to be spread around a T-junction, then up another hill and finally into the driveway of a huge sprawling house built of stone and wood.

It commanded a spectacular view in every direction, and there were big windows and furnished porches to take advantage of it from both inside and out of doors. A large swimming pool occupied one side of the grounds with what looked like sophisticated barbecue facilities under a roofed area nearby. Everything projected a casual lifestyle, not a formal one, which set Sunny more at ease.

They were met at the front door by a middle-aged

Mexican woman whom Bryce introduced as Rosita Perez, adding that Rosita ran the household.

She beamed at Sunny. 'You are very welcome. *Very* welcome. Such wonderful news!' Her dark eyes twinkled at Bryce. 'Señor Will wants fajitas for lunch. It is a good sign.'

Sunny smiled and nodded. She didn't know about fajitas but the warmth of the greeting helped to calm the butterflies in her stomach.

'Where is he?' Bryce asked.

'On his favourite balcony. I have set out drinks and dips there. Go on....' Rosita shooed them forward. '...he is waiting.'

They walked through a huge living room; big stone fireplace, big furniture in wood and black leather, brightly patterned scatter cushions and rugs featuring Indian motifs.

'What are fajitas?' Sunny whispered.

Bryce grinned. 'Dad's favourite dish. Spicy meat and vegetables wrapped in a kind of tortilla.'

'How spicy?'

'Not too spicy.' His eyes teased her concern. 'There'll be other dishes for you to choose from, so don't worry. You'll get fed.'

'Being nervous makes me hungry.'

'The avocado dip Rosita makes is great. So is the corn one. Get stuck into them,' he advised, his eyes positively laughing as he opened one of the glass doors to the designated balcony.

Sunny took a deep breath and stepped out.

It was a very wide, spacious balcony, holding a dark green wrought-iron-and-glass dining table, with

six matching chairs cushioned in green and white.
There were occasional tables, as well, serving groups
of sun loungers upholstered in the same colours.
However, the drinks and food Rosita had mentioned
were set out on the dining table.

The rustle of a newspaper being put down was the
first indication of Will Templar's presence. She
swung her gaze towards the sound and caught the
movement of legs being swung off one of the loungers…long legs encased in light grey trousers. Behind
her the door closed and she sensed Bryce stepping to
her side as the man on the lounger rose to his feet.

Her first thought was, this will be Bryce thirty years
from now. The likeness between father and son was
striking, despite the older man's white hair and the
illness that had stripped him of extra weight that
would have normally filled out his face and powerful
frame.

They shared the same impressive height and strong
facial features, as well as the air of being in command
of their world. Will Templar's heart condition certainly hadn't diminished that, Sunny thought, and fancied these father and son meetings could sometimes
develop into the clash of the Titans.

'Sunny, this is my father,' Bryce said casually.
'Dad, this is my wife.'

In the face of such an intimidating authority figure,
all her sales training leapt to the fore, pushing her
into taking the initiative. 'Hi,' she said warmly, smiling as she moved forward to offer her hand and focusing directly on his eyes, which to her surprise were

a silvery grey, different to Bryce's. 'I've been looking forward to meeting you, Mr. Templar.'

He took her hand and held it, seemingly amused by her brashly open approach. 'Impressive. A sunny disposition...' His gaze flicked to Bryce, one brow lifting. '...and the legs of a showgirl.'

'Ignore that, Sunny,' Bryce returned dryly. 'My father has a fixation on showgirls.'

Will Templar laughed and pressed her hand reassuringly. 'My son made the claim of beauty and brains. Since both are in evidence, I just thought I'd add my observations to the list. A very great pleasure to meet you, Sunny.'

The feeling of being patronised instantly raised Sunny's hackles. 'Is this a case of let the fun begin between you two?' she challenged. 'Shall I just sit down and eat while you get on with it?'

'Sassy, too.' Will Templar grinned, patting her hand in approval. 'I think I'll let you entertain me instead.'

'If you're not careful, Dad, Sunny may very well eat you for lunch.'

'I did notice her teeth, my boy,' he retorted good-humouredly. 'A smile to dazzle you with before chomping.'

'Beware the bite,' Bryce tossed back at him. 'Mine, too.'

'I do love a good fight,' Will Templar confided to Sunny, wrapping her arm around his as he drew her towards the table. 'Especially when I win.'

'I'm the winner here,' Bryce declared, his eyes hotly assuring Sunny she was the top prize to him.

'I can see that,' his father conceded. 'But who spurred you on to take a wife?'

Again the feeling of being a mere cipher between them goaded Sunny into further speech. 'Actually, Mr. Templar, I took Bryce as my husband.'

'What?' He looked flabbergasted at her temerity.

Sunny smiled. 'You could call it a mutual taking. I did have equal say in it, you know.'

Bryce laughed.

His father looked askance at her. 'You have a very smart tongue.'

'Smart brain, too,' Bryce chimed in. 'What would you like to drink, Dad?'

'I've got to stick to juice.'

'Sunny?'

'I'll have juice, too, thanks, Bryce.'

'I had Rosita bring out a bottle of Krug champagne,' his father pointed out.

'Lovely,' Sunny warmly approved, 'but not on an empty stomach.'

He pulled out a chair from the table and waved her to it. 'Then sit down and eat,' he commanded, put out at not having everything go his way.

Sunny grinned at him. 'Thank you.'

He shook a finger at her. 'You...are a very provocative young woman.'

'You mean...not a yes-woman?' Sunny tilted at him before reaching for a corn chip and the avocado dip. 'Having a mind of my own has always worked better for me, Mr. Templar. I see no reason to give it up just because I married your son.'

She coated the chip with dip and popped it in her

mouth, feeling highly invigorated for having stood up for herself.

'Here's your juice, Sunny.' Bryce set a filled glass in front of her.

'What about mine?' his father growled. 'I'm the invalid around here.'

'I thought you were fighting fit, Dad.'

'Two against one is not a fair fight.'

'You asked for it. Now if you'll stop assuming Sunny is a walkover, we could have a really pleasant lunch together.'

'Just testing her out.' He settled himself on the chair at the head of the table, gesticulating at Bryce. 'You bring a stranger into the family. How am I supposed to know her mettle if I don't test her out?'

'You could try trusting my judgment,' came the ready advice as Bryce set a glass of juice in front of his father.

'Huh! Men can get blinded by a woman's beauty.'

Bryce raised an eyebrow at Sunny. 'Am I blind?'

She grinned at him, having just tried the corn dip and found it as delicious as the avocado one. 'No. Just besotted. But that's okay because I'm besotted, too.'

Will Templar barked with laughter, vastly amused by the exchange. 'Oh, that's good! Very good! If you're not careful, Bryce, she'll be giving you the rounds of the kitchen.'

'A novel thought,' he retorted, pulling out the chair at the foot of the table and relaxing onto it.

'Novelty wears off,' came the sardonic reply. 'She might be compliant now, but...'

'You know, Mr. Templar,' Sunny cut in sweetly. 'Where I come from, it's rude to talk over a person as though she's not there.'

His silvery grey eyes narrowed on her. 'No respect for authority. I've heard that about Australians.'

'Then you've heard wrong. We do respect an authority who shows us respect.'

'Just what position do you hold in our company, young woman?'

'I do sales presentations. And I work hard at commanding respect, Mr. Templar. I do not lie down and let people steamroll over me.'

'But you're married to Bryce now,' he said sharply. 'Do you expect to keep on working?'

'Do you have a problem with that, Mr. Templar?'

'What about children? Do you figure on having any?'

She flashed a look at Bryce who smiled back at her, confident of her reply and perfectly content to let the conversation run without his interference. His eyes said she was doing fine with his father.

'Yes, we do,' she said, smiling her own pleasure in the prospect of having a family with Bryce.

'Do you intend on working then?'

'Being a mother will have priority, but it does take nine months to make a baby, Mr. Templar. Do you think I should twiddle my thumbs until one arrives?'

He frowned. 'Got to take care of yourself during pregnancy,' he said bruskly. 'My first wife—Bryce's mother—had a hard time of it. Kidney problems. Shouldn't have had a child at all. Died when Bryce was only a toddler.'

The brusk tone carried shades of old pain, instantly cooling Sunny's fighting instincts and stirring her sympathy. 'I'm sorry,' she said softly. 'I really want to have a baby, so you can be sure I'll take every care when I do fall pregnant, Mr. Templar.'

'Yes, well, no time to waste,' he said gruffly. 'Bryce isn't getting any younger. He's thirty-four, you know. Should have started a family years ago.'

'A bit difficult when I only met Sunny this week,' Bryce drawled, his eyes mocking his father's contention. 'And you can hardly accuse me of wasting time once I met the right woman.'

His gaze shifted to Sunny and she basked in the warmth of it, feeling more and more that she truly was right for him, and he was right for her. A hasty marriage it might be, but she certainly didn't repent her decision…yet.

'Got an answer for everything,' Will Templar grumbled. 'Sunny, you're hogging those dips. While I'm happy to see you have a healthy appetite, I like them, too.'

'Would you like me to spread some on the chips for you?' Sunny immediately offered.

'I can help myself if you'll kindly pass them up.'

'Not thinking of yourself as an invalid anymore?' Bryce archly commented as Sunny obliged.

'I can handle a bit of finger food.' He glowered at Bryce. 'I see you're feeling on top of things, just because you got married.'

'I generally am on top of things, Dad. I work at it. Which is why you made me CEO, remember?'

'Well, don't be getting too cocky about

it…counting chickens before they hatch. Damian called me yesterday.'

'Nice for you that he keeps in touch.' Bryce slanted a wry smile at Sunny. 'Damian is my half-brother. Dad's son by his third wife.'

'A very caring son, too,' Will Templar declared, pausing to give the statement weight, and eyeing Bryce with a very definite glint of challenge. 'Told me his wife's pregnant.'

Bryce nodded affably. 'I must call and congratulate them.'

'Giving me a grandchild before you do.'

Sunny sensed the threat behind the words and instantly felt uneasy. Was Will Templar playing one son off against another, with the position of CEO as the prize? If so, there was a factor in his marriage decision that Bryce hadn't told her about. She looked sharply at him but discerned no rise of tension in his demeanour.

He smiled, maintaining an affable front. 'I'm glad you'll be getting in some practice as a grandfather before Sunny and I have a child. In fact, maybe we should wait a while, simply enjoy having each other before Sunny gets pregnant. I believe a baby needs to be welcomed and loved for itself…' His lips were still curved into a smile but his eyes hardened to green flint as he softly added, '…not used as a pawn.'

Suddenly the air between father and son was so thick with threat and counter-threat, it could have been cut with a knife.

Sunny knew intuitively Bryce would not back off. And she didn't want him to. What he'd stated was what she believed, as well, although she didn't really want to wait. Not long, anyway. All the same, she understood that pleasing his father was one thing, being dictated to was quite another. Bryce would not be the man he was if he tamely succumbed to his father's string-pulling.

She was startled when Will Templar abruptly switched his focus to her. 'Do you want to wait a while, Sunny?' he demanded rather than asked.

'I think husband and wife should be in total agreement on when they have a baby and it's no one else's business but theirs,' she said slowly, keeping her wits alert to the undercurrents. 'I'm sure Bryce would consider what I want, every bit as much as I would consider what he wants.'

Will Templar leaned forward, boring in. 'Do you realise I still have the power to strip Bryce of his position in the company?'

Sunny felt her spine bristling. Her eyes locked onto the older man's and fought fire with fire. 'I didn't marry Bryce for *his position*, Mr. Templar.'

'What did you marry him for?'

'I fancied him rotten and I thought he'd make a great father for the children I want.'

'You fancied him *rotten?*'

Either he was unfamiliar with the term or she'd knocked him off his power perch. Sunny decided to play her hand to the hilt.

'Mmm...' She gave Bryce a smouldering look. 'He has a way of inspiring the most terrible lust in me.'

He smouldered right back. 'The inspiration goes both ways.'

'Enough!' Will Templar snapped. 'You don't have to prove you're *besotted* with each other at my table!'

Bryce shrugged. 'Actually, we don't have to prove anything, Dad. We just came to visit.'

'Fine visit this is…not even opening the bottle of champagne.'

'I'll be happy to open it,' Bryce said, lifting the bottle out of the ice bucket. 'Ready for a glass now, Sunny?'

'Yes. Thank you. These dips really are delicious.'

'Are you always so direct?' his father demanded of her.

Sunny frowned quizzically at him. 'Weren't you being direct with me, Mr. Templar?'

He looked somewhat disgruntled. 'Just testing your mettle.'

'Did I pass the test?'

He snorted. 'It's plain you and Bryce are two of a kind.'

'Is that good or bad?' Sunny queried.

For the first time she saw a flash of respect in his eyes. 'You can call me Will.'

'Thank you.' She smiled warmly. 'I take that as a real compliment.'

'So you should.' He visibly thawed. 'Just see that boy of mine starts fathering real soon. Can't wait forever for a grandchild, you know.'

From which Sunny deduced it was Bryce's child he most wanted to see, not Damian's.

That thought stayed with her long after the lunch visit was over and Will Templar had conveyed his rather crotchety blessing on the marriage and expressed his pointed hope that their honeymoon would be *productive*.

The chauffeur transported them to the L'Auberge Inn which was nestled along the bank of a pretty, tree-lined creek and surrounded by towering red cliffs. It had a European-style lodge, supplying luxurious amenities for resident guests, and the secluded cottage Bryce had booked for the night was very romantically furnished in a rich, French provincial style.

'May I say how delighted I am that you fancy me rotten,' Bryce tossed at her the moment they were alone.

She laughed and repeated her smouldering look. 'Your father clearly does not see you through the eyes of a woman.'

'I'm only interested in your eyes, Sunny,' he said seriously, enfolding her in his embrace. 'You handled my father brilliantly, but…can I believe every word you said?'

'You know the wanting is real, Bryce. How could it not be when…' She blushed at the memories of her deeply primitive response to him.

He reached up and ran his fingertips over the self-conscious heat, his eyes burning into hers as he softly asked, 'Did you fancy me rotten before you broke with Derek?'

Her skin became even hotter under his questing touch. The intensity he was projecting seeded a wild thought. Was he jealous of the relationship she'd had with her ex-fiancé?

'You must be aware of how attractive you are physically, Bryce. I think any woman would fancy you. The saleslady who sold me my wedding dress certainly did. But I didn't know you in any personal sense...'

'And now that you do?'

'Derek belongs in the past. It's you I want.'

She wound her arms around his neck and kissed him to prove there was no looking back on her part. He was her husband now and she wanted no other.

Bryce stormed her mouth with a passionate possessiveness that swiftly moved into much more than a kiss. They made love in a frenzy of desire for each other, craving an affirmation that their marriage was right and always would be.

It was hours later, when they were dressing for dinner—Bryce insisting she wear the cream lace gown again for the six-course 'wedding feast' he planned to order at the gourmet restaurant in the lodge—that Sunny recalled the question raised at lunch with Will Templar.

'Are you in competition with your half-brother, Bryce?' she asked bluntly, wanting to know the truth.

'Damian?' He looked amused, his eyes mocking the suggestion as he answered, 'My father cares too much for Templar Resources to ever put Damian in control of it, Sunny. He knows it. I know it. It's not an option.'

'Then why did he threaten it?'

Bryce shrugged. 'It's simply a measure of how much he wants me to have a child.'

She frowned. 'You played it like a power game, saying we might wait.'

'A gift is one thing, a pressured demand quite another.'

'What would you do if he did give the CEO position to Damian?'

'Go into opposition. In effect, my father would lose me.'

*And you would lose him,* she thought.

'He won't go that far, Sunny. Don't worry about it.'

All the same, she couldn't help thinking it would be best—easier all around—if they did have a child straight away. And Bryce had to be thinking that, too.

A productive honeymoon…

# CHAPTER FOURTEEN

SUNNY was not the least bit nervous about introducing Bryce to her family. She was happily looking forward to it as she settled herself to sleep away some of the hours on the long flight from Los Angeles to Sydney. Travelling first class gave her much more leg room to make herself comfortable and the wider seat took away the sense of feeling cramped. She tucked the airline blanket around her, sighed contentedly and closed her eyes.

'Sweet dreams,' Bryce murmured indulgently, leaning over from the seat beside her to drop a kiss on her forehead.

She smiled. He made her feel loved. During their whole honeymoon, which Bryce had extended to ten days, he had made her feel loved, and she knew now that she loved him. The words had not been spoken but that didn't matter. The feeling was there, which meant nothing was missing from their marriage...except a baby...and since she may well have conceived already, Sunny was not going to let that concern weigh on her mind.

She had such good memories to dwell on; action-packed days, touring the rim of the awesome Grand Canyon, cruising Lake Powell, hiking the trails through the breathtaking beauty of the hoodoos at Bryce Canyon—well named, her husband had jokingly declared—and absolutely blissful nights, revelling in the sensual pleasures of intimacy.

Her sleep on the plane was deep and untroubled. She awoke with a sense of well-being that stayed with her until the plane circled over Sydney before landing. The view of the harbour, the great Coat-hanger bridge, the gleaming white sails of the opera house, the sparkling blue of the water…it suddenly grabbed her heart and gave it a twist. *This was home.* What had she done, abandoning it for a host of unknowns?

A rush of strong emotion brought tears to her eyes. She blinked rapidly to drive them back. It was silly to let a familiar view get to her like this. People were more important than places. She had Bryce. And right on that thought, he reached across, took her hand, and gently squeezed it.

'A touch homesick?'

'It's just so beautiful,' she excused.

'Yes, it is. One of the most beautiful cities in the world,' he said warmly. 'We will be back, many times, Sunny.'

She flashed him a watery smile. 'It's okay. I do want to be with you, Bryce.'

He nodded and interlaced his fingers with hers, reinforcing their togetherness. There were times when he seemed ruthlessly intent on not allowing anything to shadow it.

He had arbitrarily dismissed the idea of staying in her Sydney apartment, booking an executive suite at the Regent Hotel for the duration of their visit. Sunny suspected he didn't care to be anywhere Derek had been, but he argued comfort and the fact that it would complicate her task of clearing everything out and ending the lease. Which was true enough.

She was thankful she and Derek had maintained separate apartments, never actually living together. At least she didn't have the complication of dividing up possessions. That would have been really messy. They had never swapped door keys, either, which was probably just as well, given their bitter parting. Sunny saw no problems in doing what had to be done today.

Although they had left Los Angeles on Wednesday night, crossing the dateline meant they were arriving in Sydney on Friday morning, and they'd be flying out again on Sunday. A packing company had already been lined up to help her at the apartment. Bryce wanted to spend the day in the Sydney headquarters of Templar Resources and he offered to collect her personal belongings from the office where she had worked.

This, Sunny realised, neatly avoided any unpleasant encounter between her and Derek, so she had agreed to the plan, but she did regret missing the opportunity to say goodbye to the people she had been friendly with. Though they were mostly men who would probably side with Derek, she argued to herself. Since her life was now with Bryce, it seemed wiser to simply stay out of the situation.

The plane landed safely at Mascot Airport. A limousine took them to the Regent Hotel. They had time to freshen up, eat a light second breakfast, and go over their plans for the day in case something had not been thought of. Satisfied that everything was in hand, Bryce left for head office and Sunny took a taxi to her old neighbourhood in the suburb of Drummoyne, only a short trip from the centre of the city.

It was strange, moving around the apartment she had occupied for the past four years, wondering what to do with everything she had collected here. There was no point in taking anything but clothes, photo albums and those personal possessions which were especially dear to her. Having spent the last day before their flight to Sydney at Bryce's home in Santa Monica, Sunny was only too aware that it wanted for nothing.

Bryce had advised sending her surplus stuff to a charity but she didn't feel right about that now. It was like irrevocably sweeping out her past—everything that had made up her life before she had gone to Las Vegas. It seemed like saying none of it had any value anymore—all she'd worked for over many years. To just get rid of it because Bryce could provide more and better…it simply didn't sit well with her.

While she waited for the packing people to arrive, she telephoned her mother, letting her know what was happening and asking if there was anything she would like from the apartment. To Sunny's intense relief, her mother suggested sending everything to her. It could be stored in the garage and the whole family could pick and choose what they could use.

'Better we keep it for you,' her mother added. 'You never know, dear. You might not be happy living so far away in another country.'

'Mum, I'm married,' Sunny protested.

'Yes, and I'm sure you're wildly in love. I truly hope this marriage works out wonderfully for you,

Sunny, but…it was rather hasty, dear. And he is an American, not…well, not what you're used to. If sometime in the future you want to come back home…'

'I'm not thinking like that, Mum.'

'I understand, dear. I'd just feel better about it if we keep things for you.'

Insurance against some unforeseen future?

Sunny frowned. Did she herself feel that? The idea warred with her sense of commitment, yet…who could really know what the future held? All she knew was that keeping her things did make her feel more comfortable.

'Okay, Mum. The boxes should arrive this afternoon.' Her mother and sisters lived at Quakers Hill, on the western outskirts of Sydney, not more than an hour away if the truck went there directly. 'Will you be home to direct where they're to be stored?'

'Yes, I'll be home. What time can I expect you and Bryce tomorrow?'

'What time do you want us there?'

'In time for morning tea. Say ten-thirty? I'm cooking your favourite carrot cake this afternoon.'

'Thanks, Mum. That's great! We'll be there soon after ten.'

'If you've got the time, Sunny, call your sisters, too. They're dying to chat to you.'

'I'll try. 'Bye for now.'

With the storage decision made, Sunny threw herself into sorting out what clothes she should take with her now, and what was to be boxed up and sent to her. As arranged, two men from the packing company turned up at ten o'clock and were amazingly efficient at their job; wrapping breakables, grouping things for easy labelling, even boxing the furniture in thick cardboard so nothing could be damaged.

By one o'clock the apartment was completely cleared. The men even carried the suitcases she'd packed down to her car for her. She drove to the local shopping centre, had a quick lunch, then dropped into the real estate agency which handled the lease of her apartment. After handing in her keys there, arranging for cleaning and settling what was owing, Sunny only had one item left on her business agenda—returning the company car which had been part of her salary package.

It was easy, at this point, to simply follow Bryce's advice. She returned to the hotel, had her luggage sent up to the suite, and instructed the concierge that the car was to be picked up by the Templar Resources company. Having now completely dismantled her previous life in Sydney, Sunny suddenly felt drained. Jetlag, she told herself, and retired to their suite to sleep it off.

Except sleep eluded her and she remembered she hadn't yet called her sisters. Or any of her old girlfriends! She started with Alyssa who wanted to hear all about her honeymoon and bubbled on about how marvellous it must be to have a really wealthy husband who could just do what he wanted without counting the cost.

'Bryce does work, too, you know,' Sunny said dryly. 'A CEO doesn't have a lot of leisure time. This was our honeymoon, Alyssa.'

'Yes, but let's face it, Sunny. Derek couldn't have given you all that. And talking of work, did you know he'd resigned from Templar Resources?'

Sunny frowned over that piece of information. 'How could I know when I've been out of the country? And how do you know, Alyssa?'

'Nadine found out. She felt sorry for him and called him.'

'I wish she hadn't done that.'

'Well, you were engaged to him for months, Sunny. Your whirlwind marriage to Bryce was a bit of a shock.'

'Derek spent every spare minute in Las Vegas gambling. Plus time he should have spent at the conference, too. Did he tell Nadine that?' Sunny demanded sharply, annoyed that her youngest sister had gone behind her back to Derek, instead of waiting for her to come home.

'Hey! I didn't do it,' Alyssa protested. 'I just thought you might want to know Derek had left your husband's company. Pride, I guess.'

A niggle of concern made Sunny ask, 'Has he got a job somewhere else?'

'He said he was going to work for the opposition. Beat Templar Resources at their own game. He was angry. You can't exactly blame him.'

*Yes, I can,* Sunny thought, remembering how he had ignored and neglected her in favour of roulette and blackjack and whatever other games he'd played.

'After what he did in Vegas, resigning was probably the best move he could make. He was well on the way to inviting being sacked, in my opinion,' she remarked stonily.

'That bad, huh?'

'Yes. I just hope he can stay out of casinos and get his life together again.'

'You still care for him?'

'No. Derek killed off any caring when...' She stopped, shying away from the ugly memory of the confrontation in the MGM lobby. She took a deep breath before firmly stating, 'I really don't want to talk about Derek, Alyssa. That's over.'

'Okay. That's fine with me,' came the quick reply. 'I'm really looking forward to meeting Bryce tomorrow.'

'Good. We'll be at Mum's about ten. See you then, Alyssa.'

Still vexed over Nadine's action, Sunny had no inclination whatsoever to call her other sister. Nadine could wait for tomorrow for whatever fuel she wanted for more gossip. She spent a couple of happy hours telephoning her long-time girlfriends, telling them her news, giving them her new address in Santa Monica and promising to keep in touch. The contact lifted her spirits. She wasn't cut off from her old life. It was simply a matter of making adjustments.

Bryce came back from the office in good spirits, too, pleased with the meeting he'd had with the managing director, and the business being done in this branch of Templar Resources. They had an early dinner and talked over what position Sunny could take on in the Los Angeles office, discussing various exciting options.

All in all, Sunny went to bed that night a happy woman, and her happiness with her new husband was shiningly evident at the family gathering the next day. Bryce's personal charisma was so powerful, doubts about *her* hasty marriage were obviously squashed within minutes, wariness switching almost instantly to pleasure in his company. Even her brothers-in-law were impressed, keen to ask Bryce's opinion on anything and everything.

He was especially good with her sisters' children, paying kind attention to the toddlers when they demanded it. Sunny was highly gratified that he fitted in as one of the family, though she doubted Bryce was used to sitting in an ordinary middle-class home, nor having the kind of rowdy lunch her family engaged in.

'Well, he's certainly something,' her mother acknowledged, when the four women were in the kitchen cleaning up after a very elaborate and celebratory meal. Her eyes twinkled delighted approval as she gave Sunny a hug.

'A hunk plus!' Alyssa agreed, rolling her eyes appreciatively.

'Yes, I can see why Derek got his nose out of joint when Bryce stopped him from seeing you,' Nadine dryly commented.

Sunny gave her an exasperated look. 'Bryce didn't *stop* Derek from seeing me. Derek waylaid us and did his nasty best to turn Bryce against me. Which, I'm thankful to say he failed to do.'

Nadine grimaced. 'I meant the night before when Derek followed your luggage to the MGM Hotel. He wanted to make up with you, and Bryce blocked him out.'

Sunny's mind whirled, remembering Bryce had left her in the bath, saying he'd been called down to the lobby to deal with an urgent problem. Derek... demanding to see her? Wanting to right the wrongs between them?

What had Bryce said to him?

Was this why Derek had been so virulent the next morning? So virulent, she had agreed to marry Bryce then and there!

'To be faced with Bryce...' Nadine went on with a shrug. '...poor Derek simply wasn't a match for him.'

'No, he's not,' Sunny grated. 'And I wish you'd drop the subject of *poor* Derek, Nadine. I was running a very *poor* second to his gambling addiction before I even met Bryce.'

'Sorry. I just meant...well, I'd choose Bryce, too.' She grinned to smooth over her gaffe. 'Who wouldn't?'

It was a question Sunny kept asking all afternoon— *who wouldn't?*—but the sparkle had gone out of the day for her. Bryce hadn't exactly lied about Derek's first foray to the MGM Hotel, but he had certainly omitted telling her. She might not have chosen to see Derek that night, but Bryce had clearly removed any choice, ruthlessly removed it, intent on keeping her with him until...until she married him.

Why?

Not out of love for her.

He needed a wife to please his father.

Kristen was demanding too much.

He preferred Sunny...*the bargain basement bride!*

It was difficult to keep up a facade of happily wedded bliss while this inner torment churned through her, but Sunny managed it. Pride made her keep pretending everything was perfect, though she barely kept her own tears at bay when her mother got teary at their leave-taking. It was an enormous relief when the chauffeured limousine pulled away from her cheerfully waving family and she could relax back in the plushly cushioned seat and close her eyes.

'Exhausted?' Bryce asked sympathetically.

'Yes,' she muttered, keeping her eyes shut, not wanting to look at him.

As he had in the plane, he took her hand, interlacing their fingers in a possessive grip. Sunny raised her lashes a little to stare down at the linked hands, at the emerald ring glinting up at her. She was married to this man, committed to having a family with him. If she didn't have his love, at the very least she needed honesty from him.

'I thought the day went well,' he commented.

'Yes, you handled my family brilliantly.'

It was what he'd said of her meeting with his father. He'd probably handled *her* brilliantly, too, all along, from the moment he decided she should be his wife instead of Kristen.

'It wasn't hard. They're nice people.'

'I'm glad you think so.'

'Need some quiet time now?'

'Yes.'

He said nothing more until they walked into their

hotel suite and the door was closed behind them. Sunny was working herself up to confront him with what Nadine had told her when he softly asked, 'Want to tell me what's wrong?'

The question hit all the raw places in Sunny's heart. She swung on him, words shooting out of her mouth in a bitter spurt. 'What? So you can fix it, Bryce?' Her eyes hotly accused as her tongue ran on. 'You're very good at that, aren't you? Fixing things to be how *you* want them.'

'And you, Sunny,' he said in a calm, quiet tone. 'I care very much about how you want them, too.'

'You have no right to decide that for me, Bryce,' she retorted fiercely, inflamed by his air of unshakeable control.

He lifted his hands in appeal. 'What have I decided without discussing it with you?'

'Derek! You stopped him from seeing me and didn't even tell me he'd come to try for a reconciliation.'

His face visibly tightened. The green eyes flared with violent feeling. 'You throw him up at me? A man who knew you so little he could abuse you in terms that I knew were false on just one day's acquaintance with you?'

'How do I know you didn't give him reason to think those things, Bryce? To get rid of him so you'd have a clear running track for what you wanted.'

'Your relationship with him was finished.' He hurled an arm out in savage dismissal. 'You acted on that. Why wouldn't I act on it?'

'He came to see me. Not you. You had no right to...'

'You gave me the right by being in *my* suite, *my* bath...' His eyes glittered with angry possessiveness as they raked her up and down. '...*my* bed!'

Sunny clenched her hands, fighting the sexual power he projected. 'You didn't *own* me, Bryce.'

'You were with me,' he asserted, his eyes burning that undeniable truth straight through her defences. 'Why would I let a drunken fool whom you had rejected, violate the intimacy you were sharing with me?'

Her mind spun on one point she hadn't known. 'He was drunk?'

'And creating trouble.'

'Trouble because you wouldn't let him see me,' she shot at him, determined not to get distracted from the main issue here.

'He had lost the right to demand anything of you, Sunny.'

The mention of *rights* exploded any gain he'd made with his picture of a drunken Derek. She stormed around the suite, putting distance between them, seething at his arrogance in making that judgment. Which he'd clearly made to suit *his purpose*.

Never mind that she'd been hurt by her belief that Derek seemingly hadn't even noticed her absence that night. Bryce hadn't cared about her feelings, except in so far as making them more positive towards him. She swung around to accuse him of it, noting he hadn't moved. He stood tautly watching her, channelling all his energy into working out how to achieve his ends this time.

'The truth is...you weren't going to give him any second chance, were you, Bryce?'

'He'd had his chance with you and blew it,' he grated.

'That was for me to decide.'

She saw him gather himself, shoulders straightening, his formidable chest lifting, strength of mind emanating powerfully from him as he stepped towards her, his gaze holding hers with mesmerising intensity.

'What are you telling me, Sunny? You would have had him back?'

It was a pertinent question, challenging where she stood as he closed on her. Sunny's chin lifted defiantly. Just because she had married him didn't mean she would overlook how he had dealt with possible opposition.

'I'll never know now, will I?' she flung at him. 'I didn't hear what he had to say.'

Bryce kept coming, relentlessly determined on his will prevailing. 'You heard him the next morning,' he pointedly reminded her.

'Yes, I heard him.' Her heart was pounding. He was so big, so indomitable, and one perverse side of her liked the fact he wouldn't be beaten. Yet he shouldn't have taken her choice out of her hands. 'And I wonder now what you said to him the night before.'

'I told him we were negotiating a new position for you in Los Angeles and I didn't care to have our discussion interrupted,' came the imperturbable reply.

'Did he fight that?' she instantly queried, knowing she would have fought, as she was fighting now for integrity in her relationship with Bryce.

'Yes.' Contempt flashed into his eyes. 'He lied, claiming you were his fiancée, which I knew you no longer were. I faced him with the lie and told him you were free to contact him at any time...*if* you wanted to.' His hands curled around her upper arms, pressing his truth. 'But you didn't want to, Sunny. You wanted to be with me.'

'I thought there was nothing left with Derek,' she argued, resenting the way he was boxing her into a corner.

'He's not worth the candle you're burning for him, and you know it,' he insisted. 'You liked what you had with me. You wanted it.'

Her eyes warred with the blazing certainty in his, yet she couldn't deny the wanton desire he stirred in her. 'What I've learnt from this, Bryce, is that you play to win,' she bit out angrily. 'Whatever it takes, you play to win.'

'You're right. I do play to win,' he conceded with ruthless intent. One hand slid up and tangled in her hair at the nape of her neck. 'That's the kind of man you married, Sunny.'

She couldn't bring herself to move or even protest. Her mind screamed it was wrong to feel excited by the electric energy swirling from him, yet her whole body was tingling, and when he spoke again, his voice seemed to throb through her bloodstream.

'I wanted you as my wife. I got you as my wife. And I'll do everything in my power to keep you as my wife.'

Then he kissed her.

# CHAPTER FIFTEEN

BRYCE lay awake in the darkness long after Sunny had fallen asleep in his arms. She had responded to him as she always did, caught up in the storm of desire that raged through them, demanding every possible satisfaction. His mind kept hotly buzzing *she was his*. But a more chilling section of his brain acknowledged he had *made* her his.

He had blocked Marsden out and seized the advantage of the rebound effect, refusing to believe that such a stupid loser could possibly be the better man for Sunny. He still didn't believe it. Yet why relationships worked for the people involved was often perplexing to an outside viewpoint. Needs could go right back to a person's roots and seem totally illogical to anyone who hadn't lived that life.

Yes, he'd won the play. Sunny was *his* wife. Yet if her emotions were still tied up with that guy...what did he have? The use of her body. Not long ago he might have thought that was enough. Certainly he'd expected no more from Kristen. But Sunny...

Somehow everything was different with Sunny. He wanted the whole package—heart, body and soul. Why she inspired this craving for all of her he didn't know, but he knew he wouldn't be content until he had it.

The black irony was he'd felt their honeymoon had

moved her much closer to him. It had been a risk coming to Sydney so soon, but it was the appropriate course to take—meeting Sunny's family and collecting what she wanted of her clothes and other possessions—and he'd thought he had the risk covered.

Sherman had straightened Marsden out about the legal consequences of malicious slander and damage during his stopover in Los Angeles. There'd been no loose talk at the Sydney office when he'd resigned— of his own free will, no pressure involved on that front. Bryce hadn't been anticipating any comebacks.

Careful questioning of the managing director had assured him the resignation was interpreted as a matter of pride. And given Marsden's lack of career interest at the conference, he wasn't considered a loss to the company. On the business side, the field had been cleared. It was the personal side that had slipped past him.

Marsden had mouthed off to one of the family.

So who had been tactless enough to face Sunny with her ex-fiancé's rantings? Her mother? No. Too kind-hearted. Alyssa? No. She'd been happily positive about the marriage. He doubted Alyssa would have done anything to take the shine off it. Which left Nadine. Little flashes of envy there. She was the most likely candidate, though she probably hadn't meant to undermine Sunny's confidence in her decision to marry him.

The critical question was how much harm had been done. Certainly Marsden had been brought right back to the forefront of Sunny's mind, and what had been clear-cut on the morning of their wedding day, was now muddied. Somehow he had to get Sunny positive about their marriage again. Wipe Marsden right out of the picture.

She was quiet the next morning. Bryce sensed she was both mentally and emotionally withdrawn from him as she moved about the suite, getting ready for their departure. He controlled his frustration as best he could, but when they sat down to the breakfast delivered by room service, and Sunny persistently evaded his gaze, the urge to confront came thundering into prominence.

'Would you prefer to be married to Marsden?' he growled.

That lifted her eyelashes. It probably wasn't the smartest question to ask but at least it got her attention.

'I'm married to you, Bryce,' she stated flatly, making it an incontravertible fact that was not up for question.

It goaded him into saying, 'Maybe I don't care for the idea of being married to a woman who's hankering after someone else.'

Her eyes flared to an intense gold. 'I'm not *hankering* after Derek. That would be really stupid, wouldn't it? Given the circumstances.'

'I would have thought so, yes,' he answered tersely.

'Do you consider me stupid?'

'No.'

'Then why do you imagine I'm hankering after him?'

'You're angry with me because I didn't allow him a second chance with you. Which suggests you would have liked that.'

She reached for a piece of toast and buttered it with

slow deliberation, her face completely closed to him. 'I might have given Derek a hearing at the time, but that time has gone,' she said, adding strawberry conserve to the toast. 'I chose to marry you and that's where I am...married to you.'

'You were happy about it until yesterday,' he reminded her.

'I didn't understand that it was about winning.' Her gaze flicked up to meet his. 'I'm sorry to report a setback in your winning play this morning.'

He frowned, completely missing what she meant. 'What do you find wrong in my wanting you as my wife?'

Her mouth curled into a wry little smile. 'Possibly the fact that I'm slow off the mark delivering the rest of what you want, Bryce.'

'Which is?' he prompted, still puzzled by her words and needing more insight on where she was coming from.

'I didn't get pregnant on our honeymoon.'

The blunt statement caught him by surprise. His entire thought process had been focused on her feelings for Marsden. He shook his head, his brain whirling to accommodate this new parameter, to fit it into her behaviour and make a different sense of it.

'Believe it, Bryce,' she said dryly, misinterpreting his confusion. 'My period came this morning.'

He watched her bite into the strawberry-laden toast as though she needed a sweetener for the sour taste that piece of news had left in her mouth.

'You're upset because you're not pregnant?' he blurted out, relieved that *this* was the problem.

'It *is* why we got married...to have a child,' she reminded him, her eyes flashing bleak irony.

'That's what you've been holding in from me this morning? You didn't want to tell me?'

'It is...' she grimaced, her eyes dulling further as she added, '...disappointing.'

Bryce instantly reached across the table and took her free hand in his, gently fondling it. 'I'm sorry you're disappointed, Sunny. But it is only early days in our marriage,' he pressed, wanting to console her. 'I'm sure it will happen. It's probably better that you're not pregnant straight off, what with having to settle into a new home and a new job.'

She stared at him in stunned disbelief. 'Aren't *you* disappointed?'

Bryce hadn't stopped to think about it. He paused for a moment, remembering the motivations he'd spelled out to her. Somehow they didn't seem quite so important now. But having a child *was* important to Sunny, he reminded himself before answering.

'We'll make a baby soon enough,' he warmly assured her.

'But...you wanted this for your father,' she said in obvious bewilderment.

'I don't see that you can force nature for anyone,' he answered reasonably.

'You wanted to give him a grandchild before...before...'

'My father is happy that I've married, Sunny. He's seen for himself we're a good match. He knows we intend to have children. It would be good to give him the news that we're expecting a baby, but it doesn't have to be immediate. Another month or two...' He shrugged, wanting to remove her anxiety.

She shook her head, still disturbed. 'I don't understand why I didn't fall pregnant. We...' She flushed, obviously recalling their intense sexual activity.

'Maybe the pills had some lingering influence. Don't worry about it, Sunny.'

'You're not worried by it?' she queried uncertainly.

'No.' He smiled. 'I'm very happy just having you as my wife.'

Sunny searched his eyes, disbelief warring with the sincerity he was projecting. Was this the truth? He wanted her as his wife first, and his father's needs came second?

'Forget about it. Enjoy your breakfast,' he urged, withdrawing his hand to continue his own meal, his whole demeanour beaming good humour. His eyes twinkled wickedly as he added, 'We have a month of high-level energy business ahead of us.'

He *was* happy. There could be no doubting it. The tense silence, which Sunny had to acknowledge causing herself as she'd battled with the emotional conflict of failing to conceive, was completely banished by a stream of plans from Bryce—plans that were clearly coated with pleasurable anticipation.

She was almost giddy with relief. When they finally left for the airport, she didn't mind at all when Bryce took her hand in the now familiar, possessive grip. It felt more like a symbol of togetherness, a warm, secure promise of his commitment to her.

*His wife...*

Her heart went all mushy at the memory of how

wildly he'd wanted her last night. He'd driven any thought of Derek right out of her mind. Besides, there had been fair reasoning in his argument for having denied Derek a reconciliation bid. Why should he let a potential rival break into the intimacy she had willingly shared with him?

That would have been stupid.

As stupid as her hankering after Derek now.

No way!

She smiled to herself over the realisation that Bryce had been nursing jealous feelings over her supposed lingering attachment to Derek. It wasn't just her body he wanted. Desire was certainly a driving force but there was also a passion for more than sex in their relationship.

A sigh of contentment whispered from her lips, bringing a swift look of concern from Bryce.

'Are you okay, Sunny? If you're in some discomfort from...'

'No.' She smiled to erase any doubt. 'Just glad you're not disappointed.'

He slanted his eyebrows ruefully. 'Well, it does curtail some rather basic pleasures but we'll probably need the rest after this trip anyhow.'

She laughed, happy that he was thinking of just the two of them and not the baby she wasn't having yet.

Next month, she thought.

Next month they would surely have good news to give to his father.

# CHAPTER SIXTEEN

FORTUNATELY there was a dispenser carrying sanitary napkins in the ladies' room. Sunny hadn't come to work prepared for such an unwelcome and demoralising eventuality. She had felt absolutely certain she would fall pregnant this month, even buying a pregnancy test kit ready to confirm the fact, counting the days to when it could be used.

Now this...

She hated her body for betraying her. Why couldn't it co-operate with her dearest wish? And how was she going to tell Bryce they had failed again?

A wave of sickening depression rolled through her. It made no sense that she hadn't conceived when they'd been making love every night. Over and over again she had lain in Bryce's arms, smiling, wondering if it was happening...the miracle of life beginning. Happy dreams...

Except they weren't coming true!

Feeling totally wretched, Sunny walked slowly back to the office Bryce had set up for her in the Los Angeles headquarters of Templar Resources. It was a wonderful office. Normally it gave her pleasure to enter this room, knowing Bryce had every confidence in her ability to carry off her new position as head of sales presentations, advising the team under her and monitoring their results. She had enjoyed the challenge of being in charge.

But she wasn't in charge of her body.

The fear of being infertile started hovering. She sat down at her desk and stared blankly at the printout of figures in front of her. Her womb ached with the draining of hope. It was impossible to concentrate on work. All she could think of was not measuring up to motherhood.

If there was something wrong with her...if she couldn't have a baby...what was this marriage worth? She loved Bryce with all her heart, but if she couldn't give him a child...it just wouldn't be right to even try to hang on to him. He wanted children, and not only to satisfy his father.

As it was, time was slipping away on giving his father a grandchild. Would Bryce start thinking Kristen Parrish might have been the better choice of wife? Sunny shuddered at the unbearable thought. He was *her* man, *her* husband. Yet if she couldn't deliver what he wanted...and he had spelled it out before he'd married her...

A hasty marriage.

Repent at leisure.

The words were coming back to haunt her now.

They should have waited. She should have had tests done first. No doubt Bryce would have insisted on tests during his premarital wrangle with his first choice of wife. Sunny couldn't bring herself to question his potency. She was sure it was beyond question. The fault had to lie with her.

Somehow she dragged herself through the rest of

the working day, though she did cancel a meeting she'd scheduled, too aware of not being able to give her best to it. Her head was pounding by the time Bryce came by her office to collect her for the trip home. She looked at him—this man amongst men— and it was totally heart-ravaging to think she couldn't give him the progeny he deserved.

'Something wrong?' he asked, frowning at her, the perceptive green eyes sharply scanning.

She grimaced. 'Raging headache.'

'Have you taken some pain-killers for it?'

'Yes.'

'Let's get you home then. You don't look at all well.' He took her bag from her, ushered her out of the office, then tucked her arm around his, keeping her close to him for support on the walk to the basement car park. 'Do you suffer from migraines, Sunny?' he asked gently.

'Not as a rule,' she muttered, feeling horribly guilty for letting his sympathy flow over her instead of telling him the cause of her pain.

'I guess you don't feel like talking,' he said, his understanding making the guilt even worse.

She had to tell him. He had the right to know. It couldn't be hidden anyhow. Sheer misery made her hold her tongue until they were in his car and heading for home, but her sense of fairness forced her to speak at the first long traffic stoppage on the freeway.

'I've got my period again,' she blurted out.

She sensed more than saw his head jerk towards her. Her own gaze was fixed on the road ahead. Her hands were clenched in her lap. She could barely stop herself from bursting into tears.

Then a big warm hand covered hers. 'I'm sorry, Sunny,' came the soft, gruff words. 'I know how much you were counting on being pregnant this time.'

The tears welled and spilled over. She had to bite her lips against breaking into sobs. Speech was impossible. The traffic started moving again and Bryce returned his hand to the driving wheel. She heard him heave a deep sigh and that was the worst thing of all…knowing how he must be feeling now.

Overlooking her first failure was one thing. They'd only been married two weeks and the contraceptive pills she'd been using might have messed up any chance of getting pregnant. There simply wasn't any reason for failing this month. If she was fertile, there should be a baby growing inside her right now. Bryce had to know that as certainly as she did.

She swiped the stream of tears from her cheeks and leaned forward, fumbling in the bag at her feet for some tissues. Her make-up was probably running everywhere. Not only was she a mess inside, she was fast becoming a mess outside, as well. She grabbed the little packet of tissues she always carried with her and sat back again, removing a couple to mop up her face.

'Please don't take it so much to heart, Sunny,' Bryce said quietly. 'It's not unusual for many couples to try for months before…'

'We're not just any couple!' she cried. 'You know we're not.'

He sighed again.

She closed her eyes and willed the tears to dry up.

'I'm sorry,' Bryce murmured. 'If you're worrying about my father...I just wish you'd stop. I hate seeing you in this state.'

She took a deep breath, trying to ease the tightness in her chest. Nothing could ease the pain in her heart. She understood that Bryce didn't want to see her weeping. Men were invariably uncomfortable with displays of deep emotional stress. Apart from which, he undoubtedly had his own inner dismay to deal with. He'd married her to have a child, the child was not forthcoming, and it was certainly not from any slack performance on his part.

Sunny had no idea how long it took to drive to their home in Santa Monica. Bryce remained silent and her mind was in a total ferment. Only the rolling open of the garage door, triggered by the remote device in the car, alerted her to the fact that the journey was over and facing up to the situation with Bryce was now imminent.

Her legs were hopelessly shaky as she walked ahead of him along the short hallway that led from the garage to the space-age kitchen with its gleaming stainless steel surfaces. Her churning stomach refuted any idea of food. Preparing any dinner for them was beyond her tonight. She went past the kitchen, wishing she could make a bolt for the staircase and a bed where she could curl up and quietly die, but there really was no hiding place.

'Sunny...'

The concern and soft appeal in Bryce's voice forced her to stop halfway across the open-plan living area. She took a deep breath, straightened her spine, and swung to look back at him. He'd halted by the kitchen serving bench. He gestured towards the refrigerator.

'Can I get you anything?'

Her heart turned over. He wanted to do something for her…help…but there was no help for this.

'A cup of tea?' he suggested, knowing she preferred it to coffee.

'Do you know where I should go to have a fertility test, Bryce?' she asked, determined on not evading the issue.

'Yes, but…' He looked pained by the question.

'I'll go next week. If it turns out that I'm…I'm barren…' What a terrible word that was, so redolent of empty devastation!

'You don't need to put yourself through this, Sunny,' he protested.

'Yes, I do. Both of us need to know if I can or can't have a baby.'

He shook his head.

'If I can't, Bryce, we get a divorce as soon as possible.'

'No!' The negative was harsh and explosive.

Sunny ignored it. 'I won't take you for anything. What's yours will remain yours. You can trust me on that. I'll just go back to Australia and get on with my life.'

'Money has nothing to do with it!' he fiercely claimed.

'I'm glad you understand that,' Sunny shot back at him, undeterred by his vehemence. 'It never did for me,' she continued flatly. 'But a child matters, Bryce. If I can't give you one, it's best we part now.'

'No!' he repeated strongly.

She looked at him with deadly calm washed out eyes. 'You know it. I know it. That's how it is.'

He stared back, his black brows beetled down over eyes burning with the need to wipe out all she'd said. But he couldn't. The equation was irrefutable.

Sunny turned away, forcing her tremulous legs to take one step after another, increasing the distance between them as she made her way up the stairs to the bedroom where their mating had been a delusion. It had not borne fruit. An empty bed…but a soft pillow to bury her misery in.


Bryce watched her walk away from him, too stunned by the bald words she had spoken to make any move. All he could think of was…*did he mean so little to her?*

He didn't want a divorce. Not for any reason. They'd been married almost two months and it had been the best two months of his entire life. He'd felt…truly not alone anymore. Not that he had ever really dwelled on loneliness. He'd considered himself self-sufficient.

But Sunny had filled all the empty spaces that he hadn't even recognised before she came into his life…filled them with warmth and joy, giving him a sheer pleasure in being, in having her with him, in sharing all the things he'd never really shared with anyone.

Divorce!

For the sake of some theoretical child he might have with a Kristen-like replacement?

Could such a child make up for a *barren* marriage?
Everything within Bryce shouted *no!*

He'd just paid out a fortune to be rid of Kristen Parrish and her self-righteous claims, a costly mistake for choosing her in the first place. But choosing Sunny was no mistake. Child or no child, he couldn't bear to even think of living the rest of his life without her.

She was his wife.

His wife in every sense.

He'd won her and nothing was going to stop him from keeping her.

Nothing!

His feet started moving. The adrenaline rush of going into battle carried him up the stairs at a pace that brooked no opposition. He was going to smash any barriers Sunny put up. He would hold her to him, no matter what! His whole body bristled with the ferocity of his feeling. He strode into their bedroom, intent on fighting with everything he could fight with, his heart thundering with the need to win.

One look at Sunny and his intent was instantly blown to pieces. She was scrunched up on the bed, her back turned to him, a back that was heaving with sobs, muffled by the pillow her face was pushed into. She was hugging another pillow for comfort. She'd kicked off her shoes and there was something terribly vulnerable about her stockinged feet, tucked up and rubbing against each other as though they were cold.

It struck him forcefully that this was grief. Heart-breaking grief. Was it possible that she didn't want their marriage to end any more than he did? Maybe she just couldn't see over the hump of not having a child. He couldn't say it didn't matter because it did to her. She wanted to be a mother. But if she couldn't be, he was still her husband and she was still his wife and he had to show her that what they had together was still worth having.

Quietly he took off his suitcoat and tie and dropped them on a chair, freeing himself of constriction. He moved over to the bed, resting one knee on the side of it to get his balance right, then slid his arms under Sunny, scooping her up against his chest, then swinging around to sit and cradle her on his lap.

'Bryce...' she choked out shakily.

'Hush now,' he soothed, pressing her head onto his shoulder and stroking her hair, trying to impart warmth and comfort. 'I want to hold you. I need to hold you, Sunny.'

She shuddered and sagged limply into the cocoon of his embrace, her strength all spent in trying to play straight with him. He simply held her for a while, stroking away the little tremors that shook her, thinking of all she meant to him.

He loved the rare integrity of her heart and mind—her whole character—the way she threw all of herself into whatever she took on, her openness and her honesty. He loved her innate decency, her caring, her sharing. He loved the feel of her, the scent of her, the wonderful sexuality of her. She was his wife.

'I want you to listen to me, Sunny,' he appealed softly. 'Just hear me out...'

\*    \*    \*

She simply didn't have the energy to argue anymore. It was easier to let his words float over her because they couldn't really mean anything. It felt bittersweet being held like this, kindly, protectively, but for a little while she wanted to wallow in the sense of closeness, of Bryce caring for her.

'I know you want to be a mother,' he started slowly. 'I think you should go and have a fertility test next week so you'll know beyond any doubt if motherhood is on the cards for you. This fear you have…you're letting it eat you up, Sunny, letting it take over as though you're not worth anything if you can't have a baby. And that's not true.'

He wasn't getting it right, she thought wearily. It wasn't the end of the world for her if she had to be childless, but it would be the end of her world with him. Why was he holding off from seeing that?

'You're worth a great deal to me,' he continued gruffly. 'You've given me more than I ever imagined any one person could give another. You've shown me…what a woman in a man's life can mean to him…in so many ways…and on so many levels…'

His voice seemed to throb into her mind, his words like slow, deep heartbeats, pulsing with the very essence of *his* life. She was stirred out of the apathy she had fallen into. Her ears prickled with the need to listen, to hear every shade of what he was saying.

His chest rose and fell as he gathered more of his thoughts. 'My father…'

A sick tension gripped Sunny again at the mention of Will Templar.

'My father…is my father.'

He spoke as if searching for a truth he needed to communicate. She found herself holding her breath, listening with every atom of energy she had.

'He's been the only real constant in my life…all my life. And I do feel…an undeniable bond with him. He's my father…'

And they were very alike, very much father and son…a bond that would never be broken, she thought, and one she couldn't fight.

'But you're my wife, Sunny…and I love you. I love you as I've never loved any other person.'

He *loved* her?

'I didn't know what love was…how it could be…'

He swept his mouth over her hair, pressing warm, lingering kisses as though wanting, needing to imprint his feeling on her, and Sunny started tingling with the sweet joy of it, unable to cling to any fearful caution.

'But I do now with you,' he went on fervently. 'And I don't want to lose it. Ever…'

She didn't, either.

'If we can't have a child…believe me, Sunny…I don't want a child with any other woman. You are more important to me than any child could ever be. Having *you* sharing my life…that comes first. I promise you…it will always come first.'

She was swamped by his caring…caring for her…only her…

His hand threaded through her hair and cradled her head, his fingers gently kneading as he made his last bid for the marriage he wanted.

'You said love to you was emotional security. I

don't know what more to do…to prove you have that with me, Sunny.' He took a deep breath and poured out his heart. 'Please…I love you so much. Can you let this pregnancy issue go, and just…*be* with me?'

How could she not?

She loved him.

# CHAPTER SEVENTEEN

SUNNY gazed in adoring fascination at the baby snuggled in the crook of her arm. Her baby. Hers and Bryce's. He was so beautiful, she couldn't stop smiling.

It was possible to look back now and be glad she hadn't fallen pregnant in those first couple of months of their marriage. To Sunny's mind, it was so much better having their child a true child of love and not the result of a marriage bargain. And that was how it had happened in the end.

The most probable cause of her initial infertility was anxiety, the doctor had told her—wanting to get it right for Bryce and his father. There'd been nothing physically wrong with her. Once she had felt emotionally secure in her marriage, she had fallen pregnant the very next month. And here she was...a mother at last.

The footsteps coming along the hospital corridor heralded Bryce's return from the airport. A glance at her watch assured her the time was about right. The clacking heels undoubtedly belonged to her mother who had flown from Sydney to see her new grandchild and stay for a while to give Sunny any help she might need in getting used to motherhood. Voices became more decipherable and she heard Will Templar giving forth.

'Oh, I knew it would be a boy. No surprise at all.'

Sunny rolled her eyes at her father-in-law's smug confidence. His flight from Sedona must have come in at approximately the same time as her mother's for them to have all met up together.

'Bryce was bound to have sons,' he went on proudly.

Sunny almost wished she'd had a daughter. Will Templar was far too fond of getting his own way. Not that she'd swap her darling little boy for any other baby. He had his tiny hand curled around her little finger, and while he might be too young to focus properly, he seemed to be looking straight into her eyes, loving her right back.

Bryce popped his head around the door and grinned at her. 'Ready for visitors?'

'It's showtime,' she said, grinning back at him.

In came her mother, beaming excitement and carrying a big bunch of irises and daffodils. 'Sunny... you look wonderful! And here he is...' She set the flowers on the bed, gave Sunny a kiss, and swept the baby up to cradle him herself. 'Oh, what a bonny boy!'

'Looks just like Bryce,' Will declared, peering over her shoulder.

'Nonsense!' her mother chided indulgently. 'See those curls? He's got Sunny's hair.'

'But it's black, like Bryce's,' Will pointed out, sticking to his judgment.

'Will, your son does not have curls,' her mother said firmly.

'Chip off the old block anyway,' Will muttered.

'Lucky your daughter's got brains as well as beauty, Marion. What we have here is a fine set of genes.'

'There's no luck involved at all, Will. Sunny married a man who matched her.'

'Well, can't go wrong with that combination,' he conceded. 'They're a good pairing. Saw it straight away.'

'Yes. They struck me that way, too. Very much in love.'

It was clear Will Templar considered this a soppy sentiment. 'What's love got to do with it?'

Her mother gave him an archly knowing look. 'Everything.' Then she smiled her perfect understanding at her daughter. 'What are you calling him, Sunny?'

'Adam,' she answered, giving Bryce a quizzical glance that encompassed their separate parents.

He rolled his eyes back at her, indicating there'd been a running altercation between them all the way here.

'Good strong name,' Will approved.

'Yes. It goes well with Templar,' her mother agreed.

'He's my grandson, too, you know,' Will reminded her mother. 'How about letting me hold him?'

'I think you'd better sit down first,' Marion York advised him. 'Sunny told me you had a heart condition.'

'Doctors are fixing that up. Gave me a whole heap of new drugs and they're working,' he declared. 'Do I look like a man with a heart condition?'

In truth, Bryce's father was looking surprisingly well, Sunny thought. He'd put on some weight and his face was a much better colour.

'Well, I must say you look like a man in his prime, Will,' Marion said admiringly, and Will Templar instantly puffed out his chest. She smiled winningly as she added, 'But why not sit down anyway? Much easier to handle a baby sitting down. You haven't had as much practice at it as I have.'

'True. But I'll have you know this grandchild is giving me a new lease on life.' He settled himself in one of the armchairs. 'Give him here.'

Sunny and Bryce exchanged highly amused looks as her mother carefully handed their baby son over to his grandfather who immediately started rocking him to show he knew exactly what a baby liked.

'Isn't he lovely?' her mother cooed.

'A real boy,' Will declared.

Her mother straightened up, positively glowing. She was wearing a plum-coloured pantsuit, a skivvy in a soft shade of wheat, a pretty scarf with a swirl of purple and plum and gold. The colours looked wonderful on her, and her eyes were sparkling, no sign at all that she'd just endured a long flight from Sydney.

'I'll go and find a vase for these flowers, Sunny. Though I don't know where we're going to put them,' she added ruefully, gazing around at the flower-filled room. 'Did Bryce buy out all the florist shops in Los Angeles?'

'Only the red roses are from me,' Bryce told her. 'Sunny has a knack of making lots of friends.'

'We can move something, Mum,' Sunny assured her. 'I love the irises and daffodils.'

'Good!' She gathered up the bouquet. 'I won't be long, dear.'

Off she went with Will Templar gazing after her admiringly before commenting to Sunny, 'Fine-looking woman, your mother. Think I'll stay on in L.A. and make sure she enjoys herself here.'

'Dad, you do have to take care with that heart of yours,' Bryce quietly reminded him.

It earned a flash of proud defiance. 'I'm not dead yet, boy.' He looked down at his new grandson. 'He's the future but I'm still very much alive,' he muttered. 'No reason I can't take a sixth wife.'

Bryce and Sunny burst into laughter.

The new grandfather didn't understand their amusement.

'You wouldn't want to be doing anything hasty, Dad,' Bryce advised with mock solemnity.

'No,' said Sunny. 'A hasty marriage might not work.'

'Did for you,' Will Templar argued. 'I don't see you two repenting at leisure.'

'No repentance at all,' Bryce agreed.

'And not likely to be,' Sunny chimed in.

Whereupon, Bryce sat on the bed next to her and drew her into his embrace. 'Hi, new Mom,' he murmured.

'Hi, new Dad,' she answered, winding her arms around his neck. 'I love you Bryce Templar, and I still fancy you rotten.'

'Likewise.'

Then he kissed her.

# INHERITED:
# ONE NANNY

## *Emma*
# DARCY

To Sue—for flaunting her fortieth birthday
with a brilliant party where my friends Dr Nick
Smith, Dr Geoffrey McCarthy and Dr Harvey
Adams happily informed me of the etiquette
in delivering the results of a pregnancy test
and insisted I acknowledge their
contribution to this story.

# CHAPTER ONE

A NANNY?

The question had niggled Beau Prescott on and off throughout the fourteen hour flight from Buenos Aires to Sydney. It had reared its tantalising head from the very first reading of his grandfather's will, pertinently included with all the other official notices sent to him in the solicitor's packet. Now that his journey home was almost over and he was about to get answers, it pushed once more to the forefront of his mind.

Why on earth had his grandfather employed a nanny for the last two years of his life? And why was she listed in the will as another responsibility to be inherited by Beau, along with the rest of the family retainers?

A nanny made no sense to him. There weren't any children living in his grandfather's household. None he knew of anyway. Certainly none had been named in the will. There seemed absolutely no point in including a nanny—whoever she was—amongst the staff who were to remain as his dependents for at least another year, if not for the rest of their lives.

It was different with the others. Beau was completely in sympathy with looking after Mrs. Featherfield who was virtually an institution as his grandfather's house-keeper. Sedgewick, the butler, and Wallace, the chauffeur, had almost equal longevity. As for Mr. Polly, the head gardener, tipping him out of his beloved grounds was inconceivable. Each one of them deserved every consideration. But a nanny-come-lately without any children to mind?

Beau turned her name over in his mind...Margaret Stowe. Margaret sounded rather old-fashioned, spinsterish. For some reason he linked Stowe with stowaway. She could be a lame-dog nanny, fallen on hard times. His grandfather had a habit of taking in the occasional oddity, putting them on their feet again. But two years of largesse and an inclusion in the will seemed a bit much.

"We will be landing at Mascot on schedule," the pilot announced. "The weather is fine, current temperature nineteen degrees Celsius. Forecast for today is..."

Beau looked out his window and felt his stomach curl, hit by a wave of grief he'd been holding at bay since he'd received the news of his grandfather's death. The distinctive features of Sydney were spread out below, the predominance of red roofs, the harbour, the bridge, the opera house. This view had always meant coming home to him. But home had also meant Vivian Prescott, the man who'd taken in his orphaned eight-year-old grandson and given him the world as his playground.

Not so much of a grandfather as a grand person, Beau thought, keenly feeling the huge bite that had been taken so abruptly, so shockingly out of his life. Vivian Prescott had lived on a grand scale, had cultivated a grand approach to everything he'd done. His heart should have been grand enough to last a lot longer.

Vivian…now there was a name that would make most men cringe. The Prescott family had a history of bestowing eccentric names. Beau had often winced over his, but his grandfather…never! He'd rejoiced in having one he considered uniquely his. "It means *life,* my boy. And *joie de vivre* is what I'm about."

He'd carried it with such panache, he'd made it perfectly acceptable, a natural extension of his highly individual personality, a positive expression of artistic flair and style, a provocative emphasis to the wickedly teasing twinkle in his ever-young eyes. It was almost impossible to believe he was actually gone and it hurt like hell not to have been there with him before he died.

A spurt of anger overlaid the grief. Damn it all! His grandfather had no business dying at eighty-six. He'd always boasted he'd live to a hundred, smoking his favourite cigars, drinking the best French champagne, a pretty woman hanging on each arm as he swanned through all the glittering charity events on his social calendar. He'd loved life too much to ever let go of it.

Beau heaved a sigh to relieve the tightness in his chest and told himself it was futile foolishness to feel cheated of more time with his grandfather. The fault was in his own complacency for letting almost three years go by without a visit home. It was all very well to excuse himself on the grounds of finding South America an explorer's paradise. A trip home now and then wouldn't have been a hardship. It simply had never occurred to him that the old man's long run of good health might be failing.

There'd been no hint of it in his letters. But then

there'd been no mention of a nanny, either. Beau frowned again over the vexing puzzle. If his grandfather had been sick, surely he would have hired a nurse, not a nanny. Unless...no, he couldn't—wouldn't—believe his grandfather had gone the least bit senile. There had to be some other answer.

The plane landed. The moment it stopped, Beau was out of his seat and opening the overhead locker for his flight bag, wanting to be off with as little delay as possible.

"May I help you, Mr. Prescott?"

It was the cute air hostess who'd been so eager and willing to look after his every need on the trip. Beau flashed her a smile. "No, I'm fine, thank you." She was a honey but he wasn't interested in taking up the invitation in her eyes. His mind was on serious business, no room for play.

Nevertheless, he was aware of her lustful once-over as he moved past her to the exit tunnel and felt a slight twinge of regret. He'd been womanless for a while, busy mapping out a new trek up the Amazon. Still, he'd never had a problem attracting a woman when he was ready for one. Being over six feet tall and having a body packed with muscles seemed to be a turn-on to most of them, even when he looked scruffy from being too long in uncivilised areas.

His mouth twitched as he remembered his grandfather calling it *his curse*. "It's too easy for you, my boy, and if you keep taking the pickings, you'll never know the fruits of settling down with a good woman."

"I have no interest in settling down, Grandpa," he'd answered.

It was still true three years later, yet his grandfather's reply plucked at his conscience now.

"Beau, you're thirty years old. It's time you thought of having children. As it stands, you're the last of our family line, and I for one, don't like the thought of our gene pool coming to an end. It's our only claim to immortality, having a line that goes on after we die."

Had the old man been feeling his mortality then?

"Grandpa, there's no time limit on a man to have children," he'd argued. "Didn't Charlie Chaplin have them into his nineties? I bet you could still have one yourself."

"You need to stick around to bring them up right. Think about it, Beau. Your parents weren't much older than you are now when their plane crashed in Antarctica. No second chances for them. If you don't take time out from your travelling to get married and start a family, it may be too late before you know it."

Too late…misery dragged at Beau's heart. Too late to say goodbye to the wonderful old man who'd given him so much. Too late to say one last thank-you. Too late to even attend the funeral, held while Beau was still deep in the Amazon valley, out of range of any modern form of communication.

All he could do now was carry out his grandfather's will as it had been set out for him, even to keeping a useless nanny in his employ for another year. And making Rosecliff—the Prescott palace—his residence for the same period of time.

Maybe the latter was his grandfather's solution to making his footloose grandson stay still for a while, long enough to marry and start a family. Beau shook his head in wry dismissal of the idea. He wasn't ready

for it. He felt no need for it. Making it happen would
be wrong for everybody concerned. Scouting Europe
was next on his agenda. He wasn't about to set that
aside, and it was plain irresponsible to establish a nest
he knew he'd be flying out of.

His long-legged stride beat all the other passengers
to the immigration counter. He was through that bit
of officialdom in no time and luckily his duffel bag
was amongst the first pieces of luggage on the carou-
sel. Having hefted it onto his back, and with nothing
to declare, Beau headed straight for the arrival hall.

As he came down the ramp he spotted Wallace, his
grandfather's chauffeur, smartly attired in the uniform
he was so proud of—convinced it added a dignified
stature to his shortness—and clearly determined on
maintaining the correct standard of service.

The sense of emptiness that had been eating at Beau
was suddenly flooded with warmth. Wallace had taught
him everything he knew about cars. Wallace had acted
as father-confessor through troubled times. Wallace
was much more than a chauffeur. He was family and
had been since Beau was eight years old.

"It is so good to see you, sir," Wallace greeted in
heartfelt welcome, his eyes moistening.

Beau hugged him, moved by affection and a rush
of protectiveness, patting him on the back as though
the wiry little man was now the child in need of comfort. He had to be feeling the loss of Vivian Prescott
as much, if not more than Beau. Wallace was in his
late fifties and though spry for his age and certainly
competent at his job, probably too old to start over with
a new employer. His future was undoubtedly feeling

very uncertain. Beau silently vowed to fix that, one way or another.

"I'm sorry I wasn't here, Wallace," he said, drawing back to re-establish appropriate dignity.

"Nothing you could have done for him, sir," came the quick assurance. "No warning. He just went in his sleep, like he always said he wanted to, right after a bang-up party. As Nanny Stowe says, the Angel of Death took him kindly."

The unctious Angel of Death declaration instantly conjured up a complacently righteous woman stuffed full of sweet homilies. Beau barely stopped himself from rolling his eyes. He had to bite his tongue, as well. Nanny Stowe clearly had Wallace's respect. Giving voice to a stomach-felt, "Yuk!" was definitely out of place.

He managed a smile. "Well, a bang-up party was certainly Grandpa's style."

"That it was, sir. Always had marvellous parties."

Beau's smile turned into a rueful grimace. "I should have at least been here to organise a fitting funeral for him."

"Not to worry, sir. Nanny Stowe took care of it."

"Did she now?"

Beau balefully added officious busybody to complacent and sickeningly righteous. How dare a mere nanny take over his grandfather's funeral? Sedgewick would have known what was required, having butlered for Vivian Prescott for nigh on thirty years, but a nanny who hadn't rated highly enough to be mentioned by his grandfather while he was alive? Beau was deeply offended at the high-handedness of the woman. Who the hell did she think she was?

"Well, let's get on home. The sooner the better," he said, feeling distinctly eager to let Nanny Stowe know her presumptuous reign of authority was over.

"Can I take your bags, sir?"

"This one." He handed over the flight bag for Wallace to feel useful. "Might as well leave the other on my back." The little man's knees would probably buckle under the weight of it.

"I could get a luggage trolley, sir."

"Waste of time." He waved towards the exit doors and set off, steering Wallace into accompanying him through the crowd of people still waiting for other arrivals. "I'd like you to tell me about the funeral," he added through gritted teeth, wanting to know the worst before he met the interloping nanny.

The chauffeur looked pleased to oblige. "We did him proud, sir. As Nanny Stowe said, it had to be a grand funeral for a grand man. And so it was, sir."

"How grand, Wallace?' Beau demanded, extremely dubious that Nanny Stowe would have a full appreciation of his grandfather's scale of grandness.

"Well, sir, we started with a splendid service in St. Andrew's Cathedral. It was packed. People overflowing outside and on the streets. Couldn't fit everyone in. Nanny Stowe got the notification list together and it included all the charity boards your grandfather sat on, all his friends from far and wide, politicians, everyone from the arts. It was a big, big turn-up."

At least she got that much right, Beau brooded.

"You know how your grandfather loved handing out red roses…"

His trademark.

"You've never seen as many red roses as there were

in that cathedral. I reckon Nanny Stowe must have cornered the market on them. They covered the casket, too. And everyone who came to the service was handed a red rose in remembrance."

A nice touch, Beau grudgingly conceded.

They emerged from the hall into bright morning sunshine. A sparkling blue-sky day, Beau thought, his spirits lifting slightly. The chauffeur pointed to where the car was parked and they turned in that direction.

"Go on, Wallace," Beau urged. "Describe the service to me."

"Well, sir, the boys' choir sang beautifully. They started off with 'Prepare ye the way for The Lord' from the musical, *Godspell*. It was one of his favourites, as you know. Loved the theatre, your grandfather did."

"Yes. It gave him a lot of pleasure," Beau agreed, beginning to have a bit more respect for Nanny Stowe. The woman did have some creative thought, though it probably stemmed from an ingrained attention to detail. A nitpicking fusspot came to mind, nothing escaping her eye or ear. Nevertheless, his grandfather would have relished the theatrical note at his funeral service so however it came about could not be overly criticised.

"Sir Roland from the Arts Council made a wonderful speech..."

His grandfather's closest friend. The obvious choice.

"The bishop got a bit heavy with his words, I thought, but the readings from the bible were just right. Nanny Stowe chose them. All about generosity of spirit."

"Mmmh...' Beau wondered if Nanny Stowe was plotting to spark generosity of spirit in him, too.

The Rolls-Royce was parked, as usual, in a No Park-

ing zone. Beau reminded himself to ask Wallace how
he got away with that, but he had other things on his
mind right now.

"The choir finished with a very stirring 'Amazing Grace.' Beautiful, it was," Wallace went on, as he
opened the trunk of the car to load in Beau's luggage.
"Then at the graveside, we had a lone piper playing
tunes of glory. Sedgewick thought of that. Your grandfather was very partial to a pipe band when he was in
his cups, if you'll pardon the expression, sir."

"Good for Sedgewick." Beau warmly approved.
Nanny Stowe hadn't known everything! She'd probably be the type to follow the "early to bed, early to
rise" maxim and had never witnessed his grandfather
in his cups.

"What about the wake?" he asked, freeing himself
of the duffel bag.

"Oh, we all knew what your grandfather would want
there, sir. Oceans of French champagne, caviar, smoked
salmon, pickled quails' eggs…everything he liked best.
Mrs. Featherfield and Sedgewick made the list and
Nanny Stowe got it all in. She said the cost was not to
be a consideration. I hope that was right, sir."

"Quite right, Wallace."

Though he'd certainly be checking the accounts. A
blithe disregard for expenses was fine for his grandfather. For such an attitude to be adopted by the ubiq-
uitous Nanny Stowe raised a few ugly suspicions about
where the money went. Feathering her own nest before
the grandson and heir arrived might be right down her
stowaway alley.

As he dumped the duffel bag in the trunk, Beau was
wondering if the family solicitor had been holding a

watching brief on his grandfather's estate while all this had been going on. Surely his legal responsibility didn't begin and end with posting off a set of official documents to Buenos Aires.

Beau was champing at the bit by the time Wallace had ushered him into the back seat of the Roller. Home first to scout the nanny situation, then straight off to check the legal position. However, there was one burning question that couldn't wait. As soon the car was in motion, he asked it.

"Why did my grandfather acquire a nanny, Wallace?"

"Well, you know how he liked to have his little jokes, sir. He said he needed to have a nanny on hand, ready to look after him when he slid into his second childhood since there was no telling when it might happen at his age."

That seemed to be taking provident care a bit far. "Was there any sign of encroaching second childhood, Wallace? Please be frank with me."

"Not at all, sir. Mr. Prescott was the same as he ever was, right up until the night he...um...passed over."

At least he was saved the Angel of Death this time. "But he kept the nanny on regardless," Beau probed for more information.

"Yes, sir. Said she was better for him than a gin and tonic."

Beau frowned. "She didn't stop him drinking, did she?"

"Oh, she wouldn't have dreamed of doing that, sir." Wallace sounded quite shocked at the idea. "Nanny Stowe is very sociable. Very sociable."

And knew which side of her bread was buttered,

Beau thought darkly, making sure she kept in good with everyone. There seemed no point in further questioning. Nanny Stowe had Wallace sucked right in. He wasn't about to say a bad word about the woman, despite her staying on so long without any nanny duties to perform. Such dalliance smacked of very dubious integrity to Beau. He was glad the chance to make his own judgment on her was fast approaching.

"Do you mind if I use the car phone to call Sedgewick, sir? He particularly asked to let him know when we were on our way."

Beau couldn't resist one dry remark. "I'm surprised it isn't Nanny Stowe who wants to know."

"Sedgewick will inform her, sir."

Of course. "Go right ahead, Wallace. I wouldn't deprive anyone of the chance to put out the welcome mat for me."

And he hoped Nanny Stowe would be standing right in the middle of it, shaking in her boots!

# CHAPTER TWO

FEELING EXTREMELY NERVOUS about meeting Beau Prescott, Maggie once more studied the photograph Vivian had insisted she keep.

"That's my boy, Beau. *The wild child.*"

Her mouth curved whimsically at the epithet given to his grandson. The photograph was three years old, taken at Vivian's eighty-second birthday party, and the handsome hunk filling out a formal dinner suit in devastating style could hardly be called a child. Though there was an air of boyish recklessness in his grin, and a wild devil dancing in his eyes.

Green eyes. They were certainly very attractive set in a deeply tanned face and framed with streaky blond hair so thick it hadn't been fully tamed for the formality of the photograph. Nevertheless, its somewhat shaggy state was rather endearing, softening the hard, ruggedness of a strong-boned face and a squarish jaw. He had a nice mouth, the lips well-defined, neither too full nor too thin. He looked good, no doubt about it, but looks weren't everything.

"Tame him long enough to get him to the marriage altar and father a child with you, and Rosecliff and all that goes with it will be yours, Maggie."

How many times had Vivian put that proposition to her in the past two years? A challenging piece of mischief, Maggie had always thought, a running bit of fun between them. She'd never taken it seriously, usually making a joke of it—"What would I want with him? You've spoilt me for younger men, Vivian. None of them have your *savoire faire* or charisma."

—or shrugging it off—"

I might not like him, Vivian. And there's no way I'd marry a man without at least liking him."

"Every woman likes Beau," was his stock answer.

"Well, he might not like me," she'd argued.

"What's not to like?"

Maggie had always let the banter slide at that point. Putting herself down in any shape or form was against her principles. She had a long history of a lot of mean people wanting to squash self-esteem out of her, treating her as worthless and of no account in the world, and she had determinedly risen above it. Nevertheless, too many disappointments had taught her liking could not be counted upon.

It had been one of the miracles of coming to this marvellous place, everyone on the staff liking her, welcoming her into the family, so to speak, and not a mean bone in any of them. Vivian had said she was his nanny and despite his highly eccentric notion of her job with him, she'd been accepted into the household as Nanny Stowe as though it were a perfectly normal position.

Vivian's oft-repeated idea of her roping in the wild child to extend the family line and ensure a succession of Prescotts at Rosecliff also met with general approval.

It was, of course, a totally mad idea.

Except it wasn't quite so mad anymore.

It was beginning to feel very much like a burden of responsibility.

Maggie shook her head, hopelessly uncomfortable with the pressure to perform. Yet it was there, and she couldn't shrug it off. Nor could she bring herself to snuff out the hope that was riding on her shoulders. People she cared about were hurting. And there was also the sense of not letting Vivian down.

"You weren't here. You have no idea how it is," she said accusingly to the photograph. "You shouldn't have been off in the wilds, Beau Prescott."

They'd had to handle it all without him. After the first couple of grief-stricken days following Vivian's untimely death, everyone had been so busy trying to get the funeral right, none of them had looked beyond it. Only when the funeral was over, did the loss really hit, and then the solicitor had come to spell out where they stood.

The one-year residency clause in the will had brought home the fact that Vivian Prescott was gone— really gone—and Rosecliff now belonged to his grandson who clearly had no use for it since he was always off travelling. After the stipulated year, the property could be sold or disposed of as he saw fit. Vivian Prescott's reign here was over, and so were their lives with him.

Maggie knew she could always fall on her feet somewhere else. At twenty-eight she was young enough to cope with a downturn in fortune and she'd had plenty of practice at making do with odd jobs in the years before meeting Vivian Prescott. Flexibility was her strong point. Though it would be hard leaving this magical mansion and its magnificent setting. Harder still leav-

ing the people who had given her the sense of being
part of a real family.

However, it was like the end of their world for Mrs.
Featherfield, and Sedgewick and Wallace and Mr.
Polly. As young at heart as they all were, they would
be viewed by other employers as at retirement age. If
Beau Prescott decided to sell Rosecliff, where would
they go? What would they do? Who would have them?

This was home to them. They didn't want to be
split up. They didn't want to be dumped on the useless
scrapheap, surviving on pensions. They weren't old.
They had at least another twenty good years in them.
Probably more.

The flurry of fear added a further weight of grief.

Then Sedgewick had remembered.

He'd stood up, elegantly tall and splendidly dignified, his ingrained authority providing a point of calm
in the storm. His big, soulful brown eyes had fastened
on Maggie, and there was not the slightest bit of tremulous doubt in his delivered opinion.

"Nanny Stowe, you can save us. Mr. Vivian wanted
you to."

She'd shaken her head sadly. "I'm terribly sorry,
Sedgewick. I simply don't have the power to change
his will."

"You promised him...I heard you...the very night
Mr. Vivian died. It was just before the guests arrived
for the party and he asked me to pour you both a glass
of champagne, remember?"

"Yes. But we were only chatting..."

"No. He said—I distinctly remember it—*Promise
me you'll give it a chance with Beau when he comes*

*home.* And you did. You clicked glasses with him and gave your promise."

"It was only funning, Sedgewick."

"Oh no! No, no, no, no!" Mrs. Featherfield had clucked. "Mr. Vivian was very serious about getting Master Beau married off to you, Nanny Stowe. He talked about it many, many times...to all of us," she'd added significantly.

"Always treated you like one of the family," Wallace had chimed in. "That's where his sights were set. Getting it legal."

Mr. Polly, his glorious gardens under threat of being taken over by someone else—or worse, destroyed by some developer—had stirred himself to put in his sage opinion. "Matter of cross-pollination, getting the two of you together."

"And in the light of Mr. Vivian's passing over that night," Sedgewick had added portentously, "I think everyone must agree you gave him a deathbed promise, Nanny Stowe. One cannot disregard the gravity of a deathbed promise."

"A chance, Sedgewick," Maggie had hastily pleaded. "I only promised to give it a chance. There's no guarantee that Beau Prescott would ever see me as...as a desirable wife. Or, indeed, that I'd see him as a desirable husband."

"But you'll give it a *good* chance, won't you, dear?' Mrs. Featherfield had pressed. "And you do have a year to make the best of it."

"Be assured you will have our every assistance," Sedgewick had declared.

"Hear, hear!" they had all agreed, their eyes pinning Maggie down with their anxious hope.

She had wanted to say again and again it was only a joke, but to Sedgewick and Mrs. Featherfield and Wallace and Mr. Polly, it was deadly serious. Their future was at stake. Making some other life was unthinkable, and their expectations of continuing the status quo into the sunset were riding on her and what Mr. Vivian had wanted.

The truly dreadful part was they had convinced themselves she could bring it off—marry the heir, have his child, and they would all live happily ever after at Rosecliff. The doubts she voiced were brushed aside. Worse…they attacked the doubts by plotting outrageous ways to get around them. The goal was now fixed in their minds and it was so blindingly wonderful, they didn't want to see anything else.

Giving it a chance did not promise a certain result, she had warned each one of them.

And what were their replies?

Sedgewick, bending his head in soulful chiding, "Nanny Stowe, you know what Mr. Vivian always preached. *You must cultivate a positive attitude.*"

Attitude did not necessarily produce miracles!

Mrs. Featherfield, doing her endearing mother hen thing, "Think of a baby. A new baby at Rosecliff. I can't imagine anything more perfect."

Babies were not high on Maggie's agenda. She was only twenty-eight, not thirty-eight!

Wallace, a lecherous twinkle in his eye as he pointedly looked at the long tumbling mass of her red-gold hair. "No need to worry, Nanny Stowe. I can assure you Master Beau will take one look at you and his brain will register—*red hot mamma.* It'll be a piece of cake."

Maggie was not interested in the brain below Beau

Prescott's belt! Not unless there was an engaging brain above it, as well.

Mr. Polly, tending his prize roses. "Nature will take its course, Nanny Stowe. A little help and care and you can always get the result you want."

Marriage, unfortunately, was not a bed of roses. It was a lot more complicated.

Maggie couldn't truthfully claim she absolutely didn't want it. Not having met the man, how could she know one way or the other? Even looking at Beau Prescott's photograph and assessing his physical attractions, she couldn't help feeling terribly uneasy with the situation.

It was fine for Vivian and all the faithful staff to dismiss the possibility of Beau Prescott's not liking her or her not liking him. They didn't *want* to admit the possibility. Maggie, however, had her reservations and many of them.

Besides, when it came to marriage, there was a matter of chemistry, too. Good-looking men had often left Maggie quite cold in the past. They were so full of themselves, there was no room for a two-way relationship. Not really. All they wanted was for a woman to fall on her back for them. Well, no thanks.

But maybe there could be magic with Beau Prescott. He did look very engaging in the photograph. If enough of Vivian had rubbed off on his grandson…

The ache in her heart intensified. Vivian Prescott had given her the most wonderful two years of her life. She hadn't realised quite how much she'd loved that old man until…suddenly he wasn't here anymore… and never would be again.

*Joie de vivre.*

Did his grandson have the same amazing zest to find pleasure in everything? Or make pleasure out of nothing! Or did one have to be old before time became so precious, the need to make the most of it inspired a creative talent for delight?

Her bedside telephone rang.

Maggie dropped the photograph back in the drawer of her writing desk, shutting it away before answering the call which would be from Sedgewick, telling her the real live flesh-and-blood Beau Prescott was on the last lap of his journey home. Her heart fluttered nervously as she picked up the receiver.

"He's earlier than we thought, Nanny Stowe." Sedgewick's plummy tones rang in her ears. "Master Beau does have a way of getting out of airports in record time." A touch of pride there.

They all loved him; Sedgewick, Mrs. Featherfield, Wallace, Mr. Polly. To them Beau Prescott was still their wild child, grown to manhood admittedly, but in no way changed from their long affectionate view of him. They wanted her to love him, too, but that was an entirely different ball game. To Maggie he was a stranger, even though he was Vivian's grandson.

"Did Wallace say how far away they are?" she asked.

"About twenty minutes." A lilt of excitement, anticipation. "I trust you are dressed and ready, Nanny Stowe."

*To knock Beau Prescott's eyes out.* That was the general advice. The plan. Consensus had been absolute—Mr. Vivian would have expected it of her.

"Yes, Sedgewick," she returned dryly. "But I think it best to give Master Beau time to greet you and Mrs. Featherfield before I intrude. After all…"

"Splendid idea! We'll hold him in the vestibule chatting. Then you make your entrance. I do hope you're wearing black, Nanny Stowe. It looks so well against the red carpet on the staircase."

Maggie rolled her eyes. "Yes, Sedgewick, I am wearing black," she assured him. "In mourning. Not for dramatic effect."

"Most appropriate," he warmly approved. "Though you must remember Mr. Vivian's principles, Nanny Stowe. You don't mourn a death. You celebrate a life. We cannot let sadness get in the way of…uh…propelling the future forward."

"Thank you, Sedgewick."

Maggie put the receiver down and heaved a long sigh, needing to relieve some of the tightness building up in her chest. She wandered around the room, trying to work off her inner agitation. Then on impulse, she opened the French doors that led onto the balcony and stepped outside.

The view drew her over to the balustrade. It was beautiful. Maggie doubted there was a more splendid position than here at Vaucluse, perched above Sydney Harbour, the magnificently kept grounds and gardens of Rosecliff spreading down to the water's edge in geometrically patterned tiers, each one featuring a fountain to delight the eye.

The mansion itself was a famous landmark for tourist cruises on the harbour. Built on a grand scale in the neoclassical style and set on five acres of prime real estate, its gleaming white-glazed terracotta exterior with its graceful Ionic columns and other lavishly decorated architectural features made it stand out, even amongst a whole shoreline of mansions. It seemed rather ironic that Vivian had made his fabulous fortune from parking lots. From the most practical of properties to the sublime, Maggie thought.

He'd taken enormous pride in what he'd privately called the Prescott Palace, using it as it should be used for splendid charity balls and fabulous fund-raising soirees. She mused over the marvellous memories Vivian had given her. He'd loved showing off his home, loved the pleasure it gave to others simply by coming here, enjoying the wonders of great wealth.

But nothing went on forever.

Nothing ever really stayed the same.

Maggie checked the time on her watch. The last bit of leeway for her was running out. She looked up at the cloudless blue sky, then down at the sparkles of sunshine on the water.

*If you're out there somewhere, Vivian, and you really want this plan to work, you'd better start waving your magic wand right now, because fairytales just don't happen without it. Okay?*

The only reply was the cry of gulls and the sounds of the city.

Maggie took a deep breath and turned to go.

The welcome mat was out for Beau Prescott.

# CHAPTER THREE

THE HUGE BLACK wrought-iron gates that guarded the entrance to Rosecliff were wide open. Wallace slowly turned the Rolls-Royce into the white-gravelled driveway, giving Beau plenty of time to get an eyeful of his home and its surrounds. As always, everything looked meticulously cared for; the lawns manicured, the rose gardens in healthy bloom, the two wings of the massive H-shaped mansion reaching out to welcome him.

It was nine o'clock and from the row of cars in the parking area for the daily staff, Beau realised nothing had been changed since his grandfather's death. The life here was flowing on as usual, waiting for him to come and make decisions. It made him doubly conscious of the responsibilities he had inherited.

Many people were employed on this estate, not only those who most concerned him. He suddenly saw the wisdom of the one-year clause in his grandfather's will. It would probably take that long to sort out what should be done with the place. Beau couldn't see himself adopting the lavish lifestyle enjoyed by his grandfather, yet it would be a shame to see Rosecliff become less than it was under some other ownership.

Wallace drove around to the east wing which housed

the entrance vestibule. He stopped the car directly in front of the great double doors, distinguished from all the other doors by a frame of elaborate wrought-iron grillwork. They were being opened, with meticulous timing, by Sedgewick.

Sure the insidious Nanny Stowe would be standing right behind the butler, Beau didn't wait for Wallace to do his ceremonial chauffeur stuff. He let himself out of the Rolls and strode straight for the meeting which had become paramount in his mind.

To his somewhat bewildered frustration, it didn't happen.

She wasn't there.

Sedgewick, as imposing as ever, his big dark eyes somehow managing to look both doleful and delighted, took his hand in both of his in a fulsome greeting. "Welcome home, sir. Welcome home."

"Sorry not to have been here before, Sedgewick," Beau said with feeling, knowing how devastating it must have been for the old butler to lose the master he'd loved and been so proud of serving.

Then Mrs. Featherfield, dabbing the corners of her eyes with her trademark lace handkerchief, her well-cushioned bosom heaving in a rush of emotion. "Thank heaven you're here at last, Master Beau. It's a sad, sad time, but it lifts our hearts to see you home again."

"Dear Feathers…" His boyhood name for her slipped out as he gave her a comforting hug. "I truly believed my grandfather would live to a hundred. I wouldn't have been gone so long if…"

"I know, dear." She patted him on the back and eased out of his embrace to address him earnestly. "But you mustn't fret. As Mr. Vivian would say, yesterday's gone, and we have to make the most of today because tomorrow's just around the corner and time does slip by on us."

He had to smile. "I remember."

"And I'm sure Nanny Stowe will fill you in on…"

"Ah, yes! Nanny Stowe." Beau pounced. "Wallace has been telling me about our new addition to the household. Where is she?"

Sedgewick cleared his throat. "A lady of deep sensitivity, Master Beau. Since Mrs. Featherfield and I have considerable longevity of service, Nanny Stowe wanted to give us a few minutes alone with you. However…" He gestured towards the stairhall. "…I expect she will be coming down any moment now."

"Yes, indeed," Mrs. Featherfield got all fluttery, urging Beau forward, leading the way under the lofty Palladian arch to where the staircase rose in elegant curves to the second-floor hall. "Nanny Stowe is so looking forward to meeting you."

No more than he was, Beau thought darkly.

As he stepped into the majestic stairhall, his gaze automatically travelled up the flight of broad steps that gradually narrowed to the first landing. A woman stood poised there, framed by the tall, arched balcony window, the light beaming in behind her seeming to set her hair aflame; glorious red-gold hair that sprang alive from her face, fanning out like a fiery halo with long glittering streamers which rippled down past her shoulders.

Beau was so stunned by this vision, it took him several moments to recollect himself enough to register more than the fabulous hair. She had skin so white it looked translucent, like the most delicate porcelain. Her face was strikingly beautiful, every feature finely balanced to please. Her neck looked almost unnaturally long, yet it, too, seemed utterly right, purposefully proportioned to hold such a face, as well as being the perfect foil for the glorious wealth of her hair.

She moved, jolting his gaze down to her feet to check he wasn't imagining what he was seeing; feet encased in black shiny shoes with a gold chain across each instep; delicately shaped ankles leading to legs in sheer black stockings; legs that went on forever, mesmerising in their long, sleek femininity.

Beau knew there were sixteen stairs from the landing to the floor and she'd come down half of them before his eyes reached the short skirt of her black dress. A gold chain curved from hipbone to hipbone, dangling over her stomach, just above the apex of her thighs.

The air Beau was breathing started to fizz. Or maybe he wasn't breathing at all and suffering from lack of oxygen. His chest felt seized up and his heart was drumming like a bongo on carnival night.

He dragged his gaze up past an impossibly small waist. A wild phrase leapt into his dazed brain…breasts like pomegranites…lush and ripe and delectable. Then he knew he was getting light-headed because his blood was all rushing down to his groin and very shortly he was going to be in big trouble.

Get back to the pure loveliness of her face, some shred of sanity shrieked. As his thigh muscles tightened to contain the hot prickling of desire, he watched the fascinating rise of a flush creep up the pearly white skin of her throat and its subsequent spread to her exotically slanted cheekbones. Then he was looking into her eyes, eyes as blue as the waters of the Caribbean, dazzling in their blueness.

"Nanny Stowe, sir," Sedgewick announced, as though he were presenting the queen.

Not even the identification jolted Beau out of his enthralment. She was stepping towards him, no longer on the staircase, and he realised she was almost as tall as he was. If he reached out and pulled her against him their bodies would be right for each other, fitting together without any manoeuvring. The thought sent another shot of excitement down to the area Beau was struggling to control.

"Please accept my deepest sympathy, Mr. Prescott."

Her soft, sexy voice caressed his spine into a sensual shiver.

"Your grandfather's death was a grievous shock to all of us. I'm sure it was very much so to you."

He belatedly noticed her hand extended to him. He grasped it, seeing its slim whiteness disappear, enfolded by his own darkly tanned hand, her fingers fluttering slightly against the strength of his. He wrenched his gaze up to hers again, fighting the fascination of the seemingly fragile extension of her femininity within his grip.

He had to think, had to speak. This woman, unbelievably, was Nanny Stowe. Sedgewick had said so. Therefore she had to be, however incredible it was.

"Wallace told me how well you arranged the funeral," Beau heard himself say in a reasonably normal voice. "I could not have done better for my grandfather. Thank you."

She nodded towards Sedgewick and Mrs. Featherfield. "Everyone helped."

"Yes." Beau forced himself to acknowledge them. "It was a grand effort and I appreciate it. Very much."

They nodded, gratified.

Nanny Stowe spoke on, her sympathy subtly shifting to eloquent appeal. "I hope you don't think it…well, unseemly…but I felt you might like to share the paying of last respects to your grandfather, so I arranged for the funeral service to be videotaped. The cassette is in the library, should you want to play it through sometime."

"It was a kind thought. Thank you again."

Beau was happily drowning in the glorious blue of her eyes, sucked right in by their seductive softness and going down for the third time. He was barely conscious of the replies he made, words dribbling out of his mouth when called for. When she fell silent he didn't really notice. Her eyes were locked on to his and he could have stood there, getting in deeper and deeper but for Sedgewick interrupting.

"We have refreshments waiting for you in the informal dining room, sir."

Her hand twitched in his, making Beau realise he was still hanging on to it. Reluctantly he let it go. Her skin was like warm silk as it slid away from his. "Yes. I could do with some coffee, Sedgewick," he answered, obviously needing something to snap him out of this entrancement. Perhaps jet lag had caught up with him. Even moving from where he was didn't occur to him.

Sedgewick orchestrated action. "Nanny Stowe, if you'd like to lead the way…"

She took a deep breath as though she, too, was feeling a lack of oxygen. "Perhaps you'd like to freshen up first, Mr. Prescott."

Did he look as though he'd been run over by a truck?

He smiled to dispel any questions about his mental and physical state, preferring to be the only one knowing how shaken he was. "No, I'm fine. Please lead on."

He was happy to stay behind her, watching her walk. Her fabulous hair reached almost to her waist, its gleaming ripples shifting with each step she took. It was so *alive,* Beau fancied there was an electric current running through it, throwing off showers of sparks that were infiltrating him. Something had to account for the weird pins and needles attacking every part of his body.

Though the jaunty roll of her very cute bottom below her impossibly tiny waist might be causing the itchy feeling in his hands. He kept them rigidly at his sides to stop them from reaching out. This woman would have to be the most stunningly gorgeous, sexiest creature he'd ever seen in his life.

And she was *Nanny Stowe?*

A sharply unsettling question darted through the fog in Beau's brain.

*What had his grandfather been doing with her?*

Two years she'd been under this roof and his grandfather, according to Wallace, had definitely not fallen into his second childhood. The more Beau thought about the situation, and all he'd heard and seen so far, it became disturbingly clear that Wallace, Sedgewick and Mrs. Featherfield viewed Nanny Stowe as mistress of the house.

And she was playing hostess to him right now!

The bottom suddenly fell out of the excitement she'd stirred in him. Beau went cold all over. It made horribly perfect sense. His grandfather had always enjoyed having a pretty woman on his arm. On both arms. But having found *this one,* why bother with any other? She had star quality on a megascale and his grandfather would have adored parading her everywhere. And probably adored her, as well! He'd loved owning beautiful things.

Beau's stomach started contracting, working up a nauseous feeling. Refreshments were certainly in order. He obviously needed food as well as coffee.

When they reached the informal dining room, his suspicion was further confirmed by the way she moved automatically to the foot of the table and Sedgewick held her chair for her. Clearly it was her place and taken for granted, even though his grandfather was no longer here.

Then Mr. Polly arrived on the scene, carrying a basket of freshly cut, dark red roses. His weather-beaten face was cracked into a benevolent smile. "I'm so sorry I missed you at the front doors, sir. Good to have you home."

Beau shook the offered hand. "Thank you, Mr. Polly. The gardens look as superb as ever."

"I keep at it, sir. I brought this basket up. Thought Nanny Stowe might like to put these roses in your room, sir." He turned to her. "They're the best of the Mr. Lincolns, Nanny Stowe. Lovely fragrance."

She blushed.

Beau was once again distracted by the fascinating flow of colour lighting up her pale skin.

Mrs. Featherfield swooped. "I'll take the basket, Mr. Polly. Let's go out to the kitchen and put the roses in water. Nanny Stowe will see to them later. She's having coffee with Master Beau right now."

Yes…they all considered Nanny Stowe a cut above

themselves, Beau thought, watching Mr. Polly being swept away. Arranging roses in a vase for a guest's room was the kind of genteel occupation suited to the mistress of the house. Except he wasn't a guest. Which probably accounted for her embarrassment. She knew, even if the others didn't yet appreciate it, his arrival changed the status quo.

Sedgewick proceeded to serve them with coffee and a selection of freshly baked croissants. "If you'd like something more substantial, sir, Jeffrey, the cook, is standing by."

"No, I did have breakfast on the plane, Sedgewick. This is more than enough, thank you."

Sedgewick stationed himself by the sideboard, ready to be attentive to every need. Nanny Stowe composed herself again, adopting a waiting attitude. Beau ate a crisp croissant and drank some coffee to wash down the flaky crumbs. It didn't really help his churning stomach but it gave him time to think.

"Did my grandfather call you Nanny Stowe?" he asked.

A wry little smile played on eminently kissable red lips. "It amused Vivian to give me that title, Mr. Prescott."

The familiarity of *Vivian* hit him in the gut. "So it was a pet name," he suggested.

She frowned. "Not exactly. It did have a sort of purpose. My job was to be with him, accompanying him wherever he wanted to go and generally looking after him. But he didn't call me Nanny himself. I was always Maggie to Vivian."

"Maggie..." he repeated, knowing it plucked at a chord of memory.

"Yes. My Christian name is Margaret, you see."

Maggie, the cat. That was it! Maggie from one of his grandfather's favourite movies, *Cat On A Hot Tin Roof.* Elizabeth Taylor had played the role. She was married to a guy whose wealthy old father was dying and to clinch her husband's inheritance she had pretended to be pregnant.

Pregnant!

Beau's mind suddenly billowed in horror at the next thought that filled it. He'd more or less challenged his grandfather to beget his own heir for Rosecliff. While his grandfather hadn't actually married Maggie Stowe, she'd lived very cosily with him for two years and she'd been given a year's grace here after his death... which could mean his grandfather had still been hoping for a result.

"More coffee, Nanny Stowe?" Sedgewick asked, holding out the coffeepot.

She shook her head. Was she being careful of her caffeine intake?

"More coffee, sir?"

He waved it away. His heart was beating so fast he didn't need any artificial stimulant. And thinking of hearts reminded him his grandfather had died of a heart attack...*before anyone expected him to!*

Doing what?

Trying to father a child?

Beau looked down the table at the blue-eyed red-haired siren who had power enough to entrance a man into attempting any reckless stupidity.

He had to know.

He had to ask.

He tried to find a way of couching the question less

shockingly. Somehow the sense of urgency mashed his brain. Nothing came but the bald need to get the issue resolved. Immediately! The words shot out of his mouth...

"Are you pregnant, Maggie?"

# CHAPTER FOUR

Sedgewick dropped the coffeepot.

The shock of this extraordinary happening momentarily distracted Maggie from the deeper shock delivered by Beau Prescott. She stared down at the broken pot and the coffee spreading across the parquet floor with a sense of disbelief. She'd never known Sedgewick to drop anything. Every one of his movements was a study in grace and dignity. Had he been as stunned as she was by the outrageous question thrown at her?

"I do beg your pardon," he intoned, his face quite blank, as though he couldn't believe the mishap, either.

"I'll get one of the maids to clean it up," Maggie said, pushing her chair back for action.

"No, no...I see I have been splashed, as well." Distress showing now. For Sedgewick it was quite impossible to tolerate any imperfection in his dress. "I shall have this...this mess...seen to immediately. Please excuse me, sir, Nanny Stowe."

Maggie was left to face Beau Prescott alone. She stared at him down the length of the table, her mind skittering over the wild hopes she'd been nursing. If he imagined her pregnant, to some other man...he couldn't be feeling as overwhelmed by her as she was by him. Which put her hopelessly at odds with the feelings he'd stirred in her.

Never in her life had she been hit so forcefully by sheer male sex appeal. When he'd entered the stairhall and looked up at her on the landing, she'd been stunned into immobility by how little the photograph had represented the real man. His skin glowed with vitality. The streaks of sunshine in his hair had gleamed like gold. His face wasn't just strongly handsome. His eyes were so magnetic they made it instantly charismatic.

His physique was no less impressive. Casually dressed in khaki shirt and trousers, he seemed almost larger than life, like a throwback to when men were hunters and survival of the fittest meant something. If his grandfather had been the ultimate sophisticate, Beau Prescott was the prime male animal, throwing out a compelling challenge to his female counterpart on some instinctive level that had nothing to do with civilisation.

She had no idea how long she'd stood on the landing, enraptured by him, but when she had finally willed her legs to move, the nylon in her tights seemed to crackle with electricity, sending little quivers of sensation through her thighs. Even more shockingly, she'd felt the hot moistness of sexual excitement as he watched her descend the stairs, his gaze travelling slowly up the length of her body until even her breasts started tingling and tightening in rampant response to the primitive charge emanating from him.

Then the mad joy of finding he was taller than she was, tall enough to make her feel they were made for each other. And his hand taking hers, like a burning brand on her skin, a claim of possession, of mating.

Utter madness in the light of the question that was still ringing in her ears and echoing around the emptiness it had opened up in her brain.

And he had seemed so nice, as well. Charming. She could have sworn the attraction was mutual...the way he'd absorbed every detail of her appearance, gazed into her eyes, held her hand. She'd been dizzy with exhilaration by the time she'd sat down at this table. Then with Mr. Polly's suggestion of putting roses in Beau Prescott's bedroom, she'd begun fantasising...

Maggie swallowed hard. She had probably needed a sobering slap in the face. The dynamic green eyes were still intensely focused on her but she found them uncomfortably piercing now. He was waiting for her reply. Not that he had any right to it—such a personal thing to ask!—but she felt pressed to clear the air between them.

Her tongue felt thick. She forced herself to produce a flat statement of fact. "The answer is no, Mr. Prescott. I'm not pregnant and not likely to be."

He looked relieved.

Maggie was goaded to ask, "Would you mind telling me what possessed you to make such an inquiry?" She couldn't help a somewhat terse note creeping into her voice. Disappointment, most probably. Or disillusionment. She must have been fooling herself over his reaction to her since he had jumped to the conclusion she was intimately involved with someone else.

He winced. "My grandfather wanted an heir."

Confusion whirled. "Aren't you his heir?"

"Yes." A heavy sigh ending in a rueful grimace. "But he was on at me to get married and have a child to safeguard the family line. The last time I was here with him, I suggested if he was so keen to pass on his gene pool he should have a child himself."

Enlightenment dawned like a white frost, covering and killing what had seemed like warm fertile ground between them. "You thought…that I…and Vivian…" Maggie choked. It was too awful a lump to swallow.

He at least had the grace to look discomforted. "It seemed…possible."

"Vivian was in his eighties!" There'd been almost sixty years between them!

"A man's libido doesn't necessarily wear out with age," came the dry observation. He offered a crooked smile. "And you are very beautiful."

Maggie was not mollified. She knew perfectly well that beauty was a learnt skill. Vivian had taught her that. He'd seen the raw potential in her and taken pride in developing it. However, beauty was not really the point at issue here. Beau Prescott was horribly mistaken in his judgment and he had to be corrected. She eyed him with searing determination as she spoke.

"Even if Vivian had felt…that way…about me, and he didn't…"

"Maggie, you exude sex. No man would be proof against it, not even an octogenarian."

"Oh!" Her face started heating up again. "You're terribly wrong." It was Beau himself who exuded sex, not her. No other man had ever made her feel so sexually aware of herself. It wasn't fair of him to transfer what had happened between them to anyone else. She tried to explain. "Vivian liked me. He was proud of me…"

"I have no doubt he adored you. From your feet up."

"He didn't want me like that!" she cried in exasperation, barely holding back the burning fact that Vivian had wanted her to want *him!* And the terrible truth was she did. Except he wasn't turning out as nice as she'd first thought him.

Blatant scepticism looked back at her.

"Your grandfather was a gentleman," she declared emphatically. Which was more than she could say for him, the way he was going.

"My grandfather enjoyed flirting with young women," he countered. "He insisted they kept him young. He boasted he'd live to a hundred. He brings you into his home and he dies at eighty-six. From a heart attack. Having met you, what am I supposed to think, Maggie?"

Her stomach revolted at the image he conjured up. Her eyes flashed fierce resentment at his offensive line of logic. "A man of any sense might have made some discreet inquiries before leaping to unwarranted conclusions," she threw at him.

"Hardly unwarranted. It wouldn't be the first time a beautiful young woman connected with an elderly millionaire. Power and wealth are well-known aphrodisiacs."

"Right!" Maggie snapped, furious with his cynical view of a relationship which had been precious to her. "I suppose you envisage me just lying back, closing my eyes and thinking of Rosecliff!"

"And all that goes with it."

Her heart lurched. Hearing Vivian's own words, though they had applied to a possible marriage to his grandson, touched a very raw place. The whole idea of *giving it a chance* with Beau Prescott suddenly became intensely repugnant to her. Mutual attraction did not suffice. He would see her as a gold-digger even if he was panting after her.

The cleaning brigade came in, two of the daily maids whose job it was to keep every room in a pristine state. Maggie greeted them and introduced them to their new employer. Apart from those few words she waited in seething silence while the mess was attended to. Beau Prescott also held his tongue, which was just as well, because she felt like biting it off.

Of course, Vivian's wealth had made life easy for her, and Rosecliff was the most beautiful place in the world to live in, but she wouldn't have come here if she hadn't liked Vivian Prescott, genuinely liked him, and she certainly wouldn't have stayed if he'd tried to come on to her. No way! She would have been out of here like greased lightning!

The maids left, their efficiency truly admirable. Probably the thick atmosphere in the room had hastened their work. Maggie braced herself for the task of setting Beau Prescott straight. In no uncertain terms!

He spoke first. "I like to know what I'm dealing with, Maggie."

"My title is *Nanny* Stowe." And she hadn't given *him* permission to call her Maggie.

"Nannies do tuck their charges into bed," he dryly pointed out.

"Not...this one," she retorted in high indignation.

He shrugged. "It seemed best to be direct. Your relationship with my grandfather..."

He stopped as Sedgewick stepped into the room, bearing another coffeepot.

Maggie was so incensed with Beau Prescott's *directness* she swung around in her chair and impulsively appealed for backup. "Sedgewick, Mr. Prescott wants to know if I was sleeping with his grandfather. Would you be so kind as to…"

The butler halted in horror. The hand holding the coffeepot shook alarmingly. Maggie held her breath, silently cursing herself for shocking the poor man again.

"Steady, Sedgewick," Beau Prescott gently advised.

The elderly butler stared at the treacherous hand until it performed as it was supposed to, holding firmly. Then he raised his eyes to the ceiling, as though appealing to the heavens beyond it. The expression on his face was easily read. What was the world coming to?

"I'm sorry for upsetting you, Sedgewick," Maggie said remorsefully.

"Not at all," he said with lofty dignity. He carried the pot to the sideboard, set it on the hotplate with due ceremony, then swung around to face *the wild child* with a look of pained reproof. "Sir, Mr. Vivian did not have an illicit liaison with Nanny Stowe," he stated unequivocally.

"Thank you, Sedgewick," Maggie leapt in before Beau Prescott could open his big mouth. "Did you ever see him kiss me other than on the cheek or on the forehead, or, in a moment of pure old-world gallantry, on the hand?"

"Never!" came the emphatic reply.

"Did you ever observe him fondle me in what could be called an intimate manner?"

"Certainly not!"

"Did he ever display any sign of being a randy old man around me?"

Sedgewick looked affronted, as well he might. "Mr.

Vivian was a gentleman." Which, to Sedgewick, was the definitive reply, delivered in ringing tones.

However, since a similar declaration by her had not cleared Beau Prescott's prejudice, Maggie continued to have the situation spelled out, her eyes glittering a proud challenge at her accuser at the other end of the table.

"In your own words, Sedgewick, what was Mr. Vivian's manner towards me?"

"I believe he thought of you as his adopted daughter whose company was always a delight to him."

"And my manner towards Mr. Vivian?"

"You wish me to be frank, Nanny Stowe?"

"Ruthlessly frank, Sedgewick."

"I believe you thought of Mr. Vivian as a benevolent godfather who made beautiful things happen. You saw it as your job to make them even more beautiful for him."

The truth. The simple truth. And it had been beautiful. It was wicked and destructive of Beau Prescott to soil it with his revolting and insulting interpretations. A rush of tears blurred her eyes and clogged her throat. "Thank you, Sedgewick," she managed huskily.

He bowed to her in a show of respect. "At your service, Nanny Stowe. Would you like your coffee cup refilled?"

"Please."

He handled the pot perfectly. Not a drop wavered or spilled. The masterly performance provided a sense of calm. "A refill for you also, sir?' he inquired.

"No. I've been refreshed enough for now, thank you. Refreshed and reassured that my house is in very clean order. For which I thank both of you."

His dry tone spurred Maggie to look at him again. He gave her a mocking glance as he rose from his chair and she knew instantly he still held suspicions about the innocence of her relationship with his grandfather, despite Sedgewick's prime witness statements. However, he wasn't about to comment any further on it at this point. He addressed himself to Sedgewick, his manner briskly purposeful.

"I trust my luggage has been taken up to my room?"

"Of course, sir."

"Good. I'll be off for the day as soon as I've showered and changed clothes. Please warn Wallace to have the car standing by."

Maggie felt impelled to say, "If I can be of any assistance…"

His eyes glittered at her. "You are not *my* nanny, Maggie."

Which swept the mat out from under her feet and left her feeling miserably hollow.

"I daresay I'll see you at dinner tonight, taking your usual place," he went on.

"If you'd prefer I didn't…"

"On the contrary, I'll look forward to the pleasure of your company."

He was plotting something. She could feel it. With malice aforethought. Every nerve in her body was twanging a warning.

He started to leave, then paused, looking back at her, a sizzling challenge in his eyes. "Oh, and don't put roses in my room, Maggie. I am not my grandfather."

# CHAPTER FIVE

BEAU STOOD UNDER the shower, willing the hard spray of water to beat out the sexual edginess Maggie Stowe had implanted. The woman was a witch. His grandfather had obviously been enchanted by her and she had Sedgewick curled around her little finger, too. Not to mention the rest of the household staff; Wallace singing her praises, Mr. Polly bringing her roses, Mrs. Featherfield star-struck by her stunning beauty.

No doubt about it, she cast a powerful spell.

Beau savagely promised himself he would not fall victim to it.

She'd had him captivated at the start but he wouldn't go under like that again. He was wise to her now. Maggie Stowe was out for all she could get. If she thought she could turn him into another godfather, making beautiful things happen for her, she'd find herself frustrated at every turn.

It was bad enough that his grandfather had blindly doted on her. Beau was glad there'd been no physical intimacy between them. Not that he would have begrudged his grandfather the right to have his sexual needs satisfied. A man was a man, regardless of age. But taking a woman as *young* as Maggie Stowe was a bit much for Beau's stomach. She could only be in her twenties.

Though she certainly knew how to use her assets! No grass growing under *those* expensively shod feet. The question was…how much hay had she made during the two sunshine years of prettily playing pet daughter to a besotted old man who had the means to indulge her every whim?

Making things more beautiful for him…huh! Making herself more beautiful with nice little items of jewellery would be her line. He'd bet his boots on it. Lucky his grandfather hadn't adopted her legally. A fine old mess that would have made of the will. As it was, she didn't have a leg to stand on in claiming anything apart from a year's free housing and wages.

Though God knew what she'd picked up in gifts while his grandfather was alive. Well, he was about to look into that. She'd invited him to make discreet inquiries before leaping to unwarranted conclusions. Little mistake there. Beau was going to make exhaustive inquiries and he didn't care whose feet he trod on in getting to the truth. If she expected him to be *a gentleman* of the old ilk, overlooking unpleasant little realities, she was in for a few nasty shocks!

He stepped out of the shower with all mental motors running. While he dressed he telephoned the family solicitor and the firm of accountants who handled his grandfather's finances, giving fair warning of an imminent visit from him. He didn't want condolences. He didn't want any pussyfooting around the situation. He wanted answers, and woe betide anyone who didn't have them ready for him.

The ride into the city from Vaucluse was accom-

plished in brooding silence. Wallace, possibly advised
by Sedgewick to keep his mouth shut unless called
upon to answer questions, offered no comment about
anything, and Beau didn't care to have any interruption
to the plan of action fermenting in his brain.

The solicitor's offices were in Philip Street. Once
there, he told Wallace not to wait around. He'd catch
taxis wherever else he wanted to go. Privately, he
didn't want Wallace reporting his every move to *Nanny*
Stowe.

Beau was ushered straight into Lionel Armstrong's
executive suite, greeted warmly by the man himself,
and offered refreshments which he declined. They sat
in leather chairs across a magnificent mahogany desk
and Beau tried to repress the feeling he was dealing
with a self-satisfied man who needed stirring.

Lionel Armstrong was just a bit too sleekly well-fed
for his liking. The man was in his fifties, handsome in
a heavy-set way, vainly proud of his thick white hair
which was carefully styled and groomed, and he made
almost a fetish of the trappings of success.

"Well, Beau, I'm happy to say there are no tricky
problems with your grandfather's estate. Vivian made
a straightforward will and the process towards probate
is in hand."

"I'm glad you consider it straightforward, Lionel. I
consider it somewhat surprising. Firstly, I thought he
would have made more provision for those who had
been with him longest."

"Ah, you mean the faithful four. No need for con-
cern on their behalf. Sedgewick, Mrs. Featherfield,
Wallace and Mr. Polly have been well taken care of.
Your grandfather set up superannuation funds for them.

John Neville, the head accountant can fill you in on those. I believe the settlement for each one after the stipulated year is up will be well into six figures."

"And Margaret Stowe?"

"The nanny?" Lionel looked amused.

Beau was not amused. "Yes. The nanny who has a year's grace along with the others."

"Oh, that was one of Vivian's little quirks. Wouldn't be talked out of it. Said the others depended on her to do the right thing. And I must say she did a splendid job of organising the funeral. Splendid!"

"The cost of which was claimed against the estate?"

"Of course. Everything in order. All accounts checked. If you're going to see John Neville, he'll show you."

"Fine. Does Nanny Stowe have a superannuation fund, too?"

"Every permanent employee on the estate has. It's the law. However, since she'll only be in service for three years altogether, it will not amount to much. Nothing there for you to worry about."

"I'd like to see her file."

Lionel frowned. "What file?"

"You know and I know my grandfather kept a file on all his employees. References, résumés, and any other information that seemed pertinent. It was your responsibility to run a check on them. For live-in staff taking up positions of trust, it was a mandatory precaution."

"True." His mouth twisted over the word. He leaned back in his chair, linked his hands across his stomach, and viewed Beau with a wry expression. "I have no answer to the mystery of Margaret Stowe."

Beau's sense of anticipation turned into unpleasant tension. "What the hell is that supposed to mean?"

"Ask me for a file on anyone else and I can supply it. All I can give you on Margaret Stowe is a copy of her birth certificate. It states she was a foundling. The informant is a doctor and apparently he gave an estimated date of birth. No parents. No witnesses."

"Where did her name come from then?"

"Perhaps a note was pinned to the baby. Perhaps the doctor or a nurse gave it to her. Nobody knows. The doctor died eight years ago. He operated from a home surgery. The house burnt down and all his medical records were destroyed. That line of investigation came to a dead end. As did every other line." He unlinked his hands to gesture helplessly. "It was as though Margaret Stowe lived in a vacuum until her meeting with your grandfather."

"Oh, come on. You expect me to believe that?" It was looking like a straight case of dereliction of duty to Beau.

"It's the truth," came the hasty assurance.

"You must have put a private investigator onto her," Beau pressed, not prepared to accept a whitewash.

"With zero results. Apart from her birth certificate, she had no official existence. She had never filed a tax return, never owned a credit card. No record of education or employment…"

"What about social security? She could have been raking in unemployment benefits."

"She was not listed on any register. No passport. No driver's licence. I assure you, every avenue of information was thoroughly checked. More than once.

When the first investigator failed to uncover anything, I hired another. With no better outcome."

Someone has always kept her, Beau thought. She's probably had a string of godfathers since her teens.

Lionel Armstrong shrugged off the failure. "Her known life began the night Vivian met her and offered her the job as his nanny."

"Well, she very conveniently sprang alive then," Beau commented acidly. "How did he meet her?"

"He said she was selling roses."

Beau barely refrained from rolling his eyes. Maggie Stowe had done her homework on Vivian Prescott. He'd been her mark and he'd fallen for her; hook, line, and sinker.

"What did my grandfather say when you put it to him that you could collect no background on her?"

"He laughed and dismissed it as of no importance."

Lionel Armstrong's *laissez-faire* attitude niggled Beau. "Didn't you argue with him? Point out the dangers?" he accused more than asked.

"Naturally. But to no effect. Your grandfather did have a mind of his own, Beau, and there was no changing it on Margaret Stowe."

Bewitched, Beau thought broodingly.

"In fact, he said something I've never forgotten," the solicitor went on musingly. "And I must say, he did seem to have taken on a new lease of life."

"What were the unforgettable words?' Beau demanded tersely, unable to suppress his frustration over getting nothing tangible to hang on Maggie Stowe.

"I think Vivian revelled in her nonentity status. He said, "'She's going to be my creation, Lionel. And very possibly my salvation.'" And his eyes were twinkling in that impish way he had."

"Salvation?"

The solicitor shrugged. "Your guess is as good as mine. Maybe he thought he'd found an angel."

"If she sprouts wings, I'll start believing it," Beau said caustically. He'd had enough talk of angels.

"Disturbs you, does she?" The solicitor eyed him with speculative interest.

"I don't like mysteries," Beau growled.

"Well, perhaps being such an experienced explorer, you'll dig it out."

Beau intended to, one way or another.

After he left the solicitor's office, he stopped at a street café to grab some lunch and chew over what he'd learnt so far. Which wasn't much. Maggie Stowe was twenty-eight years old and she was the only one who could tell him about herself. It would probably be a stack of lies he'd get from her but at least he could have the lies checked.

He'd blundered in being too direct this morning, putting her offside. He would have to smooth that over this evening, lull her into feeling he accepted her at face value. It would be stupid to give offence again. Better to charm the information out of her. Let her think she was winning.

He thought briefly of dropping in at the head office of the travel agency he'd established in Australia. It was hardly urgent. Helen Carter had been running the business efficiently for the past three years. It was a courtesy to tell her he was back home again, but it could wait another day. He was too obsessed with

Maggie Stowe to give Helen or anything else his un-
divided attention.

The firm of accountants was housed in the MLC
building, right in the city centre. With clients as
wealthy as Vivian Prescott, they could well afford such
premises. Beau thought of all the parking stations and
lots his grandfather owned—*he* now owned—around
Sydney. With traffic the way it was, and ownership of
cars always on the up and up, the business of providing parking was probably the most solid investment of
all in a fast-moving world.

Beau had no intention of interfering with it. John
Neville and his associates had been handling the family finances for many years and were very proficient
at it. They earned their fees. Beau had no doubt everything would be in order on the business side. It was his
grandfather's personal expenses over the past two years
that interested him, particularly in regard to their connection with Maggie Stowe.

John Neville was happy to oblige him with this information. He was a small, neat, precise man, proud
of his meticulous bookkeeping. For some reason, Beau
found Neville's bald head reassuring. His gold-rimmed
spectacles also seemed to add an air of no-nonsense
professionalism.

"Miss Stowe's salary was generous." He pointed
out the figure from the wages book. "But, as you can
see, not outrageously so, considering she was always
on call. Never had days off."

"Never?"

"Not even a vacation. Vivian took her everywhere
with him and he paid for what he called her appearance clothes out of his own pocket. Naturally, he used

credit cards. Everything he bought for Miss Stowe to wear has been itemised."

He passed over a detailed printout for Beau to peruse. Dresses, suits, hats, shoes, handbags…practically all designer wear if the steep cost was anything to go by.

"As you know, your grandfather enjoyed a very full social calendar with his many charities and he liked Miss Stowe to shine at his side."

"From the look of this, she certainly shone. What about jewellery?"

"Rented for any big occasion. Miss Stowe would not accept jewellery from your grandfather. In fact, she sold some of the evening gowns Vivian didn't want her to wear again and returned the price she got to us. All properly docketed. The accounts for the funeral were scrupulously kept, as well."

"No discrepancies?" Beau queried. His "feathering her nest" theory was being shot down and that didn't make sense to him.

"None," came the firm reply.

"Nothing missing?" Beau pressed.

John Neville looked uncomfortable. "There is and there isn't. I find it very vexing. Nothing I could do about it but I strongly dislike not having everything accounted for."

"Please explain," Beau encouraged, his interest sparked again.

"Oh, it has nothing to do with Miss Stowe." He beetled a frown over his glasses. "Vivian could be a very wilful man. When he didn't want to take advice, he wouldn't."

Beau had more or less heard the same from Lionel

Armstrong and the matter was very definitely con-nected to Maggie Stowe. He waited for John Neville to enlighten him further.

"He came in one day, about two months before his death, and asked me to get him a million dollars in cash."

Two months before his grandfather's death rang a bell in Beau's brain. That was when his last will and testament had been made...including Margaret Stowe.

John Neville pursed his lips in disapproval. "Now that amount of money one simply does not carry around in cash. Legitimate transactions are all paperwork. Nat-urally I inquired the reason for such a request."

"And the answer?' Beau prompted.

"He said it was his money and he could do what he liked with it and it was none of my business." The af-front of that statement coloured John Neville's voice. "I could not shake him into telling me what he wanted it for. He stubbornly insisted I get the cash for him. I had no other choice. It was his money."

"Did you find out where it went?"

He dolefully shook his head. "I expected it to turn up. A purchase. A land deal. Something. I looked for it. I even asked around in certain circles. Very dis-creetly, of course. Not a trace, not a hint. I can show you the paperwork attached to the handing over of the million dollars to your grandfather. He took it. I have witnesses to his taking it. But what he did with it was, and still is, a complete mystery."

Beau now had two mysteries.

The case of the woman from nowhere.

The case of the missing million.

He also had a very strong conviction…find out the background of Maggie Stowe and he'd find the missing million.

# CHAPTER SIX

MAGGIE STARED GLOOMILY at the vast array of very expensive clothes in her wardrobe. Vivian had made dressing up fun. She'd seen no harm in giving him the pleasure of it and there was no denying she had enjoyed feeling wonderfully glamorous, swishing around in gorgeous outfits.

She didn't think Beau Prescott was going to view any of this as fun, though. The money Vivian had spent on making her look splendid was sure to bring his grandson's censure down upon her head. He'd more or less accused her of being a whore this morning. Milking an old man's indulgence was bound to come next. She wished she could shrug it off, not care, but it hurt having Vivian's grandson think badly of her. It hurt all the more because she'd felt so instantly, so strongly attracted to him.

A knock on her bedroom door broke into her misery-laden thoughts. "Yes?" she called despondently.

Mrs. Featherfield came bustling in, brimming with excited anticipation. "He's home, dear. Sedgewick suggested predinner drinks in the salon at six-thirty. That gives you half an hour to get ready." She eyed the opened wardrobe with avid interest. "He's still in his suit so you could wear something really pretty."

Maggie grimaced. "It's no use, Mrs. Featherfield. He doesn't like me."

"Nonsense! Master Beau was well and truly bowled over this morning. Saw it with my own eyes."

"Well, he very quickly recovered and bowled me out of any getting together with him," Maggie said dryly.

"Now that's not it at all. Sedgewick and I agree that Master Beau liked you so much he got jealous at the thought of you and Mr. Vivian...being close. He wanted you for himself."

Maggie found herself at a loss as to how to argue with such triumphant satisfaction.

"So don't you worry, dear," Mrs. Featherfield rushed on. "Wallace said Master Beau was very quiet on the way into town. Sedgewick feels that setting the record straight about you and Mr. Vivian gave him food for thought and reconsideration."

All of it bad, Maggie figured, remembering the spark of malice in his eyes as he'd left her.

"Shock can do funny things to people," Mrs. Featherfield remarked with a wise look. "We all need a period of adjustment. Master Beau will have settled himself down by now and I'm sure he'll be charming to you this evening. You must give him another chance, dear."

He was going to make mincemeat of her. Still, if she didn't put on a show, Mrs. Featherfield, Sedgewick and the others would feel she was letting down the side. Maggie forced a smile. "I'll do my best."

The housekeeper beamed happily at this reassurance. As she hurried out of the bedroom she warned,

"Six-thirty, mind. Jeffrey's cooking Beef Wellington for dinner and he's very particular about the timing."

No doubt there'd be romantic candles on the table, too, Maggie thought, her heart sinking at the prospect of bearing the cynicism in Beau Prescott's eyes. She hoped Sedgewick wouldn't suggest champagne. The foreboding words, *I am not my grandfather,* were still ringing in her ears.

In a spurt of defiance, Maggie pulled out her red poppy dress. Since Beau Prescott viewed her as a scarlet woman, she would throw it right in his face. She had nothing to be ashamed of in her relationship with Vivian and she'd be damned if she would let his grandson turn it into something it wasn't. Vivian had adored the boldness of her wearing red with her red hair, declaring it both daring and dazzling. Certainly the poppy dress would do away with any accusation she was not trying hard enough.

Maggie had always thought of it as a flirty little dress. It wasn't exactly figure-hugging. The silk chiffon with its vibrant pattern of scarlet blooms splashed over a white background, more or less slid and shifted over her curves, falling to a cute short skirt with an underfrill rippling softly around her thighs. At the back, the skirt was looped up at the centre to showcase rows of flouncy underfrills that took on a life of their own when she moved.

Definitely a flirty dress. One could even say it flaunted her femininity. With malice aforethought, Maggie proceeded to complement the dress with appropriate accoutrements; sheer, pale flesh-coloured tights, high-heeled red sandals that strapped up to above her ankles, and long, dangly crystal earrings to reflect colour as they sparkled against her hair.

She sprayed her neck and wrists with Christian Dior's "Poison" for good measure, then pranced downstairs, all flags flying for the cause, although to her mind, the cause was already dead and beyond revival. Nevertheless, Sedgewick could not fail to be pleased with her appearance and any further debacle between her and Beau Prescott would not be laid at her door.

She swept into the salon, walking to the strong beat of rebellion. Sedgewick was serving her antagonist with a freshly made martini. Beau Prescott, standing in a commanding position in front of the French marble mantelpiece, above which hung a romantic painting of Cupid at play—definitely a perverse comment on what was going on here—took the martini from the silver tray, looked at Maggie who had paused to take in the scene, and gave her the full force of a brilliant smile.

Her heart tripped.

"Good evening, Maggie," he said pleasantly, lifting his glass a little as though toasting her appearance. "You make me see you would brighten any man's world, regardless of age or circumstance."

Unsure whether or not she had just received a compliment, Maggie seized on another implication in his greeting. "Did you have a difficult day?" she asked.

"Mmmh…" His eyebrows slanted musingly, attractively. "…I'd call it a three martini day. Will you join me in one? It may help smooth over my *faux pas* of this morning."

An apology? Maggie was dumbfounded. She'd come to do battle and here he was in retreat. A very graceful retreat, too. And he looked so heart-meltingly hand-

some, a twinkling appeal in his eyes, a smile still playing on his lips, the compelling power of his masculinity
given a tantalisingly civilised veneer by a perfectly tailored three-piece suit.

Her mind belatedly dictated a "Yes, I will, thank
you," reply, and a smile to match his. With Sedgewick
looking on benevolently, she could hardly do anything
else. Besides, she really did want to give Beau Prescott
another chance, so long as he was being nice to her.

Maggie was instantly outmanoeuvred from adopting her usual hostess role. Beau Prescott took charge,
very much the master of the house as he gave orders
to Sedgewick, directed Maggie to sit on the sofa of
his choosing and invited her to sample Jeffrey's hors
d'ouevres—his best creations—artistically arranged
on an exquisite platter.

The little puff balls filled with creamed egg and
topped with sour cream and caviar were irresistible.
Besides, Maggie needed something to settle the sudden attack of flutters in her stomach. She was very,
very conscious of Beau Prescott as he took the armchair closest to her, facing her across the oval end of
the gilt-legged marble table which served both pieces
of furniture.

He chose one of the fine pastry boats contain-ing
Jeffrey's special crab mixture. Undoubtedly, Sedgewick had instructed the cook to pull out all stops tonight. After all, it was Master Beau's homecoming.
Maggie hoped it would be interpreted that way by the
man who was now viewing her with speculative interest.

"I imagined you very differently, you know," he
confessed with an appealing twist of irony. "I guess,

because you were linked in the will with Sedgewick and the others, I automatically put you in the same age bracket. Or thereabouts."

It was an understandable assumption. "Then I must have come as a shock," Maggie offered, remembering Mrs. Featherstone had excused his behaviour on that basis. She was prepared to be as generous.

He nodded. "To put it mildly. I'd be grateful if you'd fill me in on a few things that have been teasing me all day."

"What do you want to know?" Maggie asked warily, willing to meet him halfway if this was a genuine offering of goodwill.

"Well…" He gestured helplessness. "How did you come here? Did my grandfather advertise for a nanny?"

The questions sounded like pure curiosity, nothing judgmental about them. Maggie's nervous tension eased a little. Such curiosity was fair enough in the circumstances.

"I don't think the idea had even occurred to him until after he'd met me," she answered, shaking her head as she remembered back. "I'm sure it was just one of those things that grew on him and he kept adding to it as he went along." Wanting Beau Prescott to understand she looked at him appealingly. "It was like a game to Vivian."

"To you, too?"

Maggie felt she was on trickier ground here. She answered cautiously. "He made it fun. But he taught me a lot, too." The sense of loss welled up in her again. "Your grandfather was a wonderful person and he gave me the best years of my life," she said in a burst of fierce feeling.

The intent green eyes seemed to probe her emotion, measuring it. Maggie's nerves tensed up so much she was almost driven to challenge any disbelief he had, but she held her tongue. She couldn't make him believe her. He either did or he didn't.

Luckily Sedgewick picked that touchy moment to serve her the martini she'd agreed to have and Maggie gratefully grabbed the glass, hating the searching silence. She gulped some of the strong liquor, barely stopped herself from choking on it, then sought further distraction in selecting one of Jeffrey's dainty pizza circles with cheese, tomato and olives baked into it.

"I know what you mean," Beau Prescott said quietly, startling her into looking at him again. His expression was soft, fondly reminiscent. "He had such a zest for life it was infectious. He opened windows to the world for me."

"Yes. Oh, yes! That was just how it was." The words tripped out, surprised delight lifting her heart.

His head tilted inquiringly. "How did the two of you meet?"

She relaxed into a smile. "It was the most amazing encounter. I was out of work at the time and just scraping a living by peddling single roses. I bought them at the markets, and prettied them up with foil paper and ribbons. I did the rounds of fancy restaurants in the evening and a lot of guys would buy one for the woman they were dining with. A romantic gesture, you know?"

He grinned. "How much did you charge?"

She grinned back, pleased he didn't disapprove of her enterprise. "Five dollars. I figured for an elevation of mood, it was worth at least as much as a glass of wine."

"Perfectly reasonable," he agreed encouragingly. "I guess my grandfather couldn't resist buying one from you."

"Well, not exactly. He was with a large party of people at one of the restaurants I visited. Parties like that didn't usually buy so I was concentrating on the smaller tables. Twosomes were always more promising. Your grandfather must have been watching me because he caught my eye and beckoned me to his table. To my astonishment he insisted on buying the lot, every rose in my basket. He said a pretty girl should be partying on a Saturday night and I should sit down and join *his* party if I had nowhere better to go."

Beau Prescott laughed, his good humour wafting over Maggie like a seductive caress. "That sounds so typical," he said, his green eyes dancing at her, enticing her into telling him anything he wanted to know. "Whom did he have with him?"

"It was a group of artists who'd won awards."

"Anyone well-known?"

"I don't really know. I never met them again."

A slight frown.

"You could ask Sir Roland," Maggie suggested helpfully. "He was there. I guess it was an Arts Council thing."

"Ah!" The frown smoothed away. He smiled. "How many roses did you have left?"

"Twenty. For me it was a great sale. And then being offered free food, too...I was only too happy to sit down and join them. I ended up having a marvellous time."

"My grandfather had a great talent for parties," he said fondly.

"He certainly loved being the ringmaster and he did it superbly," she warmly agreed.

They both sipped their martinis as memories lingered, their mutual affection for a grand old man subtly linking them and pushing their differences away. The silent hum of harmony filled Maggie's heart with pleasure. This is how it should be, she thought, and imagined Vivian smiling down at them.

Beau leaned over and helped himself to an egg and caviar puff. The movement instantly restirred her awareness of the man; the fabric of his trousers tightening across a width of thigh that looked so hard and strong, Maggie's breath caught in her throat as her mind flashed to how he might look naked, might feel against her own nakedness. She quickly shifted her gaze to his hand before a betraying blush erupted. It was just as fascinating in its maleness. A sure hand, she thought, capable of anything, and a little quiver of possibilities raced through her, further undermining her composure.

"So how did the nanny idea come up?"

The light, quizzical words shot through her ears and forced her to refocus. Maggie took a quick breath and almost gabbled in her haste to resume a natural flow of conversation.

"Oh, Vivian asked me about my life and I gave him a potted history, making it more colourful than it really was." She shrugged. "You know how you do with strangers whom you never expect to meet again. It's easier, more entertaining than laying out the less pleasant bits."

"You mean you made up stuff?"

"No. What I said was true," Maggie rushed to assure him. "I did travel with a circus…' The moment the word was out, Maggie caught her breath, looking to see if there was an adverse reaction. Some people considered a circus unsavoury.

No frown. If anything, an increase in interest. Maggie braved going on.

"I worked as a nanny for the family who owned it. I also worked as a nanny on an outback station. I've done lots of other jobs, as well, but those were the two that evoked the most interest the night I met Vivian."

He looked bemused. "What was the name of the circus?"

"Zabini's. It was a relatively small outfit, family owned and run. It toured country towns."

"I would have thought that kind of thing was out of date now," he remarked.

She nodded in quick agreement. "It was having trouble pulling in crowds when I was with it and that was over ten years ago. The problem was, the family didn't know any other way of life. I was only with them for one tour. They didn't need me after they went into recess so I don't know what happened to them."

"And that's when you headed into the outback?"

"Yes." She smiled ruefully. "It seemed like another adventure. I had experience as a nanny and there was plenty of employment available in that area."

"Where did you end up?"

His obvious desire to know and the lack of any critical air released Maggie from caution. She happily painted the picture for him.

"On a big cattle station in the Northern Territory. A place called Wilgilag. Which means 'red' in the Aboriginal language. And it sure was. Red earth as far as the eye could see. Endless red. The cattle roamed over hundreds of square kilometres in search of feed. It was like another world. A different life."

She caught herself back from rattling on too much and waved a dismissive hand, consigning Wilgilag to the past. "It was all a long time ago. Lots of water under the bridge since then, but that was the background of the nanny business."

He smiled, obviously content with her explanation and amused by the situation. "I see how you could make it sound very colourful and my grandfather would have enjoyed it immensely. Did he latch on to you straight away for the nanny job?"

"No. I was really surprised when the party broke up and he gave me his card, saying if I wanted a steady job, to come and see him the next day."

"He didn't specify the job?"

She shook her head. "It made me wonder. But he'd been so charming. I'd liked him. And curiosity got the better of me. I couldn't see any harm in finding out what kind of job. I mean, I wasn't exactly doing anything wonderful, just making do until something interesting turned up."

"Then Rosecliff must have come as another surprise to you."

His eyes were twinkling, teasing, and his ready acceptance of everything she said was so exhilarating, Maggie didn't feel she had to watch her tongue or manner with him anymore. Her natural exuberance came bursting forth, eyes sparkling, hands flying, words bubbling.

"Was it ever! I couldn't believe anyone actually lived here at first. I thought I must have somehow got it wrong. Even after Sedgewick admitted me to the house—a real live butler, for heaven's sake!—and ushered me into Vivian's presence, it felt as though I'd stepped through the looking glass like Alice, and sooner or later something would snap me back to reality."

He smiled.

Maggie happily beamed a smile right back at him, not noticing anything amiss in his. The circus hadn't owned a tiger. She had never seen a live one. She had no point of comparison.

"What did you think of the nanny proposition?' he prompted, still smiling.

She rolled her eyes. "Wild! But just the thought of living here was wild. It was all so impossibly wild I couldn't resist giving it a try. After all, I could always walk away if I didn't like it. But it just escalated into something more and more wonderful."

He looked quizzically at her. "You didn't ever feel the lack of...well...younger company?"

She might have, if Beau Prescott had come home before this. He was very acutely reminding her she was a young woman with a whole stack of unfulfilled needs, clamouring to be met. There seemed to be a simmering invitation in his eyes. It kicked her pulse into such rapid action it was difficult to concentrate on giving him an answer to his question. She blurted out the truth.

"I was too busy to think of it."

"For two years?" he queried, his gaze wandering over her with a sizzling male appreciation that said more clearly than words she had been wasted in a limbo of nonsexuality.

Maggie's skin started prickling. She gulped some more of her martini and shoved a crab boat into her mouth, desperate to stop the rise of heat. She crossed her legs, inadvertently drawing Beau Prescott's attention to them, and wished she could uncross them again as she inwardly squirmed under his gaze. Afraid more leg action could only be seen as provocative, Maggie plunged into speech.

"I'd been in the company of heaps of young men before I came here. None of them were capable of giving me what Vivian did."

His gaze flicked up and there wasn't the slightest haze of warmth in his eyes. Two green shards of ice sliced into her, cold and deadly. "I don't suppose any of them were millionaires."

The comfort zone created by his earlier geniality was comprehensively shattered. Maggie felt a chill deep in her bones. He'd been putting on an act, drawing her out to get something bad on her.

"Apart from my salary, I never took any money from Vivian, Mr. Prescott," she stated, a bitter defiance edging her voice.

He let her denial hang for several moments before drawling, "I wasn't suggesting you did. But a lot of money was spent on you, Maggie. Your clothes…"

Her chin went up. "Yes and tickets to the opera, the theatre, concerts, balls…you name it, Mr. Prescott, and I certainly was given a free ride to all of them. No question. I'm guilty of going along with everything Vivian wanted. And I'm guilty of loving it, too. I'm sorry it sticks in your craw so much. Maybe you'd like to ask Sedgewick for another martini. Make it four for the day."

She set her own glass on the table and stood up, bristling with angry disillusionment. "Shall I ring for him to come?"

He waved a dismissive hand and tried an appeasing smile. "I was merely remarking on the obvious. Why take offence?"

"You could have tried looking beyond the obvious, Mr. Prescott."

The pretence of a smile twisted into a grimace. "You call my grandfather by his first name. Why not use mine?"

"Because I don't assume familiarities. I never have. In my experience it's asking to be slapped down if you do," she answered tersely.

"Oh, come on! Not in Australia," he protested. "It's the most egalitarian society in the world."

"That depends on where you're coming from," she mocked. "You've never lived an underprivileged life, have you? Never had to learn to be subservient. You have no idea what it's like to live that kind of life."

He frowned, unable to deny the charge.

Sick at heart, Maggie turned away from him and walked around the table, moving to stand where he had stood earlier, in front of the fireplace. She felt too agitated to sit down again. She glanced up at the painting of Cupid frolicking in a garden and a rueful smile curled her lips. The arrows being shot here tonight weren't dipped in a love potion. More like poison.

When she swung around, Beau Prescott was keenly observing her, a perplexed V drawing his eyebrows together.

"I'll tell you what Vivian gave me," she shot at him. "Acceptance, approval, liking, respect. He took me in and made me one of his family. He transformed me into something more than I was and showed me what was possible. He educated me in so many ways—books, music, art—opening my mind to things I'd never known and would never have learnt without his guidance and tuition."

She paused, showing her contempt for his shallow judgment of the situation. "I don't know why your grandfather did it. Perhaps he was lonely. Perhaps he enjoyed playing Henry Higgins, turning me into 'His Fair Lady.' Perhaps he liked having an eager pupil. And I was certainly that. I was hungry for all he gave me and I did my best to live up to all he wanted for me."

Her sense of rightness urged her to add, "I'm not ashamed of that, Mr. Prescott. I'm proud of it because I did Vivian proud. I loved your grandfather. I really did. And whether you like it or not, that's the truth."

He said nothing, retaining an intense air of listening as though waiting to hear more. She held his gaze in fierce challenge. The silence lengthened. The tension between them thickened.

Sedgewick stepped into the room and cleared his throat. "Dinner is ready, sir."

It was so pedantic, such a ridiculous anticlimax, Maggie broke into a peal of laughter. "I do assure you, Mr. Prescott, our cook's Beef Wellington will be much tastier than sinking your teeth into me. Best that we answer his call immediately."

She set off for the dining room, not waiting for any response, savagely berating herself for being a gullible fool. Never again, she vowed. Beau Prescott might be capable of charming birds off trees, but this bird was going to keep her wings tightly folded against him.

# CHAPTER SEVEN

BEAU FORCED HIS jaw to keep working, doggedly chewing up each mouthful of the Beef Wellington to the point where he could swallow it. At the other end of the table, Maggie Stowe was carving through her dinner with military precision, and he'd be damned if he was going to let her see she'd robbed him of his appetite. The woman had too much power as it was.

She tapped straight into every male hormone he had, setting them more abuzz than they'd ever been, regardless of the dictates of his brain. She messed with his mind, too, blurring what should be completely clear, straight-line logic. He couldn't decide whether she was a superb actress or completely for real. If it wasn't for the missing million, he'd be tempted—strongly tempted—to accept her story at face value.

At least he now had some facts to check. Sir Roland would be a reliable eyewitness to the first meeting in the restaurant and he wouldn't mind Beau questioning him about it. Zabini's Circus and the cattle station, Wilgilag, were items he could pass on to Lionel Armstrong. Any competent private investigator should be able to get some character references out of them. *If* she'd told the truth about her *nanny* background.

He glanced down the table. Her face was in shadow, frustrating his need to see past her polished facade. "Sedgewick, would you please switch on the overhead light and remove the candelabra? I can hardly see what I'm eating."

"As you wish, sir."

Beau could feel his irritation growing as Sedgewick complied with ponderous dignity. The disapproval emanating from the old butler was so thick it could be cut with a knife. Maggie Stowe was clearly upset. With all the subtle skill at Sedgewick's command, he kept letting Beau know who was at fault and it wasn't the nanny.

The brighter illumination of the room didn't really help. Maggie's face was like a white mask, completely expressionless. Beau watched her pick up her glass of claret and take a swig. Not champagne tonight, he thought with acid satisfaction. He'd told Sedgewick to serve a good red. The champagne days were over for Nanny Stowe at Rosecliff. No doubt she could buy it for herself soon enough with the missing million.

She had to have that million squirrelled away somewhere.

It was the obvious answer.

Yet she had flatly denied taking any money from his grandfather apart from her wage. And she had scorned him for not looking beyond the obvious.

The woman was a wretched torment. He glared at her as he picked up his glass of wine, needing a good dose of full-bodied claret to ease the angst she'd given him. She didn't look up from her dinner. Since she'd sat down to it, she hadn't met his gaze once. Beau was left with the strong impression she had wrapped a shield around herself and comprehensively shut him out. Her stony silence reinforced it.

The urge to smash it down spurred him into speech. "What did you do after you left Wilgilag?"

Very slowly, reluctantly, she lifted her head. Her eyes glittered like sapphires. "If you want ammunition against me, find it yourself, Mr. Prescott," she said flatly.

Her reply gave him no joy nor satisfaction. Having made him feel like a slime, she returned her attention to her meal and continued eating. Beau couldn't stomach any more food. She had his gut twisted into knots.

"I simply want to know more about you, Maggie," he defended, trying to beat off the sense of being in the wrong. Very badly in the wrong.

She shook her head, not bothering to even glance up at him.

Beau seethed with frustration. He couldn't make her talk. He recalled the artless, open way she had bubbled on before he'd put in the jab about millionaires and savagely wished he'd held his tongue on that point.

Yet had it been artless or artful? Truth or lies? Impossible to know until he'd checked out what she'd told him. One thing was certain. Because of his stupid gaffe in revealing his own train of thought, she was not about to hand him any more information about herself.

He emptied his glass and signalled to Sedgewick to refill it. The action was performed without comment, without eye contact. Beau felt himself being cold-shouldered on more than one front.

Was he wrong about Maggie Stowe? Was he hopelessly, foolishly, hurtfully wrong? He couldn't deny that her passionate defence of her relationship with his grandfather had struck chords of truth. And guilt.

*Perhaps he'd been lonely.*

Those words hit hard. Beau doubted this situation would ever have arisen if he hadn't stayed away so long. Or if he'd found the time and the woman to marry and have children—which was what his grandfather had most wanted, an extension of the family line. Having plenty of friends did not provide the same sense of closeness and caring as having someone who belonged to you, who was there all the time.

Beau could even see now why his grandfather had chosen to take Maggie Stowe in and make her one of his family...a flower-seller with the potential to be much more, given the means and the guidance. "She's going to be my creation," he'd boasted to Lionel Armstrong, and he would have revelled in the role of Henry Higgins; the achievement of it, the sheer theatre of making someone over and producing a star, the heady reward of her appreciative response to his teaching.

If Maggie Stowe had really had an underprivileged life, why wouldn't she be eager to try everything on offer, hungry for it, loving it? It made sense. The only fly in that ointment was the missing million, which suggested she could be a very clever con woman.

Beau just couldn't let that go. Not without knowing more. A lot more. He cursed himself again for letting his advantage slip. She was on guard against him now. He'd have to work other angles and hope something pertinent would turn up.

It startled him out of his dark reverie when she rose abruptly from her chair. She laid her refolded napkin on the table and looked directly at him, making his heart kick at the renewed link between them.

"I beg to be excused, Mr. Prescott," she said with quiet dignity. "I am not feeling well."

Which left him no loophole for insisting she stay. Beau set his glass down and rose to his feet, courtesy demanding he let her go gracefully. "I'm sorry. If there's anything you require…"

"No. Thank you." She turned to the butler. "Sedgewick, please apologise to Jeffrey for me. I know he will have prepared a special sweets course. Perhaps Mr. Prescott will have two helpings to make up for my leaving it."

"I'll ensure Jeffrey understands, Nanny Stowe," Sedgewick returned kindly, drawing her chair back for easier movement.

"Thank you."

She walked the length of the table with the carriage of a queen, yet when she paused by Beau, he saw she was trembling, and her face was so bloodless he wondered if she were really ill. Her eyes were no longer glittering. They reflected a sickness of soul that screwed Beau up even further.

"I've been presuming too much. I won't sit at table with you again, Mr. Prescott. As you said this morning, you are not your grandfather."

Beau opened his mouth to argue, everything within him rebelling against the evasion she intended. The mystery of her was not resolved. He wanted the challenge of her presence. He wanted more of her than he could admit to. But before he could voice the words of protest tumbling through his mind, her eyes misted with tears, making him recoil from saying anything.

"Goodnight," she whispered huskily and moved on, walking briskly from the dining room, leaving him feeling like a monster for making her cry.

He watched her go, the flouncy little frills of the sexy red dress taunting him with what she might have given him if he'd acted differently. His loins ached with thwarted desire. His mind raged against the circumstances that trapped him into keeping his distance. The angry frustration welling up in him could barely be contained.

Sedgewick proceeded to clear her end of the table, apparently unconcerned by the incident, carrying on with his job, transferring her plates and glass to the traymobile. Beau, still on his feet, his napkin crumpled in his hand, glared at the old butler for being so deliberately officious about his duties.

"If you've got something to say, Sedgewick, spit it out!"

A dignified pause. A slight raising of eyebrows. A look down his noble nose at Beau. "I was thinking, sir, I have served many people in my years at Rose-cliff. Amongst them, the high and mighty of this country, one might say. People who thought their wealth or power put them above others. Nanny Stowe may have come here without much to recommend her, sir, but she is a genuine lady. Mr. Vivian certainly thought so, too."

"You don't know what I know, Sedgewick," Beau retorted in dark fury.

His lofty mien became ever loftier as he answered, "Possibly not, sir. I have only had two years' close acquaintance with Nanny Stowe."

Which neatly sliced Beau's feet out from under him. He threw the napkin on the table, picked up his glass and strode to the sideboard to collect the decanter of claret. "Please inform Jeffrey I won't be wanting sweets, either. Nor anything else tonight, thank you, Sedgewick," he said in savage dismissal.

"Very well, sir."

Armed with what was left of the good red he'd insisted upon, Beau headed for the library, haunted by a glorious mane of red hair, a red dress that was too damned bold to be worn by a woman with that shade of hair, and the authoritative words of a man who should know what he was talking about.

He found the videotape of his grandfather's funeral and slotted it into the machine ready to play. Left to himself, he automatically shed the constraints of formality, taking off his coat, vest and tie, then rolling up his shirt sleeves and undoing the collar button. Getting rid of his excess clothes, however, did not ease his pent-up tension.

He poured himself a glass of wine, picked up the remote control panel, and tried to find some comfort in one of the leather armchairs. His thumb was hovering over the play button when he realised his anger was inappropriate for watching the funeral of a man who'd raised him from boyhood, a man he'd revered and loved.

He waited a while, occasionally sipping the claret, clearing his head of Maggie Stowe and filling it with memories of happy times with his grandfather; the adventures they'd had together—cruising The Great Barrier Reef, seeing the wildlife of Kakadu National Park, exploring the underground world of Coober Pedy—then in his teens, the trip to Europe where his grandfather had made history come alive for him.

It had been Vivian Prescott's gift, to make the world
a marvellous place. And he'd chosen to bestow this gift
on a woman he'd picked up one night. Right or wrong,
it had been *his* choice. *His* choice, too, to take a million
dollars and do whatever he'd done with it.

Beau wanted to respect those choices. He really did.

*A genuine lady...*

God! He even wanted to believe Sedgewick was
right!

He just couldn't bear the thought his grandfather
had been fooled.

With a heavy sigh, Beau pressed the play button and
set the footage of the funeral rolling.

He found the service intensely moving...the songs,
the words spoken, the roses, the cathedral packed to
overflowing by those whose lives had been touched
by Vivian Prescott. Then, at the cemetery, it was indeed a fine, fine touch, having a piper in full Scottish
dress, lead the carrying of the coffin to the graveside,
the age-old wail of pipes ringing down the last curtain.

The final ceremonial words floated past Beau un-
heard, his attention fastened on the little group of
people standing a few metres behind the bishop, his
grandfather's family, for lack of anyone closer.

He was inexorably drawn into studying the woman
who had most recently come amongst them, the woman
at the centre of his grandfather's last years. He focused
his entire mind on setting aside his prejudices and seeing her as objectively as he could.

She looked magnificent in a tailored black suit and
a broad-brimmed black hat that managed to be both
sober and stylish. *Doing Vivian proud,* Beau thought,
finding himself admiring her stance, despite his suspi-

cions about her character. Not once did she look down at the grave. She held her single rose clutched to her chest, and her face was lifted to the sky.

She didn't appear to be aware of the tears trickling down her cheeks from the corners of her eyes. Or she determinedly ignored them. She kept her gaze fixed upwards, as though she wouldn't let herself believe Vivian Prescott was in that coffin. His spirit was out there somewhere, soaring free, not tied to the earth in any shape or form. The Angel of Death had come kindly...

Beau winced at the thought, yet ironically found himself in sympathy with it. He switched off the video, having seen enough. His glass was empty but he didn't feel like drinking more anyway. The sense of having done Maggie Stowe an injustice was strong. Even if she'd had her eye on the main chance, capitalising on all she could, she certainly hadn't failed her benefactor at the end.

*I loved your grandfather. I really did. And whether you like it or not, that's the truth.*

He might not like it, but Beau was beginning to believe it. The whole funeral was an act of love, getting it right, doing his grandfather proud. He could no longer see it as putting on a show. There was too much care, too much feeling behind it for him to dismiss as an exercise in showmanship.

So where did that leave him? An unappreciative, ungrateful, blundering clod? Driving a woman to tears instead of giving her her just due?

Wretchedly at odds with himself, Beau pushed out of his armchair and paced restlessly around the library. He'd set about this nanny business all wrong, shooting off with bees in his bonnet, right from the start, making assumptions without the evidence to back them up.

What if Maggie Stowe was *a genuine lady,* as Sedgewick claimed?

He'd virtually accused her of being a whore and a gold-digger. There could be no doubt he was wrong on the first count. As to the second…God only knew!

She'd gone off to her room in obvious distress because of him. His grandfather had installed her in a position of respect here and he'd cast her as unworthy of it, cross-examining her like a criminal in the hot seat and judging before she'd had a proper hearing. Was that fair? Would his grandfather be proud of him?

Shame wormed through Beau. His grandfather had trusted him to let everything at Rosecliff carry on as dictated in the will and he hadn't even let one day pass without blowing it apart. Not one day. What he personally thought was irrelevant. This was a matter of trust to be kept, and keeping it was the least he could do since he hadn't been here to do more when it would have truly counted.

He checked his watch. It wasn't too late to straighten things out with Maggie Stowe. Best to do it right now. That way they could start afresh tomorrow. And he'd get to go to bed with a clear conscience.

Fired with resolute purpose, Beau left the library, only realising when he was halfway up the stairs, he didn't know where Maggie Stowe was. A moment's thought gave him the answer. His grandfather would have given her the Rose Suite. Their relationship had begun and ended with roses. It fitted. And whatever his grandfather had ordained for her, had to be carried on for a year, come what may.

# CHAPTER EIGHT

MAGGIE DIDN'T WANT to answer the knock on her door. It was bound to be Mrs Featherfield, anxious to smooth things over again, offering excuses and pleading for more time and tolerance, probably bringing a soothing cup of hot chocolate to settle her down. Impossible mission, Maggie thought, inwardly recoiling from having to cope with it. Better to ignore the knock. She'd done enough answering.

She stayed out on the balcony, ending more than the long day of emotional battering. Her life with Vivian...Rosecliff...this view over the harbour...she had to say goodbye to all of it. There was not going to be any flow-on with Beau Prescott.

Another knock, louder, more insistent than before.

Maggie frowned. Was her silence giving Mrs Featherfield concern? She didn't want to worry the housekeeper. Sedgewick would have reported the scene in the dining room to her and she might start thinking of real illness if she wasn't answered. Better to let her check and have done with it.

Reluctantly but resignedly Maggie moved back to the French doors and called, "Come in," hoping a minute or two would see the end of any fussing.

Beau Prescott stepped into her bedroom.

Disbelief dizzied her. Shock hit in waves. He'd actually come after her, right into her room, invading her privacy, making nowhere at Rosecliff safe from him. The civilised veneer had been cast off; his suitcoat, vest and tie gone. She was swamped by his sheer maleness, the physical dominance of the man, the aggressive masculinity that seemed to swirl from him and draw on her like a powerful magnet.

She stared at his muscular forearms, bared to the elbow as though ready for action. Her heart skittered. She wrenched her gaze up but it moved erratically over his chest, finding the arrow of flesh where his shirt was opened and fastening on the base of his throat where the throb of his pulse was clearly visible. Another shock. Tension tearing at her, forcing her to lift her eyes to his, to see what was driving his heart faster.

A blast of raw desire plastered her with a hot awareness of what she was wearing. She hadn't thought of it, her mind scrambled by the impact he was having on her. The slinky nightgown had been a personal purchase, its sensual appeal irresistible, a clinging creation of navy silk and lace that slid over her skin and snugly moulded her breasts.

It wasn't transparent and Mrs Featherfield had seen and admired it, but the lace-trimmed V neckline revealed more cleavage than she would normally put on public view, especially to Beau Prescott who already saw her as having no morals at all. It didn't stop him looking at her with lust, though, and Maggie felt a quite vixenish satisfaction in stirring him on a primitive level when he couldn't possibly approve of himself being attracted to her.

Rebellion simmered through the heat he aroused. She'd be damned if she'd make any move to cover up. She was in her own bedroom. She enjoyed wearing this nightgown. It was one little pleasure he couldn't take away from her. Besides, a belated attempt at modesty wouldn't impress him. He thought badly of her anyway. So let him stare. Let him burn as much as she was burning.

Her breathing quickened with the reckless, dangerous excitement of challenging him on the most basic level of all. She felt her breasts rising, falling, straining against the flimsy silk, her nipples hardening, flaunting themselves through the provocative arrangement of lace. And she didn't care. She revelled in the feverish glitter in his green eyes, exulted when splashes of red speared across his cheekbones betraying *his* rush of blood, *his* discomfiture with what was happening to him, *his* response to the stimulus of her femininity.

Her mind boiled over the memory of her first sight of him this morning, the sizzle of sexual awareness, the pleasure, the tingling anticipation of thinking they were made for each other, the sense of at last having found a man she wanted, with whom it would be right to mate. Frustration seethed through her as her eyes raked down his body. This man should have been hers. Her bones ached with the sense of loss.

"Maggie…"

The low, gutteral uttering of her name snapped her gaze up to his again, violent emotion coursing through her at the violation of possibilities he'd ripped away before they could grow. Damn him! she thought in bitter fury. Damn him for not recognising what should have been!

It was true...*Hell hath no fury like a woman scorned.* But he wasn't scorning her now. Not now. Whatever barriers he'd imposed between them were gone and *the wild child* had been let loose. Except there was no child in those blazing eyes. It was rampant manhood on the move and he was coming at her, tearing off his shirt, blinding her with a broad expanse of bronzed masculinity.

His clothes were dragged off and hurled away with lightning speed. No hesitation. No inhibitions. Maggie did nothing, said nothing to stop him. She was totally mesmerised by the splendour of the nakedness emerging. He was stunningly beautiful and compellingly, enthrallingly, majestically *male.* Her whole body was seized by an intense lust for the touch of him, the taste of him, the complete and utter experience of him.

She'd barely had time to want when the want was answered, a strong, binding arm scooping her against him, the thin film of silk between them heightening the physical sensations of their bodies meeting, impressing, exulting in the intimate contact, his hand burrowing under her hair to curl around the nape of her neck, and his mouth crashing onto hers, hot and hungry, intent on plunder.

He kissed her deeply, a strong, sweeping possession determined on tasting all of her. Electric tingles shot straight through the roof of her mouth and exploded any inhibitions she might have had. A fever of passionate need took hold, inciting a wild response to his aggression. They ravished each other in a tumult of kisses, laying an erotic siege that pushed for more to give under the urgent escalation of the desire to take everything—everything they could—here and now.

His fingers hooked into her hair, tilting her head back to expose her long throat to a burning trail of kisses, and she arched into him, loving the sensation of hard unyielding thighs against hers, the thick roll of his manhood pressing into her stomach, the heave of his chest compressing her breasts.

He dragged the shoulder straps of her nightgown down with his teeth, then lifted her off her feet, one arm under her thighs, the other under her back, lifting her high, shoulder high, draping her over his arms like a taut bow, her naked breasts pointing up for his mouth to take, the swell of her flesh taut and tingling, drowning in fierce waves of pleasure from the hot suction of his kisses as he carried her across the room.

Then the bed was beneath her and the silk was stripped from her body, leaving her open and utterly vulnerable to the eyes glittering down in rapturous thrall. "The same colour...the same colour..." he murmured, his voice furred with sensual satisfaction, and he thrust his fingers through the red-gold silkiness at the apex of her thighs, parting it, sliding down to caress the soft, intimate folds it hid...hidden no more as he buried his face there, tasting her sex, driving fierce spasms of sensation through her, making her jerk and twist and tremble with the intensity of his pleasuring.

She felt herself poised on a perilous edge, her muscles melting, contracting in need for him to be inside her, filling the aching emptiness, easing the screaming desire for full possession. She was dying for him... dying for the proving of the promise, the final plunge that would make order of chaos. She clawed at his head, silently begging, urging him to come to her.

He lifted himself over her, kissed her, his mouth

invading hers with fast, darting thrusts that drove her wild, taunting her with what he withheld. She bucked in fierce incitement and he rolled, carrying her, lifting her to straddle him, challenging her to take what she wanted, how she wanted. He was there for her, primed and positioned, and his hands slid to her buttocks, squeezing them, urging her into aggressive action.

She took him, lowering herself slowly, feeling herself stretching to encompass him, feeling her muscles convulse around him in response to the exquisite sensation of him moving into her, deeper and deeper, like a delicious fullness pushing through a long swelling stem to a place that seemed to blossom with soft inner petals opening to ecstasy.

She closed her eyes, focusing on that fantastic inner world, and she lifted herself, revelling in the reverse slide, wanting to feel it all over again, exulting in the control he'd given her. His hands stroked up her back and lifted her hair forward, over her shoulders. As she undulated over him, he curtained her breasts with the long silky tresses, caressing them through the soft, tantalising texture in the same rhythmic movement she used on him, evoking a wild eroticism that drove her into pumping faster, until suddenly she was shaking, unable to direct anything.

He whirled her onto her back and took command, poised over her with all his dominant power and the stroking inside her was different now, like a steam train charging towards some zenith she couldn't even imagine, the rails sparking with showers of electricity—speed, power, action—and a scream of achievement building, building, rushing through her, pushing her to an incredible peak and bursting into an explosion of intense melting sweetness that fused their bodies together and left them collapsed on each other, saturated in heat, all energy pooled and drained.

Maggie had no idea how long they stayed like that, limp and damp and dazed in the aftermath of passion. Eventually Beau dragged himself aside and lay on his back, apart from her. She didn't mind the separation. Her brain was in some strange limbo where thoughts could not be defined, let alone caught and held. Somehow what had happened was too much to grasp, too difficult to sort out. It hadn't really been she who had shared in all those wild actions. Some kind of madness had possessed her.

As though this recognition and acknowledgment cleared the haze a little, various ideas darted through. The madness was his fault. He had incited it. After all, she had never done anything like this before. Though it shook her that she'd let it happen, in a way, she had actually wanted it to happen. However, wanting him was no excuse when she knew perfectly well *his* wanting would stop right here in this bedroom.

He didn't like her.

And she didn't like him, either.

So what on earth were they going to do now?

The silence and stillness stretched on, humming with an awareness which was no longer sexual but gathering just as much electric tension. However exhausted they were, sleep was definitely not in the air. Maggie suspected Beau Prescott was nursing the very same thoughts that were plaguing her.

"It's been a long time since I've been with a woman,"

he said at last, making it a quiet statement of fact, all
emotional judgment strained out of it.

He hadn't turned to her, hadn't moved at all. He
spoke to the ceiling. Maggie understood this. It was
easier to converse without looking at each other. The
excuse he offered sounded reasonable enough for her
to use, as well.

"Same here," she answered, speaking just as carefully. "With a man, I mean," she added for clarity.

"I didn't come in here to do that." A trace of shock
in his voice.

"I didn't expect you at all." Maggie was pleased to
make that point. "I thought it was Mrs Featherfield
knocking."

Another silence, not quite so tense, carrying more
a stunned quality which they both accepted now they
had spoken. Maggie thought how strange it was…both
of them sprawled stark naked on the bed, yet wrapped
in separate worlds, despite the incredible intimacies
there'd been between them. Clothes didn't seem to matter. Nothing could cover up what they'd done together.
It felt ridiculous to even try.

"I watched the funeral," he said.

"Oh!" Maggie puzzled over why that was relevant in
the current circumstances. "I hope it was all you would
have wanted for your grandfather," she said gently,
wondering if grief had knocked him sideways.

"Yes."

At least she had done something right in his eyes.
Though it was a bit late to change anything between
them.

"I wanted to tell you…wanted to apologise for my
attitude today," he said in a rush. "I should have re-

spected the position my grandfather gave you. And I will," he added determinedly.

Maggie gave it some thought but couldn't see how it would work, given his predilection to always thinking the worst of her. "I was planning to leave tomorrow," she stated bluntly.

She could feel him frowning. It took him a while to reply. "I don't want to drive you out." It was said stiffly.

He didn't really want her here, either. He'd made it perfectly clear their connection tonight was a total aberration. As it was for her. She found it difficult to even look at facing him tomorrow.

"It's best I leave. You needn't worry I'll take much with me. I tend to travel lightly and most of the clothes Vivian bought me won't fit into my usual life. You can sell them. The accountant, John Neville, will tell you where."

"But it's right for you to stay," he argued, uncomfortable with the outcome of his gold-digging accusations. It stirred him to move. He propped himself up on his elbow and frowned down at her. "It's in the will. My grandfather wanted it."

Even with a beetling frown on his face, he was an incredibly handsome man. But looks weren't everything. Sex wasn't, either. With a heavy sigh, filled with disappointment and resignation, she stated the reality she had faced earlier.

"Vivian is gone. You made me realise that today."

He expelled a deeper sigh. "I'm sorry. I don't know what else to say. Except I do want you to stay."

She searched the shadowed green eyes, trying to see what was driving him now. Was it only the will? Was tonight's cataclysmic folly influencing him? Was he thinking he might want more of her? Horror suddenly billowed through her mind. She jackknifed up, sitting with her hands clapped to her face before jerking around to face him with the dreadful truth.

"You didn't use protection!"

He shot up from an elbow to a hand prop. Her shock was echoed in his fast retort. "You're not on the pill?"

"No. I had no reason to be."

"Hell!" He thumped his forehead with the heel of his palm.

Maggie was struck by visions of him having explosive one-night stands all over South America. "Are you safe? I mean...medically clear of..."

"Damned right I am!" He whipped away the hand that had slid from his forehead to pinch his eyes. "Are you?"

"Yes. I haven't had sex for years!" she defended hotly.

The green laser beams retracted into dark turbulence. "Is there a chance of...of your falling pregnant?"

Maggie took a deep breath and calculated. It was the worst possible time. Which had probably contributed to the mad wanting to mate with him. Didn't they always say that was the danger period for women to fall to temptation?

"Yes. I'm afraid there is," she said flatly, scarcely able to believe she had been so stupid, so wilfully, wantonly stupid.

"Bloody hell!" he said, not liking it any more than she did. He swung his legs off the bed and sat hunched away from her, his head in his hands.

Maggie drew up her knees, hugging them, feeling more alone than ever.

The silence was filled with pregnant things.

"Well, you can't leave now," Beau said tersely, twisting around to direct his decision at her. "Not with this hanging over our heads."

Like the sword of doom, she thought, her heart sinking on the horns of their dilemma. She met his eyes, schooling herself to expect nothing. "Would you want the baby if I had one?' she asked, hating the idea of forced acceptance.

"Of course, I would!" He stood up, stiff with indignation. "Do you think I'm the kind of man who'd abandon his own child?"

People did.

Who knew that better than she?

Maggie never would. She couldn't. Impossible for her to trust anyone but herself to do right by her child. If she had one.

"I don't know you," she said. "I only met you today and you certainly haven't struck me as someone I could trust and depend upon. I think you'd do what suits you."

"Well, you're wrong," he declared, affronted by her opinion of his character. "And there's plenty of people who'd back me up on that."

She shrugged noncommittally. "I guess time will tell."

"Yes, it will."

He left her with that dark comment as he walked around the room collecting his scattered clothes.

Maggie sagged into dismal despondency. Maybe God would be merciful and let her get away with this one night of madness. When she did have a child she wanted to be in a true love relationship where abandonment would never be a possibility. She had no idea what kind of father Beau Prescott would make. Probably a resentful one and what good was that?

She didn't look at him. Didn't want to. In her mind he'd moved from being a possible mate to one who'd hate a lasting connection with her. Yet if he had fathered a child on her she couldn't shut him out of their lives. Not if he wanted in. She couldn't deprive her child of its natural father, couldn't let it feel abandoned by him.

"It's settled then," he said decisively, having gathered up his clothes and hung them over his arm, still careless of his nakedness. The green eyes held steely resolution. "You stay, Maggie. At least until we find out if you're pregnant."

"Yes," she agreed. It was the only sensible course to take.

*Trapped,* she thought.

Satisfied the matter *was* settled, he left, shutting her door on the most regrettable episode of her life.

# CHAPTER NINE

BEAU LEANED BACK against the door to the Rose Suite and shut his eyes in sheer anguish at having committed the worst folly of his life.

*Trapped!*

Trapped by the oldest method in the world.

Impossible for him to shun a woman he might have made pregnant. What's more, if she had his child he was tied to her for life!

And he'd walked right into it like one of those suicidal animals—lemmings—that threw themselves off cliffs. No rationality to what he'd done. No stopping for wiser consideration. His brain had fused and animal instinct had taken over the driving seat. He should have shot himself in the foot before going into Maggie Stowe's bedroom. It might have kept him sane.

Summoning up the last shreds of his utterly depleted energy, he pushed away from the door and plodded down the corridor to his own suite. One hell of a day, he thought, and hell's fires were still burning. He'd be damned lucky if he wasn't scorched forever from this night's work. Never in his life had he lost his head so completely. Never! He had no answer to it.

Sweet relief to reach his own bedroom and crawl

between the sheets. He was wrecked. In every sense. Maggie, the cat, had clawed him inside out and finished up with a dish of cream that would never run dry...if she was pregnant and carried it through. Which she would. Beau had no doubt about it. The way she'd checked his attitude about fatherhood made that course a certainty.

Not that he'd want her to sneak off and have an abortion. His child was his child. Getting rid of it was not an option in his book. All the same, he desperately hoped there would be no consequences from tonight's madness.

In all fairness to Maggie Stowe, he couldn't say she'd planned it. There was no way she could have anticipated his visit to her suite. He had to believe her claim that she hadn't expected to see him, so she hadn't set out to seduce him by wearing the sinfully provocative slip of silk and lace.

No, she definitely hadn't planned it, but she was a dead-set opportunist. Why else would she have flaunted herself in a sizzling challenge to him? It was a carnal come-on if ever he saw one. No protest from her when he'd responded to it. No attempt to stop him. She'd been right with him from the start, revelling in the whole mad ride.

For a moment, his body gripped with the memory of how fantastic it had been, the incredibly intense excitement of... But it still shouldn't have happened. Giving great sex was fine but it wasn't all he wanted in a woman. For the mother of his child he'd want a few other attributes, especially someone he could *trust!*

And what did he have in Maggie Stowe?

A woman from nowhere!

Still, worrying about what couldn't be changed wasn't going to get him anywhere, either. Sleep was what he needed. He'd face whatever he had to face tomorrow. Besides, there'd be time before the pregnancy deadline for him to get a handle on Maggie Stowe. She couldn't stay a mystery forever. The more he knew, the better equipped he'd be to make the right choices.

Beau blanked his mind and slipped into sweet oblivion.

The first day after *the night of the disastrous mistake* did not start well for Beau. Maggie failed to appear for breakfast. It was an ominous sign. They might have come to an understanding about her staying on at Rosecliff but goodwill had not been established. Sedgewick subtly let him know this was not a situation he favoured. The cold shoulder continued.

After breakfast, Beau took refuge in the library, a private domain where he could get on with his agenda for the day. He settled himself behind his grandfather's splendid mahogany desk—used more for the business of keeping his social diary and planning charity functions than anything else. The computer, fax machine and photocopier in the far corner of the room had also been used for these purposes but they were handy for Beau, as well.

Top priority was to telephone Lionel Armstrong and get another investigation started. Happily the solicitor was in his office and took the call immediately. Beau related the facts he now knew about Margaret Stowe and demanded immediate action. Urgent action. And reports coming in as fast as possible.

"I want those employers milked of everything they

know about her. Character references, background, even impressions if they don't have facts. Photographs, records...whatever can be dug up."

"Beau..." A hesitation. "...Is all this necessary? I mean...why go to town on her at this point? Is there good reason for it?"

Beau gritted his teeth. Good reasons abounded! Maggie Stowe might be the mother of his child. And there was still the missing million.

"Just do it, Lionel," he bit out.

A resigned sigh. "Vivian wouldn't listen to my advice, either. Makes me wonder what it is about this woman."

"The point, Lionel, is I want to *stop* wondering."

Beau had no idea when or how a pregnancy test could be taken but he had the strong feeling he shouldn't let the grass grow under his feet while he was waiting.

"Put two investigators on it. One for Zabini's Circus, one for Wilgilag. Time is of the essence," he said emphatically. "Reports within a week would be good."

"It will cost..." the solicitor began to warn.

"Irrelevant. Tell the guys to fax or phone me here. I want progress reports. Is that clear, Lionel?"

"Yes. Very clear. I'll get two top investigators to work immediately, giving your precise instructions."

"Thank you."

He was trying to get his thoughts in order for a call to Helen Carter at the head office of his travel agency when there was a knock on the library door.

Maggie, he thought, and his heart did a weird somersault and sent a buzz through his veins. Steady does it, he sternly commanded. Wayward responses and wrong reactions could do untold damage. Control had to be maintained. Firm control.

First and foremost he had to establish goodwill and push table-sharing at meals, get things back to normal, do what his grandfather would have expected of him. Courtesy was the key. Courtesy and control. Best to stay right where he was, seated behind the desk and looking at ease.

"Come in," he called, pitching his voice to a bright, welcoming note.

Mrs Featherfield entered, carrying what looked like a large ledger under her arm. "I hope I'm not interrupting anything important, Master Beau," she rushed out, beaming a hopeful and eager smile at him.

He felt absurdly deflated, like having a prize whipped away from him at the last moment. It made him effusive in denial. "Not at all, Feathers. I always have time for you."

"Oh! How nice!" She came forward with an air of happy anticipation. "I wanted to show you my scrapbook."

Beau was surprised. "What have you been collecting?"

The book was placed on the desk in front of him. "They're all the newspaper and magazine cuttings about Mr. Vivian. I thought you might like to see them. Especially the more recent ones, since you've been away so long."

Beau opened the book and started leafing through. "This is amazing! I had no idea you were keeping such a record."

"Well, they are lovely memories, Master Beau. Your

grandfather was such a gentleman. Being in service to him was a real privilege."

"I'm glad you felt that, Feathers," Beau said warmly.

"Indeed, I do. Nanny Stowe used to say he turned life into a rainbow."

With a pot of gold at the end of it?

Or was it simply colour after rain?

Beau frowned as he recalled Maggie's claim of having led a very underprivileged life before coming to Rosecliff. *Without much to recommend her,* Sedgewick had said.

"Mr. Vivian loved having her with him," the housekeeper went on. "And he was always determined she'd be the belle of the ball when he took her to those big charity dos." She leaned over the desk and turned a chunk of pages. "Here they are!"

A photo of Maggie with his grandfather leapt out at him in full technicolour; his grandfather an elegant figure—as always—in a black dress suit and bow tie, turned admiringly towards a magnificent Maggie, wearing a stunning evening gown in black and burgundy, with exotic jet jewellery gleaming on her white skin and against her vivid hair.

"I remember that night well," Feathers said fondly. "Mr. Vivian called us into the hall to watch her come down the staircase. He twirled his walking cane like a magician and called out, 'Hey, Presto!' and we clapped when she appeared. It was such fun! Mr. Vivian was delighted. He was so very, very proud of her."

The scene described lingered in Beau's mind. He could see it quite vividly and it made poignant sense of all he had heard about the relationship between his grandfather and Maggie. It also made him feel mean-spirited for thinking badly of her. Of course, his grand-father had been the ringmaster. It was completely in character for him. As for Maggie...well, who would knock back the opportunity to be turned into a star?

"What was she like when she first came here, Feath-ers?"

"Nanny Stowe?"

"Yes." He turned to her with keen interest. "What impression did you have of her at the start...say, her first week at Rosecliff?"

No immediate answer...pensive...thinking back. When she spoke, the words came slowly. "It was like she'd been transported to another world and she couldn't quite believe it. Excited by the adventure but frightened of putting a foot wrong. And surprised. Mostly surprised."

"By what?' Beau prompted.

Feathers frowned. "I think...that we'd let her fit in here. I had the sense she wasn't used to belonging any-where. What she brought with her...well, it was really pitiful. Some well-worn jeans and T-shirts, a couple of those cheap Indian dresses..." A shake of the head. "...The bare minimum of everything."

*I tend to travel lightly.*

"Of course, Mr. Vivian soon fixed that. I suggested she throw out her old clothes but she wouldn't." An-other frown. "She said they were the only things that were hers."

*The clothes Vivian bought me won't fit into my usual life.*

"She had no idea how to make the most of herself, either. Seeing her now, you would hardly recognise her as the same girl who came here. No make-up, her glorious hair stuck into a plait. And she was thin. Too thin. All bones. Mr. Vivian said she was a thoroughbred racehorse who needed grooming and training. I remember how surprised she was when he showed her how she could look. Like she couldn't believe it was her."

*Vivian is gone.*

So was his magic wand, Beau thought. It's over for Maggie and she knows it.

*You made me realise that today.*

"She needed looking after," came the motherly opinion. "That's what I thought of her. She was like a waif of the world who'd never had anyone to look after her."

*It's best I leave.*

Beau was suddenly seized by a heart-squeezing suspicion. Maggie was gone. That was why she hadn't come down to breakfast. She had already left. Packed the things belonging to her and stepped back through the looking glass to the reality that had been hers before coming here.

He leapt up from his chair and barely quelled the impulse to go racing up to the Rose Suite. Her bedroom was off-limits for him. Absolutely. If she was there and he went banging on her door...it would be gross behaviour, open to distasteful interpretation.

"Is something wrong, Master Beau?"

The concern voiced by the housekeeper burrowed through his inner agitation. He looked at her distractedly, his mind dictating that any meeting with Maggie would have to be conducted on neutral ground.

"Feathers, I would like to talk to Nanny Stowe. Would you please go and ask her to join me here?"

"You mean...now?"

"Yes. Please."

"Shall I leave my scrapbook with you?"

"Yes. Thank you." He could barely curb his impatience. "It is rather urgent I see her," he pressed.

The housekeeper looked pleased. "I'll be as quick as I can, Master Beau."

She sailed off with an air of triumph. Beau was left with the strong impression she was in league with Sedgewick to *set him straight* on the subject of Nanny Stowe. However, neither of them could have any idea of what had transpired between him and Maggie last night. It complicated everything. There was no longer a simple line to take. Maggie may well have decided the game wasn't worth the candle if she had to take him into her life.

And if she had the missing million, why stay? Why put up with the aggravation of him when he couldn't get a damned thing right?

Beau paced around the library like a caged tiger. He'd messed up big-time, not giving Maggie Stowe the benefit of the doubt. He would have to chase after her if she'd gone. Which could present one hell of a problem. A woman from nowhere could easily slip back into nowhere, especially with a million untraceable dollars at her disposal.

He'd hate not knowing about the child, if there was to be one. To be left wondering would be a dreadful torture. It didn't matter that it hadn't been planned. His child was his child. A fiercely paternal possessiveness swamped every other consideration and Beau was on a feverish roll of resolution to pursue his bloodline to the ends of the earth, if necessary, when a knock on the door delivered a swift kick to his heart.

"Yes," he snapped, expecting bad news.

Maggie Stowe stepped into the library.

Disbelief choked Beau for a moment. The subsequent relief at seeing her was short-lived. She wore jeans and a T-shirt and her gorgeous hair was confined to a plait, making the contours of her face sharper and the blue of her eyes more blue...guarded eyes, wary and watchful as though he were a wild animal who might strike at her, and she hugged the door, keeping her escape route handy.

Beau's hand came up, a finger stabbing emphatically at her. "You are not to leave, Maggie."

Her chin came up. Defiance flared. "I don't believe you have the right to tell me what to do, Mr. Prescott."

"Oh, for God's sake, call me Beau! After what we've shared, it's ridiculous to stick to formalities."

A flush stained her cheeks.

He was doing this wrong. Beau knew it but somehow couldn't stop it. Every time he saw her he went haywire. "Relax! I'm not going to assault you," he shot at her as he turned aside to walk to the desk and put it between them. "Not that I did last night," he added with a warning look over his shoulder. She was not going to pin that on him. No way! He might be guilty of a lot of things but he wasn't guilty of taking an unwilling woman to bed with him.

"I have no intention of accusing you of anything, Mr. Prescott."

"Beau," he repeated with fierce insistence, glowering at her from behind the desk. "You are perfectly safe with me, I promise you. I just want to talk."

"Surely the simplest solution is for me to leave."

"No!"

"You could pretend this never happened. Out of sight, out of mind," she quietly argued.

"That won't work."

She looked bleakly at him. "What *will* work? You hate this. You're obviously upset. Why make a meal of it when I'm willing to walk away?"

"Is that what you were preparing to do? Without telling me?' Just the thought made him feel hollow inside.

"No. I agreed to wait until we know," she answered flatly.

"Why didn't you come down to breakfast?"

"I overslept."

"My grandfather wouldn't have bought those clothes for you," he pointed out.

"No. They are rightly mine." A flash of pride. "Vivian did pay me a salary and I bought some things for myself."

"Why are you wearing them?"

"I feel more comfortable in them."

"Because of me? Because of what I implied?"

She shrugged. "There's no reason to dress up anymore."

"I've spoilt it," he said regretfully.

"It doesn't matter."

"Yes, it does. I'm sorry. I really am."

She stared at him.

He could feel her scepticism and the turbulence of spirit behind it. He held her gaze, projecting sincerity, determined she know he genuinely rued the way he'd treated her. Whoever she was, whatever she was, she'd given something special to the last years of his grandfather's life and he did respect that.

"Please...I'd be grateful if you could overlook

my manner to you regarding the clothes…and other things," he said, desperate to break the tension between them. "I've been very wrong to cast any aspersion on what gave everyone here pleasure. Most of all, my grandfather."

Her gaze slid away. Sadness was etched on her face. Beau wanted to reach out to her but didn't know how without seeming to be threatening. He searched his mind for a more effective peace-offering and couldn't come up with anything.

"I called a women's clinic." The soft words were directed at the carpet. It obviously took an act of will to bring her gaze up to his again and the resolution in her eyes didn't quite cover the fear and anguish behind it. "I can have a blood test in four days. It takes one working day for the results to be determined. A week all up, and we'll know one way or the other."

She didn't want to be pregnant. The realisation thumped into Beau's heart. He'd been wrong about that, too. Whatever had driven her response to him last night, it wasn't the possibility of having him father a child on her.

"They say a blood test is definitive," she added.

"I'll go with you," he said, impelled to stand by her and give what support he could.

Her mouth twisted. "Don't you trust me to do it right?"

He frowned, shook his head. "I just want to be there. Some people faint at having a blood test taken. You shouldn't be alone. I'm involved in this."

She looked at him quizzically, reassessingly, and Beau felt his pulse quicken with the hope he *was* getting through to her, touching a base that was more than physical.

Finally an ironic smile. "I guess it is a togetherness project. And it's best you are with me to make sure everything's correct. It removes all doubt."

Practical. The hope withered. She didn't trust him, didn't believe he would actually be concerned about her.

"If the test is positive, I *will* look after you, Maggie. And the child. I'll look after both of you," he declared emphatically.

Again she stared at him. He saw her throat move in a convulsive swallow. "It's my responsibility, too," she said huskily. "You don't have to feel...I don't want to be a loadstone around your neck. And there's nothing worse for a child than to feel...unwanted."

As she had been.

An abandoned baby.

"I promise you it won't be like that," he said with a fervour that rose so strongly in him Beau had to fight the impulse to cross the room and enfold her in a comforting embrace, promising her all the security he could provide.

"Well, if the test is negative, there won't be any problems," she said flatly.

Beau felt his whole body clench in rejection of that outcome. It was utter madness, he told himself. She was doing it to him again, getting under his skin, twisting him around, raising instincts that raged through him, robbing him of any common sense.

He wanted the child.

He wanted her.

And it didn't seem to matter that it made no sense at all.

Control and courtesy, his mind screamed, trying to hold on to the course of action he'd set himself. He took a deep breath, willing some oxygen into his brain.

"Maggie...could we start again?' His voice was hopelessly strained.

She looked blankly at him. "Where?"

He tried to sort through the chaos she wrought in him and realised it was impossible to wipe the slate clean and pretend they were meeting for the first time.

"I'm sorry. I've given you every reason to think badly of me," he said in wretched disarray. "I guess... what I want...is the chance to show I would be worth having around...if it comes to being parents."

She eyed him thoughtfully. "Yes. I would need to know that."

"So, we have a truce?' he pressed.

She slowly nodded.

Relief drained through him. He gestured his willingness to give. "Is there anything I can do for you today?"

She shook her head, still wary of him, unsure where this was going. Beau cautioned himself against pushing too far.

"Well, I have some business with my travel agency so I'd better get on with it. I may go in to head office but I'll be back this evening. You'll join me for dinner?"

"If you like."

"Yes. And I'd feel better—everyone here would— if you'd wear whatever you'd normally wear for my grandfather. Please don't feel uncomfortable with it. I don't want to negate what he did."

She heaved a shaky sigh. "Are you sure about this, Beau? I don't like treading a minefield."

She'd called him Beau. He smiled, struggling to project reassurance rather than the sudden rush of exultation he felt. "I'm all out of bombs, Maggie."

The missing million could stay missing until further notice. He had other priorities right now.

"Well, I suppose a truce is a truce," she said without much conviction. "Tonight then," she said, a ghost of a smile on her lips. Having given the agreement, she slipped out of the library, closing the door quickly behind her.

It reminded Beau of leaving her suite last night.

*Trapped.*

The realisation struck. She was feeling it, too. With far more reason than he had! He wasn't the one who had to carry the pregnancy, give birth, bear all the burdens of becoming a mother.

He had to try to make this waiting time easier for her. It was the decent thing to do. Besides, he needed to score some positive points. Whether a baby eventuated or not, there was something about Maggie Stowe that got to him and he couldn't let her go. Not until he was…satisfied. Yes, satisfied. About everything.

# CHAPTER TEN

MAGGIE FELT MISERABLY alone in her big bed, lying in the darkness, endlessly reviewing the past six days.

Playing with fire, she thought. Every time she was with Beau Prescott, it was playing with fire. And she was bound to get burnt.

It would have been better, safer, to have kept a solid distance from him since their night of madness which had so insidiously locked them into this waiting together. Instead, she had left the door open for him to infiltrate all her defences.

Just being with him put her at hazard, his physical presence playing havoc with her senses. The daily doses of charm and caring interest made her feel even more vulnerable, seeding hopes she knew had no solid basis for growing into something good.

If it all stopped tomorrow, if the test result was negative and he gave vent to any expression of "Thank God I'm saved!" Maggie knew she would shrivel up and die inside.

Yet if the test result was positive, how much weight could she attach to his turnaround in behaviour towards her? The paternal instinct might be aroused, but how long would it survive if resentment set in? *The wild*

*child* might start chaffing against any tie. The will
to be honourable could conflict very badly with the
need to be free.

Maggie was acutely aware of his holding a rigid control, especially over the simmering sexual attraction
which neither of them admitted to on the surface. He
didn't want to compound the problem they already had,
didn't want to get so close there was no room for an
easy retreat. The truce was simply a truce from which
either of them could withdraw, no promises made, no
obligations entered into. It was important to remember that when the deadline came tomorrow. She would
hate to make a fool of herself.

The awful part was, no matter how complicated it
made her future, she wanted to be pregnant with his
child. Somehow—underneath all the conflicts between
them—she still wanted to believe they were meant to
mate. Surely when he had come to her, she had instinctively responded to that primitive urge. It was the only
excuse she had for doing what she'd never done before…putting herself in jeopardy, in a position where
there might be no way out.

The old fear suddenly seized her. She determinedly
beat it away. There *was* a way out of this web of circumstances. She could simply step back into the life
she'd had before coming here and leave all this behind.

She shifted restlessly, fervently wishing the long
hours of this night were already over. Her bed offered
no comfort. It kept evoking erotic memories, memories that made her feel a deep sensual craving for
the same sexual experience to be repeated. Except she
wanted the intimacies to be on more levels than the
strictly physical. She was hopelessly obsessed with

Beau Prescott, even though common sense dictated he was probably more her enemy than her friend.

Feeling torn by too many conflicting feelings, Maggie tried to will herself to sleep. At least tomorrow would bring answers, whether she liked them or not. The doctor had promised the result would be telephoned and faxed through to them as soon as it came in, which would surely be tomorrow morning.

Answers were better than being in the dark.

Beau shifted restlessly in his bed. He'd used every relaxing technique he knew and they were all useless. His body knew damned well what it wanted—Maggie Stowe—and there was no telling it otherwise. Every night he craved to be in bed with her, wanting the wild heat of their coming together again. And every night he had to exercise this constant control over the torturous desires raging through him.

Thank God the truce would be over tomorrow. This limbo of waiting was killing him. After the result of the blood test came through he could move their relationship onto a different plane. If it was positive, surely the pregnancy would grant him the leeway to get closer to her. Closer in every sense. If it was negative, he would probably have to fight her decision to leave. Either way, it meant action…change…and he would have some barometer of what she was feeling towards him.

She couldn't deny there was a hell of a lot of chemistry between them. These things weren't one-sided and he had the evidence of that one night together to prove it. Nevertheless, he doubted sexual attraction was enough to hold her here.

This past week she had been very wary of him, certainly not inviting any touching. Even in conversation she'd been cautious, weighing her replies before giving them. It was obvious she didn't trust any spontaneity with him, probably believing it had led her astray and she wasn't about to repeat that mistake. He suspected, in her mind, it was a huge mistake.

He now knew she usually shied clear of ties, never staying long in one place, never attempting to put down any roots. She frankly admitted to having been a drifter, taking up an amazing array of jobs; crewing on a yacht, picking tomatoes, waitressing, helping to run camping tours, being a clown at children's parties.

She wouldn't be pinned down to when and where, clearly suspicious of his motives for questioning her, but the experiences she had related over these past few days had a credibility he couldn't doubt. Besides which, when he'd questioned Sir Roland about the first meeting with his grandfather in the restaurant, both accounts of the evening dovetailed. Maggie had not lied nor embroidered the story in any way.

Having a string of godfathers did not fit what he knew of her now. The missing million didn't fit, either. She had a strong streak of independence and an untouchable inner core which he equated with the will of a survivor.

Remaining for two years at Rosecliff with his grandfather was something exceptional in her life. He was sure of that. But then the climate here had been exceptional for her under his grandfather's rule...acceptance without question, approval, liking, respect. When those personal values were threatened she moved on. At least, that was what had stood out to him in the investigators' reports.

Beau knew those reports, word for word, having read them so many times, endlessly analysing, trying to solve the enigma of the woman from nowhere. Mrs. Zabini's statement still teased him with its implication of a harsh, subservient upbringing.

"I think she a runaway. No papers. Very few clothes. She say eighteen, but I think younger, maybe sixteen. Is difficult to get nanny to travel with circus so I not question too much. She say she come from big foster family and used to looking after little ones. Whether true or not, she very good with children. Do everything. No complaining.

"But not comfortable with people. Very shy. Keep to herself. I think she afraid of people. When policemen come round circus she hide. But she no thief. She never make trouble. I think she not want to be found. I think she run from bad things so I let be. The Zabinis know of running from bad things in old world. She not of old world, but fear is same.

"When we stop for our resting she leave. No want to stay in one place. My husband, he write reference for her. A good girl. Good nanny. She go with our blessing."

From Wilgilag, the story was much the same.

Very good with the children, but shied from adult company. Didn't talk about herself. No family. No connections. No mail ever came for her and she never wrote letters. Everything was smooth sailing—no problems, no trouble—until the owner's sister arrived for a visit. Her curiosity about the nanny, nagging her with questions, apparently drove the girl away. A cattletrain came in, loaded up, and she left with it. No goodbyes. No reference. Never heard anything more of her.

Beau wondered how long and how far Maggie had kept running before she began to feel safe. The fear Mrs. Zabini had spoken of must have dissipated somewhere along the line before she'd met his grandfather or she wouldn't have been a participant in the publicity he invited. On the other hand, maybe she felt she looked so different, no one would identify her as the Margaret Stowe who had gone missing over ten years ago. She was also under the protection of a very wealthy man with influence in high places.

The situation had now changed and she could be getting ready to run again. Beau knew she didn't feel safe with him. The trick tomorrow would be to convince her she was. Especially if the test proved positive.

If it was negative...

Well, he wasn't really prepared for fatherhood. It hadn't been on his agenda. Having it thrust upon him was hardly ideal. Yet he knew he would be disappointed if a negative result came in.

Crazy...

As crazy as wanting Maggie Stowe so much, every cell in his body ached.

He didn't have the solution to anything.

He only knew that tomorrow had to move him closer to it.

## CHAPTER ELEVEN

D-DAY, AS MAGGIE thought of it, could not have been more sparkling. The morning was bathed in brilliant sunshine, the sky and harbour bright blue, not a cloud anywhere, no smear of city pollution. It could have been midsummer instead of autumn. It was the kind of day to make one say, "God's in His heaven, all's right with the world."

Except it wasn't all right for Maggie.

She tried to brighten herself up by wearing yellow. When she went down to breakfast, Beau was already at the table, perusing a newspaper. Sedgewick was re-filling his glass with orange juice. The "Good mornings" exchanged rang with good cheer, sincerely so on Sedgewick's part.

Beau looked tired around the eyes, as though he hadn't slept any better than she had. The strain of this entrapped situation was beginning to show, Maggie thought, her heart sinking even lower at the prospect of the news to come…the news which would almost certainly blast this beautiful day and bring the winds of change.

"Jeffrey is preparing a special treat this morning,"

Sedgewick informed them as he poured her a glass of juice.

Maggie's stomach hosted so many butterflies she didn't feel like eating anything.

"He is an exceptionally good chef," Beau remarked.

And well he might, Maggie thought, considering the stream of *treats* that had been coming from the kitchen all week. In Sedgewick's opinion, good food promoted good humour and the butler was leaving no stone unturned in encouraging what he now saw as a promising relationship. Jeffrey undoubtedly had orders to soothe with excellence and titillate with innovation.

"He considers himself an artist, Master Beau," Sedgewick answered, beaming benevolent approval at the reformed *wild child*.

"So what gourmet delight is he producing this morning?" Beau asked with a show of eager interest.

Was it forced? Maggie wondered. How could his stomach not be in knots? Was he confident of taking *any outcome* in his stride?

"Jeffrey has a friend, sir, who comes from Louisiana. I understand the dish is a favourite there. Fried green tomatoes. Quite delectable, sir. I have sampled it. I promise you are sure to enjoy it."

"*Green* tomatoes?" Maggie questioned.

"Yes, indeed. Slices of them coated in a golden crust which has a subtle taste of garlic and onion."

Garlic was the last thing Maggie needed this morning.

"Tell Jeffrey we await the pleasure," Beau said, apparently relishing a new eating experience. His eyes were twinkling, despite the look of fatigue on his face.

His happy air of anticipation was absolutely incomprehensible to Maggie.

Sedgewick served her with her usual fruit compote and sailed off to the kitchen to deliver the good news. She picked up her spoon and stared at the fruit—slices of peach, pear and mango. Easy enough to slide down, she thought. Maybe she should leave them until after the fried green tomatoes. They might kill the aftertaste of garlic and settle any queeziness in her stomach.

"That yellow dress looks wonderful on you, Maggie," Beau said warmly. "I must say it's very heartlifting to see."

The compliment startled her. She looked at him, wondering what he meant by it.

He offered an appealing smile. "I do hope it means I'm forgiven for my trespasses."

Her mind remained blank, unable to find any connection to what he was saying.

"I was sitting here, dreading the possibility you might appear in your jeans, ready for a quick take off," he explained.

Finally it clicked. He was thinking of their meeting in the library, the morning after…when she'd offered to leave then and there, only agreeing to stay until the results were known and they were clear of the pregnancy fear.

"You don't want me to go…no matter what?' she tested, wary of taking anything for granted with him.

"Absolutely not," he answered firmly.

Her heart hopped, skipped and jumped. His niceness to her over this past week couldn't have been a pretence. Why would he invite a longer pretence than he had to? Maybe he really had begun to like her as a person. Or…maybe he was still feeling guilty about not treating her as his grandfather would have wanted, still doing penance for his *trespasses*.

Before she could form a question that might ascertain his motives, Mr. Polly intruded, carrying in a basket of roses, his weather-beaten face wreathed in pleasure.

"Please excuse me, Master Beau…"

"Of course, Mr. Polly."

"…Prize blooms, these are. I told Mr. Vivian they would be this year. He said to enter them in the Royal Easter Show if they came out this good."

"Well, go right ahead and do it," Beau encouraged. "They look like winners to me."

"Double Delight," Mr. Polly almost crooned as he held one up for them to admire. "That's what they're called. Because of the red and white in the petals."

"What a perfect rose!" Maggie exclaimed.

"Perfect for you, Nanny Stowe. I thought you might like these for your room."

He was such a sweetie. "How kind! They're so beautiful!" she said warmly.

"I'll take them to Mrs. Featherfield to put them in water for you. And may I say, you've always been a Double Delight, Nanny Stowe." He looked meaningly at Beau. "I felt sure you would see a prize in them, sir. Thank you for your permission to put an entry in the show."

Maggie felt herself colouring red on white as the head gardener took his leave of them, having delivered a remark which had the subtlety of a sledgehammer. She quickly picked up her spoon and delved into the fruit compote, hoping Beau was oblivious to her being labelled as a prize worth recognising. To her, the whole staff were embarrassingly obvious with wanting *the chance* for their relationship to develop into a happy-ever-after and secure future for everyone.

"You see? My life here wouldn't be worth living if you left, Maggie," Beau said in dry amusement.

Reluctantly she met his gaze and he grinned at her as he expounded on the situation. "Sedgewick would order Jeffrey to dish up slops for each meal. I'd be sent to coventry by Mrs. Featherfield. Wallace would un-doubtedly ensure the grumpiest, bumpiest ride in the Rolls. And Mr. Polly would grow thorns."

She couldn't grin back. It wasn't funny. "They've been with your grandfather a long time, Beau," she reminded him. "They're frightened of change. You should understand that before deciding on whatever course you'll take."

He weighed her words. "You care about them."

"They've all contributed to giving me the best part of my life. Of course, I care about them. They're good people. With the kindest of hearts."

"All the more reason for you to stay on then."

Maggie wasn't sure of that. It could be prolonging hopes that were better cut dead so they didn't obscure the realities to be faced.

"We'll see," she said noncommittally.

The reasons Beau was giving were centred on him—his comfort—not on any feelings for her. The hope that had danced through her bloodstream a few minutes ago, fell limply by the wayside. She ate the fruit without thinking about it, without even tasting it.

Sedgewick returned. The fried green tomatoes were served. Beau was suitably complimentary about the

Louisiana dish. Maggie made agreeable murmurs and washed the glug in her mouth down with coffee. Nothing more of any importance was said.

After breakfast, Maggie excused herself to see to the roses Mr. Polly had left with Mrs. Featherfield.

"I'll be in the library," Beau said pointedly.

Where the fax machine was, Maggie thought, and found herself trembling. She clenched her hands, stiffened her spine and sternly told herself she would cope with everything better once she knew the test result.

In the end, she didn't join Beau in the library, waiting for the news. She simply couldn't bear to be with him. Having arranged the perfect Double Delight blooms in a vase, she carried it up to her suite, placed it on her dressing table, then wandered around the bedroom that had once seemed like a place fit for a princess.

It still was, but it no longer made her feel like a princess. The rosewood antique furniture was beautiful, gleaming with a perfect polish and set off with ornate brass handles. The pink silk canopy above the bed was splendidly draped, adding its richness to the rose print bedspread. Deeply sashed pink curtains dressed the French doors, falling into luxurious pools on a floor thickly carpeted in the palest of green. She loved it all. She had been very happy here. Yet now she felt outside it.

She stopped in front of the cheval mirror and stared at her reflection. Vivian's re-imaged Maggie Stowe looked back at her. Strange how the outer shell could almost make one believe the inner self had been changed, too, but it wasn't really so. Right now this image superimposed a lot of other Maggie Stowes but they still existed in her heart.

There was the unpolished, uncultured young woman Vivian had met. Maggie could still see her peering through the added gloss and style...a streetwise survivor who'd learnt most of the games people played and how to duck or slide past them. Life wasn't easy without paper qualifications. Exploitation was not uncommon in the casual job market, especially when the employee had no family to back her up and no easy recourse to the law. Maggie never let herself get caught in webs like that. Just a touch of it and she moved on.

The mirror shimmered as her vision reached further into the past...to the fear-filled girl/woman who'd found safe refuge with Zabini's Circus as she struggled to come to terms with a world teeming with all sorts of different people and different places and different ways of life. Impossible to have envisaged what she'd meet once she left the restricted world of the compound.

Her mind flicked at the suppressed memories of that earlier life...the discipline, the subservience, the constant demand to respect the good teachings, the secret growth of resistance, rebellion, and the need to keep it hidden until she was old enough, grown up enough to escape.

*You with the red curls, cast your eyes down, girl!*

Maggie saw herself at six, a thin child, all eyes and hair. She couldn't hide her hair. Confining it in a plait had made it less obvious. But she'd learnt the lesson of casting her eyes down because it hid her thoughts and feelings.

She'd learnt the wisdom in the kind advice from her first housemother who had probably recognised a rebellious spirit…best to bow the head, best to obey, best to keep in line, best not to bring any notice to herself. That way she could live in her mind, in the dream worlds she kept to herself.

She couldn't remember when she'd begun to believe there had to be a bigger, better life outside the compound. The fence was to keep them protected from bad things, they were told. But the grown-ups came and went. They didn't seem to mind going out there to whatever existed beyond the fence. When she was grown up enough she would go and find out for herself.

And she had.

Then she knew the fence hadn't been about protection at all. It had been about power. And the compound had been a prison, although supposedly a benevolent one. She'd never let anything become a prison again. The sense of anything closing in on her set nerves jangling. Freedom had become an important value in her life. Or maybe it always had been…something genetic that not even the commune discipline could crush out of her.

Where had these genes come from? If her mother and father had ever lived in the compound, she'd never recognised them and they'd never acknowledged her. None of the grown-ups she'd seen had red hair, although she realised that was not conclusive. Who were they…the man and woman who had created the person she was?

The mirror didn't give up those answers.

They were forever lost to Maggie.

Her mind slowly swam up through the layers of the past, back to the reflection in front of her…Vivian's sculpture from the material she'd been, the material

she still was within the different shaping. It had been
Vivian who had held her together like this. Without
him…it was getting harder to hold on to it, to keep
believing it was real.

The faithful four—Sedgewick, Mrs. Featherfield,
Wallace, Mr. Polly—were trying to hold on to it, but
it wasn't the same without Vivian. Beau didn't believe
in her. That was the crux of it. He didn't see what his
grandfather had seen and Vivian's Maggie Stowe was
beginning to lose her reality.

She moved away from the mirror and sat down on
the edge of the bed, wrapped in a sense of hiatus as
she waited for the news which would form decisions
and directions for her. Eventually a knock came on
the door and Beau called out to her. His voice echoed
through her head, forcing a set of instructions to form.

*Get up.*

She pushed herself onto her feet.

*Go and open the door to him.*

Her legs were shaky. She felt sick, dizzy. The news
he was bringing to her carried such enormous import.
She sat down again, trembling.

Another knock. Another call. It had to be answered.
She took a deep breath, trying to ease the fierce grip
of tension. Words still had to be forced.

"Come in."

The old training suddenly slid out and took over. She
sat very still, her fingers interlaced on her lap, head
bent, eyes cast down, mental shield up. No one could
get at her that way. She could take in what she needed
to and leave out the rest.

She heard Beau come in and close the door behind
him. It didn't occur to her it might be inappropriate to

invite him into her bedroom. In her mind she wasn't really anywhere…just waiting.

He didn't say anything. She felt his eyes on her, scrutinising, assessing, felt his approach, the energy of him coming closer and closer, saw his feet, pressing into the thick carpet in front of her. He held out a sheet of fax paper for her to read. It took several moments for her to focus her eyes on the typewritten message.

The test result was positive.

# CHAPTER TWELVE

BEAU COULD FEEL his heart thumping wildly as he waited for a reaction. The printed result had to snap Maggie out of whatever far place she had retreated to. He wanted to speak to her, yet his mind was such a jumble of thoughts and concerns, he was riven with uncertainty over what to say. Fact—proven fact—had a shattering effect on preconceived suppositions and her withdrawal from him wasn't helping to put anything sensible together.

He'd stepped into this room with a sense of honourable purpose. The seemingly frozen image of her, sitting in a pose of passive submission, had instantly unsettled him. There was something terribly wrong about it. The vibrant vitality he associated with her wasn't simply guarded. It had receded. He felt as though he was looking at an uninhabited shell.

The urge to pick her up and shake life back into her was almost irresistible. His mind cautioned that any touching might trigger an extremely adverse response. His body desperately wanted to heat hers to a sizzling awareness of what they had shared while creating the result he now held out to her.

"I think we should get married, Maggie."

Her head jerked up, her vivid blue eyes wide and whirling with shock.

Beau was shocked, too. It wasn't what he had planned to say. He didn't know where the words had come from. They'd spilled off his lips before he could think better of them.

"No!" She leapt up, suddenly, explosively invigorated, colour shooting into her face, a bright flash of recoil in her eyes as she palmed him aside in her agitated move away from him. "No!" Her head shook in vehement denial. She walked in an erratic course around the room. "No, I can't! I can't!" she cried, then made a beeline for the French doors, clearly driven towards escape.

"Why not?" Beau demanded aggressively, any common sense completely smashed by her extreme reaction. Never mind that he'd only meant to suggest marriage as a possibility to consider. Wasn't he one of the most eligible bachelors around? He was in a position to virtually offer her the world on a silver platter. Why the hell wasn't she seeing that and evaluating the advantages?

She paused, her hands curled around the knobs of the doors. She didn't turn back to him. Her shoulders heaved. Tension screamed from her. "It would be...*a prison,*" she said, the dark revulsion in her voice slicing straight into his heart.

A prison? Beau was stunned speechless. The concept of marriage to him being a prison was horrifying enough, but the way she'd said it...as though it would be an unbearable torture!

The doors were opened and she was out on the balcony before he could raise a protest. Escaping from

him, as though his offer had conjured up something
monstrous. Beau's insides twisted into knots. This
wasn't right. It was no more right than the way she
had been sitting when he'd come in.

He stared down at the paper in his hand. Maggie
Stowe was pregnant with *his* child. Whatever was disturbing her so deeply had to be resolved. He couldn't
let her move on from him, dropping out of sight and
out of contact. His whole being revolted against that
eventuality. He had to reach out to her, into her, and
somehow hold her to him.

Pumped up to fight for the outcome he wanted, Beau
tossed the fax sheet on the bed and followed her out to
the balcony. She was standing against the balustrade,
as far away from him as she could get. Her gaze was
aimed at the far north shore of the harbour, above and
beyond the artfully landscaped gardens of Rosecliff, as
though her immediate surroundings—however beautiful—were part and parcel of what she needed to get
away from.

"How can you call Rosecliff a prison?"

The question shot from his mouth as he stepped up
to the balustrade, turning to scrutinise her profile and
discern whatever he could from her expression. He
had to start with something and hopefully she'd give
him enough signals to find a path to an understanding between them.

She rigidly ignored him. Or rigidly held herself in.

"You could have all this…" He waved at the grounds
below them, property that would be coveted by anyone. "…If you married me."

She closed her eyes. Her fingers curled more tightly
over the curved top of the balustrade. Her body wa-

vered slightly. Beau waited, not prepared to rush into any judgment. He'd already made too many mistakes with Maggie Stowe.

"It's people who make a prison, not a property," she answered, as though dragging the words from some deep place inside her.

People? What people?

She turned her head and looked at him, her eyes burning with unshakable conviction and an accusation that reduced his material argument to ashes in the wind. "It's the people in charge of the compound. The people in power. They make the prison."

Him? How could she equate him with a prison?

He stared at the searing knowledge in her eyes and his stomach curled. This wasn't some theoretical philosophy. She had lived through what she was saying and it was still very real to her, traumatically real. He'd wanted to learn what drove Maggie Stowe and here it was…an experience so soul-scarring she couldn't move past it, not even with all the running she'd done over the years.

She turned her gaze back to the far horizon. "I won't live like that," she said with fierce determination. "I won't let my child be subjected to it. I'll keep us both safe. And *free*."

Her voice shook with the emphasis she gave to freedom. Beau found himself intensely moved by it. He understood the desire for freedom, empathised with it, but he knew intuitively this was more than desire. It was need…deep-rooted need.

His mind flicked to Mrs. Zabini's statement. Not a runaway, he thought, an escapee from a prison. Though it couldn't have been a government institution…nothing criminal. The investigators hired by Lionel Armstrong would have turned up any official records of her. Maybe the prison had been some private orphanage. A big foster family, she'd told Mrs. Zabini. Yet surely those also came under the jurisdiction of the social welfare arm of government.

She'd used the word, *compound.* Beau had an instant vision of high, secure fences. Illegal immigrants were kept in a compound until their cases could be evaluated. But once again, that was government business. How had Maggie remained outside the official net until she was—Mrs. Zabini's guess—sixteen?

Whatever the answer, that wasn't his immediate problem and he doubted she'd tell him anyway. She was equating him with *the people in charge, the people in power.* He had to change that view of him and do it convincingly or she would disappear from his life. The issue was not material advantages to her.

*Acceptance, approval, liking, respect...*those values overrode everything else in Maggie Stowe's mind. That was decisively brought home to him now. If he couldn't answer them...

He took a deep breath. The sense of being on the edge of a precipice was very strong. One careless step and he was gone. He'd wanted action with Maggie... any action. He'd had no idea the ground was so perilous.

A trapped animal will always turn on its captor, he thought. He had to soothe, win her trust, move them both back to a safe place where they could negotiate with each other.

"Why do you see marriage to me as a prison, Maggie?' he asked quietly, careful to keep any judgmental note out of his voice.

She shivered. "You're only thinking of what you want, Beau."

It was a flat statement, uncoloured by the emotions he suspected were still ripping through her. The truth of it was undeniable.

"I want what would be best for all three of us, Maggie, not only myself," he countered softly.

"I haven't given you the right to judge what's best for me. And I'll fight you over judging for my child, as well." She turned to him, eyes blazing in challenge. "No one will ever take from me the right to be my own person and make my own judgments."

He frowned. "I'm sorry. I didn't mean to do that."

"Yes, you did. Why else would you want marriage if not to lock me and our child into your life where you'll be in legal charge of us?"

"I just wanted to be in a position where I could take care of both of you," he argued, sincere in this belief of himself.

"You wouldn't respect my wishes. You don't care about my feelings."

Another flat statement. He struggled against it. He did care. He felt a tumult of caring right now. But he could see she wouldn't believe it. "I have tried to show you differently this past week," he said, searching for some way to appease the hurt he'd given.

She shook her head. There was a twist of irony on her lips as she answered, "There's a difference between being civilised and actually accepting a person in your heart. Liking them. Wishing them well. You think I don't know it?"

He'd done his best to stand back from the attraction he felt, seeking the truth about her. He hadn't wanted to be any more stupid than he had been. But he couldn't offer those reasons as excuses for his manner towards her.

Her eyes mocked his dilemma. "From the very start you didn't trust me, Beau. You still don't. That's why you want to lock me in."

It was terribly disconcerting that she saw him so clearly, saw what he himself hadn't quite grasped until she laid it out to him. She shamed him with her truths. All his actions had been motivated by what *he* wanted while she had been the hub of endlessly rotating wheels of suspicion.

"Maggie, is the pregnancy a prison? I mean...not thinking about its tie to me. Apart from that..." He hated asking this question but he had to, in fairness to her, aware that *he* had driven the course to these consequences and wanting to remove the trapped feeling she had to have. "...Do you want to have the child?"

"Yes. Yes, I do," she answered decisively, without even a slight hesitation.

Beau breathed a huge sigh of relief. "So do I."

She slanted him a look, checking if he meant it.

He tried an appealing smile. "I know it's not the most propitious circumstances, Maggie, but I can't help feeling excited about it."

She frowned. "You don't mind about me being the mother?"

"I can't imagine anyone better."

It bewildered her. "But you don't like me."

With a devastating jolt, Beau realised this was the crux of her flight from his proposal of marriage. Without liking, there couldn't be respect or approval or acceptance. Her logic could not be faulted. And he *was* guilty of doubting her fitness as the mother of his child. But he'd learnt so much more about her since then.

"That's not true, Maggie," he said with passionate insistence. "You blew my mind the day I arrived home and I've been struggling to get it together ever since. I now believe a woman who could make my discerning grandfather so happy and so proud of her, is a woman well worth knowing. And I believe a woman who inspires so much caring from our live-in staff has to have a very caring heart herself."

He saw her face tightening, felt her resistance to what he was saying, and in sheer desperation, cried, "Maggie, I swear to you, I no longer see in you anything not to like."

He knew, the moment the words were out, he'd emphasised a negative instead of a positive. He saw the recoil in her eyes, the bleak dismissal of this line of pursuit even before she spoke.

"I guess it suits you to say such things, now that I have something you want."

It was a judgment he deserved, but it hurt. The rejection of his earnest endeavours to alter her impression of him hurt, too. He realised he'd delivered too many hurts himself, striking at vulnerabilities he hadn't known existed, hadn't stopped to look for them behind his grandfather's *creation*.

Blinded by prejudice.

Too many prejudices.

Where was his salvation now?

Despair dragged at his determination. He'd dug his own grave and made the walls too high for him to climb out of it. Or maybe he was using the wrong approach. He had to keep trying, no matter what.

"What do you want to do, Maggie?" he asked, humbled by her painfully accurate reading of the situation. "What would make you feel...right?"

# CHAPTER THIRTEEN

MAGGIE DIDN'T KNOW what would make her feel right.
She didn't know what to do. She lifted her gaze to a
sky so endlessly blue it seemed to stretch on to infin-
ity. Her heart ached with so many griefs, her mind
couldn't encompass them all. They slid into a desperate, silent plea for help.

*Vivian...Vivian...*

Where was he? Did he see it had gone terribly
wrong? It was such wicked, painful irony...the marriage he'd wanted between her and Beau...the child to
carry on his family line...it was in her power to deliver
on the promise...yet her soul revolted against accepting the form it was taking.

*Give it a chance...*

I did. I tried. It can't work like this, she cried, exon-
erating herself from the burden laid on her.

Yet the needs of others kept pulling her back to it,
denying her release.

Sedgewick... *You must cultivate a positive attitude.*
Was she being too negative in the face of Beau's desire
to keep her and the child?

Mrs. Featherfield... *A new baby at Rosecliff. I can't*

*imagine anything more perfect.* Was it fair to deprive
her child of its natural inheritance?

Wallace seeing sexual attraction as the answer...
and she couldn't deny it had led to this shared parent-
hood. Given more open expression, might it not bridge
this dreadful gap between them and soften their differences?

Mr. Polly... *Nature will take its course. A little help
and care and you can always get the result you want.*

Could Beau learn to care?

Did a baby help?

Would anything change if she gave it more of a
chance, or would the prison gates inexorably close her
in if she stayed on here?

She took a deep breath and looked at him...this man
who knew her intimately yet did not know her at all.
Vivian's grandson. The father of her child.

Her heart fluttered at that last thought. It was real
now. The father of her child. She couldn't deny him,
yet...what would it lead to?

"How can I trust you?" she blurted out, anguished
by her uncertainties.

A muscle in his cheek contracted but his eyes didn't
waver from hers, dark pools of green, seemingly reflecting the pain she felt. "It would need you to take a
risk, Maggie," he said quietly. "I can't prove your trust
is not misplaced unless you're willing to chance it."

"Marriage is too big a risk for me, Beau."

He nodded, then managed a wry smile. "A classic
case of fools rushing in... I'm sorry, Maggie. My understanding has been very amiss. I seem to have blundered all the way along the line with you and I wish

like hell I'd done everything differently. But I know that doesn't make anything better for you."

His regretful attitude soothed some of her jangling nerves. He probably thought she was mad, rejecting his offer of marriage out of hand, and so fiercely. Impossible to explain just how threatened she'd felt at that moment, with him looming over her in a pose of commanding authority and the bank of distrust forming too dangerous a current for her to ride.

He looked...almost kind now. Caring. Of course, it could be another pose. On the other hand, there had to be good in him. Everyone at Rosecliff couldn't be entirely deceived on that point. Maybe with their child, he would show his best side. He couldn't hang anything nasty on an innocent baby.

What was it about her that brought out the mean judgments he made? If they were to be linked by their child, she needed to understand where he was coming from with her. At least that way she would be more prepared for handling the situation. She searched for some meeting ground and instinctively homed in on the person who'd brought them together.

"Vivian loved you, Beau. Very much."

"I know," he murmured encouragingly.

"He expected...because we were both dear to him... he wanted us to like each other."

"Yes, he would," came the ready agreement.

"I warned him it might not happen. I was always prepared to leave if you didn't like me. After all, you were his grandson. His real family. I thought you might see me as a usurper of his affections..."

"Maggie, I don't see you like that," he quickly assured her. "Nothing and no one could have changed the bond between my grandfather and me. It was unique to us. Just as I'm sure what you shared with him was unique to you."

Yes it was. Wonderfully, unbelievably unique. No one could ever guess, ever comprehend what it had meant to her. Which was why she had to be as fair as it was reasonably possible to Vivian's grandson.

"You could have been jealous," she suggested, still unsure of his feelings where she was concerned.

"No. Not in any possessive way, Maggie. My grandfather gave of himself to many people. It never diminished what he gave to me."

He sounded so genuine, so reasonable, it made no sense of what he'd done. "Then why have you been so mean to me?" she bluntly asked, searching his eyes for the true answer.

He grimaced, guilt and shame flicking over his face. "I was upset over not having seen my grandfather for so long. I guess I felt cheated by his dying when he did. And when I first arrived home you did seem like a usurper, acting the mistress of the house, the staff taking their lead from you. I simply wasn't prepared for what I walked into, Maggie, and it chewed me up. I'm sorry you became a target of distrust."

A target...the focus of all his bad feelings. Yes, she could accept that explanation. But it didn't make her feel any safer with him.

"You aren't anymore, Maggie," he assured her, an earnest plea for forgiveness in his eyes. "I realise they're probably empty words to you but they're true."

She wished she could believe them. "Vivian asked me...he made me promise...to give it a chance. Liking you, I mean. Being open to liking. He knew...under-stood...I tend to be wary of people."

"I wish he'd still been here to say the same to me," Beau said ruefully. "It would have been different, Maggie. I am genuinely sorry for all the misunderstand-ings."

"I'm sorry, too. Because I don't trust you now, Beau. I'd leave here today except...it's Vivian's grandchild and I know I wouldn't feel right, not giving it every chance to work out something we can live with...am-icably."

"Then may I make a suggestion?"

She nodded, having no ready answers in her own mind.

"Come away with me for a while. People get to know each other very well when travelling together. I want to scout a tour through Europe so it'll be a busi-ness trip for me." He suddenly grinned, a sparkle of gentle teasing in his eyes. "You can accompany me as my nanny, if you like, looking after the kind of things you did for my grandfather."

Laughter bubbled out of her throat. Maybe it was the absurdity of the idea or some form of hysterical relief from nervous tension. Maggie shook her head, feeling too limp and drained to care.

"No pressures, I promise you," Beau went on, his voice eager with the wish to persuade. "Separate rooms. And you'll have your ticket home so you can leave me anytime you choose."

A trip to Europe...fantasy, she thought, but a very seductive one. Vivian had always been referring to places there.

"It's a break away from here, Maggie. It'll make it

easier for you to leave Rosecliff, if you must. You won't
be upsetting Sedgewick and the others. I think they'd
all approve of me taking you with me."

He was right about that, she thought ironically,
though it couldn't really be done.

"And I will look after you, Maggie," Beau pressed.
"If you'll risk the chance to let me show you, it's a step
towards resolving the future, isn't it?"

He looked so keen. Her heart jiggled painfully.
"It's…it's a good suggestion, Beau. I'd like to try it…
but…it just isn't possible."

He frowned. "Why not?"

She flushed at the hopelessness of a situation he
probably couldn't comprehend. "Apart from the bank
account Vivian organised for me with his accountant,
for my salary to be paid into, I have nothing to prove
who or what I am. Vivian and Mr. Neville were refer-
ees for me to the bank manager because I didn't have
any of the usual forms of identification. But that won't
do for a passport."

"You have your birth certificate…"

"No. I don't. I tried to get a copy once but the regis-
try wanted information I didn't know," she confessed.
"And it's no use looking for the answers. No one would
admit anything now. I may not have even been registered."

She turned her gaze out to the harbour, once more
awash with the helpless feeling of a dislocated person
with no roots and nothing to steer by. I'm like a piece of
flotsam on the water, she thought, but at least I'm still
afloat. Better than being submerged in hopelessness.

"Maggie, let me help you with this. There must be
people who know…"

She shook her head. "You don't understand, Beau. It's not there anymore. They've gone. If there were records, they've gone, too."

"What's not there, Maggie?" he asked quietly.

She'd said too much. It was really better not to say anything. People didn't—couldn't—relate to something so far outside their experience. She remembered telling a workmate once. It made the woman look at her differently, as though she were some kind of freak.

"Are you afraid of…whatever's gone?" It was a soft, tentative question, sensitive to her feelings.

She had no reason to be anymore. No one could take her back to that life in the compound. She'd been free of that fear for many years, but the sense of having a big chunk of her life stolen and used for the supposedly higher purposes of others never left her.

"Maggie…will you trust me with this? You can stand on judgment of me right now. I want to help, to move forward with you."

She heard the plea in his voice and it touched her. The father of my child, she thought. Was it right to drop the shield with him? If she did, would they move forward or would he back off?

Best to know.

"All right."

She shifted to the corner of the balcony, instinctively putting distance between them before she turned to face him. A challenge like this required space. He stood side on to the balustrade, watching her, waiting, maintaining an air of confidence that encouraged her to unburden herself on him.

Maggie put the past at a distance, too. It was easier to pretend it had happened to someone else, a part of her that she was now separated from, a different person. She knew it wasn't really true but the disconnection allowed her to speak more objectively.

"I was brought up in a kind of commune. There were about fifty children. Different ages. Eight to a house with a housemother in charge. None of us knew who our real parents were or if we had any at all. None of us had any memory of a life outside the compound."

He didn't show any shock at all. "You were always kept inside it?" he asked, gently inquisitive.

"Yes. The idea was...we were the innocent children of God and we were to be kept pure from the world. It was a cult thing. I guess you could call it a social experiment."

His face tightened but he nodded for her to go on.

"We were taught to read and write but had no formal schooling or examinations as I later discovered the children outside took for granted. Music was a big part of our daily routine, singing and playing hymns and good songs. If you didn't question anything, it wasn't a bad life. Very regimented, very disciplined, very...stifling."

"It was a prison to you," he said softly.

She winced, aware of having given that away too tellingly to refute. "There was no freedom...for anything. No privacy except in your own mind. I escaped when I was fourteen."

He looked surprised. "That young?"

"I was tall. I could pass for older."

"Where was the compound, Maggie?"

"Northwest New South Wales. Deep country. It's been abandoned."

"How long ago?"

"Eight years. I was twenty when the news of its existence broke. I don't know who or what tipped off government officials but the compound was raided and the children were taken away and put in the hands of welfare people to sort out. Those who were in charge of the compound—they were called The Inner Circle—destroyed whatever records they'd kept and skipped the country."

"They weren't pursued?"

"Traced to Hawaii, but they disappeared from there. There was a flurry of investigative journalism. More sensational than helpful. Problems with the children being assimilated into normal society. The older ones found it most difficult, wanting to go back to the safety of the compound."

"You didn't think of coming forward at that time and telling your story?"

"It came out in the newspaper stories that there were professional people—doctors and lawyers—who'd helped the Inner Circle get children who were given up for adoption. Abandoned babies. I didn't trust the people in power. I didn't know what they might do to me. Besides, I was making my own way. I didn't want what they might think of as help."

"Fair enough." No criticism. He seemed to understand the dilemma she'd faced. "Did you tell my grandfather any of this, Maggie?"

"Yes. But not for a long time. It's hardly a subject I care to bring up. To begin with, when he wanted to know my bank account, which I didn't have, I just told him I'd always worked for cash in hand and most of that went in day-to-day living." She shrugged. "It was the truth. There was no other way to avoid the paper-work I had no answers for."

"He didn't press you about your lack of official sta-tus?"

"Why should he? The accountant made me official enough to cover Vivian's requirements. The question of a passport never came up."

"I see," Beau murmured, then looked at her quiz-zically. "When did you tell him what you've just told me?"

She paused for thought. "He was talking about fam-ily lines. He wanted to know my...my background. It would have been about two months before he died."

Beau heaved a sigh that seemed to hold both relief and satisfaction. "Thank you for confiding in me. It answers a lot."

Maggie didn't want to ask what it answered. If he was now seeing her in a different light, it didn't show. It didn't seem to be affecting him one way or another.

"Will you come with me to Europe, Maggie?' he asked.

"I told you..."

"I'll get you a passport. I'll get you all the official identification you'll need for anything, whether you come with me or not."

"But how?"

"Believe me, I have the power and the resources to do it."

She stared at the resolution stamped on his face and felt something hard and cold inside her start to warm and melt. "You'd do that for me?" Her voice was a bare whisper.

"Yes. I'll put it in motion at once."

Decisive, confident, fearless. Maggie was sharply reminded of her first impression of him…the aggressive vitality of the man, the flow of positive energy, the innate power that seemed to proclaim he could overcome anything or anyone, a hunter who always succeeded in attaining his goal, no matter what road he had to take or what hardship he had to endure.

A mate worth having…fighting for her…

She felt the stirring of desire again, the pins and needles of promising possibilities. Hope danced in and out of her brain, taunting her caution, fraying her doubts. He was waiting on her answer to the suggestion he'd made. Not forcing. Waiting for her to choose, of her own free will. Her heart insistently pumped one message…give it a chance.

"Then I will," she said huskily. "I will come with you to Europe." She managed a wobbly smile. "As a nanny."

# CHAPTER FOURTEEN

"This is so exciting!" Mrs. Featherfield bubbled, her eyes darting around the Rose Suite to check for any item that might have been overlooked. "Are you sure you have everything packed?"

"The list has all been ticked off," Maggie assured her, almost light-headed with the enormity of the step she was about to take. "And I put it in the lid of the suitcase as you told me so I won't leave anything behind."

The housekeeper's smile beamed with pleasure and self-satisfaction. "I taught Master Beau that a long time ago." Tears suddenly welled into her eyes. "I remember when Mr. Vivian took him off to Europe. I'm sure Mr. Vivian would be delighted this has come about with you, my dear."

Maggie gave her a quick hug, barely containing her own flood of emotion. "It was good of Beau to think of it," she said huskily.

"He has a generous heart. Just like his grandfather. You'll be safe with him, dear."

Maggie was beginning to believe it. He'd been so different to her these past four weeks, treating her as an equal, caring, considerate, including her in planning the itinerary so she could read about the places and have the pleasure of anticipation, answering all her questions with good-natured patience and obvious enjoyment.

Best of all, he'd done what he said he'd do. Amazingly, she now had a birth certificate, credit cards and a passport, which made her feel like a real person. Even though there were no names of a mother and father on her birth certificate, it hadn't been a deep disappointment. Somehow she'd accepted having no parents a long time ago. It was better not to have them, knowing they'd cared so little for her they'd abandoned her to the unknown…a foundling.

Besides, it was more than heart-warming to know that Beau cared about her feelings. As well as everything else, he'd insisted on arranging driving lessons, which she'd duly taken—with Wallace aiding and abetting—so she also had a provisional driver's licence. She was suddenly, wonderfully, overwhelmed with identification papers, all of which were now securely tucked away in her newly bought traveller's handbag.

Mrs. Featherfield pulled back and dabbed at her eyes. "Well, we mustn't keep them waiting. I'll carry your coat. You look so smart in those clothes, it would be a pity to clutter you up before Master Beau sees you."

Maggie's heart instantly kicked into overdrive. She had tried not to think of how alone together she was going to be with Beau on this trip. He had booked separate rooms, as promised, and he hadn't once presumed on the attraction between them. Both of them did their best to ignore it, yet it was there, stronger than ever for Maggie since Beau's attitude no longer carried any discernible trace of hostility. Sooner or later the temptation to give in to expressing it was bound to arise.

Would it be right or wrong?

She'd know when it came, she nervously assured herself.

Beau and Sedgewick were in the stairhall. Both of them turned to watch her come down as she and Mrs. Featherfield reached the balcony landing. Benevolent approval was written all over the butler's face. Beau looked relaxed and happy. Nevertheless, Maggie felt there was more than a simmer of pleasure in his eyes as they skimmed her appearance.

She'd donned comfortable clothes, as advised, teaming black trousers and skivvy with a leopard-print velvet vest, a gold-buckled belt and her gold anchor-chain. The outfit wasn't spectacular, just well put together, as Vivian had taught her. It was Beau's gaze on her that made her feel it was sensational and sexy.

Or maybe it was because he looked that way to her, dressed in sage green trousers, a fawn ribbed skivvy, and a dark brown leather jacket, casually hooked over one shoulder. He had such a magnificent physique, it was difficult not to let her gaze linger on his powerfully muscled body.

"I take it all the luggage is already in the car," she said brightly, trying to settle the flutters in her stomach with a concentration on practicalities.

"Wallace has it stowed and is standing by," Beau answered, grinning at the efficiency with which everyone was seeing them off. It was impossible to be unaware of the staff conspiracy to encourage every move towards a harmonious and happy togetherness.

"Perhaps you will send us the occasional postcard,

Nanny Stowe," Sedgewick said, his eyebrows raised in pointed appeal.

Wanting to be kept posted on any promising developments, Maggie interpreted. "Of course I will, Sedgewick," she assured him, hoping her smile didn't look as stiff as it felt.

Both he and Mrs. Featherfield escorted them out to the car. Mr. Polly was standing beside Wallace, waiting for them, intent on adding his good wishes to everyone else's.

"Mr. Vivian always reckoned the gardens at Versailles were something special. Should have a look at them when you get to Paris," he advised.

"We will," Beau promised.

"You have a good time now, Nanny Stowe. Mr. Vivian would be real pleased about Master Beau taking you off around the world."

"Thank you, Mr. Polly. I can't imagine I'll see any roses better than yours..." He *had* won first prize at the Royal Easter Show with his Double Delight. "...But I will check out the gardens in Europe."

He nodded and smiled. "Bit of care. That's all it takes," he said as Wallace ushered her into the back seat of the Rolls.

Beau said his last goodbyes and settled onto the seat beside her. Wallace shut the door and with an air of a dignified custodian in control of his charges. He saluted those who'd delivered them to him, took the driver's seat, and set the trip in motion.

"Got the tickets?" Beau asked her, his green eyes twinkling with good humour.

A nanny's job in travelling, he'd declared, was to look after tickets, see that schedules were kept, en-

sure that nothing was left in planes, trains, restaurants
and hotels, hold ready supplies of first-aid items and
emergency medications, and generally see that proper
meals were taken so appropriate energy levels were
maintained.

Maggie suspected that putting her in charge of the
tickets was meant to make her feel she always had a
passport to freedom. Beau would not hold her with
him. The choice was hers.

She patted her handbag. "All correct and double-
checked." A blissful sigh of satisfaction accompanied
the welling sense of a dream turning into fact. "We're
really on our way."

Beau laughed. "You'll feel even more so once the
plane takes off. It's always a buzz."

It reminded Maggie that Beau was more than a seasoned traveller. Exploring the world was what he'd chosen to do with his life. She wondered how he thought
fatherhood would fit into it, whether he imagined her
and their child tagging along with him wherever he
went.

On the other hand, when he'd proposed marriage,
he'd linked Rosecliff with it, so maybe he envisaged
settling there for a while. Or settling *her* there with the
child while he came and went. Maggie wasn't sure she
liked that idea but it was premature to be considering
it anyway. This was a time for gathering a true sense
of what life with Beau Prescott might be like.

"I checked the weather report for London, sir.
They're having a very cool spring. Nine to fifteen degrees Celsius. You'll have to be snuggling up," Wallace cheerily advised.

"Thank you, Wallace. We do have coats with us," Beau dryly replied.

"Same in Paris and Berlin. Much warmer in Rome. Twenty-four degrees Celsius there. You'll be able to thaw out once you're in sunny Italy. Won't need your heavy clothes on."

"I dare say it will be a pleasant change," Maggie commented, hoping Wallace wouldn't go so far as to suggest stripping off entirely.

"Speaking of Italy, I saw a TV program on the Amalfi Coast the other night," he went on. "A couple zooming around in a red Ferrari. Great car. They stopped at a fantastic village that was built like it was hanging on to a cliff. Positano it was called. Looked very romantic."

"Well, we may make it there," Beau said agreeably.

Wallace continued to be a font of information all the way to the airport. He didn't precisely suggest Beau and Maggie become lovers but the implication was in everything he said. Maggie tried not to feel awkward about it. Beau was very smooth in making light of the more pointed comments. Nevertheless, the pressure to deliver on the promise got to her again.

It was a relief to say goodbye to Wallace but she was hopelessly tense once she was alone with Beau, keeping a rigid distance so there'd be no accidental touching in the airport terminal, fumbling with the tickets at the check-in counter, looking anywhere but directly at him. She found herself tongue-tied, too, nodding when he spoke to her, unable to offer any conversation as they made their way to the first-class lounge to await their flight.

She had a craven urge to run away. People in power

make prisons but people you care about also make prisons, she thought. Before coming to Rosecliff, she'd only been responsible for herself. She hadn't let herself become too emotionally involved with anyone or any place. Now she couldn't shrug off those who cared about her and she also had to consider what was best for the baby. Running away wasn't really an option anymore. It wouldn't be fair.

She took a chair by the window in the lounge and stared out at a line of huge jet aeroplanes, waiting for their loads of passengers and cargoes. The only plane she'd ever been in was a four-seat Cessna, commonly used in the Australian outback. How these enormous machines lifted off the ground was a marvel. Soon she would be on one, flying off to the other side of the world. But not alone.

Never alone again, she thought, one hand straying to her stomach. She'd missed a period and the tightness in her breasts was another physical manifestation of her pregnancy. The changes in her body heralded changes in her life she couldn't turn back from. Nor did she want to. Yet she couldn't help feeling apprehensive about the future.

Beau brought her a cup of tea—she'd gone off coffee—and settled into the armchair beside hers. She muttered a "Thank you," still not looking him in the eye.

"You don't have to live up to others' expectations, Maggie," he said quietly. "Especially if it creates a conflict within yourself."

She glanced up, oddly relieved he understood.

He caught her gaze and transmitted an empathy that stroked her troubled heart. "Stay true to whatever you believe is right for you," he advised. "In the end, that's what works best. For everyone. An unhappy person spreads unhappiness."

She recognised the truth in what he said and felt the strength of mind and purpose he'd harnessed to follow his own path in life. In this respect, he was very similar to his grandfather, a natural leader, exuding confidence. It didn't matter that he poured his energy into something different to Vivian. The charismatic power that drew others to him was the same. It made them feel safe within the radius of such strength.

*He has a generous heart. Just like his grandfather. You'll be safe with him, dear.*

The insight suddenly burst upon her. "It's you they need, not me. Do you realise that, Beau?"

"You mean Feathers and Sedgewick and…"

"Yes. Vivian was the focus of their lives. They're clinging on to him through me because…" She hesitated, reluctant to starkly state what they wanted of her.

"They see you as a way to hold on to their lives at Rosecliff," he said, openly revealing his perception and encouraging her to speak hers.

She leaned forward, earnestly pressing the truth she had just comprehended. "It's not the place so much. It's you. You're Vivian's natural heir, and I'm not referring to simply inheriting his property. They want you to give their lives purpose, providing a hub for them to work around as your grandfather did, and they're afraid you won't, afraid you'll let them go and they won't know what to do then."

"You don't have to worry about that, Maggie. They're my family. One way or another, I'll answer their needs. You can count on it."

In so saying, he lifted all responsibility from her shoulders and the burden on her heart. She sat back and smiled, happy he understood.

They *were* safe with him.

Beau had made her feel very unsafe but she realised now he had felt unsafe with her, too. It had been right to tell him about herself, good to clear the air between them. She relaxed, enjoying a sense of freedom in exploring more with him.

"Any other worries?' he asked, obviously wanting to erase her fears.

"No. Except…" She nodded to the view outside the window. "…I hope our plane doesn't crash."

He grinned. "We're flying with an airline that has an excellent safety record."

"Those jumbo jets are so huge."

"I'll hold your hand."

She laughed as warmth flooded through her. Maybe she and their child would be safe in his keeping. A strong man with a generous heart would surely make a good father. Would he be her mate for life?

An hour later Maggie was strapped into a spacious and comfortable window seat, being treated to the privileges of a first-class passenger on a flight to London. The plane was zooming down the runway, picking up enormous speed. Just as she was tensing for the lift-off, Beau reached over and took her hand.

She felt the warmth and comfort of the reassuring gesture as she watched the ground fall away beneath them and experienced the exhilaration of climbing up to the sky. Once she was confident they were not about to drop out of it, she turned her head from the window and smiled at the man who was looking after her,

her whole body humming with a wonderful sense of sharing.

"My grandfather called this the great adventure," he said, returning her smile.

"Thank you for taking me on it, Beau."

In more ways than one, she thought, looking down at their linked hands, liking the togetherness.

It was a journey towards trust.

The greatest adventure of all.

And the most dangerous.

# CHAPTER FIFTEEN

BEAU VERY QUICKLY understood his grandfather's enchantment with Maggie Stowe. She was so eager for knowledge, she soaked up everything she could, loving the experience of a wider world, the wonder of it sparkling in her eyes. Fatigue, hunger, discomfort… none of it meant anything to her if there was something more to take in and savour. London was a historical feast and even its present living culture was endlessly fascinating to her.

She wasn't a tourist as Beau knew tourists, notching up places they'd been. She wasn't interested in buying souvenirs, nor even looking at them. That took up time better spent in active pursuit of a bigger treasure house of memories to be kept in her mind and heart and soul. So she said.

Beau suspected she automatically dismissed souvenirs as excess baggage. In a life led *travelling lightly,* books and ornaments would simply weigh her down. She didn't have a family home where she could store them. What most people took for granted had not been available to Maggie Stowe.

To have carried through such an isolated and alienated existence and still have an open-hearted zest for exploring more and more of life, showed a truly amazing resilience. Gutsy and grand, Beau thought, and found himself admiring her more than he usually admired anyone.

Even with places he had already seen, she revitalised his interest and extended it. He remembered on his previous visit to the Tower of London with his grandfather, he'd been captivated by its fortress aspect, the rooms where famous people had been imprisoned, the instruments of torture, suits of armour. Maggie was more enthralled with the Queens of England who'd been buried in the chapel, and shocked by the wealth of the British Empire, embedded in the Crown Jewels.

It was fun to be with her. She brought a kind of magical joy to each day with her vibrant enthusiasm, a dancing smile and evocative comments inviting him to share everything that touched her. He loved her uninhibited reactions, enjoyed her perceptions, found intense pleasure in her company, and thought how much he'd like spending the rest of his life with her.

He took her to Harrods since a visit to London wouldn't be complete without a look at the famous store. It was a natural expectation that Maggie would be tempted into buying something from the rich array of goods on display, if only one of the exotic pastries from the food hall. She did end up making a purchase, but not for herself, for Sedgewick.

"Look, Beau! A silver stopper for bottles of champagne. It's to keep the bubbles in after the bottle's been opened." Her eyes sparkled with glee. "Sedgewick will love it!"

"Why?" he asked, bemused by her pleasure in it.

"Oh, he looks so pained when nobody wants any

more champagne and there's still some left in the bottle. With this stopper he can keep it for later and enjoy it himself. He never drinks while he's on duty and he hates waste. I must buy it for him."

She was being served when she was struck by second thoughts, turning to Beau in agitated uncertainty. "Maybe I shouldn't. You don't drink champagne as Vivian did. If you don't intend to throw any more parties or do functions at Rosecliff..."

"Buy it," he said decisively. When still she doubted, he added, "I won't be dropping my grandfather's charity balls. If I'm not there to host them, I'll put Sedgewick in charge."

And on such an off-the-cuff incident, the future of Rosecliff suddenly turned. Or maybe the decision had been building up in him from the day he'd first returned home to a heritage he couldn't quite disown. Rosecliff represented home to him and having a home with a sense of continuity to it had a value now it didn't have before getting to know Maggie Stowe. Every child deserved a proper family home and Beau was determined on giving their child the best he could offer.

Having said what he'd said, it felt right. He'd make it happen. And Maggie was an integral part of it. Somehow he'd make her realise that before this trip was over.

They caught the Eurostar train from Waterloo to Paris, travelling under the English Channel and speeding across the countryside of France faster than any cars they saw on the roads. They both gave the trip top marks for inclusion on a tour.

To Beau, in his teens, Paris had been a city of stupendous grandeur, dominated by the architectural splendour of its public buildings and monuments, the marvellous precision of their mathematical alignment, the spirit of Napoleon and the fantastic Eiffel Tower. He hadn't seen it as a romantic city for lovers. He did now.

Spring in Paris. There was a nip in the air as Wallace had forewarned but the sun shone on them as he and Maggie followed the walking tours he'd planned; enjoying the pretty tree-lined streets that led up to the Sacre-Coeur, stopping to watch the clever acts of mime artists; strolling from the Louvre, through the Tuileries and all the way down the Champs-élysées, pausing to cast a critical eye over an exhibition of sculptures, admiring the massed displays of flowers in the gardens, having fun simply people-watching.

On the very first day, he'd caught her hand when she'd stumbled over uneven cobblestones. He hadn't relinquished it and she hadn't withdrawn it. The tacit acceptance emboldened him to take her hand every day. Beau could hardly believe how good it felt…this least intimate of physical links. In his mind he tied it to liking, approval, acceptance and respect, and his heart swelled with the sense of achievement this gave him. He was breaking down the barriers between them, winning her trust.

They spent a day at Versailles, marvelling at the incredible artistry involved in supplying the best of everything to the Sun-King of France; the riches of the palace, the extravagance of Le Trianon, the breathtaking design of the forest and fountains and gardens. Maggie bought a book of photographs of the latter to give to Mr. Polly.

"Just to satisfy his curiosity," she remarked. "He's such a master gardener himself, he'll appreciate the attention to detail in all of this."

Another day, they wandered around an antique fair, set up along the banks of the Seine near the Bastille. On one of the stalls Maggie saw a collection of elaborately designed brass buttons. "For Wallace," she cried excitedly. "He'd just love these on his chauffeur's uniform. Help me choose, Beau. I'll buy them and sew them on his jacket for him."

"You're right," he agreed, surprised by her perception. "Short of a red Ferrari, you couldn't buy him anything better. Wallace will be puffing his chest out everywhere."

They both grinned over the little vanity, enjoying their shared knowledge of the chauffeur's pride in his uniform. Once again Beau was touched by Maggie's thoughtfulness in the gift.

He was further struck by her caring perception when she pulled him into a lingerie boutique in the Place des Voges. He initially thought she was finally going to buy something for herself, but it was Mrs. Featherfield she had in mind.

"A nightgown from Paris with real French lace. She'll adore it, Beau."

The saleswoman obligingly laid out several on the counter. Beau eyed the sexy gown Maggie was fingering, trying to see it objectively instead of envisaging her in it. So far he'd managed to keep his desire for her under control, but willpower couldn't quell the needs she stirred and the display of highly erotic lingerie was dangerously arousing.

"You don't think that's a bit…well, Feathers isn't exactly young and she is rather buxom," he commented critically, thinking the sooner they got out of this shop, the better.

Maggie laughed, her eyes teasing his ignorance. "A woman is never too old or plump to enjoy feeling feminine and deliciously sensual," she declared knowingly. "Mrs. Featherfield loves the nightie I…"

She stopped, biting her lips as heat flared into her cheeks. Beau knew instantly what she was remembering. The image of her in the navy silk and lace gown burst into his mind, tempting him beyond endurance. He sensed her own sharp awareness of it, the flash flood of desire sweeping through her, the struggle to contain it. A wild exultation possessed him. It was the same for her…the want…the need…*the same for her!*

Beau didn't pause to question the compulsion that seized him. He swept the array of nighties on the counter over his arm. "Trying them on," he threw at the saleswoman, nodding to the change cubicles at the back of the shop. He scooped Maggie along with him and she came unresistingly, hustled into movement, catching her breath, looking hotly confused but not protesting.

His heart was hammering as he yanked the curtain of the cubicle closed behind them and tossed the nightgowns on a padded stool. His whole body was tingling with feverish anticipation as he turned to gather Maggie to him. She dropped the bags she'd been holding, her emptied hands lifting, but not to push him away. No. They slid inside his jacket, wanting to touch, wanting to feel him, and the intense yearning in her eyes set him on fire.

He wrapped her in his arms and kissed her with all the pent-up hunger of weeks pouring into a passionate need for her wholehearted response. She left him in no doubt of it, her mouth as urgent as his in tasting and accelerating the intensity of sensation generated by their mutual desire for each other. He covered her face with kisses, breathed in the seductive scent of her hair, moved her back against the wall for support as they both trembled with the force of their release from the restriction they'd imposed on themselves.

With his hands free to revel in the soft curves of her femininity, his mouth sought hers again, loving it, caressing it, savouring its hot sensuality. It was like drinking champagne on an empty stomach. His head swam with the exhilarating intoxication of it and he couldn't put a stopper on the bottle. Her arms were around his neck, her body arched excitingly against his, her fingers curling into his hair, holding him to her, wanting him.

His erection was painfully hard, fighting the constriction of his jeans, throbbing for release, desperately seeking its home within the soft cradle of her hips. And Maggie was burrowing closer to him, the thrust of her breasts pressing deliciously against his chest, her stomach curling around his hard shaft, relishing it, inviting him, encouraging him, the quiver of her thighs revealing the same feverish desire that gripped him.

His hands scrabbled at the cloth of her long skirt until they found the hem and pulled it up. Then came the fierce delight of finding she was wearing garterless stockings, not tights, and the silky scrap of her panties gave easy access to the intimacy he craved. She was already wet with need for him, and she shuddered and gasped as he stroked her.

A purring sound came from her throat, music to Beau's ears, but not to hers. Her eyes opened wide, the sudden realisation of where they were and what was being done rocketing through the sensual haze of satisfaction.

"Beau, we can't…" The shocked whisper fell from lips swollen with his kisses and tremulous with a denial she didn't really want to make. Her body was straining to give, to feel all he would give her.

"Maggie, I'm dying for you…" He pinned her skirt up with his thighs and tore his zip open.

Then as he guided his own hot flesh along the soft path of her other lips, already so sexually aroused they welcomed him in convulsive ecstasy, she sighed with exquisite pleasure, "Yes…yes…" and her eyes swam with sweet relief and a wild, reckless acceptance of any time, place or circumstance.

She lifted a leg, opening herself further, sensuously stroking his leg with it. Only a shallow penetration was possible and the teasing of it was driving him crazy with excitement. He shoved his jeans down his thighs, filled his hands with the soft roundness of her buttocks and hoisted her up, the explosive tension inside him demanding the thrust that took him deep inside her, fast and strong and intensely fulfilling.

She wound her legs around his hips, sinking him even further. And there was a moment to die for, a moment of stillness, of exquisite appreciation of how it was to be together like this, so deeply co-joined, owning an inner world that was uniquely theirs, that drummed only to their beat.

Her hands clutched his shoulders, fingers digging into his flesh as though they, too, would claw inside, holding and possessing what they shared by any primitive means. Her head was thrown back, exposing her long throat, and there at the base of it her pulse visibly throbbed. He kissed it, drew on it, loving the sense of her heart thrumming with his.

He felt her muscles start to spasm around him and he abandoned the kiss to ride the gathering storm of sensation, driving ahead of it, pushing it, rushing along with it, plunging from crest to crest, as the waves of her climax rolled through him and the sheer wild glory of it caught up with him and spilled him into the sweet peace of heaven.

She slumped over him, hugging his head, and he buried his face in the heaving softness of her breasts. He wrapped her fiercely in his arms to prevent her slipping away from him, holding on to their intimacy as long as he could. Her fingers stroked his neck as though gentling him and he felt a rush of tenderness for the woman she was, the mother she would be.

He listened to her heartbeat, feeling an emotional intensity he'd never felt before. This woman belonged to him. He would never let her go. Never. He would fight whatever he had to fight to keep her.

Only when she stirred did he become aware of external sounds; footsteps, a burst of conversation in French, the click of hangers on racks. "Beau…" she whispered, her breath warm on his skin, fingers stroking his hair, alerting him to the shift that had to be made.

She leaned back against the wall. He lifted his head. Her face was flushed, her eyes brilliantly luminous, her mouth slightly parted as though her lips were too sensitised to close. She met his gaze unflinchingly, locking on to it, determined on open honesty yet unable to hide a shimmer of intense vulnerability.

"Other customers have come in. This isn't exactly a safe place," she murmured shakily.

"Doesn't matter. They're strangers we'll never meet again," he answered. "This…us…is far more important, Maggie."

Her smile was wry. "I can't believe I let this happen again. It's crazy."

"But you wanted it," Beau pressed, alarmed at the thought of her backing off from him.

"Yes," she said helplessly.

His fear dissolved into a relieved and happy grin. "Maybe it seemed crazy the first time, when we didn't really know each other, but this time it makes perfect sense."

She giggled. "In a change cubicle?"

"Marks a change, doesn't it?"

She shook her head in bemusement. "I didn't imagine change would come quite like this."

She accepted it though, Beau thought exultantly. "Spontaneous combustion," he explained. "I promise I'll romance you tonight. How about a dinner cruise on the Seine? The lights of Paris, seductive food, French champagne…"

Her eyes softened. She stroked his cheek. "You don't have to, Beau. It's not really about romance, is it?"

"No. It's about what we give to each other. Very basic. But there's no reason we can't put a shine on it, Maggie, and I want to give you all the highlights the world has to offer." He meant it, too. There was nothing glib about what he felt for her.

She expelled a deep sigh. To his ears it was the sound of contentment in their understanding. Her eyes flirted with the confidence he'd imparted. "Well, I think it's time you put my feet back on the ground so we can resume our journey."

He kissed her to make up for the more intimate disconnection and there was no awkwardness at all about fixing themselves up before rejoining the public world. Acceptance, approval, liking, respect, Beau happily recited to himself as he waited for Maggie to complete the purchase of a sinful piece of sensuality for Mrs. Featherfield.

There was one thing wrong with the list, he decided. *Liking* wasn't strong enough.

He *loved* Maggie Stowe.

He felt he couldn't bear her out of his sight, let alone out of his life. It wasn't simply the part of him she carried inside her—their child—that made it essential to convince her that marriage to him could never conceivably be a prison. It was the person she was...his mate in every sense he could think of. He wanted—*needed* from her—the commitment of marriage.

# CHAPTER SIXTEEN

IT WAS STRANGE for Maggie to be so *close* to another person. It felt right. Everything with Beau now *felt* right. But it was strange, having someone close who seemed to understand whatever was going on in her mind, who could virtually anticipate her impulses, who was constantly there for her.

She wasn't used to it. She'd never had a relationship like this. Even the mental affinity and affection she'd shared with Vivian did not approach the depth of this closeness with Beau. She missed Vivian, but she had never doubted she could go on without him. With Beau it was different. He pervaded almost every breath she breathed, giving it a buoyant happiness she had never known. Take him away...she shied from thinking about that, afraid of how bereft she might feel.

Enjoy the moment, she kept telling herself. Worrying about tomorrow was a waste of the present. Maybe she was living in a fool's paradise, but it was paradise.

The days were filled with amazing sights; the towering black cathedral at Cologne, the fairytale castles along the Rhine River, the majestic mountains of Austria. Once they reached Italy, it became impossible to categorise the sheer romance of the places they ex-

plored…Lake Como, Verona, Venice with its intriguing history and location.

The nights were so intimate, Maggie forgot what it
was like to be alone. Which was scary, since she had
spent so many years on her own. Even when she had
shared rooms, slept in dormitories of bunks, or camped
out with a group, the sense of being an independent
individual had never left her. Yet the longer she was
with Beau, the more blurred became the line of separation between them.

From Paris onwards, he had rebooked their accom-
modation. Separate rooms were pointless. Neither of
them wanted to be parted. There were moments when
just looking at him—this man who excited all her
senses—evoked the most extraordinary feelings of
intense possessiveness.

He was a lover of great tenderness, as well as passion. He could draw her into sex, into *loving,* with a
slow gentleness that eased her into new territories, new
discoveries about herself, then take her with him to
heights so wild and wonderful, her body would lurch
with delight at the memory of it for days afterwards.
He was inventive, thoughtful, responsive, challenging,
and she didn't have the slightest regret about giving in
to the sexual attraction she'd wanted to explore with
him. However, she did sometimes wonder if its potency
coloured everything else they shared.

How long did passion last?

She had no answer to that question. No one to ask.
No one to tell her. Impossible to bring it up with Beau.
She couldn't forget he had a vested interest in tying her
to him, so how could she trust anything he said about

the future? She could only trust what she knew they felt together now.

He rented a villa in Tuscany, intending it as a base for forays into Florence and other outings around the beautiful countryside. The villa was situated on a hill, giving a lovely view of olive groves and green fields dotted with wild red poppies. Maggie was instantly captivated by the soft quality of the light in Tuscany. It seemed to deepen colours and spread a magical sense of peace and well-being.

Having been situated in cities for most of their travelling, their move to the quiet and slower pace of this relaxing location had a strong appeal. It was also timely for Maggie. Apart from the tightness in her breasts, she had barely been aware of her pregnancy. Morning sickness hit with debilitating results.

At first she struggled to carry on as Beau's tour companion, but three days of trying to ignore how unwell she felt, proved the impossibility of this endeavour. Each morning she had to ask Beau to stop their rental car so she could be sick on the side of the road. They missed out on getting into the Uffizi Palace in Florence because standing in the long queue for over an hour had resulted in her fainting. An unfightable fatigue swept over her in the afternoons, sapping her enthusiasm for sightseeing, and she dropped off to sleep during the return trips to the villa.

Beau's kindness and patience and consideration for her were exemplary but she felt miserably guilty for holding him up, wasting his time and giving him the general unpleasantness of worrying about her. On the fourth day, she decided to beg off going anywhere, too conscious of being a drag on him to enjoy being a tourist.

When she'd rolled out of bed, the room had spun, forcing her to lie down again and keep very still until everything righted itself. Beau had gone to make her a cup of tea, hoping it would help to settle the queaziness she felt. When he came back, he was frowning in concern.

"Would you like to see a doctor, Maggie?" he asked, setting the tea on the bedside table. "Maybe you need iron tablets or…"

"No, I'll be fine soon," she quickly assured him, hating the thought of causing any fuss. "I'm sure this is just a phase, Beau. I'm sorry it's inconveniencing you."

"Inconveniencing…" It was plain he didn't like the word, stiffening up and looking sharply at her.

Maggie sighed her impatience with any pretence. She didn't feel like arguing the point so she simply said, "I want to stay here today, Beau. There's no need to worry about me. I'll just lie around and relax and…"

"Are you suggesting I leave you here and go off to Sienna as planned?" he broke in tersely.

"Why not? I'm perfectly capable of looking after myself," she answered reasonably.

"Even if you are, it's a hell of a judgment on me, Maggie, sending me off as though I wouldn't care about you."

He was offended, she realised, deeply offended by her assumption he would leave her to her own resources in these circumstances. As she stared at him, taking in his viewpoint, his face twisted with frustration.

"Damn it, Maggie! I said I'd look after you. It's you

who's insisted on carrying on these past few days. Do you think I've enjoyed watching you push yourself?"

She frowned, confused by this further critical note on her handling of the situation. Didn't he realise she'd been considering his needs?

He gestured hopelessly and turned away, walking to the end of the bed. His shoulders heaved and he swung around, his face anguished by some inner torment. "I kept telling myself to respect your right to make your own decisions, but I have the same right, Maggie, so don't take it upon yourself to make decisions for me. Your welfare and that of our child is as much my responsibility as it is yours. It's wrong for you to take that away from me, too."

"Beau, this is a business trip for you," she reminded him.

"Is that your excuse for holding yourself in and shutting me out?" he threw at her.

Maggie stared at him in bewilderment.

He expelled a sigh of deep exasperation and shook his head. "You still don't trust me, do you?" he said dully, the anger gone as abruptly as it had burst forth.

"I'm not sure I know what you mean," she said tentatively.

His bleak look smote her heart. "Never mind. I'm sorry for losing my temper when you're not well." He grimaced. "I never seem to get my timing right with you."

"That's not true." It was more an offer of appeasement than a comment.

"Isn't it?" He shrugged and walked to the door. He paused there a moment, then looked back, his eyes raking hers with pain. "If you want anything, call out. I'll be in hearing range. As unbelievable as you might find it, Maggie, business doesn't come first with me. You do. You and our child. You always will."

He left her with that quiet statement of fact and Maggie couldn't block a rush of tears. A huge lump of emotion constricted her throat. It was impossible to call him back right then, and perhaps it was better not to. She needed time to think, to sort herself out in the light of how Beau perceived her.

For a while, her mind couldn't move past his assertion that she came first with him. She and their child. It was such a huge thing to comprehend. She hadn't expected him—anyone—to put her needs ahead of his... to care so much...for her to be so important to him.

She'd never been that important to anybody.

She'd stifled the urge to cling to him this morning, to ask him to stay with her, dismissing it as silly weakness and unfair to him. Now the accusation of holding herself in and shutting him out hit home. She had been doing that, automatically shying away from expecting anything of him, not *trusting*.

Yet what was there not to trust in Beau? What more did he have to prove to her? Hadn't he done everything he said he would? And given her much more!

So they'd had an unfortunate start. He'd explained what he'd felt and why he'd acted as he had. He'd more than compensated for his errors in judgment where she was concerned. It was wrong not to trust him.

He'd left the bedroom door open. She was free to call on him anytime. He'd invited her to. There was no reason to feel inhibited about it. Whether he responded or not was his decision, his choice. It finally dawned on her that without open communication, trust couldn't grow and she was denying any chance of that with second-guessing him, as well as burying her head in the sand rather than look at the future.

Maggie sipped the tea Beau had brought her as new resolutions formed in her mind. He'd put some cookies on the saucer. She ate one slowly, testing her stomach's reaction. Feeling no ill effects, she finished the lot, then tentatively got out of bed again.

The world remained normal.

She dressed quickly and went in search of Beau. He was sitting at the table under the vine-covered pergola which spread along the front of the villa. A notebook and Biro were at hand but he wasn't writing anything, just staring out at the view, apparently in deep thought.

When she stepped out on the flagstoned terrace, his head jerked around as though he had been listening for any noise, reacting instantly to it. The tension in his body leapt out at her. She hesitated, suddenly uncertain of her welcome. Then he visibly relaxed, his mouth curling into an ironic smile as his gaze swept over her appearance.

"Well, I guess you've shown you didn't need my help."

"Yes, I did," she quickly corrected. "The tea and cookies helped a lot. I feel much better now."

"Glad to hear it." He gestured to a chair. "It's very pleasant sitting out here. Would you care to join me?"

She nodded. "Don't get up. I'm fine now. Really."

He subsided in his seat and watched her sit down. Maggie's nerves jangled. Had she done the wrong thing again, rejecting the courtesy of seeing her seated? Heat rushed into her cheeks and just as quickly receded, reflecting the emotional mess she was in.

"I'm sorry I offended you earlier," she gabbled, her eyes pleading his forgiveness. "I didn't mean to make you feel unwanted. I'm just not used to...to depending on other people."

He shrugged. "No need to apologise. It's not your fault. I do appreciate it's difficult for you, Maggie. With your background."

He turned his gaze away to the view spread out below them. Maggie wanted to dismiss his reference to her past, yet it was relevant. Somehow his sympathy and understanding shamed her. She shouldn't be letting the far past taint her judgment. There were no points of comparison to it in her relationship with Beau. None at all.

"My grandfather used to call me the wild child," he said whimsically. "Not undeserved. But I think the name more aptly fits you."

"Me?' Maggie frowned, not seeing the parallel.

He sliced her a darkly knowing look. "Not even the compound could tame you, Maggie. And you've been roaming free ever since you got out of there."

Only because I never felt I really belonged anywhere, she thought.

He shifted his attention back to the view. "I was looking down at that field of poppies earlier, before you came out. All those flowers growing wild and free, so vibrant with their red petals. The thought came to me that they probably wouldn't thrive nearly so well, transplanted to a formal garden. Better to let them grow their own way. Let them shine how they will."

She sensed melancholy and despair and inwardly railed against the darkness falling between them. He was withdrawing from her. She could feel it. He swung his gaze to her again and she saw it, the deep personal pain behind the restraint he was grimly holding.

"I've done everything wrong with you, Maggie. I thought I could right it. Sheer blind arrogance on my part." He managed a travesty of a smile. "The pushing stops here. If you want us to lead separate lives… well, it's up to you to decide on what arrangement suits you best."

She understood then. It was she who'd been blind. Beau loved her. And she had wounded his generous heart to the point of giving up on ever winning her love. She also knew words would be meaningless, as meaningless as they'd been to her without the right actions to back them up.

She rose from her chair, her heart gripped by a panicky urgency. She had to prove to him that all his gifts of love to her had not been in vain. She had learnt. The past was not going to blight her life with him. It wasn't going to touch them anymore.

Without a word she turned and walked away, heading straight down the hill to the field of red poppies. A feverish energy pumped through her veins. A sense of destiny pounded through her brain. Beau Prescott was her mate. She was going to spend the rest of her life with him. She was not going to be afraid of anything.

Once amongst the wildflowers, she stooped to pick a bouquet of them, gathering them up as fast as she could. When she had an armful, she took a deep breath to steady herself, then started the return journey to the villa.

It startled her to see Beau had followed her and was standing only a few metres away, watching her intently, obviously worried over her physical or mental state.

She smiled to ease his concern and headed straight for him. There was puzzlement in his eyes as she offered him the bouquet of poppies.

"I give them into your keeping, Beau," she softly explained, her eyes begging him to understand. "With them comes my absolute trust. And my love. And my life."

"Maggie…" Hope conflicted with doubt.

"Please?"

"Dear God!" He took the flowers, though his eyes said they were no substitute for her. "I thought…"

"I think we do much better together when we stop thinking, Beau."

He laughed and tossed the poppies aside to wrap her in his arms. "I love you, Maggie Stowe. You are where I want to be for the rest of my life."

Her heart caught, then soared. She slid her arms around his neck, pressing closer as she kissed him, the great surge of feeling between them pouring into the swift, fierce passion they had known from the very beginning. For a long, long time, they lay amongst the wild poppies in the field, bathed in the soft mystical light of Tuscany, loving each other in the full knowledge of their love.

Not once did Maggie think of Vivian's wishes. Nor did she think of Rosecliff or those wanting this happy outcome, nor of the child conceived before either she or Beau had considered such a possibility. She thought only of being with this man, where she would always belong. This was *their* chance, and she didn't want to waste a moment of it.

# CHAPTER SEVENTEEN

ST. ANDREW'S CATHEDRAL was packed for what was being called The Wedding of the Year—Beau Prescott, heir to the Prescott millions and owner of Rosecliff, marrying his grandfather's beautiful protége, Margaret Stowe, with the bishop performing the ceremony and the boys' choir giving voice to songs of joy.

It was what Mr. Vivian would have wanted, Sedgewick had declared, informing Beau and Maggie in no uncertain terms, and volubly backed up by Mrs. Featherfield, Wallace and Mr. Polly, that this wedding had to be the grandest party of them all.

Beau smiled to himself as he waited at the head of the aisle for his bride to appear. He hadn't argued with them. He wanted to give Maggie the best of everything, especially on their wedding day. And no way would he spoil the pleasure of the faithful four in contributing to the event.

Sedgewick was undoubtedly in his element, supervising all the arrangements in the ballroom at Rosecliff, getting ready to distribute oceans of the best French champagne. Feathers would have revelled in helping Maggie to dress. Wallace would be as proud as punch, chauffeuring the bride in the most brilliantly polished Rolls in the city. Mr. Polly's roses were on prime display and would undoubtedly feature in Maggie's bouquet.

They were all delighted with his and Maggie's plans for the future, too, keeping Rosecliff as their home and a centre for supporting his grandfather's charities, while taking time away each year to explore and organise a new package tour for their travel agency. Beau couldn't help grinning as he remembered planning this with Maggie.

"We will have a child to consider," she'd reminded him.

"Any child with our genes is bound to be a wild child," he'd declared. "It will just be one big adventure after another."

"You mean we take our family with us?"

"Why not? We'll open all the windows on the world."

To which she'd laughingly agreed.

And he'd teasingly added, "Of course we'll need a nanny to come with us to give us time to ourselves. Or for the occasional short trip, we can leave nanny and child at home for Feathers and Sedgewick and Wallace and Mr. Polly to spoil outrageously."

With which *they* had heartily agreed.

The fulsome tones of the pipe organ faded into silence. Beau's heart kicked. This was it. He turned as the first chords of Mendelssohn's "Wedding March" rang through the cathedral. And there she was, hugging Sir Roland's arm, starting down the long aisle towards him.

At first he thought she looked like a Medieval princess. Her high-waisted ivory silk gown was embroidered in gold and rich in elegance, shimmering with each step she took. Then he focused on her radiant face, framed by her glorious hair and haloed by her bridal veil and he thought…an angel. The Angel of Life.

The dress artfully covered her four months' pregnancy but the thought of the child she carried in her womb—their child-filled Beau with a special sense of awe as he watched her come to him. The words his grandfather had once spoken to Lionel Armstrong slid into his mind…creation…salvation…and they suddenly had meaning, beautiful magical meaning.

The family line would go on through him and Maggie. Had his grandfather foreseen that? Was his spirit somewhere close, smiling over them, giving them his blessing?

Then Maggie was beside him, giving him her hand in trust and in love, and Beau held it safe as they pledged themselves to each other, husband and wife. The cathedral filled with song, voices soaring in joyful celebration. It was a pale echo of what they felt in their hearts, what was reflected in their eyes. All the years of their lives had been leading to this moment…the mating that was meant to be…and this was their wedding.

The reception in the ballroom at Rosecliff was every bit as splendid as Sedgewick ordained it should be. It was the most glittering evening anyone could ever remember. Jeffrey cracked the whip over the caterers who served superb food. Champagne flowed. Mrs. Featherfield kept the maids on their toes. The floral arrangements were fantastic. Sir Roland led off the

speeches, all of which were warm and witty and wonderful.

When it was time for the Bridal Waltz, because of
certain information imparted to Beau by Wallace, the
band didn't play a waltz at all. The Bridal Dance was
announced and to the opening strains of one of Abba's
hit songs, "Dancing Queen," Beau proudly led Maggie out to the centre of the floor, parading her to the
guests who spontaneously and loudly applauded. She
was laughing in delight when he turned her into in his
arms, the song in full swing as he took her dancing.

"Who told you it was an old favourite of mine?"
she asked.

"Wallace. And what more appropriate?" He grinned
at her. "I'm dancing with the queen of my heart."

"And I with my king."

The look in her eyes was almost Beau's undoing, especially when the band moved into playing "I do, I do, I
do, I do, I do," but he manfully restrained himself from
racing his newly wedded wife off to a private place. It
was probably fortunate that Sir Roland claimed Maggie for his dance, thus removing temptation.

Lionel Armstrong took the opportunity to draw
Beau aside and pass him an envelope. "It's from your
grandfather. I was instructed to give it to you in the
event of your marriage to Margaret Stowe."

Beau was astounded. "How could he possibly know
it would happen?"

"He didn't. I was given another envelope to be
handed to you when the stipulated year in the will
was up if you hadn't married Margaret Stowe."

Beau shook his head in total bemusement. "So what
happens to the second envelope now?"

"It has already been destroyed as per Vivian's instructions. He said the marriage would make it irrelevant. I was further instructed to tell you that this…" he tapped the envelope in Beau's hands "…should be read by both of you on your wedding night."

It gave Beau important cause to whiz Maggie off to a private place. She was as deeply intrigued as he by this extraordinary action by his grandfather and they sought brief refuge in the library. The envelope contained a letter and a set of keys which puzzled them both, making them all the more eager to read what Vivian Prescott had written.

*My dear Beau,*
*I am delighted you've had the good sense to marry Maggie. She is my wedding present to you since I found her, having despaired of you ever staying still long enough to recognise a soulmate.*

Beau chuckled. "The old devil. I bet he was planning this from day one of meeting you."

"You don't mind?' Maggie queried.

"Why should I mind? He got it right."

Her smile glowed with love. "Yes, he did."

They read on…

*The keys are to open a safe-deposit box—details next page. In it is my wedding gift to Maggie. She has a need to feel free, Beau, which is a need you must understand if you are to sustain a happy marriage. To ensure this in a financial sense, I have put a million dollars in the box for her to use as she wills.*

The missing million!

"Oh!" Maggie slapped her hands to flaming cheeks. "How could he? All that money!"

Beau grinned at her. The mystery was solved at last. "He could because he loved you, Maggie. And that money's going to be yours to do whatever you like with it."

"Well, thank heaven we're married so I won't feel wrong about him giving it to me."

"You would have had to take it anyway."

"What?"

"Look for yourself."

*If you had been foolish enough to let Maggie slip away from you, my instruction would have been to give this amount to her so she would never again feel the insecurity she was burdened with through no fault of her own. I trust you would have done that, Beau, without contesting my wish on this matter.*

Beau instantly saw his grandfather's wisdom in taking this bequest out of the will. With a year's grace, he wouldn't have begrudged Maggie the million, but faced with it straight away, he probably would have raised even worse hell than he had.

"He was so kind to me," was her heartfelt murmur.

"Maggie, you did a lot for him, too," Beau assured her, feeling fine about everything until he read the next paragraph.

*I have one request to make. When my great-grandson is born, I would like you to follow the tradition of the Prescott family in assigning a name which will develop strength of mind and character and lend a unique individuality to live up to. My personal fancy is Marian.*

"Over my dead body!" Beau growled.

"Marian!" Maggie exclaimed. "I thought that was a girl's name."

"Yes! Like Vivian and Beverly and… Goddamn it! I am not going to saddle a son of mine with a name like that! Beau was bad enough."

"I like Beau. It suits you. I liked Vivian, too. It suited him. Maybe…"

"Don't say it! I will not consider Marian."

"Well, maybe we'll only have daughters."

"Let's hope." He lovingly patted her stomach. "You'd better be a girl in there."

The letter finished off with his grandfather saying he was now off on the greatest adventure of all and he wished them both the very best of this world.

It left them smiling.

"I guess you could say he came to our wedding," Beau said with a warm glow of contentment.

"I think he's been here all day."

"Yes. But the night is definitely ours, Maggie."

He drew her into his arms and their kiss excluded everyone else, a long, satisfying private celebration of a togetherness that was uniquely theirs.

Five months later a boy was born.

He was christened Marian John Richard Prescott.

Beau insisted it was up to the boy himself to choose what name he wanted to live with and that his great-grandfather couldn't have his way about everything. In the meantime, Maggie could call him Marian. If she really, really wanted to. He wouldn't deny her that right as long as she understood it was an act of love on his part.

Maggie smiled very lovingly at both him and their son and said she thought family tradition was nice.

Beau remembered she had come from nowhere, saw her need, understood it, and surrendered with a sigh of resignation to the inevitable.

Marian Prescott developed a lot of character.

* * * * *

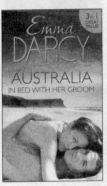

# *Special Offers*

Every month we put together collections and longer reads written by your favourite authors.

Here are some of next month's highlights— and don't miss our fabulous discount online!

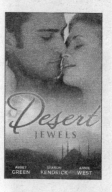 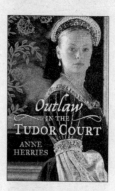 

On sale 21st March  On sale 4th April  On sale 4th April

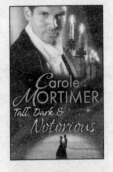
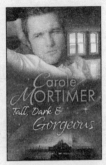
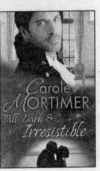
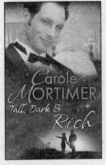

Discover more romance at

# www.millsandboon.co.uk

- ❤ WIN great prizes in our exclusive competitions
- ❤ BUY new titles before they hit the shops
- ❤ BROWSE new books and REVIEW your favourites
- ❤ SAVE on new books with the Mills & Boon® Bookclub™
- ❤ DISCOVER new authors

PLUS, to chat about your favourite reads, get the latest news and find special offers:

- 📘 Find us on facebook.com/millsandboon
- 🐦 Follow us on twitter.com/millsandboonuk
- ❤ Sign up to our newsletter at millsandboon.co.uk